SYMPATHY

Dede Crane

SYMPATHY

RAINCOAST BOOKS

Vancouver

Raincoast Books gratefully acknowledges the ongoing support of the
Canada Council for the Arts, the British Columbia Arts Council and
the Government of Canada through the Book Publishing Industry
Development Program (BPIDP).

Edited by Lynn Henry
Cover design by Bill Douglas
Interior design by Teresa Bubela

LIBRARY AND ARCHIVES CANADA CATALOGUING IN PUBLICATION
Crane, Dede
        Sympathy / Dede Crane.
ISBN 1-55192-781-0
        I. Title.
PS8605.R35S94 2006   C813'.6   C2005-903576-5

LIBRARY OF CONGRESS CATALOGUE NUMBER: 2005928389

Raincoast Books   *In the United States:*
9050 Shaughnessy Street   Publishers Group West
Vancouver, British Columbia   1700 Fourth Street
Canada v6p 6e5   Berkeley, California
www.raincoast.com   94710

At Raincoast Books we are committed to protecting the environment
and to the responsible use of natural resources. We are working with our
suppliers and printers to phase out our use of paper produced from
ancient forests. This book is printed with vegetable-based inks on 100%
ancient-forest-free paper (100% post-consumer recycled), processed
chlorine- and acid-free. For further information, visit our website at
www.raincoast.com/publishing. We are working with Markets Initiative
(www.oldgrowthfree.com) on this project.

Printed in Canada by Friesens.

10 9 8 7 6 5 4 3 2 1

For my parents,
Millicent A. Crane
and
Thomas B. Crane (1914 – 2000)

Contents

sympathy *noun* **1) a** the state of being simultaneously affected with a feeling similar or corresponding to that of another. **b** the capacity for this. **2) a** the act of sharing in or responding to an emotion, sensation or condition of another person or thing. **b** the capacity for this. **3)** compassion or commiseration, condolence.

— *The Oxford English Reference Dictionary*

Prologue

"Dear Diary" feels too much like I'm talking to myself, so I'll imagine I'm talking to you.

Dear Hugo, Don't know if I can put anything coherent into this beautiful book you gave me, but I'll try. Occasionally, when younger, I recorded the odd thought, even the odd "poem," but have never kept a journal before. Have always considered English my second language. Dance my first. I never feel words represent the world properly, the way music can, or touch; even a simple gesture feels more substantial. Words take the stuffing out of things for me, flatten them when they're so much crazy bigger. Maybe if I think of these words I'm writing as musical, find some sort of rhythm and flow with them, that'll fatten them up.

So, hi, Hugo. It's a wind-washed Wednesday and raucous ravens pit themselves against the westerly wind as I query quietly: what started me on the road to dance?

Sorry, that was just stupid. Besides, it's Thursday.

I believe my first inspiration to dance happened at home, but not from anything I'd seen on television. I remember it was the official pre-dinner hour, when Dad and Mom had their measured whiskey sours, one apiece, never two. I can see my dad smashing ice cubes with the ice whip, as I called it, and dropping them into two diamond-cut whiskey glasses. Then came the thick-bottomed shot glass quavering with copper liquid before it was dumped into the sour mix, diluted with OJ and stirred with a long glass stick. People had the good gadgetry back then.

My parents' life seemed so smooth, so well-rehearsed, like a long-running Broadway play — a slow one, like The Gin Game. *My life with Allan, on the other hand, is fly-by-our-pants chaos. Though, now that I've retired maybe it'll settle into something more predictable. Hah! Allan's out right now, talking to some guy starting up a small farms magazine. As if Allan knows anything about farming or starting a magazine. Says he wants to figure out how to build a solar-heated chicken coop, which is one of the things he'll put in the magazine. Says he'll be the carpenter expert, wants to call himself "Hammerhead." If he really builds a coop, that'll probably mean owning chickens. And after he loses interest, those chickens will end up my responsibility. I'm afraid of chickens. I think domestication has made them insane. Didn't they used to be able to fly?*

Anyway, my story: I was five and I know it was winter because inside-out time had happened before dinner. That's what I called it when the windows switched over from showing the outside world to reflecting the inside. In other words, it was dark early. God, it's embarrassing when I think how much I used to watch myself in window mirrors, adjusting my posture, pulling in my stomach. I don't know how many times, eyes glued to storefront reflections, I bumped into people on the streets of Manhattan.

It may not have actually been the first time it happened, but it's the first memory I have of music playing in our apartment. My parents were TV watchers and owned only one record, a forty-five of Bobby Darin singing "Mack the Knife." Once a year it somehow made its way to the record player. That first time the music seemed to filter down from the ceiling, like magic dust, and the world inched to the right. The light intensified, the air got thicker and my parents weren't my parents anymore. The regulation, sober adults I knew and trusted had kicked off their shoes and their feet were stamping on the notes of the music as if they were little flames bursting out on the floor. And their arms were doing all these snakey loops, like the boneless woman I'd seen that year at Barnum and Bailey. Then Dad started whipping Mom around as if she had wheels for feet and both their faces became entirely new thoughts. I remember my brother and sister hopping up from their Chinese checkers game to copy them, hold hands, Richard looking seriously cool, Patricia laughing nervously as Richard jerked her around by the arm.

I couldn't stop watching my mother. If you can, Hugo, picture a thirty-something Arlene, her eyes all glittery, head thrown back, square pearls for teeth, her hair stiff water splashing against her cheeks. She was beautiful in the way something willingly tossed around by wind is beautiful. Self-abandoned and unrecognizable. Then the record came to an end and everything hardened up, shrink-wrapped back to the same old. I started crying for more music but the roast was ready, Mom all right angles again, her hair lifeless. Dad ordering us to wash our hands.

I asked for dancing lessons the next morning and my mother promptly enrolled me in a ballet class at the local elementary school where, assuming these were the necessary preliminaries, I obediently learned to plié and tendu, all the while waiting for the day my creased-faced teacher threw off her shoes and knocked a hip out of line. She did have hands that whispered secrets, I'll give her that.

Hey, just figured out what to do with my class of ten-year-olds for the spring recital. Cross-dress them like mini-men, give them all a mop for a partner and choreograph to "Mack the Knife." They can all crumple to the floor in death throes at the end, a big flourishing kiss to their dames. How do you like that idea? Now I just have to come up with some damn steps. Wish you were here. I still go into stun-mode when the word "choreography" comes up.

Remember that time you "amended" Stuart's steps during a performance? He was so pissed at you. Of course he loved me, the brilliant taker of orders. "The waitress," as you called me. I really don't know why I love you so much.

God, it was nerve-wracking having you as a partner. The way you'd let go of my waist in those pirouettes at the end of Don Q. And I was never sure you were going to catch me in the flying fish in the Sugar Plum pas de deux. I could feel you wondering which would be more exciting from a performance point of view — catching me or not catching me. Each time, I would say a little prayer and just go for it, and each time felt like I was hurling myself off a cliff.

So, thanks for not letting me break any bones in our short-sweet partnership because, I know, in the name of art, it was tempting for you.

Blackjack's barking insanely, my sweet boy must be home from school. Ciao.

METHODOLOGY

In order to uncover the original shock experienced by post-traumatic stress disorder (PTSD) patients, we must turn our attention to that which houses the shock: the physical body. Why? Because psychological shock is experienced through the parasympathetic nervous system, which, in turn, encodes the original trauma in the body. Since the original trauma is often entirely repressed or forgotten by the reasoning mind, the body becomes our only reliable witness. We should pay heed to the wisdom of the adage the body never lies. This approach is a far cry from our usual concentration, as therapists, on sifting through the patient's endless rhetoric, searching for clues.

It is time we approach psychotherapy from a more "elementary" angle and focus greater attention on the sympathetic relationship between mind and body. Mind and body should not be seen as separate or distinct from each other; instead, they should be understood as one and the same expression. I am convinced that unearthing the physically stored traumatic memory and integrating it into the patient's cognitive awareness is the most effective way to build a sound foundation for mental health.

—Michael Myatt, PhD

EN ROUTE to the newest option for her youngest child, Arlene Taylor drives past her favourite shop in Alexandria, eyeballing the outfits in the window. In one of the few boutiques that offers a senior's discount, the glint of a gold sweater catches her eye. It's only mid-August but like a beacon of the future, of days still to come, fall fashions have arrived. And a future implies that the world isn't ending, even if last September she, and everyone else on the Eastern seaboard, assumed otherwise. Nothing infuses the future with hope like a new outfit. Miraculously, there is a parking space just a couple doors down from the store, a sign from above to go have a gander. Arlene checks her watch and then her daughter, expressionless in the seat beside her. There's almost a half-hour's grace before the meeting with Dr. Myatt and the clinic is only five minutes away.

"I won't be long, Kerry-Ann. Just sit tight."

Leaving the windows cracked a few inches like others would do for a dog, Arlene slips out of the car and locks all the doors with a magical press of her key chain. As she puts a couple of quarters in the parking meter, she wishes she had one of those Walkman things to put on her daughter's head. It would make her look occupied at least.

Between trying on clothes and consulting with salesgirls, Arlene keeps an eye on the car and on the back of her thirty-four-year-old daughter's statuesque head, still motionless and showing no evidence of difficulty, or of anything else for that matter. Five minutes becomes fifteen, then twenty, before Arlene emerges from the store in creamy-gold linen pants and an ivory shirt silk-screened with gold and red leaves. Luckily she'd worn her tan slingbacks this morning and not her white sandals.

"It's been a while since I've treated myself to something new," she says, climbing in beside Kerry. "What do you think? It's a suit, actually. The jacket's in the bag."

ROSEWOOD'S SIMPLE architecture is unassuming, its sure lines giving an appearance of neatness and clarity, as if this is truly a place where loose ends are tied up, wrinkles smoothed. With its large blocks of limestone, the four-storey building looks modelled after D.C.'s Hirshhorn Museum — except for the fact it has windows, big ones. And, if it weren't for the lack of balconies, Arlene would have assumed the building was a classy new apartment complex, a gated community. A handsome stone wall surrounds the property and wrought iron gates with arrowed tips mark the entrance. The architects have worked hard, she figures, to help neighbours ignore what goes on inside.

"Terrific how convenient Rosewood is to the Torpedo Factory," Arlene remarks to Kerry as she turns into the adjacent parking lot. "Do you remember me taking you there? It's that wartime factory they turned into art studios and galleries?"

She pulls into the handicapped space and pops the trunk.

"My *Pumpkin Cart* has been accepted for their fall festival," she informs Kerry now that the conversation has turned to art. "Sold my *Georgetown Townhouses* for a couple hundred last year."

Out of the car, Arlene lifts the collapsible wheelchair from the trunk with a groan. As she struggles to unfold the thing, she breaks a nail. "Damn it, I just had those done." She bats at the chair, then discreetly tears off the rest of the nail with her teeth and hopes there's an emery board in her purse. Finally she manages to get the wheelchair open and secured.

"Okay, out we go." With a firm hold on Kerry's elbow, Arlene guides her daughter out of the car and over the couple of steps into the wheelchair. Gaze fixed on nothing, her face composed yet blank, Kerry responds to commands like a docile sleepwalker. Her steps are as light as the arm under Arlene's hand. Arlene pictures her daughter's bones filled with nothing but air and squeezes Kerry's arm harder. She has given up trying to understand why Kerry moves when prodded but doesn't talk, shop or think. Doesn't even feed herself. Her daughter is a mystery Arlene's looking for someone finally to solve.

At the front gate Arlene announces herself into an intercom. A buzzer sounds, she pushes at the gate and it magically opens. As she enters the property, she smoothes her hair and looks for a hidden camera to no avail. She takes in the grounds: casually trimmed bushes, feathery grass devoid of dandelions or buttercups, clusters of petunias dribbling out from under shrubs, tall stands of mums and lilies toppling into each other. Everything looks strategically neglected, *faux naturel*. The overall effect is of a garden where fragmented minds will feel neither outdone nor out of place. The ten-foot-high walls enclosing the property are alive with flowering vines clipped to remain inside only. The amount of flowering things is impressive for this late in the summer.

At the building's entrance, Arlene watches a white-smocked nurse take the last luxurious drag of her cigarette before blowing it apologetically out the corner of her mouth. The nurse twists the butt into the white sand of a silver ashcan and then walks into the garden. An old man wearing a Tilley hat and Hawaiian shirt gestures to the nurse with a feeble hand to come share his bench. Arlene notes that the nurse greets him by name before passing by. His gesturing continues, his gaze slowly swinging over to Arlene who, feeling like a voyeur caught out, continues wheeling her daughter up to the building. Beside the plate glass doors is an engraved brass plaque. Arlene just has time to read THE ROSEWOOD CLINIC, ESTABLISHED 1973 when the doors are opened by a security guard with a buzz cut and a shadowy attempt at a moustache. Biceps challenge his short sleeves.

"Another hot one today," the guard says in gracious Southern tones.

"Lovely, but getting cooler in the evenings," Arlene responds, in defence of her outfit.

"Fall's just around the corner," he says agreeably. "Looking forward to some cooler weather."

The guard's smile tells her he takes pride in his practised way with small talk. Arlene smiles back, pleased with the Rosewood she's seen so far.

"And you're here to see?" His grey eyes discreetly scan Kerry top to bottom. Arlene, vicariously flattered, smoothes back Kerry's long hair. The youngest child isn't classically pretty like her sister, but she carries herself with a certain gloss, even mute in a wheelchair.

"Dr. Michael Myatt."

He scrolls down names on his computer screen, clicks his mouse. Beside this screen sits a second screen divided into four views of the property. One view takes in the area outside the front gate.

"Dr. Michael's the PTSD wing and the blue elevators," he says, pointing down the hall. "Third floor west is where you want to go."

"Thank you," nods Arlene, pushing on.

The third floor is done up in shades of grey and maroon. A dreary and outdated colour-combination, but at least it looks kept up. Arlene gives her name to a round-eyed receptionist, young, barely thirty, who directs her to the waiting area by the windows. Parking Kerry at the end of the coffee table, she notices upholstered couches in place of the sticky hospital vinyl she's come to know. As a private institution, Rosewood must be able to afford the cleaning bill. The windows overlook the garden at the back of the building. She's glad to see that patients aren't issued some sort of uniform. A bank of red roses marches up and down the back wall like a thorny deterrent to thoughts of escape. Of course, people pay to be here, they're not committed, she reminds herself, and is relieved to note that no one's in restraints. Perhaps the majority of Rosewood patients are wealthy neurotics trying out the latest thing in therapy. Maybe people come here for a dose of mental health the same way they go to a fat farm to lose weight.

A gawky young man with orange hair and a terrible complexion is now standing against the wall staring bug-eyed at the receptionist behind the desk. He is voraciously sucking one of his fingers, the longest, nastiest finger, and a towel dangles from this hand to cover his chest like a bib. Arlene acts unaware, not wanting to grant the young man any satisfaction in case he looks in her direction.

"Can I help you, Johnny?" asks the receptionist, and the young man cowers his head and shrinks off down the hall.

Arlene sighs and wishes Beresford were here to help decide if this is the place for their daughter. She picks a brochure from the coffee table and reads: "The Rosewood Clinic was founded in 1973 by Dr. Philip McGuire in cooperation with the American League of Psychologists and Psychiatrists. Its mandate is to remain on the cutting edge of psychotherapy, to hire forerunners in the field and to strive to discover compassionate and successful treatments for the victims of mental illness. Rosewood's two-acre parcel was donated by local entrepreneur, Donald Hager, whose late wife, Marel Rose Hager, suffered a debilitating mental disorder that was never conclusively diagnosed nor cured. She committed suicide at the age of thirty-nine."

What other choice do we have, she thinks, looking out beyond the garden wall to the sluggish, murky-brown Potomac. Hard to believe she used to swim in that water. On the far bank, concealing roads and warehouses, the leafy tops of trees shimmer in the sun. The view will be rather spectacular when the leaves turn.

Turning from the window, she notes the graceful gait of an approaching man dressed all in green — forest green pants and a sage green shirt. Only trees should wear green, she thinks, and decides his oval glasses don't suit his squarish face. Nice skin tone, though. Arlene has always appreciated a tanned look, natural or otherwise, and maintains a moderate tan year-round herself, never having felt she has the complexion to go pale. This man's about the same age as her son, she muses — thirty-eight, thirty-nine? Realizing his destination appears to be her, she turns back to the window and discreetly checks the corners of her eyes for wandering bits of mascara.

"Mrs. Taylor?"

His voice is almost courtly and his head tilts back ever so slightly as he shakes her hand. It's a meticulous handshake that makes Arlene wish she'd filed her ruined nail.

"Pleased to meet you. I'm Michael Myatt."

"You're Dr. Myatt?" Arlene has been expecting someone older, someone with a white lab coat, a clipboard at least. His eyes alight on hers for the briefest second before slipping to the left and past her entirely.

"That would be me. Please," he says, gesturing down the hall, "we can speak privately in my office."

There's a nice depth to his voice, thinks Arlene, moving toward the wheelchair. She could never trust a man with a shrill voice.

"Here, I can push," he offers.

Following behind, she notices he's wearing sandals. With socks? Is it sanitary to be wearing sandals in a place like this?

Expecting the usual grey display of textbooks and framed credentials, Arlene is pleasantly surprised by this so-called doctor's office. The grey linoleum is camouflaged by a vibrant Tibetan carpet, dark-red with a navy border, swirling gold clouds. Azure-blue blinds stripe the window and two large abstracts decorate the walls. One is humped with curving shapes in hot oranges and reds; the other is painted in soothing lavenders, hazels and pale greens that explore the angular and the vertical. Though Arlene prefers realism, she recognizes that these works are of high quality. There is one diploma above the bookcase, but all she can decipher from here is the dark calligraphy of his name, Michael Paul Myatt. The room smells clean, as if devoid of scent, like plain paper. No, she decides, there's a faint smell of hand soap, of freshly washed skin.

A large oak desk is sparsely set with a table lamp, phone and a single framed picture. A cartridge pen lies tightly perpendicular to a pad of buff paper. Arlene has an irrational urge to flick it into a spin and see where it ends up.

"Please have a seat, Mrs. Taylor. I'll just place Ms. Taylor here between us. She goes by her maiden name?"

"Yes, but that was mostly for stage purposes." Arlene emphasizes the word "stage" hoping to spark some curiosity in the reserved brown eyes. Can a therapist be shy?

She settles herself into one of two wingback chairs, the kind she'd expect to find in someone's living room, not a doctor's office. She waits for Dr. Myatt to move to the leather chair behind his desk and resists the impulse to fold her arms in front of her as he takes the adjacent wing-back instead. She looks away, craning her neck slightly to see the photo on his desk.

"My father," explains Dr. Myatt, as the frame is whisked across the desk toward her. "He's a scientist. Used to teach botany at the University of Washington."

Arlene is embarrassed that her nosiness is so obvious but quickly recoups to feel slighted at Dr. Myatt's presumption, not to mention his lack, thus far, of appropriate eye contact.

"Handsome man," she says curtly, glancing from father to son and back again. "You must have your mother's colouring," she can't help adding.

"Yes, she was Italian. My father's a Brit."

Dr. Myatt's conversational tone is flat and uninspired — he'd be someone to avoid at a party. Why no picture of the mother in his office, Arlene wants to know, but doesn't dare ask. He's obviously not a married man. Dr. Myatt returns the frame to its place and changes the subject.

"Kerry-Ann is it?"

"She goes by Kerry. I'm afraid I'm the only one who calls her by her full name. Ann was my mother's name."

Dr. Myatt gets out of his chair and squats in front of the wheelchair, his face level with Kerry's. Her eyes blink once but remain in their fixed position as if staring at his tie. The tie resembles something by M. C. Escher, stairways leading back onto themselves, leading nowhere.

"And there was no brain damage from the accident?"

"The doctors all say the same thing. She's physically sound, no injury whatsoever to her brain or throat. The larynx and vocal cords fine. Apparently she wasn't even bruised. Tests show normal brain activity and that there's no physical reason for the catatonia."

"Her age?"

"Just turned thirty-four last week." Arlene sighs, thinking how silly her ministrations of cake and song had felt last Thursday. Kerry showed not the least glimmer of response and Patricia cried like a baby.

"I'm very sorry for your loss," Dr. Myatt says to Kerry with what Arlene gauges to be genuine concern. He seems to deliberately pause before adding, "I would prefer if you and your mother call me Michael."

A nicely personal gesture, thinks Arlene, for a rather impersonal man, though why he's telling this to Kerry-Ann and not to her ... There's another pause before Dr. Myatt offers Kerry his hand, palm up and level with her throat, as if greeting a strange dog. Arlene looks on critically, caught between finding fault with this young man and hoping he is the answer to her prayers. He remains perfectly still and Kerry audibly increases the strength of her next inhalation, as if to draw in the warmth or scent of his hand. He slowly retracts his hand.

"Very good," he says, as much to himself as to Arlene's stone-faced daughter. He rises and, this time, takes the seat behind his desk.

The strangeness of the exchange leaves Arlene with a sense of help-lessness she refuses to entertain. She crosses her legs and adjusts the peaked crease of her new pants over her knee, pleased to see how the cotton-linen blend picks up the light. He sits for so long looking at Kerry and nodding that Arlene jumps in.

"Since the medical doctors have been ineffective, I've brought Kerry-Ann here on a friend's recommendation," she begins. "He's a physician himself and was familiar with your work in Kosovo? With trauma victims?" She widens her eyes in admiration but he's not looking at her. "And you didn't even speak the language?"

"I picked up enough," says Dr. Myatt, carefully taking up his pen.

"My son, Richard, was able to read about your methods on the internet. And your successes with patients deemed unreachable." Arlene raises her voice in a congratulatory tone but still receives no eye contact. He should get rid of those funny glasses and wear contacts. She tries a direct question. "My son says post-traumatic stress is what the army used to call shell shock. Is that true?"

"They called it shell shock in the Second World War and battle fatigue in the First World War. And nostalgia in the Civil War."

"Nostalgia, that's curious. A longing for the familiar," she thinks aloud.

"It's more nostalgia for the traumatic moment itself," interjects Dr. Myatt. "An addiction of sorts that keeps returning its sufferers to that heightened state, but only because the incident hasn't been physiologically processed and digested. So they can't move forward in real time." He blinks hard, as if a gnat had just flown in his eyes, and abruptly stops talking.

"Oh." Arlene takes a breath, hopes he'll say more. He doesn't. "Well, Kerry-Ann's been insensible since the accident, almost six weeks now. My other daughter, Patricia, Kerry-Ann's older sister, tried giving her daily doses of some sort of nature medicine called aconite. She's into alternative mumbo ..." Remembering where she is, Arlene stops short of saying "jumbo."

"It's a homeopathic remedy for shock," Dr. Myatt says dryly.

"Yes, that's it. Well, it did absolutely nothing but neither did the drug the specialist prescribed. It's supposed to be the standard drug for catatonia, I forget the name. Something barbie."

"Amobarbital." Dr. Myatt uncaps his pen and places the cap perfectly perpendicular to the pad of paper.

"Yes, well, it just put her to sleep. Took me two weeks to get her out of bed and walking to the john again. I prefer the catatonia to a coma. Nor did antidepressants accomplish anything." She waves the memory away. "I was getting fed up with the drug experimentation, so we're here to explore other options. My husband would have joined me but he's recovering from a recent heart attack." Arlene stops. She hadn't meant to share this more personal information, at least not yet.

As if she'd finally said something of interest, Dr. Myatt's eyes meet hers for the barest second, then he speaks to her forehead. "This must be a very difficult time." Arlene raises her chin to try to line up his eyes with hers, but he returns his gaze to his pad of paper.

"I *will* say that I feel Kerry is an excellent candidate for the therapies I employ."

"Oh?"

"From your application I understand Kerry lived in Canada, in Victoria, British Columbia."

"She and her husband and son moved to Victoria about six months ago. They'd been living in Vancouver before that, for the past several years. Allan was from Vancouver. His family's still there." She pauses, leaving room for him to respond, but Dr. Myatt remains as still as her catatonic daughter. "Kerry-Ann ended up falling in love with Canada and the West Coast. These days we should all like to be living up there." It's approaching the one-year anniversary of 9/11, so Arlene assumes he understands her meaning. "Kerry's father hailed from a small city in Saskatchewan, so Canada's in her blood. After Kerry-Ann retired from her dance career, just last January, they bought a little place with help from his family, on Vancouver Island." She smiles sadly at her daughter, inviting the doctor to do the same. "Still has her dancer's figure." Dr. Myatt doesn't look. Instead he tips back in his chair and writes something on the pad now perched on his knee.

Despite Arlene's suspicion that she's talking to herself, she continues. "It was more of a cottage than a house they bought, a fixer-upper. Outside of town in a rather rural area." The word "rural" pushes off her tongue like a bad taste. "But it was close to the water. We Taylors love the ocean." Arlene clears her throat, but the doctor's attention doesn't leave his pad. She can't tell if he's writing notes or doodling like a schoolboy. "We brought her home to care for her. All *her* family lives here in northern Virginia."

"I'm from the Northwest myself," Dr. Myatt ventures. "Seattle."

There's a small contribution to the conversation, thinks Arlene, and for the first time notices the substantial gap between his two front teeth. Why was *that* never fixed? Gives him a bumpkin look. Surely it's easily corrected with braces, even a simple white filling of some kind.

"I miss the landscape," he continues. "But not the rain."

"Is that so?" The computer hums mulishly from the corner.

"She was a very talented young lady, a ballerina, you know." Arlene plucks some fluff off the lap of Kerry's dress and sprinkles it to the floor. "Only seventeen when she was asked to join the Capitol Ballet here in D.C., which, of course, we were very sorry she left. Her father spent more time at the ballet than at the Redskins games." Arlene's laugh doesn't even warrant a glance much less a smile. "But our little girl had bigger fish to fry with the NYCB." She waits for the question with no luck. "New York City Ballet," she relinquishes, "a *soloist*. She met Allan when the company played in Toronto. He was a stage hand or a set builder, I never got that straight," she says, shaking her head. "She joined up with Ballet B.C. after the move. A virtual star with that fledgling troupe. We were always so proud of her. Since retiring she'd started teaching kids in Victoria. Everyone was dying to hire her, as you could imagine."

Tired of speaking to Dr. Myatt's eyelids, Arlene stops. The doctor swivels his chair to look out the window behind him. Clasping her hands together in her lap, Arlene drums her fingers along her knuckles. Is she wasting her time here? Obviously she's wasting his. Arrogant. Is that what he is? The hole in the conversation widens and her back begins to itch under the new shirt. Perhaps he's partially deaf? She leans forward and raises her voice a notch. "I would like to hear more of what this clinic has to offer my daughter. I understand that patients are admitted as fulltime residents. My first question is how often family is allowed to visit?"

Dr. Myatt's chair swings back around. "Visitation can be daily until we begin intensive treatment. Then it will be reduced to weekly, at which time we can meet to discuss Kerry's progress. The number of visitors should be limited, though — just yourself or Mr. Taylor."

It's as if someone has flipped a switch on his back. "We boast a higher than average caregiver to patient ratio than any private clinic in the country. We don't rely on drugs for mood stabilization and we employ only the most current methods, all of which take a hands-on approach, so to speak. We have our own resident medical staff who monitor the patients' physical health and prescribe appropriate medications only when absolutely necessary."

Rattling off this information, he speaks to the photo on his desk, to Kerry's wooden face and to a spot somewhere over Arlene's head. Arlene raises her hand to smooth the top of her hair, thinking Dr. Myatt would starve if he were in sales.

"I see," Arlene says, her back suddenly crawling with itches in unreachable places. Is she really to believe that this gap-toothed, sandalled doctor with his grave lack of social skills will be able to re-humanize her daughter?

"I will also require some grasp of Kerry's background," says Dr. Myatt. "Her childhood and upbringing. All these factors are pertinent to her present condition." For the first time, he makes solid, sustained eye contact with Arlene.

It's a wholly unexpected and accusatory stare and she feels caught out, as if she'd forgotten to put on her face this morning, remove the curlers from her hair. He may as well have held up a finger and said: "Mothers are the axis of evil." She pulls in her stomach and tucks in her chin. "Other than the fact that we were and still are a happy, well-adjusted family, I'm not sure what to tell you."

Arlene is propelled by her outrage out of her chair to her daughter's side. She plants a tense hand on Kerry's shoulder, the bone disconcertingly sharp. "Kerry-Ann has had every advantage, and really, Doctor, if you could have seen that car with its top shaved off and begin to imagine what it was like seeing your spouse and your only child mangled like —"

Arlene yelps and snatches back her hand as Kerry shoots violently forward, then slams back against the wheelchair only to do it again and again. She is mortified watching her daughter's bloodless hands grip the chair arms, her blank eyes bulging, her jaw suddenly oddly slack. She has heard of, but never witnessed, Kerry's attacks. The slamming picks up force, Kerry's breath shrinks to quick gasps and the chair's off-angled wheels squeal, metal on metal.

Dr. Myatt urges Arlene aside and plants himself behind the wheelchair to catch Kerry's next head slam in the stomach. Planting his feet well apart, he takes hold of the wheelchair's handles as Kerry's head whacks him again, a dull smack that makes him cough. Arlene watches in embarrassed silence as Dr. Myatt closes his eyes, then eases his shoulders up by his ears and slowly lets them drop. His chest rises with an audible breath and slowly deflates. What in the world is he doing?

Kerry's next smack forces the air, *ooph*, past now parted lips and his face begins to look as slack and witless as her daughter's. Shouldn't he be calling in a medical doctor to give her a shot of something?

"It's awfully, bright, in here, with the, overhead, light on," he says, as if nothing's out of the ordinary, his words bumped along by Kerry's rhythmic assaults to his diaphragm. "The carpet, looks, to me, as if, it could, use, a going over, with the, vacuum."

Since Dr. Myatt's eyes are closed, Arlene doesn't know if he's talking to her or Kerry. It's ridiculous. Whatever does he think he's doing? *Stop her*, she wants to scream, barely able to contain her horror at her daughter's graceless, open-mouthed display.

"The duty nurse, should be, here soon, to take you, for a tour, of the, facility, and the garden, Kerry," Dr. Myatt oophs along. "She'll show, you around, the dining room, the, recreation, facilities, and the grounds. The roses are still in bloom."

Still absorbing Kerry's blows, Dr. Myatt starts in on the weather, of all things. Arlene is about to call for a doctor herself when Kerry's rocking begins tapering off, diminishing in force and size until she wobbles to a stop. Her face is flushed and her long neck juts awkwardly forward, pigeon-like, as she gulps mouthfuls of air. Arlene feels the tension drain from her shoulders and reaches for the chair back for support. Her instinct is to apologize for her blunder in mentioning the accident, but she's afraid the sound of her voice may trigger another scene. She waits for Dr. Myatt to say something. His eyes are still closed as he remains standing, perfectly still behind Kerry.

At least this outburst has enabled her to see him at work, thinks Arlene. In the hospital, the only way they could calm Kerry's fits was to hold her down and give her a needle. She can't help but be impressed. Dr. Myatt's not one for small talk, she decides, watching his closed face, because he's single-minded. Many intelligent men can't think and talk at the same time.

Finally Dr. Myatt's eyes open and he backs up two slow steps from the wheelchair, his shirt rumpled where Kerry's head has landed.

"That's excellent," Dr. Myatt says quietly as Kerry's breathing begins to normalize. Her mouth, thankfully, is closed again. He turns now to Arlene, eyes focused on her hairline as if addressing her brain. "It would have been wiser of me to have had the duty nurse take Kerry for a tour of the facility before we discussed certain issues. I apologize." He reaches for a button on his phone.

He's assuming the blame for her indiscretion, Arlene realizes. A lovely gesture and something Beresford would do. Pleased, Arlene sits back in her chair. She's met many bright, successful men who are social bores. This doctor is obviously quite capable and she'll have no hesitation signing the forms necessary for him to supervise Kerry-Ann's recovery.

Minutes later, Arlene is watching her daughter being wheeled away down the hall. Kerry's long hair, combed so carefully this morning, now hangs over her ears instead of behind, some caught up in her collar and ballooning out in an oblong puff. Hopefully the nurse will notice and do something about it.

"How long it will take to bring her safely back to full cognitive functioning I can't answer," Dr. Myatt says, closing the office door. "Shall we sit down, Mrs. Taylor?"

Now that Kerry is gone, Arlene detects an undertone to his voice, a melancholy she'd failed to notice before. What makes a person choose such a pain-ridden profession? Dr. Myatt sits at his desk and with precise movements caps his pen and replaces it alongside his pad of paper, now laying face-down on the desk.

"Because Kerry was a contributing member of society before this tragedy, we can hope for a complete recovery," he says. "The recovery rate of PTSD patients with secondary traumas, stemming from their childhood, for example, is far less predictable. We might have her home by Christmas —but, of course, I can't promise. And then, after recovery, there's always a grieving period, healed only by life's inevitable carrying on."

These last words sound so defeatist that Arlene's attention shifts to the lavender abstract on the wall.

"After residency is terminated," Dr. Myatt continues, "we recommend follow-up therapy on an outpatient basis."

As he finishes these words, there's a rapping at the door. It eases open and a young woman peers in, a girlish grin on her face, and Arlene recognizes the receptionist from the front desk. Cute, thinks Arlene and she peers around the door to assess the rest of her. A little thick through the ribs and bustline but nice slender legs. Arlene smiles and the young woman smiles back. Deep dimples indent the woman's broad cheeks and little brown curls escape her hair combs. Arlene can't help but think of Betty Boop.

"Excuse me. Michael, here are the papers you asked for."

"Thank you, Terese," Dr. Myatt says, getting up from his chair. "These are the necessary consent forms, Mrs. Taylor, if you decide to place your daughter in our care. And this," he waves the thin document like a flag, "is a brief outline of my program, laid out in five main stages, which I have put in layman's terms as best I could. Something for you to take home."

Arlene notes that Terese has remained in the doorway, her back against the door frame. Judging from the height of her heels and shortness of her skirt, she's dressed for more than a day behind a desk, Arlene thinks. In her stocking feet she couldn't be more than five foot two.

Dr. Myatt nods at Terese and smiles warmly, magically releasing her from the room. He *can* smile, thinks Arlene teasingly.

"The techniques I employ are non-invasive and kinetic," says Dr. Myatt, addressing the window and world at large. "To put it as simply as I can, we will be tapping into the underground spring of our survival instinct — our healthy, pre-trauma physiology that I refer to in my outline as our basic will to thrive. Kerry's connection to this inherent drive has been," he hesitates, as if searching for an appropriate word, "derailed. This will is born simultaneous with physical and sensory development and I have developed a series of exercises that reconnect the patient to this early state. My view treats the patient with the understanding that the mind and body are inseparable, that they reveal each other simultaneously."

Arlene has no idea what he's talking about. No wonder he's single.

"It sounds like an approach Kerry-Ann would appreciate, being a dancer," she says politely. "She was always very in tune with her body."

"Well, this document will explain my approach more thoroughly."

Arlene looks down at the papers on her lap. "Sympathetic Exchange" reads the title page, "Michael Myatt, PhD" appears across the bottom. She flips to the table of contents:

METHODOLOGY

ORIENTATION

Stage I — THE WILL TO THRIVE

Stage II — THE WILL TO WONDER

Stage III — THE WILL TO KNOW

Stage IV — THE WILL TO LOVE

Stage V — THE WILL TO CHOOSE

The affirmative "will" as opposed to "won't" is all she registers and all she needs.

"That won't be necessary," Arlene says, unleashing a pen from her purse. She's tired now and tells herself that this man is well-intentioned and without guile. He'd even be an interesting-looking man if only he'd fix that gap in his teeth. "Where do I sign?"

She signs the consent forms in three places, then takes the papers outlining Dr. Myatt's methodology and rolls them up to fit in her bag. She can use the backs as drawing paper for the grandchildren. She rises and Dr. Myatt moves to open the door for her. "Frieda Carter is the head nurse for our wing," he tells her. "She'll be able to answer any questions you might have regarding clinic procedure and patient care. I'll introduce you on the way out."

Together they walk down the hall.

"Oh, I forgot to mention," she says. "I found a book Kerry had been keeping since her retirement. Just some of her thoughts on her career, I believe, but I thought it might be helpful."

"Yes, I'd certainly like to take a look at it. I last saw the ballet, maybe a dozen years ago now. I enjoyed it very much," he says. "It obviously requires tremendous discipline."

So he was listening. "Well, yes, Kerry-Ann is doggedly determined.

But, of course, she received tremendous support from her family."

Arlene smiles, satisfied by the opportunity to make this final remark.

⚬⚬⚬

MRS. TAYLOR speaks in mauve tones, thinks Michael on his way back to his office. And why does he keep kowtowing to Frieda Carter? When he introduced Mrs. Taylor he felt himself bowing slightly to the head nurse. His subordinate. Why is he trying so hard? Because he's on probation is why. A one-year trial contract. He knows it, and for sure Frieda knows it. And because he's never had such generous means before to put his therapeutic ideas to test, he's anxious to do well. Nor has he had the privilege of intensive daily interactions with such a small group of patients. Another precious rarity in his field.

He shuts his office door to sit in peace for his five minutes to spare before trying again with Johnny Bourne.

Angling his father's photo toward his chair, Michael admires the cool serenity in the man's face, the careless regard for the camera, and recognizes the ability to "step back" as something they shared. His father had been a contented man, needing no one else to enrich his world, his family a kind of background noise. He and Michael hardly spoke those last few years, Michael too busy rebelling, his father wordless porridge at the best of times. And then the man was gone — disappeared. Michael never thought, back then, to track him down. Rather he dismissed his father's disappearance the way only adolescents can. Michael had left home himself shortly after, to attend university in California, and whatever resentment and anger he might have harboured for his father, his mother aside, was channelled into his studies.

Now Michael removes from his top drawer a letter he'd received just this morning. For as long as he can remember he'd received two cards a year from Eden, one on his birthday and one at Christmas. Like a stalker, she'd somehow always managed to track his whereabouts despite frequent changes of address. Her cards, complete with maudlin rhyme, had never contained anything more than a signature. But today's letter is different.

Today he's not only learned where his father has been hiding all these years but that the man is sick and maybe dying. The cabin at Lake Bernard was the place Michael had more or less assumed his father had gone, but since Eden never said anything, he'd dismissed the idea. Instead, every few years, whenever his curiosity got the best of him, he made all sorts of useless inquiries, racking up his long-distance bill and spending fruitless hours on the Net. So what does Eden expect him to do now? Care? Take him off her hands? A month into his new posting at one of the most prestigious clinics in the country, and she expects him to drop everything and hop on a plane, come hold his father's hand? He removes the letter from its envelope, opens it and almost winces at its crude lettering. He rereads the last lines: *Your father doesn't know I write this but he will love you when he sees you. Please come before too much time passes. You are missed.*

If *he* doesn't want me there why should *she*? Michael wonders if his sister received a similar letter, then remembers Isabelle never knew about Eden, his father's much younger lover, and the affair that has apparently lasted a lifetime. He folds the letter back into its envelope and, with one accusing finger, pushes it away from him until it touches the foot of his father's photograph.

The photo was one of the few things Michael took from his mother's house after she died, besides his father's favourite sports coat and a brand new dress coat Isabelle insisted was too good to give away. Mostly he was amazed and saddened that his mother had clung to his father's things for all those years. Isabelle also insisted Michael take the matching photograph of their mother. The photos had been taken at the same time, plus a third one, that Isabelle claimed for herself, of his parents together, arms around waists, smiles hard-won by some joke made by the photographer. The professional photo shoot was something his mother would have arranged and his father would have consented in order to avoid a scene. Michael can't say what happened to the photo of his mother, only that he misplaced it somewhere along the line. A subconscious forgetting perhaps. His mother had willed the house to Isabelle, while Michael was left with some bonds worth around ten thousand dollars. He wasn't surprised.

His mother had never treated her children equally in life so why would that change in death? Isabelle had been embarrassed by the disparity and offered to sell the house and give him half. But he knew she loved the old place and he truly wanted her to have it. He didn't need the money.

Michael picks up the photo and examines his father's face. A face not much older than Michael's is now. How often has he imagined those eyes watching him, noticing his choice of tie, admiring a clever retort, being impressed, for example, by the way he was able to calm the dancer in the wheelchair. To think that the man's been alive and well all this time and Eden, that dull-witted woman, has known all along ...

He takes a breath and calmly puts down the photo, replaces the letter in his desk drawer. Back to the living, he thinks, checking his agenda: Johnny Bourne. Taking up his notepad, he carefully tears off the top piece of paper. He glances at his sketch of a dancer, the long hair fused with her dress in a twine of motion, then crumples it up and overhand shoots it into the recycle box. Two points.

THOUGH MICHAEL'S trying to make a habit of taking the stairs, he sees Terese stepping into a nearly full elevator and hurries to catch up.

"Michael," acknowledges the man behind Terese, a Dr. Stemple from fourth floor, schizophrenia. Michael gives Dr. Stemple a friendly nod, hoping a silent reply thwarts any conversation in this public a space. The doors close and Michael and Terese are forced to stand so close as to be almost touching. Terese smiles up at him, dimples indenting her cheeks. Elfin, he thinks, keeping his eyes on the cold, grey steel doors.

Michael is now acutely attuned to the tension of her presence beside him — a high-wire tension, as if she's speaking in a frequency only a dog can hear. Michael turns his attention to the whisper of a voice behind him, something about "remembering to pick up Charlotte." When he first feels Terese's fingernail on the side of his palm, he starts, yet doesn't move his hand. She slowly drags the nail downward. He stares ahead for several seconds before risking a glance. Her eyes are fixed on the elevator doors but there's a hint of a smile on her lips.

She might be more lively than he'd imagined, he thinks, as the elevator dings and the doors slide open. He follows her outside, in the direction of the parking lot, neither of them speaking until they're out of earshot of other people.

"Need a ride home?" she asks, jingling her car keys.

"I prefer to walk," he says. "It's my only exercise, but thanks."

"Walk me to my car, then?" A saucier look, one brown curl springing free to frame an eye.

"Sure."

Standing alongside her rusty Toyota Tercel, he finds out Terese lives alone, "a one bedroom in Abingdon Apartments just across from the Bradlee Shopping Center," has a cat named Jinx, "who is always breaking things," and that she broke up with her last boyfriend seven months ago. She pauses after this last bit of information but Michael doesn't know how he's supposed to respond and just nods. She asks if he eats shellfish.

"There's a restaurant near my place called The Crab Pot. It's a casual, plastic bib kind of joint, but if you like crabs and beer, you can't beat it."

They make a tentative date for Saturday and he watches her drive away waving in the rearview mirror. She's not shy, he'll give her that.

To bypass the retail commotion of King Street, Michael keeps to Olde Town's residential streets, those reminiscent of horse-drawn carriages and musket-carting soldiers. This block of Prince Street is humped with cobblestones, the placement of each rounded rock a work of art in comparison to the black smear of asphalt elsewhere. He admires the knitted brickwork of the sidewalks and how seamlessly the townhouses appear to grow out of them, shoulder to shoulder, marching uniformly up and down the block, the residents marking their individuality by the colour of their front doors — fuchsia, lemon, a dignified navy — and choice of door knocker. The painted shutters and windowboxes match the door, any lingering flowers depressed-looking by this late in summer. Almost every house has an American flag waving beside it.

A sign of a country-wide PTSD, thinks Michael, a nationalistic panic to create the illusion of solidarity, of safety in numbers. He never saw this profusion of flags before 9/11. God bless America and to hell with everyone else is what the flags say to him. He remembers this time last year and that amazing softening and dissolution of borders between people. Overnight, there was a sense of connection with the past, present and future terrors that people everywhere experience. And there was such sympathetic outpouring toward America from around the world that for a time the whole incident felt like a blessing in disguise. Then dualistic, isolationist thinking took over. The government reduced everything to "us against them," "good versus evil," and the softness turned to stone. In his psychotherapy, this is just the sort of disassociative thinking Michael is trying to undo. As a therapist, separating oneself to try to remain physically, emotionally and intellectually superior to one's patients undermines the psychological support needed to penetrate to the root of a disorder. And in the long run it creates a dependent therapist–patient relationship. At least, this is part of the theory Michael's hoping to prove.

A jogger trots toward him, an attractive woman with the tattooed head of a serpent or dragon poking out of the waistband of her shorts. She gives him a passing smile and he can't resist a brief glance back, to see if she does the same. She doesn't, and he thinks of Terese. Spunky, a little untamed. They can have some fun, he imagines, without it interfering with their lives. It's amazing to him how long his father's affair with Eden has lasted. Of course, for all he knows, the man had plenty of other women in-between leaving Michael's mother and ending up with her. Though his father doesn't seem the type to spend time and energy seducing women. Ending up with a compliant pudding-head like Eden was probably more a case of needing someone to cook and clean for him while he lost himself in his spores and fungi.

He passes St. Andrew's Cathedral with its alpine spires, then sees the Masonic Temple on the hill in the distance like something out of ancient Greece. Here on the East Coast, he thinks, the spirit of the landscape lies in what's been built on top of the land, its buildings, bridges and monuments; on the West Coast, the trees, rocks and shore still outshout the man-made. Even the weather seems more in your face out West.

An analogy occurs to him: Manhattan losing the Twin Towers is akin to Seattle losing Mount Rainier. He pictures the great mountain on fire before crumpling to the ground — bears, mountain goats and various rodents leaping into the sky and falling to their deaths. Turning onto his street, Michael suddenly misses the cooler and much cleaner Pacific air.

His apartment occupies the main floor of a townhouse built in the 1930s. The place has been recently renovated, the plaster walls replaced with drywall, the plate-glass windows double glazed. The original wood-work was salvaged and painted a bright white, the oak floors preserved under glassy layers of varnish. Only after moving in did he discover that the two fireplaces, which had sold him on the place, had been choked with bricks. The landlord blustered on about the charm they added, never once mentioning that they no longer worked. He fishes his key from his pocket and opens the door, hearing the murmur of the radio he deliberately left on this morning.

ORIENTATION

In examining the nature of non-congenital mental illness, I maintain that most can claim as their trigger a single, traumatic event. The traumatic event, however, is not the ongoing cause of illness. The ongoing cause of mental illness is something I will refer to as "deliberated ignorance," otherwise known as associative disorder. This is the mind disassociating from the body and losing touch with normal narrative memory that locates the patient in time and space.

This deliberated ignorance is instinctive, a reptilian-brain survival tactic. Initially helpful, it serves as a buffer between the victim and his pain. But as time progresses, if the original trauma is left unaddressed and buried from the victim's conscious awareness, the emotional energy of the trauma will remain trapped in the victim's physical body. Like an infection festering beneath the skin, the physiological wound fails to heal because it has never been properly exposed and tended. This suppression, or deliberated ignorance, ultimately serves to create a deeper, more insidious grasping of the painful event and stores the trauma, quite literally, in the bowels of one's being.

My approach traces its lineage to pioneers Ida Rolf, Carl Rogers and Bonnie Bainbridge-Cohen, therapists whose work acknowledges and addresses the sympathetic relationship between the psyche and the soma, and between healer and healing. To become effective therapists, we must awaken our own physiological or psychokinetic awareness and recognize interpersonal sympathy as the most expedient way to unearth internalized trauma. This level of exchange entails "taking on" the physiological state of the patient, helping to bear the burden, and guiding the healing process from firsthand experience.

Dear Hugo, Remember performing together as kids at the Lisner? How old were we that first year, eight? You were the delinquent Fritz, and I your sweet older sister, Clara. I'll never forget when you tripped me with your sword. What was it, our second show? And I nearly landed in the orchestra pit? I remember how the whole audience gasped and made this sound as if they were sucking all the air out of the theatre. I was completely mortified and ready to cry until I saw that mocking frown on your face. I'm still waiting for an apology, you know. Your claim of innocence is refutable.

My favourite part of dancing Clara was getting to ride up and down in that creaky balloon at the end of the second act and waving goodbye to everyone below in the Land of the Sweets, especially that most handsome of cavaliers, Ivan Nagy. Ooh, he was hot.

How many collective Nutcrackers have we been in over the years? Over five hundred easy, I bet. I've done nearly every dance in that damn show with one exception: the Spanish Dance. I'm too lyrical, I guess, and too blonde. Though they let me do the Arabian Princess in Vancouver. Just had to darken my skin with makeup. I loved that seductive dance. Every performance, I'd pick out some guy in the audience near the front and imagine I was doing a tortuous striptease for him. I on my pedestal stage and the guy not allowed to get anywhere near me — it was a safe seduction. Or so I thought. This one time, a guy was waiting at the stage door after the show. As soon as I saw him I knew it was the man I'd played to in the audience. He had his little girl with him, who was maybe seven years old, and he nudged her forward to ask me for my autograph. When I passed back her program, he touched my arm and whispered if he might see me sometime. He had these intense, manic eyes and I was sure I was going to have a stalker on my hands. I told him I was married and had a son about his daughter's age. Then I got the hell out of there. Next time I danced the Arabian dance, I played to the blind spot and imagined Johnny Depp sitting out there.

Sometimes I wonder who I might have ended up with if I hadn't become pregnant with Thomas. Not that I can complain. It's not like Allan screws around on me or gambles away the family non-fortune. And he does have a good sense of humour, which Thomas and I both need. He's great in the hay which, of course, was my downfall in the first place. How can someone be sensitive in the bedroom and insensitive in every other room? Unless he wants to have sex, he never touches me in any affectionate way. It's like he sees right past me unless he's horny.

I thought my being retired would bring us closer together, but now I'm thinking we're as close as we're going to get. I mean we share things, but they're practical things related to the house, food, Thomas, music. Well, music's not practical, but Allan's relationship to it is. He just hears the lyrics and the beat, nothing else. He doesn't hear the person who wrote the song and the place it came from, if you know what I mean. You know, Allan never liked ballet. "Didn't get it," as he once said. "But appreciated the dancers' flexibility." I ask you: Are all men so basic?

I need to find myself a new girlfriend to talk to because you, Hugo, are just too far away.

꧁꧂

MICHAEL ENTERS the orientation room and pauses. He ignores Johnny for a moment to take in the feeling of the space designed to create what he calls "a balanced environment." The soft yellow walls are dispassionate yet soothing, the darker wood floor (floors must always be darker than walls and ceiling so as not to confuse our primal expectations of earth and sky) provides a secure sense of ground, the salmon-coloured blinds offer a hint of challenge similar to that of the sun and, yes, the collage, a fragmented mash of dyed paper, is disorienting, but not too much so. Physical environments, Michael believes, and this includes art, affect and influence a person's state of mind. Fortunately for him, the director for the third floor, Dr. Gerald Scully — though he looks like A-flat sounds — is something of an art collector. He was the one who approved Michael's budget for "restorative art." Save for a table and half dozen chairs stacked in the corner, the room is clean and bare. Pleased with himself, Michael walks to the window and adjusts the blinds, irritated by how one lifts slightly higher than the others.

"Good morning, Johnny. We're going to have another go today. All right?" He removes a chair from the stack. "Remember, I'm only here to help you."

Johnny B., as he calls himself, crouches on a chair and his arms, like thick rubber bands, are wrapped tight around his knees. Spotless white socks, looking fresh out of their wrapper, exaggerate his long thin feet. He follows Michael's every move with loud, saucer eyes and, as if chewing old gum, his jaw muscles roll the skin of his cheeks. Michael's glad to see that Johnny was able to leave his towel behind today and that his fingers are starting out of his mouth for once.

"It's okay, Johnny." Michael adjusts his chair to face his patient square on. "A nice day out there. Did you get a walk in?"

Johnny nods once, more of a jerk than a nod. His fear is bright green, thinks Michael, who is a longtime believer of synesthesia, the mixing of the senses. It was more than just a whimsical belief on his part; it applied to his work in a curious way. In fact, he considered it practice in keeping his senses alert and receptive.

Today will be Michael's third attempt at treating Johnny, who has never remained in the room long enough for Michael to make any real headway. Frieda, with her trumpet-like manner, believes Johnny needs more time to feel at home, to get his bearings without another doctor messing with him. At least this is what Terese overheard. Michael, on the other hand, believes Frieda has become possessive of the boy in the gap between Dr. Weber's leaving and Michael's coming on board.

Johnny is twenty-four, his face scored with equal parts pimples and freckles. He was passed around the hospital system until he was finally assessed by specialists as emotionally delayed but not clinically insane. He was promptly labelled PTSD, for the district's want of further diagnosis, and is the one government-sponsored patient under Michael's care. Johnny had no family to claim responsibility for him after police discovered him in a rank, mouse-infested apartment nestled alongside his mother's corpse. A reported suicide by barbiturate overdose, rigor mortis was well established by the time the police were called in. Apparently, the call was from Johnny himself.

If it hadn't been for the Kilney statute, Johnny would never have stepped foot in a place like Rosewood. With the new statute, Virginia had a mandate to control the number of homeless people littering the streets. Johnny had "homeless" written all over him. Johnny's fees were being paid by state tax and the balance swallowed by Rosewood, so there was pressure to progress Johnny through therapy as quickly as possible. With results. It was a constraint Michael did his best to ignore.

"Okay, Johnny. Stay with me this time?"

Johnny stares harder, wider.

"Good," confirms Michael as Johnny sucks his breath past clenched teeth and lets it out his nose.

Michael brings his awareness to his own body. He slowly guides it from the soles of his feet to the top of his head, along the way discerning and then releasing the subtlest of tensions. He visualizes internal trap doors swinging open and wind moving freely through the open tunnel of his body. Within minutes his facial muscles let go, his jaw droops, easing his lips apart, and as he releases the surface tension of his skull even the lines of his forehead come smooth. His lids drape heavily around the eyeballs' curve and his gaze comes to rest about mid-shin of Johnny's frog-like posture. Michael turns next to the rhythm of his own breathing, in … and out … allowing thoughts to arise, clarify themselves and dissolve without association. In … out … in … out … he rides the brief tides of his breathing until the detached clarity he has honed over the years begins to brighten the edges of his peripheral vision. Three feet away, Johnny's coiled apprehension looms large.

Minutes pass before Michael feels a constriction at the back of his throat. When he sees his patient begin a confined rocking, he trusts that the feeling is significant and gives the throat sensation room to expand. Johnny's head now wrenches side to side in an unspoken "no" and Michael experiences a sensation of his eyes sinking into their sockets.

"Mrs. Carter!" Johnny screeches, puncturing Michael's concentration.

Lurching from his chair, Johnny's stocking feet slip as he scrambles like a tragic clown toward the door. He manages to pull it open and Frieda is already there, waiting on the other side. Michael doesn't miss her "I told you so" expression as she takes Johnny's hand in hers.

"Hope his funding doesn't dry up before we even get started," Michael says under his breath, yet hoping Frieda hears.

∽◦∾

MICHAEL EASES his weight off his elbows and flips onto his back, his breath beginning to slow. He reaches across Terese's searching face for his wine, which is on the side table — he and she somehow ended up on the other side than they'd started on — then settles himself upright against the headboard.

"Cheers," he says, taking a sip. Cheers?

He's embarrassed, as always, by those last primitive minutes of mindless thrusting. He's always thought that men fall asleep after sex because of a subconscious need to disassociate themselves from the stupid animal they've become. The first time with someone new is always the worst, he reminds himself, stifling a yawn.

"Can I have a sip?" Terese reaches for his wineglass but he stretches for hers and passes it over, instinctively wanting to create boundaries again.

"Australian Shiraz," he says. "Aussie wine just keeps getting better."

"As long as it gives a good buzz, it works for me." Terese takes a noisy sip and passes back the glass.

Cute, vivacious and with lovely breasts, Terese made a lot of noise during sex, but nothing in her body indicated to him that she'd had an orgasm. He should have asked her what she likes but it's a point of pride for him to figure such things out himself. He wants his eyeglasses now, craves definition. "Can you see my glasses on that side table?" he asks.

"You look much sexier without them, you know," says Terese, hesitating before handing them over. She nestles her head against his chest then and traces a nipple with one finger.

Michael can't stand his nipples being touched. He takes her hand and kisses it.

"You must not have eaten your cabbage growing up," she says.

"What?"

"My mother used to tell my brothers that if they ate their cabbage, it would put hair on their chests."

"What about you?" Michael lifts up the covers for a teasing peek.

"Wax. Keeps it in check," she says. "I love cabbage." She laughs, then gives the side of his face a lick.

He wants to wipe off the lingering wetness but doesn't. He glances at the clock. How to gently make her leave? He won't get a wink with a strange body in bed with him.

"So, Mrs. Carter tells me you were sought out after your writing appeared in some bigwig journals."

"Maybe," Michael teases.

She smiles. "*Real different* is what she calls you."

"Frieda seems to have it in for me for some reason."

"Yeah, she gave me a hard time when I started, too. A control freak, I guess, wary of new people in her territory. She's, like, been there forever and everyone says it's because of her that the PTSD wing's the smoothest run in the whole shebang."

Shebang?

"I know she doesn't like that you ask people to call you Michael and not Dr. Myatt. Thinks it's unprofessional."

Michael considers defending himself but Terese keeps going, her voice an insistent red. "And she's shocked by the money the board approved for you. Is it true we're getting a hot tub?"

"Flotation pool, for therapeutic purposes only."

"Too bad." She slips her hand under the covers and around his waist.

"I love what you did with your office, by the way, and told Mrs. Carter

I thought it was warm and inviting. Just so you know, I stood up for you."

"Why. What did she say?"

"She said it looks expensive."

Michael sighs.

"She'll get used to you and your shoes." Terese gives his waist a tickling squeeze. "Your dorkenstocks."

"Birkenstocks."

"Birkenstocks," she whispers, then looks up at him with such needy eyes that he checks the time again. Terese notices and speaks more quickly.

"Mrs. Carter does seem more severe than usual, though. One of the nurses told me her youngest son's been stationed over in Afghanistan."

"That's no fun," says Michael, trying unsuccessfully to feel sympathetic.

"She's got five kids, you know, all boys."

"Hmm."

"I wonder if she kept trying for a girl. I know I would," Terese says, her hand suddenly self-conscious as it slides over his chest.

Michael desperately wants to be alone now. It's late and he's hungry. They'd shared some nachos at the bar but that was hours ago and then Terese was all over him. He glances down and sees that she's closed her eyes. Better make his move before she falls asleep.

"Are you hungry, Terese?" Michael says, neatening her hair.

"Depends." Sounds like she's expecting him to whip up an omelette.

"Does a donair sound good to you or is it just me? There's a place between here and the clinic that's open late."

"Oh?"

"I'm on call and it's just a matter of time before my beeper goes off. Johnny B.'s meds either aren't working or he's flushing them. He's been sneaking around after lights out and ending up in other patients' rooms. Patient Taylor's twice now."

"The ballerina? Is she really catatonic or just a snob?"

Michael ignores this cattiness. "He doesn't usually wake anyone, but he scared the hell out of patient Daily last night."

"I'd heard Norma had a fright," Terese says with a forced laugh.

"Took an hour to quiet her down."

"She's a talker, that one, but sweet."

"It's not a bad development for Johnny, though," Michael says, thinking aloud. "An attempt at socialization. However primitive."

"He wouldn't try and leave the building?"

"It's hard enough to get him outside to the garden. And it would take some planning to get past Jeremy or Hogie."

"It's Hootie, not Hogie." Terese smiles as if thrilled by an opportunity to correct him.

"What sort of name is Hootie?"

"What sort of name is Hogie? The guy's from Georgia. That's all the explanation one needs," says Terese. "I once dated a fellow from Macon named Denmark Groover III. With a goofy name like that I assumed he had to be rich. Turned out to be a cad. Denmark Groover the cad." She laughs, then keeps talking. "Can't help notice that Johnny has a hard time keeping his eyes on my face whenever he comes asking after Mrs. Carter. It's a little disconcerting being ogled by someone who sucks his fingers and carries a blanket. Like being ogled by Linus."

Michael's stopped listening. He wants her gone.

"You know, the Charlie Brown comic character?"

"Yeah."

"Has Johnny asked you for your autograph yet?"

"No."

"He's asked just about everyone else. Apparently he keeps them in his bedside drawer. Not sure what he does with them, but —"

"So, how about a hot donair with creamy aioli sauce and then I'll drive you home." Michael eases himself out from under her head, forcing her to sit up.

"Okay, sounds good." Terese sounds disappointed.

As Michael tugs on his clothes, he sees her studying the print over the bed.

"That's something I picked up years ago, when I was at UCLA."

"*Driving to Venus* by Christopher Pratt," reads Terese.

Michael sees the print anew, as if through her eyes. He's always found a sort of cool comfort in this ribboned highway emptying into a deserted landscape. It's painted from the perspective of a person behind a windshield, driving a car. There's an even coastline on one side and flat grassland supporting a line of diminishing telephone poles on the other. Most of the canvas shows pale early-morning sky.

"How many people do you think there are in that car?" Terese asks unexpectedly.

"How many would *you* say?"

"Two, with a dog in the back seat."

"Interesting," says Michael.

"You?" Terese asks again.

"I've always thought the guy was alone."

"You would," Terese responds softly, though Michael detects an edge.

He leaves it at that. He doesn't want to feed any unrealistic notions she might harbour about a budding romance.

∞∞

LYING IN the hospital bed, her husband's shrinking form makes Arlene's five-foot-ten Norwegian build appear immense, endowed with super strength. Under the bullying fluorescent lights, Beresford's receding lips have paled, the dry skin puckered into tiny pleats. Arlene tries to conjure up the tall, broad-shouldered man with the bedroom eyes she once enjoyed kissing. She fails. Luckily, Beresford's mental acuity is unchanged and when he speaks she recognizes the person she knows and loves and her scrutiny dissolves.

"So Kerry's finally all settled in?" Beresford's voice, hoarse and weak, retains its chipper inflection. An effort for both their sakes, Arlene knows.

"Yes, I had her room changed this morning so she has a view of the Potomac. At the price she's paying, I was not going to be shy to ask. I just hope Allan's insurance is going to cover this."

"Depends on how long she stays," ventures Beresford.

"The rooms have decent furnishings. Arborite, not real wood, but at least it's not this cold metal stuff." She looks around the room. "Her bed is a regular old mattress and box spring, even has a bedskirt. Has these guardrails, though." She takes hold of the rail on Beresford's bed and gives it a shake. Beresford's eyes close for a second, as if feeling some new pain, and Arlene waits.

"That's nice," he says, slowly opening his eyes.

"I'm going to bring in some things to spruce it up. A painting or two. And that linoleum could sure use a rug. Maybe I'll buy her one of those hooked rugs. They're inexpensive. Unless you think we could spare the Persian in the den."

"Sure, sure. Poor baby," says Beresford with a shake of his head.

"I told you the doctor said she may very well be home by Christmas."

"She'll get past it. She's got a lot of life ahead of her yet. You tell her I'm counting on those chocolate cookies of hers for Christmas," he says, raising his index finger. "And I won't be disappointed." This command, from a shrivelled king, is all heart.

"I'll pass it on."

"I sure hope this is the man who pulls her through. My God, I never felt so powerless in all my life when I was trying to get that child to look at me." Fatigue drains his voice to a whisper.

"Don't go making yourself sicker. I'm expecting both of you around for Christmas." Arlene props the pillows behind his back. "The head nurse told me that Dr. Myatt was top of his class at UCLA."

"Glad to hear it," he says.

She passes him his glasses, then the front page of the *Post*, and takes the entertainment section for herself before dropping heavily into the chair. When she stops moving, she's always surprised at how tired she is.

Much of Arlene's day is spent driving the half hour to Arlington Hospital, another forty to the Rosewood Clinic in Alexandria and then the twenty-five minutes back to Falls Church and her white-cushioned condo on the seventeenth floor. Most nights she's back at the hospital for an hour or two. She is thankful for an air-conditioned car, simulated leather seats and her *Les Mis* tape. Despite these added commitments and their emotional toll, she's been maintaining her morning tennis games at the club, at least one lunch per week with the girls, her Tuesday evening Scrabble with Dorothy and time for her painting. She refuses to let herself worry about things that are beyond her control. A big waste of energy is what that is.

"They're never going to catch that bin Laden," says Beresford with a smirk, shaking the paper into a neater fold. "He's the type who thrives on outmanoeuvring the enemy."

"If we had stayed out of their business from the start, this would have never happened." Arlene has said this before and she'll say it again.

"There'll always be extremists and someone's got to take control of them," objects Beresford. "Especially now with all the deadly weapons around. And, frankly, I'd rather our government be the ones in control."

An imperialist attitude, thinks Arlene, but as usual she allows her husband the last word. She notices Beresford's left foot is uncovered and reaches down to adjust the covers. His toes are an anemic colour blue and cold to the touch.

"Your feet cold?" she asks.

"More numb than anything."

"Well, you need to move them around a little, get your circulation going."

They read in silence as Arlene uses one hand to rub his feet, one at a time, through the blanket.

Beresford Taylor, twelve years her senior, is seventy-eight years old but recovering well from yet another minor heart attack. Arlene expects him home by the week's end, propped up in his chair in the den, his will to live much hardier than his failing heart and strangled arteries. The specialist says it's only a matter of time before he suffers a massive coronary or stroke. Having given home care to her dying mother, Arlene has no qualms about looking after her husband until the end. That's what family's for. She expects as much from her children when her time comes, hospitals being no place to live, much less die. Arlene just hopes she doesn't survive past the point of looking all right. Old age does terrible things to a woman's face and she's spent too much of her life working at looking good, beautiful even (in her day), to have her final impression rendered grotesque.

"Let's see the mail," says Beresford, handing back the paper.

Arlene pulls a handful of envelopes from her purse. She reads each bill out loud before passing it over. The chequebook and pen follow. As Beresford writes out the cheques, Arlene addresses the envelopes. She saves any scarf business for last. This sideline enterprise is something Beresford has taken up since retiring and selling his rattan furniture store. The scarves keep his hand in a world he loves, keep alive a young man's dream of hitting it rich.

"An order from the gift shop at the Smithsonian is all we've got. For fifty," she says, handing over the fax.

"It was two hundred this time last year," he sighs. "Nothing from the Memorial gift shops?"

"Not yet."

"Tourists are staying home," says Beresford, taking up the chequebook again. "Can't blame them."

"Not with armed guards checking your trunk and glove compartment at every parking garage." Arlene and Dorothy had suffered through this indignity last month at the National Theatre. And not only was their car searched on their way in, but again on the way out.

Back in 1976, Beresford had come up with the idea of making an accessory scarf boasting the signatures of each U.S. President. His intent was to capitalize on the millions who came to the Nation's Capital for the bicentennial celebrations. Arlene came up with the design, placing each signature inside a white rectangle and scattering the boxes over a navy background, with a red and white stripe trimming the border. The scarf pulled in sixty-thousand dollars that first year and has given their retirement a cushion ever since. Arlene keeps one tied to the strap of her tennis bag and another on her purse while Beresford never forgets to bring one to a party or restaurant to leave with the hostess or manager. No guest leaves the Taylor home without a signature scarf.

"But you can't live life worrying about all the bad things that could happen," says Arlene, thinking of Dini, her former tennis partner at the Army-Navy Club. "The worst is over in my book, and we need to get on with it."

Dini was at the club a year ago when that plane crashed into the Pentagon. Arlene would have been there, too, except that she and Beresford happened to be in their time-share at Myrtle Beach. The Army-Navy Country Club, minutes from the Pentagon, is in the direct flight path of Reagan National. Planes roar overhead all day. But Dini had described this plane as "flying so low it bent the top of the trees." She'd told Arlene the sound was deafening, but the worst part was seeing "terrified faces pressed up against the windows, waving and pounding on the glass." Dini always overreacted and Arlene didn't completely believe her. But after that day, whenever Dini heard a plane overhead, she'd feel faint and weak in the chest. So she upped and moved to Wisconsin, where her eldest daughter lives, and it took Arlene two months before she found a tennis replacement. The new gal isn't half the player Dini was.

Arlene helps Beresford put the cheques into the correct envelopes, then licks the stamps.

"Don't forget to mail those," he says, finger rising again, as if she's not to be trusted with such an important task.

"I will."

He pats the covers, searching for the TV remote, and finds it just as a nurse whips aside the curtained door.

"Good day, Mr. Taylor," she says crisply as she wheels in a cart carrying needles and test tubes.

A minute later, she is injecting a series of silver needles into his already bruised arms, setting off more purple and red explosions. Like spider mums under a layer of yellowed gauze, Arlene thinks.

"Excuse me. Krista, is it?" asks Beresford when his arms are his again.

"That's me," smiles the nurse as she holds a vial of his blood up to the light.

He clears his throat and attempts to sit up a little straighter. "Have I given you one of our signature scarves?"

⌒o⌒

KERRY LIES in her new bed in this foreign-smelling room, struggling to keep her eyes open, struggling to pay attention. She is dressed in a white cotton nightgown with lace trim, a Victorian remake, one of two her mother bought for her stay. Kerry gave up wearing nightgowns when she was twelve, her spirited legs straining against the nightgown's skirt until it would end hiked-up, lumpy and bothersome around her waist. Even as a child she preferred sleeping in the nude or in an old Italian undershirt of her father's, rescued from the garbage, his Old Spice lingering in the fibres.

Tonight she's flat on her back, encased in a paper diaper, then a nightgown, then in a sheet and blanket. The metal bed rails are raised and a safety strap lies across her waist, just loose enough for her to turn over. These security measures increase the vigilance of the surface of her skin but, as fatigue finds its way in, her eyelids begin to betray her. Her waiting concentrates into a single point of light and finally gives up, imploding into an oddly determined sleep.

A shadow on the cold floor, Johnny B. sits in silent adoration of the new patient's profile, watching eagerly as her eyelashes flutter to a close. He had seen her being wheeled around the gardens and saw a marble angel with honeyed hair and sweet tangerine lips. Her silence called to him but he was too shy to answer and could only watch as she disappeared and reappeared between the bushes. Her room smells like fresh-cut flowers, but perhaps it's just the smell of an angel's lair, or just her smell. He doesn't know why but he feels safer in her presence. She makes this unfamiliar place he's been put seem smaller, better. Sucking on his finger, he rubs his towel back and forth on the skin between his top lip and his nose, enjoying the terrycloth's bumpy texture against his whiskers. In his free left hand, he holds his droopy penis, awaiting his angel's blessing.

I love my dog, Hugo. I've never been able to say that before because I never had a dog before. I love my dog.

We got a pup for a housewarming gift, an adorable black mutt with a white diamond chest and white socks on his two left feet. Funny how animals really do have two left feet. Remember Vanessa yelling that: whadoya have, two left feet? Why did the left foot always get the bad rap. Why not two right feet? Being left-handed, I take that personally. Blackjack's feet are enormous which I'm told means that the rest of him is going to follow suit. He's got this handsome border collie face, a thick body like a lab's and this upright bushy tail that curls around itself like a husky. He's completely orally fixated and was chewing everything in sight until a neighbour turned us on to pig's ears. Yes. Real ear of sow, dried like leather to a beautiful copper-brown. It's not as gross as it sounds.

As I thought, it's ending up that I'm the one that walks the dog and feeds him and is trying to train him. Now he's totally devoted to me, follows me around like a sheep and growls at Allan if he touches me. My own little bodyguard. He loves Thomas, of course, sleeps with him every night, so now everybody has a bedmate. It's stopped Thomas from coming in our bed at night and I have to say I miss snuggling my big boy. I dread the day when he won't let me hold him anymore.

I just remembered all the animals I rescued as a kid. The "dirty beasts" as my mother called them. Our next door neighbour's cat was a hunter and always bringing "gifts" home to his master. The neighbour would haul the cat inside and leave these in-shock animals, birds and voles mostly, paralyzed on the welcome mat. I couldn't just leave them there for the cat to get again. I'd make sure they could see me coming and approach soft as nothing, trying to breathe calm into the frozen wild of their eyes. Then I'd make a hammock out of my shirt and lift them into it as gently as I could, their tiny hearts thrumming against my fingers. I guess they were too stunned to strike out at me because, oddly enough, I don't recall ever being bitten or anything. With that little bundle of heat against my stomach, I'd tiptoe around locating a shoebox (a hospital) and filling it with nesting materials, grass and leaves. Before putting them in the box, I can remember rocking them and singing wordless songs. Repetitious syllables, really, sounds that I thought soothing, even healing if I found the right frequency. Then, having punched holes in the top, I'd carefully transfer them into the box, and tuck them away at the back of the walk-in closet in Patricia's and my bedroom. I'd feed them water with an eye dropper and figure out what food they ate. Lettuce, worms, dead flies. And when I'd hear a little head knocking against the top, I knew it was time to let them go.

You know, I buried only a few, the rest scurrying off or taking flight with a blast of freedom that always startled me.

∽o∾

MICHAEL KNOCKS — two sharp raps — before entering the orientation room for his first session with Kerry Taylor. She sits in sunlight, framed by the collage he'd discovered in a gallery in downtown Seattle, an abstract mash of paper tinted with dyes made from fruit and vegetables. He'd found the picture's blend of colours unpredictably fluid and therefore useful in freeing both the eyes and the conceptual mind. Now, as the muted turquoise, golds and blues of Kerry's Indian cotton dress merge with the collage, he finds himself newly disoriented. He closes the door behind him.

"Good morning, Kerry," Michael says, and pauses to leave room for a standard reply.

"You slept comfortably?" he continues "... Mrs. Carter tells me you're eating well, which is terrific ... Well, I'd like to begin right away, if I could ... I will simply be sitting with you this first week."

As if answering for her, a starling flutters momentarily at the window, then flies off. Kerry doesn't blink.

"And please know," Michael adds, his voice slowing with a practised sincerity, "that I am here for you, to share your burden."

Head poised, collarbones lifting against white skin, long straight hair brushed down her back, Kerry looks like a dancer posing for a portrait. Michael pulls up a chair opposite her and finds himself adjusting his posture to match his patient's.

"Lovely day out there … Okay, let's begin, shall we?"

Not wanting to rouse self-consciousness, he avoids looking directly at the patient's face. He settles his gaze to where her dress drapes the rounds of her knees. In the sunlight the fabric is slightly transparent and he discerns the long muscles of her thighs before quickly blinking his attention back to the cotton surface. His eyes flicker to Kerry's vacant eyes. Since she seems to register neither his presence nor any hint of self-consciousness, he indulges the temptation for a quick visual study before getting down to work. He notes the high cheekbones, tapered nose and plump, almost babyish lips. And though it probably wouldn't be noticeable if she wasn't so immobile, the two sides of her face seem mismatched, one nostril, eye and eyebrow sitting a fraction higher than the other. Even her lips look fuller on the left side. A gentle Picasso. A ropy muscularity shapes the thin arms and there is pride in the pulled-back shoulders and lifted chest. Despite the vacant face, her physical presence feels vital and alive. Michael's eyes trace the small mounds of her breasts, move to her waist and down to linger on her boyishly narrow hips. Again, he guiltily checks in on her face. The smooth skin of her forehead seems active to him now, as if slightly compressed, especially on the right.

Michael centres his attention and discerns that his own forehead appears to be pulsing slightly. There's a sensation of heat, of blood pooling, there on the right side — right frontal brain activity, perhaps, which is the area that interprets non-verbal cues, that "reads people." He wonders how active Kerry's brain is despite the lack of response. The soft arc of her eyebrows frame round, silvery-blue eyes that appear almost quartz-like. Windows on her catatonia, Michael jokes to himself. The colour is cold, unearthly, like a winter sky reflected off the frozen surface of a lake. Like Lake Bernard in December, he thinks, picturing the rough cabin where his father took him each year for the week following Christmas Day, to celebrate Christmas a second time, just the two of them, and Eden. These backwoods trips were repeated each summer, but for three weeks, sometimes longer. Michael complied only until he was old enough to refuse.

His attention is quickly brought back by the movement of Kerry's hand. Like a trusting dog showing its belly, her right then her left hand turn from palm down on the wheelchair armrests to palm up. Caught off guard by this unsolicited gesture, he takes a couple of focusing breaths, chiding himself for allowing his attention to wander. He looks harder at Kerry's facial expression: nothing. He realizes he's holding his breath and lets it go.

The initial meeting with Kerry comes back to him — she responded to his proffered palms in his office. He slowly turns over his hands, one, then the other, to mirror his patient's and centres himself to begin. He focuses near her feet this time. Are those ballet slippers she's wearing? He casts Kerry in his peripheral vision and lets his breathing and concentration deepen. He rides the full swell and dissolve of his breath until a resonance, like a bat's echolocation, delineates the room and its objects. Minutes pass before he realizes his patient's breathing is lifting and falling in unison with his. For a brief moment, he entertains the thought that she's mimicking him, making fun of the obvious, but there's no visible intention emanating from the face across from him. He can't tell who's initiating this breathing rhythm and holds his breath just long enough to break stride. Her breathing continues as it was.

Michael then notices that his palms feel clammy, as if a layer of moisture is evaporating. Are Kerry's palms feeling similarly? Glancing up to confirm that her forehead is no longer active, he's surprised by a new somatic shift as a gust of what feels like brightness invades the cave of his chest. It's a disconcerting feeling, as if someone's fingering the inner edges of his ribs and prying them apart. His attempt to draw this sensation closer on his next in-breath causes his chest to involuntarily tighten and he checks an urge to turn over his open palms. Keeping his hands where they are, he focuses on relaxing his chest area. He still can't get a good breath and a tickle in his larynx starts him coughing.

"Excuse me," he says, then stands and moves over to a table in the corner that holds a tray with two glasses and a pitcher of water.

He pours himself a glass and takes a sip, then another. He looks back at Kerry sitting there, facing his empty chair.

"That's better," he says aloud. He returns to his seat and places his glass on the floor. He wants to apologize but that would be putting himself in a position of weakness. Maintaining one's authority instills confidence in the patient.

He begins again, palms down this time, in a more grounded and less vulnerable posture, then re-establishes a full and relaxed breathing pattern. A few minutes in, he sees that the fingers of her bared palms have softened and bend inward, a shrivelled look. The tickle starts up in his throat again and though he tries to suppress it, he can't. Maybe he's coming down with something. Excusing himself again, he reaches for his water glass. Though Kerry's expression remains as neutral as chalk, he notices that her physical presence is diminished, her posture fatigued. Or is it disappointed?

"Maybe that's enough for today," he says to Kerry, thinking this such an odd beginning, that perhaps it would be best to start fresh tomorrow. Clearing his throat, he sees by his watch that only fifteen of the allotted forty minutes has passed. "Thank you for joining me," he says in a more authoritative tone. "Your experience today is good and trustworthy," he adds mechanically, then moves toward the intercom to summon the duty nurse.

Catching the top corner of his chair with a hip, he skews it off angle. Kerry's set gaze seems directed at the shifted legs of the chair, her curled, upturned palms horribly empty. He wants to straighten the chair but something makes him resist.

IN THE WASHROOM, Michael removes his glasses and vigorously soaps up his hands, then face, cleansing himself of the residual kinetic energy that clings like off-key noise to the surface of his skin. He rinses with hot water followed by a blast of cold. As he pats himself dry with a paper towel, he looks in the mirror. Without his glasses, his face appears as ill-defined as cafeteria food. What just happened in there? He was distracted, didn't give the patient enough credit for a fully operable consciousness beneath the catatonia. Loud forebrain activity.

Michael replaces his glasses, turns off the light and rests his hand on the doorknob. Standing in the dark, he listens to the leaky faucet mark the seconds. It's like a fluid finger tapping him on the shoulder.

In his office, he sits for several minutes before a blank pad of paper centred on his desk. He picks up his pen, testing its weight in an open palm before beginning.

Responsive despite the Face
dance for Two
Who's leading Whom
frozen lake Eyes ... expectant

He notes the use of capital letters before ripping the page from the pad and placing it to one side. Then he opens his top drawer and chooses a red and an orange marker. Uncapping the red, his hand moves deftly, making hills and valleys across the page before a smile-like scoop at the base to connect up with the initial line. Replacing the red marker with orange, he draws a meandering fissure down the empty centre of the red outline. He puts the pens aside and reviews what's happened on the paper. A crimson hand, a left hand, seems to wave back at him, an empty palm split down the middle by an orange line. He thinks back to his sister Isabelle's teenage dabble in palmistry. What placement on the palm is that? The lifeline? The heart line? Both severed in Kerry's case. But palmistry didn't interest him then, nor does it interest him now.

Michael files the two pages of "sympathetic exchange diagnosis" in the bottom drawer of his desk. These sheets are for his personal reference only. At the week's end he will type and print out a formal report for the official file kept at the front desk, the file that's used as reference for his superiors as well as for Frieda and her staff. He gets up to head to the staff room for a cup of tea. These carefully established routines have proved effective in clearing his senses, disinfecting his instruments, as it were, before he encounters his next patient.

THIS TIME of morning, so close to lunch, Michael usually has the staff room to himself, so he is surprised to see Terese sitting on the couch eating an apple. Bryson, one of the few male nurses on the floor, one of the "brawns" as Michael's heard them called, is there, too, pouring milk into his coffee. Bryson looks like he's about to leave.

"Hey, Michael. Come sit," calls Terese, patting the cushion beside her.

Michael notices the male nurse glance from Terese to him and back to Terese.

"Just need to make a cup of tea first," Michael says, careful not to sound too familiar.

"Water's hot," says Bryson with a crooked smile. Michael stiffens and looks away. He certainly hopes Terese hasn't been talking.

"Thanks." Michael turns to Terese. "I think the faucet in the bathroom across from my office needs a new washer. It's dripping." He keeps his voice impersonal, businesslike.

"I'll put in a call to maintenance."

"I'd appreciate that." He pours hot water over his tea bag.

He deliberately takes the chair beside the couch and relaxes his tone only after Bryson's gone.

Terese's crossed leg, swinging freely, is causing the bottom of her shoe to thwap rhythmically against her heel. The mindlessness of the sound irks him.

Terese cocks her head to one side and smiles. "It's warm enough to sit outside at Duck's Inn. Free for lunch today?"

Michael pauses a moment. He's just here to regroup between patients and doesn't want a question requiring decision making. He feels her eyes on him as he dunks his tea bag. He doesn't want to put her off entirely.

"Terese, it's difficult to get away now that I've begun therapy," he says. "That's why I requested the catered lunches. My resources are really taxed." He shoots her an apologetic smile, wrings out his tea bag and stands up to toss it in the wastebasket. At home he'd put this in the compost bucket.

Terese uncrosses her legs and fusses with her skirt. "That's okay."

"This is a very important posting for me and my particular approach calls for one hundred percent of —"

"You don't have to explain. Maybe over the weekend."

"There *is* the Asian collection at the Smithsonian I've hoped to —"

"We can take a picnic and sit by the reflecting pool. The sun's supposed to continue." She gets up from the couch and confirms the date with a squeeze of his knee he's glad no one's around to see. "I should get back to it. Phone calls to make, catered *lunches* to order." She rises and drops her apple core in the wastebasket. "Do you really want the same turkey club for lunch every day?" she asks, turning around. "Why don't you let me surprise you?"

"Umm … that would be fine, I guess."

"Oh, and did Mrs. Carter mention that the Wednesday socials are starting back up? It's a time for staff and patients to have tea together. You know," she pumps her index fingers down and up, "to 'bond' outside of therapy."

"She's mentioned it twice and twice I've sent a memo saying I won't be attending."

"Because you're anti-social?" Terese's tongue pushes out the dimple in one cheek.

"I prefer not to socialize with my patients is all." He makes a point of looking her in the eye and adds, "Mixing work and pleasure is not the way I operate."

Terese looks sideways out the window. "Yes, Doctor. Turkey club it is."

He's offended her now, but maybe that's okay. A woman like Terese needs clear boundaries.

MICHAEL IS well into the taking and sending technique and Johnny, radiant in his peripheral vision, has miraculously remained seated. Johnny's arms are tightly crossed over his chest and his tongue flicks in and out of his mouth like an inquisitive snake. His breathing is rapid but evenly spaced. A sign of willingness, thinks Michael, surprised they've gotten this far.

Soon, a hollow nervousness enters Michael's awareness, a loneliness, a timidity. This he merges with his exhalations, letting it dissolve into thin air. He considers such feelings as a patient's first layer of defence against more relevant responses.

After a few more minutes of the same, Johnny's breathing slows and deepens. Good, thinks Michael, and as he takes in his next breath, he feels his stomach involuntarily contract. *Now we're starting. How about that.* He hones in on the sensation, allowing it to intensify. The herbal tea Michael consumed before the session begins to pitch and heave like a miniature ocean storm. Soon it seems to be lifting in swells of nausea, then smashing against a hard-fisted determination not to vomit. Michael inhales the queasiness, invites it closer, until its claustrophobia is thick and airless. Johnny has begun a confined rocking, but his breath remains relatively steady. Michael switches his focus to releasing, softening the knotted tension around his stomach and sending out relief on a breezy exhale. He continues this process, working to introduce even an instant's freedom from memory and fixation. *Come on, Johnny,* he silently urges. *You can let it go for just a second.* This bartering carries on for what seems like an eternity until there's a gap in their joined clenching, a chink in the armour. *Yes.* It's just a tiny slit at first, fit for a shaving of light, soon big enough for a probing fingernail, then a greased finger, a warmed hand as Michael breathes himself open and gently invites Johnny along. *Let's go. We can do it together.* Therapist and patient enter a near hypnotic trance and Michael's vision begins to blur.

Ten minutes later, the air is dense and agitated, a bath of anxiety. Johnny's rocking has condensed to a shiver, as though the temperature has dropped. His eyes rotate up into their sockets as if trying to escape his body. Somewhere, something is coming unglued. Michael's breath catches, the air forcing itself in and out as if he's running a race. He rides a wave of stomach pain approaching the unbearable, and then the shift happens. A small hard ball seems to catch in the back of Michael's throat, forcing a violent cough. Johnny shrieks, lifting clear off his seat, then buries his face in his hands, rooting for a finger to suck.

Michael's nausea has vanished, the blocked feeling in his throat now full-blown. And, Michael realizes, his anus has gone stiff with one steady contraction. Johnny releases a low moan, like a threatened animal, his body collapsing into itself as if to deflect more notice.

The therapist must not be too eager for results, Michael reminds himself, and must allow the patient to guide the process.

"Johnny, we're finished for today," Michael says to the top of Johnny's buried head. He gets up to buzz for Frieda. "You should rest now. Thank you for joining me. I'll have Frieda bring your snack to your room." And, yes: End each session with a phrase of positive reinforcement. "Everything we have experienced here is good and trustworthy. That was excellent work. Believe me. You're going to feel better."

Frieda is at the door, a cold smile for Michael before she takes Johnny's hand. "He's shaking," she whispers over her shoulder.

"He did very well," says Michael, looking past her to Johnny. "Excellent work."

Tomorrow, he muses after they've gone, he and Johnny can spend less time on the stomach business and begin to dissect the blockage in the throat. Maybe work the moan up to a small shout or something vaguely assertive. He tongues the space between his front teeth, a childhood habit and a sensation he finds comforting, self-affirming. Michael suddenly recalls his father laughing at his early attempts at whistling. It wasn't a disparaging laugh — more of a breathy chuckle, the sort of laugh that sounded like pipe smoke — but it was enough to make a proud seven-year-old practice incessantly until he found a way around the gap in his teeth. Just like he's found a way around the gap in his life. If the man died tomorrow, Michael thinks, it really wouldn't make a hell of a lot of difference to him. On his way to the washroom, he finds himself whistling the song sung in baseball's seventh innings these edgy days — "God Bless America."

Later he writes in Johnny's file:

narrowed Anal and Oral channels, twin tunnels

Conflicted Longings knotted at solar plexus
the tie that binds

Opening his desk drawer, he chooses a blue and then a black marker. Locating his mind in his hand, he first draws a blue spiral wide at its centre and tightening into corkscrews at either end. Exchanging the blue marker for the black, his hand moves in furious circles directly below the blue spiral until he has created a solid black inverted triangle. He sits back and regards the shapes. The inverted triangle, elongated at its bottom point, resembles a funnel. It is nearly twice the size of the blue spiral and looks as if it's about to vacuum the spiral out of existence.

∽o∽

ARLENE HAMMERS a nail in the wall over her daughter's dresser as quietly as possible. She hasn't bothered to get the clinic's permission to hang artwork, but surely they couldn't object to her painting. She steps back to make sure it's hanging straight and feels frustration all over again at having never quite got the colour of the leaves right. She turns her hand to arranging the flowers that arrived for Kerry today — turquoise orchids in a snare of baby's breath. "Never liked baby's breath," she says, and chucks the small white buds in the garbage. After trimming the stems, she places the orchids in a vase brought from home, begins fanning them out.

"They're from your old ballet master, Sebastian Stuart," she tells Kerry. "Or is it Stuart Sebastian? I left the card at home. Orchids, nice choice. They must use dye to get such a colour, don't you think?" She glances quickly at Kerry, imagining she might catch her silent daughter off guard. Like in the game Simon Says, perhaps Kerry will answer and be instantly cured. But no.

Arlene wheels Kerry over beside the one comfortable chair in the room, places the vase on the table beside her. She holds her daughter's floppy hand and resumes the one-way conversation.

"I promise to bring you a rug this week. Ooh, that painting makes a difference. I'm going to bring my daisy painting next time, for over your bed.

Five dozen showering out of my cut crystal vase. The round vase with the pleated sides?"

She relays Beresford's motivational words, talks of his progress (in only the most positive terms) and moves on to discuss the unusually warm weather for September and the goings-on with Kerry-Ann's sister and brother, careful to avoid mentioning their children. She reports on the sympathy cards that are still arriving from dancer friends and colleagues scattered around the globe, censoring out the words of condolence. Most of the cards are from New York and Vancouver but some hail from as far away as Israel and Japan.

"One from your old rival, I mean roommate, Dasha. She had such a pinched look, really. And those funny little ears. Oh, did I tell you Janice Healy called the other day, your buddy from Blessed Sacrament? You probably haven't heard from her in twenty years. I told you that she was our waitress one day, years back, at that good chili place just up the street. Well, she ended up marrying the restaurant's owner, if you can believe it, and now has four kids. Why anyone needs more than two ..." Wrong thing to say, she realizes, nervously checking her daughter's face. Not a blink. Arlene had only wanted two children, but Beresford, being a good Catholic, didn't believe in birth control. After three children in as many years, Pope or no Pope, Arlene put her foot down.

She turns back to the mail. "Another from Hugo in Frankfurt. Very strange picture on the front," she says, not bothering to show Kerry the black and white photo of two scruffy, unnatural-looking kids, a girl and a boy, holding up their middle fingers. "I'll never forget that camel hair coat he wore to your retirement party," she says, shaking her head. "Wow, did he look smashing. Homosexuals do have a sense of style. I look forward to his call each week, he's always so entertaining. Yesterday he told me that one of his new recruits was so nervous on opening night that she peed while perched on her partner's shoulder. Can you imagine? Said it dripped right onto the floor and that the shoulder of the man's grey unitard turned black." Arlene covers her mouth with the back of her hand. "He must be exaggerating."

She has saved Hugo's card for last, and, reading it to herself first, dispenses the highlights. "Got mixed reviews for his new ballet, *Circling the Sun*. Says nobody seemed to grasp that it was about society's obsession with the masculine principle. He says Big Daddy's Girl would have understood. Who's Big Daddy's Girl?"

Arlene glances at Kerry's empty face.

"Says he loves you very much and will come visit in early December. He's offered to come sooner, but I've put him off. By December, I'm sure we'll all be up for visitors."

Placing Kerry's hand on her lap, Arlene rises to fetch the brush and hairpins on the dresser.

"Beat Dorothy last night at Scrabble, went out with a seven-letter word, *umiacks*. Some kind of boat. Left her stranded with the 'Q.' You know, we play with the timer now, just like the pros."

As Arlene brushes her hair, Kerry sits with the erect posture of a dancer, her eyes fixed on the grey-spackled linoleum. The slight tug of resistance in her daughter's long neck cautions Arlene not to pull too tightly. For a person whose mind seems so blank, thinks Arlene, Kerry's body feels oddly alert.

"All you kids were so blonde once upon a time," says Arlene, imagining painting a few highlights in the darkening strands. She torques the hair into a French twist and secures it with the pins, thinking that the last time she did this, Kerry was in grade school. But Mrs. Carter told Arlene that physical contact is beneficial under these circumstances, as are casual reminders of happier memories. She may not respond, but there is absolutely nothing wrong with her hearing, the head nurse had assured her.

"I've always liked you with your hair off your face," says Arlene. "The bunhead babes, as your brother used to call you and your friends." She smiles at the memory. "Richard is so clever in the word department."

Arlene was taken with Frieda Carter, impressed by her thorough, no-nonsense approach. The towering black nurse with her powerful arms and beautiful pale-chocolate skin brought to mind Amazonian matriarchs from those ancient tribes ruled by women. She understands Mrs. Carter's been working at the clinic since its inception and that it's her doing that Kerry is eating as well as she is and finally gaining some weight back. Nursing is obviously more than just a job for this woman, thinks Arlene, then wonders if she may have to watch that Kerry isn't being overfed. She isn't getting the exercise she's used to, so probably doesn't need that much food.

Before wheeling her daughter outside for her daily air, Arlene stoops to turn up the collar on Kerry's shirt to frame her face. "I wish you and your sister would wear a little lip colour," she says, rummaging in her purse. "Salmon coral would bring out the tones in your skin and, look at that," she exclaims, unsheathing a lipstick from its golden cylinder, "it matches the flowers in your skirt."

Arlene listens for footfall before gingerly applying two fingers to her daughter's chin and tilting it upward. Kerry's gaze remains lost on the floor as Arlene pushes colour onto the puttyish lips.

"Hold still," she reprimands the utterly mobile flesh, then tries less pressure.

This reminds her of assisting with her daughter's makeup at dance recitals. But, back then, Kerry's pale blue eyes would be staring up at her, roaming her face, filled, or so it seemed, with questions that never formed. It's discomforting how one's own child can feel so foreign, she thinks, and is momentarily grateful for Kerry's infant-like oblivion.

Kerry always abhorred the smell of lipstick, she remembers now with chagrin, only wore it for the stage and even then it was those odourless lip pencils. Well, maybe that's changed, she tells herself. And who's to complain? Arlene touches up her own brandy-wine lips, grinding them together before a stretching pucker.

"Come on, gorgeous, let's go wow the menagerie on the lawn."

Outside, Arlene wheels past patients and their visitors while those that look like Rosewood staff receive animated smiles, notes on the weather. A little PR never hurt. That reminds her, she should bring along a signature scarf for Dr. Myatt. Being new to the area, he'd probably like that. The latest batch even has George W. Bush's signature, illegible as it is.

After their stroll, Arlene feeds Kerry an early dinner of Ensure, puréed beef, mashed potatoes and mashed mixed vegetables. She coaxes the food into the disinterested mouth as she once did when Kerry was a baby, never expecting to have to repeat the process thirty-four years later. When she wipes the excess food off her daughter's lips, lipstick streaks the napkin an alarming orange.

∽o∾

IN A FITFUL sleep, Kerry wrestles against the belt strapped around her waist, her knees stabbing up white cotton hills. The police car's red light swings in circles, tinting and untinting her view, making it hard for her to see. Must keep her head up. On either side of her, wearing white, then red-splashed jumpsuits, they are holding her back, bruising her arms, keeping her from returning to the car, a convertible? *Lakmé*'s "Flower Duet" raging overhead. She desperately needs to feel the warm skin of the man and boy under her palms. Their names scream until they are echo-fixed inside her skull, a skull without nerves, without feeling, as it cracks against the headboard behind her. She opens her eyes to a figure in white, then red holding her arm, bruising her arm, before a sudden sting spreads a haze of sleep up her veins. The swinging light illuminates the masked head in the corner, his frightened eyes pleading with her to love him. She tries to go to him but her legs have been filled with wet sand. The siren of applause rings wild in her ears and the stage goes to black.

Dear Hugo, After all those years and God knows how many shows, I never got over pre-performance nerves. What's it like to wait in the wings? Hell, pure and simple — stomach churning, heart racing, debating whether I had time to visit the bathroom again. I remember that herbal nerve stuff you sent me from France. It smelled like bad breath and didn't work, by the way, and I quickly came to the conclusion that it was just another one of your mind-over-matter games. But I kept taking it anyway. Why, you ask? Because I'm a masochist? Yes, I am. I missed how you would torture me before shows and this herbal poison was the closest I could get. I can hear you now: "You're going to fall, Kerry, fall on your knobby ass and they're going to laugh and point. It's going to be baaad. Ha ha bad." And I'd hit you, which was helpful. But you know, you always lowered my expectations of myself — no, destroyed my expectations — and in that hopeless state, I'd get onstage and focus on just the music, because that's all I had.

After you left NYCB, my pre-performance terror got even worse. The other dancers would say things like, "You can do it. Knock 'em dead." Even "merde" was said with a smile. I kept having to imagine you beside me, sneering and calling me a loser. Although now that I think of it, you did say one or two nice things to me before a show. Must have forgotten to take your medication that day. One was: "Only amateurs aren't nervous." I loved you for that one. And what was another one? "The true artist is in a constant state of panic." That one wasn't as helpful, but on some level I understood what you meant. I do pity the kids in your company. They must be nervous wrecks.

I don't know why I suffered so much before a show, because as soon as

I stepped onstage, I was okay. Why I couldn't use that knowledge to calm myself before the next show is one of life's stupid riddles. Once onstage I'd be moving inside a vast, almost magnified stillness, a quiet that seemed to be at the heart or centre of the music, if that makes any sense. And in that place, thoughts of myself would evaporate like steam, even the pain in my feet would disappear.

Maybe an orgasm comes closest to describing it. A stillness that roars with life. That dissolves the boundaries between you and whatever it is that's supposedly not you. Sorry, I can't express it better. Now that I've retired, I guess more orgasms are in order. How many would you say make up for dancing both Concerto Barocco and The Four Temperaments in the same evening? Three, four? Of course four is probably an off morning for you.

You know, it sounds cliché but nature — trees and rocks and stuff — isn't a bad substitute for the performance rush. I find B.C.'s landscape draws me out of myself and into that bigger reference point. And does so without having to have diarrhea first. I'm starting to believe what those tree huggers say: "Trees yodel if you know how to listen." Don't I sound so West Coast?

Allan's been taking us camping. It's a little grimy and the food tastes suspiciously like dirt, but after three days with the sky as your ceiling, time starts to decompose. It's like the fourth wall of the world just falls away and there's so much more room to relax. Despite his hunting and gathering everything that's supposedly edible — dandelions, mushrooms (no not that kind), limpets, salmonberries, clams, oysters — and building beach forts, lean-tos and a portable campfire, even Allan slows down, a little.

Until I lived outdoors for days on end, I had no idea how much weather changes. Not just hour-to-hour changes, but minute-to-minute. The whole earth, sky and whatever's in-between, seems to be moving and breathing like some giant organism. Well, I guess we're the in-between. Which makes us part of this constant heave and push, this constant change. So maybe my mood swings are a natural phenomenon and not altogether my fault. Sometimes I look at a tree and think that I'm just like that tree. Standing upright with all these roots reaching into and feeding off my past, branches like arms grasping toward the future, each leaf another new thought that eventually withers and blows away.

Good thing you're not really reading this or you'd be mocking me, merci-lessly — "I'm a tree, blowing in the wind, reaching and bending." But you'd like camping, Hugo, because you'd get to buy a new wardrobe in khaki and camouflage, lace-up boots, sun hats. Oh, I do miss you.

Hey, Thomas is intent on taking dance classes this summer. Breakdance, that is. He tries to copy moves off MTV and is really pretty smooth. Obviously gets it from me. Remember going to that disco bar in Amsterdam with Allan? We thought he was trying to be funny, but that was how he really danced? "Spastic," I think you termed it. Watching the way his body moved to music should have clued me into his lack of attention span. His latest project: he's decided to take up sheep-shearing. The magazine thing didn't pan out. What a surprise.

∽✤∾

MICHAEL HAS just finished an encouraging session with the new, forty-two-year-old resident patient, Marcus Novakowski, or Manic Marcus as he overheard Nurse Bryson call him. Michael stands in the staff room wringing the remaining flavour from his tea bag. He smirks as he recalls how Marcus' verbal diarrhea loped from insults to riddles.

"Hey, Moron, what walks on four feet in the morning, two feet in the afternoon and three feet at night? Get it? Got it? Get it? Too slow. Even for a moron. Want me to tell you the answer?" A stocky, compact man, Marcus planted his mitt-like hands on his knees, his stubbled chin jut-ting comically forward. "Ready?" He smacked his legs with a force that must have stung. "It's a moron like you. Crawling on all fours in the morning of your shitty life, walking on two legs in the prime of your shitty life and using a moron cane for the twilight of your shitty life. Get it now? Are they paying you to just sit there and do nothing? My insurance better cover this bullshit."

In just one session, and without Michael saying a word, Marcus pro-gressed to swaggering around the room yelling his insults, arms jabbing the air for emphasis, until he began shouting "Shut up" and actually shut himself up. Before any more verbiage could start, Michael confirmed the session over and called the duty nurse.

Now he tosses the tea bag in the garbage under the sink, thinking he should definitely suggest starting a compost program at the clinic, maybe create a vegetable patch in a sunny corner out back that the patients could help tend. Better to take things slowly, wait until he's been here longer; then he'll speak to Dr. Scully about it.

Marcus Novakowski has filled the last available space in Michael's program, bringing the total number of resident patients up to eight. The PTSD wing houses twelve, but the number of Michael's patients, both resident and outpatients, has been restricted this first year, in order to give him the time and space needed to refine his methodologies. Rosewood's board of directors is banking on Dr. Myatt's prototypical work to bring not only prestige to Rosewood but an increase in funding from both the public and private sectors.

The staff room hums with a dozen people, nurses and cleaning staff, arranged in familiar cliques, chatting about anything but work. Michael receives a few noncommittal smiles; no one goes so far out of their comfort zone as to offer a chair to the new guy. He's a doctor, after all, and hardly in need of a favour or of further confirmation of his status. He finds a lone chair against the far wall, and as soon as he's seated, Frieda Carter is looming over him.

"Doctor Myatt," she says, still using the formal address despite his attempts otherwise, "*your* patient, Ms. Taylor, may be a little less wakeful for her session today." She's speaking at a volume that includes the room. "I just wanted to warn you and to apprise you that she became highly agitated last night and needed attending to."

Is she blaming him? Like police officers and border guards, Frieda makes Michael feel inherently criminal. He notices that the base of his tongue has become taut and the tiny muscles around his eyes constricted. Is this a reflection of Frieda's present somatic state or his own defensive posturing? The room has quieted, every ear primed for a battle. He and Frieda make decent entertainment, he imagines, for ten in the morning. Instead of answering, Michael takes a cooling slurp of his tea.

"The duty nurse couldn't calm her down so she was given a sedative." Her enunciation clipped, Frieda's tongue seems to lash against her teeth.

"This is the first intervention that patient Taylor has required."

Unstated is: And it happened right after your first session with her, thinks Michael. "Okay, thank you, Frieda," he answers in a quiet voice. "This is recorded on her chart?"

"Yes, it is."

Michael is silent. After a few uncomfortable seconds, the other staff quickly resume their conversation.

"Don't be overly concerned," he hears Frieda mutter as she strides away. What has he done to make this woman mistrust him so?

MICHAEL'S SECOND session with Kerry is a disappointment. Slumped in her chair, Kerry's breathing is shallow, her head hangs forward on a protruding neck, goose-like, a portrait of a mind willing itself to die. Michael can hardly believe this is the same person he worked with yesterday. The only sensation he receives is of a weakness in the chest area and he makes a note to have the resident physician check her heart and blood pressure. Twenty minutes into the session she falls asleep in her chair, head hanging to one side, spittle bubbling at the corner of her mouth. Unable to wake her, and beginning to feel drowsy himself, he cuts the session short. As he gets up to summon the nurse, a soft fart startles him. He looks back at his patient and she begins a watery snore. How strong was that sedative? He doesn't like that this patient, in particular, has been humanized in so pathetic a way.

THOUGH KERRY receives no medication that night, the following day's session is even worse. Five minutes after Michael walks into the orientation room, his patient is asleep. He tries switching her next session from the morning to the afternoon, but again Kerry slumps asleep in her chair, small snorting sounds issuing from her nose. What has changed over the past few days? Perhaps his patient misses her mother's daily visits. He asks Terese to invite Mrs. Taylor to come the following morning. He'll try again with Kerry in the afternoon.

After lunch, Michael has an appointment with outpatient Tia Long. Michael meets his outpatients in the non-clinical setting of his office and serves them tea and cookies. He believes that a homey environment will blur the distinction between talking with a therapist and talking with a friend over a kitchen table, his office serving as a kind of halfway house. He wants these individuals to feel less like patients and more like guests.

Michael's inherited Tia from his predecessor, Dr. Viet Weber. A gregarious German fellow with permanently blackened fingernails from his hobby as a blacksmith, Dr. Weber was a professed Jungian, who, in his years at Rosewood, experimented with role play and re-enacting traumatic episodes. In these dramatic plays, patients were encouraged to re-enact not *what* happened to them but *how* they responded to what had happened. Michael has read with amusement some of his case studies. In Weber's words: *He bleated like a goat. All day like a goat. Next afternoon, more with the goat. Some patients responded like royalty.* The point of the exercise was to provide psychic distance between patient and traumatic incident and thereby empower the patient with the possibility of choice. Michael imagines that, for the majority of patients, it was a highly conceptual and subjective exercise. In any case, most of Dr. Weber's former patients have been deemed functional and are now being reintegrated into society.

Though Michael's first two sessions with Tia were unremarkable, this, their third meeting in as many weeks, promises to be anything but. Dressed in a black velour track suit and fitted white T-shirt, Tia arrives short of breath, as if she jogged here. Before today, Michael has seen her in matronly skirts, loose-fitting blouses and pin-straight greying hair. The hair has become a mass of black ruffian curls, and Michael realizes that, if he were to pass her in the hall, he wouldn't recognize her. As she leans forward to sit in the offered chair, Tia's V-neck exposes a dark tunnel of cleavage.

"It's a new you," says Michael tentatively.

Tia fixes one eye on him and tilts her head at a rakish angle. "You like?"

Michael gives her a noncommittal smile and moves to sit behind his desk. Though in their former two meetings, Michael experienced nothing more threatening than a testing pinch of his waistline and a lingering hand hold, Dr. Weber's warning rings loud in his head. "Keep a firm and respectable distance from her." Weber's notes also suggested having something nearby to occupy the patient's hands. Today, for the first time, Michael understands why: Tia's hands are in constant motion and seem to belong to someone else entirely, or to two other people. He marvels at how she can rub one hand on the arm of the chair while feathering her lips with the fingers of the other. It reminds him of the childhood coordination game of rubbing your stomach while patting your head.

Diagnosed with borderline personality disorder, Tia is forty-six years old, twice divorced, and suffers from episodic bouts of exhibitionism and nymphomania. Raised in a devout Catholic family of Italian descent, Tia was the only girl amid three brothers, two older and one younger. Apparently, as a preteen, she was regularly fondled by her two older brothers under the knowing ogle of her father and blind eye of her mother. "Harmless fun," her father called it, and withdrew his affections if she didn't "play along." So, as she stood brushing her teeth at the bathroom sink, her father watching from and guarding the doorway, her brothers lifted her nightie and with tentative, curious hands caressed her budding breasts and explored between her legs. She had described their touch as gentle and said that exposing themselves was never part of the game. Despite her confusion and guilt, or perhaps because of it, Tia would be aroused and masturbate afterward in her bedroom. She'd imagine her brothers and father off doing the same, the four of them climaxing together, rattling the roof while Tia's mother ruthlessly scoured out the kitchen sink. The fondling stopped when her father feared she was starting to enjoy it.

"Apparently rubbing myself against the smooth corner of the sink uglied his fantasy," were her words.

At fifteen she lost her virginity to her high school principal. Lovers came in all ages and sizes after that and at age nineteen she offered herself to her virginal younger brother on his sixteenth birthday. She cared deeply for this brother and had never gotten over how quickly her gift was unwrapped, used once, then discarded.

Tia and Michael chat about the cooler weather, the parking problem in Olde Towne and this morning's arson attack at a Muslim school in Maryland. Soon, a practicum nurse arrives with a tray of tea and cookies and, with a shaky hand, pours tea into the sudden silence. As soon as the nurse has left, Tia peers at Michael over her tea cup, her black-lined eyes noisy with secrets.

"Speaking of religion," she says, perching on the edge of her chair, "I need to confess my sins, Doctor."

She places her tea cup on Michael's desk, and he quickly tucks a napkin underneath. While the fingers of her one hand drum along the desktop, the index finger of her other traces the circle of an earlier stain as though it were the lips of an open mouth. Although Michael finds it helpful to finally see Tia's disorder in action, he doesn't want to encourage it. He picks up the plate of cookies.

"Cookie?"

She snickers as if he's being silly and waves the plate away. "Two handsome, clean-cut Jehovah's Witnesses, you know the look, rang my doorbell Saturday morning. It was awfully warm that day." Her voice drops, takes on the thickness of a Tennessee Williams character. Leaning back in her chair, Tia scrunches her curls with one hand and illustrates her words with the other. "Young things they were, armed with nothing but pamphlets and salvation ..." She licks her lip as if tasting the word salvation. "They asked if I wanted to go to Paradise, and I said you betcha ..."

"Tia, let's stay present, please," Michael says simply and without looking at her. He removes a pen from his desk drawer and begins to take notes.

"It was only ten o'clock, maybe eleven, and I was still in my bathrobe." Tia's voice grows distant as her right hand, as if with a mind of its own, slides down the elasticized waistband of her pants. To show he is unmoved by her performance, Michael noisily sips his tea.

"Maybe you could pick up your tea now, Tia?" he suggests. "With two hands?"

Eyes shut, Tia doesn't appear to hear him. Her free hand cups one breast through her T-shirt. "My robe somehow lost its tie," she pants, pinching her nipple between thumb and forefinger. "And my breasts escaped when ... I ... I ... aah ... went for the pamphlet."

"Tia," Michael tries again, louder, but his admonition is useless. Tia proceeds to vigorously masturbate in the chair, her chest arching, the exposed flesh of her midriff jiggling.

"Ooh ... both pairs of creased ... polyester pants, shifted ... eee ... to the left ... yes ... yes, oh, yes, sir!"

Angling his chair so that only his profile faces Tia, Michael picks a book off his shelf and flips the pages. Tia, hair tossing side to side, peaks in tones of tinny, punted aahs.

When she finally returns to herself, her cheeks are flushed and her eyes glassy, one tight black curl sweat-plastered to her forehead like a bullet hole. Michael lowers his book and nonchalantly offers her more tea.

"Oh, I'm so sorry," Tia says, suddenly tearful. One hand whips a Handi-wipe from her purse while the other readjusts her shirt over her pants. She washes her hands with meticulous care, groaning as if she has a headache. "What the hell am I going to do, Doctor Myatt — I mean Michael. Those poor boys. They're probably scrubbing themselves with sandpaper as we speak." She puts the wipe on the desk and Michael whisks it into the trash can. "I'm so embarrassed. Please forgive my awful, terrible, unforgivable behaviour."

"They made their own choices and you should enjoy your body while you can," Michael says flatly, working to dismantle the guilt that fuels his patient's destructive pattern. He believes "talking through" the patient's confused behaviour at this point, only serves to reinforce it.

"I'm very, very bad," Tia persists. Her voice dips dangerously south on the word "bad."

"I'd like to do a guided relaxation exercise now and, on your drive home today, Tia, I suggest tuning your radio to a classical music station or, better yet, I could lend you a tape of female sopranos. The high notes help stimulate pituitary function and can relieve the congestion in your lower energy centres. Maybe also check with your physician to rule out a bladder or urinary tract infection."

Tia's vitality deflates like a popped balloon. "You know, coming three or four times used to be nothing," she says, her voice flatlining back to normal.

"Now I've got to work real hard for one. Perimenopause the doctor calls it."

"Tia, you've a healthy lust for life," Michael says kindly, "and physical changes are worth celebrating. But right now, we've —"

These comments have elicited a sly sideways smile from the patient and, before Michael can stop her, she is out of her chair and moving around the desk like a starved cat.

"Tia," says Michael firmly. "You can return to your seat now."

But instead she lowers herself onto the arm of his chair, her hand a small animal scurrying across his shoulders. Abruptly Michael stands, forcing Tia to do the same. She hangs onto his shoulder and Michael feels her nails claw the back of his neck as he slips in behind her to pin her arms to her side. He begins to lead her back to her chair. "That's excellent," he confirms as Tia fights to turn into him, her hands flailing like flippers at her side. "You can let the impulse pass." She is panting, as speechless as a savage. Her head lolls back as if trying to touch him and he can smell her perspiration now, mingled with her odd perfume, a young scent. Patchouli? Sandalwood? Having made it back to her chair, he's afraid if he lets her go she'll spring at him. "Have a seat and we'll begin that relaxation exercise now. This exercise will be something you can practise on your own."

Tia is still struggling against his grip, so he has no choice but to be brusque.

"Sit," he barks.

Tia startles and drops into her seat, which emits a little squeak. She looks up at him with the injured eyes of a scolded child and bursts into tears.

EMERGING FROM the washroom, Michael sees Frieda striding down the hall in his direction, carrying herself like Beethoven's Ninth. He steadies himself with one hand on the doorknob. Her nurse's dress looks cleaner than white, almost luminescent, her white stockings turning her sturdy brown legs a ghostly grey. Her black hair, etched with grey, is neatly hairnetted into a bun at the nape of her neck. He admires her disciplined appearance and is impressed by the fact that she never looks frazzled. She is more or less Michael's height which, combined with her confidence, is disconcerting and he instinctively avoids making eye contact.

"Dr. Myatt."

He'll make one last attempt. "Please, call me Michael."

Frieda pauses, "Yes, well." She takes an impatient breath. "Johnny," here she concedes him a first name, "is still in the garden. I'm just going to fetch him, so he'll be few minutes late for his session. He must have forgotten the time."

"Nice to see him getting outside."

"Yes, it's an improvement. At the moment, he's helping push patient Taylor around the courtyard."

"Highly social behaviour. Apparently he's drawn to Kerry."

"Yes, and I am aware of the night visits to her room. I'm considering a tracking device."

"I'd rather hold off. He's just starting to open up a little and I don't want him to feel like we don't trust him."

"But Ms. Taylor can't shoo him away like the others can."

"Yeah, but he's harmless."

"I agree." This exchange is the closest to civil they've come yet, thinks Michael. Perhaps if he keeps conversations brief and doesn't challenge her opinions, they'll do all right. A crooked expression comes over her face. A smile?

"Are you bleeding, Dr. Myatt?"

Michael puts a hand to his neck and comes away with a finger streaked with blood. Oh, shit.

"How did that happen?" she asks, her eyebrows rising with suspicion.

"No idea," Michael says a little too quickly. He's not a good liar and can feel himself blushing. He's not about to tell her about Tia, though, knowing she'd blame him for letting the situation get out of hand.

Frieda starts backing away from him.

"You can buzz me in my office when Johnny's ready," Michael says, changing the subject.

"I will," she says without turning around. She holds up one hand in a gesture that is part wave, part stop sign.

Michael waits until she's turned the corner then slips back into the bathroom to wash what turns out to be two sizable scratches.

❧

ARRIVING HOME from the hospital, Arlene pours herself a glass of Chablis over ice, kicks off her shoes and puts her feet up in front of the news. She wonders what possible colour of skirt the newscaster's chosen to wear with that wine-coloured top and leans forward for a peak over the desk. She'd expected the TV camera to follow her lead and, embarrassed by her mistake, takes a long sip of wine. George W. comes on, dredging up more enemies of the nation and throwing around the word "evil" like a cartoon hero. His self-conscious smirk makes her palms itch and she switches to "Who Wants to Be a Millionaire." After a spiffy dinner of cheese, crackers and raw veggies, she sits at her easel in front of her latest watercolour. She paints from a photo taken last May of her favourite hillside in Rock Creek Park: a brooding rock face, slick with rain, yellow daffodils bloom from its black fissures. Using an ice cream lid as a palette, she mixes brown and black, then adds a touch of white. Her man-sized hands exchange strength for delicacy as the bristles skim over the paper, bleeding colour into the paper's finely pressed pores. The events of the day fade to a distant hum.

Arlene changes into pajamas, brushes her teeth and takes off her face. After applying night creams to various parts of her body, she sinks into the mattress with a groan. Reaching to turn off the bedside lamp she sees, as if for the first time, the rose vine design along the lamp's base. In the dark, she pictures the 'David Austen' roses, the purebreds as she thought of them, that she grew in the backyard of the garden apartment where she and Beresford raised the three children. The ones at Rosewood, with their weak scents and flaccid petals, can't begin to compete. She remembers the velvet sweetness that infiltrated their small yard during that one glorious week of summer. She'd anticipate their heady culmination, sniffing the air, listening for the increased buzz of insects, feeding and watering them just the right amount. When the days finally arrived, she spent as much time as possible outside. In the morning, alone with her coffee, admiring how the dewdrops with their tiny doors of light wobbled on their petal thrones. In the afternoon, reading in the lounger, stopping every few pages to smell the air, then stroke the flowers' outlandish softness. She'd insist on barbequing dinner and eating at the picnic table under the locust tree and then come out again later to inhale their persistence in the dark. Five, maybe six days pass and, as if conquered by their own splendour, their peak was over. Arlene would cut them and fill the house with rose bouquets, expediting their red death.

✼

KERRY IS ASLEEP and dreaming that her teeth are not teeth, but rose petals, white rose petals, stuck to her gums with just the smallest amount of saliva. She has something she needs to say but knows the slightest breath will make her lovely petal teeth float from her mouth, drift away and be lost. His back to her, Allan is pounding nails into even-length boards laid down over crossbeams. He's building a porch deck but it is narrow and long like a bed, a coffin. Allan's curly brown hair has turned darker, straighter and it is now Dr. Myatt raising the hammer. She holds one careful hand over her mouth, keeping her lips close together, and speaks with the least possible force.

"I can't open my mouth very much," she says, careful her tongue doesn't lick away her front petals. He doesn't look up, can't hear over the hammer. Dr. Allan never listens. She murmurs louder, "I need to talk to you. You have to listen. You have to pay attention."

The faintest tinkle of bells and she is pulled awake, is reminded to keep watch. Someone is here, again. In her half-sleep she welcomes the intruder as she would her own child during a thunderstorm. The shy silence tweaks a memory of a warm body next to hers, toothpaste breath, powdery skin, pokey elbows. As the image threatens to come clear, her eyes tumble to the back of an emptied head.

Sucking his pinky and ring finger together, Johnny bunches his towel into a kind of pillow on the cold floor. He settles his head and inhales the towel's soapy smell. He prefers Ivory but Tide will do. He watches his angel's lips parting and closing, parting and closing in her sleep and imagines phantom music rising from her throat. She's singing for him, he thinks, and he slips his free hand down his pajama pants to hold himself. Momentarily content.

Dear Hugo, It was good to hear your inimitable voice Wednesday, though you sounded so heartbroken and I desperately wished I could cheer you up. I suspect you will have gotten my card and flowers by now. Hope the photo on the card brought a small smile. I feel so guilty having told you I thought Frederick was too young for you. Look how wrong I was. He did sound like an old soul and I wish I'd gotten a chance to meet him. Shit, it's awful how many dancers we've lost. Tell me you're being careful. Please. I can't lose you. I wish I could talk to Allan as I can to you. We'd be an old married couple by now if only you didn't bend the other way. Allan's good at looking as if he's listening to me but behind his cocked head and sympathetic squint, I can tell his thoughts are elsewhere and elsewhere again. Attention deficit disorder I think is the term. I try not to take it personally, but, God, it's hard to get things off your chest if the person that's sitting on it can't hear you. I know what you'd say, Hugo, "Allan's Allan. He's restless, he's funny and he's good with his hands. Appreciate that." And I do appreciate that but, sometimes, especially now that we're spending more time together and all my close friends are in other cities, I need more. If I could afford to call you on a regular basis, maybe I wouldn't feel this way. I want Allan to be like you and know what I need when I don't even know what I need. Why do I want so much attention, anyway? I sound like a spoiled brat. Pathetic.

Just got off the phone with Mom. She's heading down to Tabasco, Mexico, next week for a tennis tournament. Gotta love it — Arlene and her blonde pals taking on the Mexicans. She says they always lose when they play there because Mexican women are built closer to the ground, which gives them the advantage. I didn't ask.

Anyway, I'm continually wandering from the matter at hand. My life in dance. That's what this journal is for, no?

Recently I've been thinking a lot about what it takes to be a dancer. I read in the paper that anybody can master any discipline after approximately three thousand hours of practice. That's about three hours a day, every day for three years. Interesting, eh? As if it all comes down to discipline and applying yourself, and not necessarily talent. Which made me think of all the kids, the spontaneous talents, like Esther or Jonathan, who end up quitting. Maybe all that praise takes the challenge out of it, while the rest of us work our butts off just to get the teacher to look at us. Now that I'm a teacher, I'll have to try to remember that. I've got this one girl, Marta, who's leagues above the others and I have been having her demonstrate things and putting her in the front row, etc. Now I wonder if I'm risking her career. I'm going to start ignoring her.

Our old teacher Vanessa was an expert at lavishing just the right amount of attention and encouragement to make me utterly in love and in need of her, then taking that attention away and lavishing it on someone else, to make me work all the harder to win it back. I can hear her gangster voice, cigarette dangling from the corner of her red-lipsticked mouth, "To be a dancer, you need grace and good taste."

Gotta love her.

I know you didn't feel this way, but Vanessa was the be-all-and-end-all teacher for me. The one who put it all together. The teachers at the Academy taught me the external stuff, the steps and terminology, the placements of head and arms, but Vanessa made my feet feel like hands (though I could never pick up marbles with my metatarsus the way she could, and not because I didn't try), my legs feels like arms, and she freed the rest of me to express the inner stuff. In short, she taught me how to truly move within the technique, which I believe is called dance.

I think it was because she started so late in life that she had consciously, even mathematically, figured out where each movement initiated from. Like how turns came from your heels and from anticipating with your eyes. She knew the control for fouettés came from the knee down, that piqué turns happened from the inner thigh and developés from raising the toe and pushing the knee down. No other teacher would break it down the way she did, teach the form from the inside out. She was pure genius. I mean, who else would tell you: "Put your eyes in your feet!"

I remember that awful week, her standing next to me, tapping her ringed finger on the side of my head all through the grand battement exercise. "Don't think," she kept barking inches from my ear. "Your body's smarter than you are." It was so embarrassing, and infuriating, yet I loved the attention. I can still taste how badly I wanted to please her.

"Like pearls to swine," she'd say, blowing smoke rings and adjusting her wig in the mirror. But, the thing was, her frustration with us was real, not contrived. She was that much more dedicated to dance, to achieving perfection than we were, her passion like an infectious disease. I swear she could teach a monkey to dance. Remember stubby-legged Stacey? How Vanessa had her doing triple turns and those beautiful tour jetes?

Val Warden from Toronto. I wonder who thought up the stage name Vanessa Hargrove — a name chock full of grace and good taste. Frog Lady, as you so graciously called her. She was froggish with her wide mouth and beady eyes, that short torso and those long legs. I forgot to tell you on the phone that I recently found out that Vanessa was the dancer doing the absurdly fast dance sections in the movie, The Red Shoes. That those were her frog legs.

Speaking of leggy wet creatures, Allan and Thomas are out crabbing. They borrowed a neighbour's car top; Allan bought a couple of crab traps and some chicken-backs for bait. Allan's been talking a lot about living off the land and sea, growing our own food, foraging for berries, dandelion greens, lamb's quarters. I think it's code for him remaining unemployed. They're back, I hear Thomas yelling. They must have caught something. Ciao!

∽o∾

MICHAEL MAKES a couple of phone calls to ensure the flotation pool will be filled and ready to go for next week. He'd made do with bathtubs in Kosovo, hot tubs in California, and can hardly believe an institution is financing his ideal set-up. Chuckling to himself, he checks his Day-timer. Johnny B. in ten minutes, then Kerry Taylor and Norma Daily this afternoon. Michael stands up to stretch, and from his office window, sees

Johnny pushing Kerry around the courtyard, Johnny's face as mute as hers, his rust-coloured hair a lesson in contrast to his bright green sweatpants. Thus far, Johnny has refused to let Rosewood's barber cut his hair, which now moulds over his ears to resemble a toque. His wardrobe consists of sweatpants and striped T-shirts of deviant primary colours — a wardrobe for the colour-blind, thinks Michael. Bright white socks flash beneath his elasticized pant legs and match the white towel laid over his shoulder like a wine steward's. Michael compares Johnny's boyish uniform to Manic Marcus' black Ts and regulation army pants — both wardrobes good mirrors of arrested youths. After Frieda found a pocketknife in one of Marcus' pockets, her staff was instructed to pat him down on a regular basis.

Michael takes out Johnny's file and flips it open. High school must have been brutal for a thumb-sucker like Johnny. His hair colour alone would have been an invitation to heckle. Michael pictures him in these same dime-store clothes and bad haircut, the same circles ringing his eyes, sporting even more pimples, if that's possible. Johnny would have been the type of spooky, unhygienic kid that even teachers disliked. "Grade ten education" is indicated on his file though Michael's surprised he made it that far. Frieda, who allows Johnny to play games on her office computer, has assured him that Johnny can read and write. Michael recalls what Terese said about Johnny's signature collection and wonders what that's about. He won't ask, though, knowing Johnny needs to keep some secrets in order to relinquish others.

Michael watches as Johnny picks up a fallen rose, holds it under his nose and then tentatively under Kerry's. For no reason, Michael imagines Kerry biting Johnny's hand. He laughs at the thought, not bothering to analyze it, and turns back to Johnny's file. He's pleased with Johnny's recent progress. In yesterday's session, the boy was growling and sucking his fingers openly, the blocked energy in his throat area definitely moving. How the nurses miss his nightly disappearing acts is incomprehensible. Michael will suggest putting sound monitors in both Kerry's and Johnny's room and an old-fashioned string of bells around their doorknobs. Hopefully, the nurses are not hard of hearing.

MRS. TAYLOR appears in high spirits when Michael runs into her in the hall.

"Just on my way to visit Kerry-Ann. How is she doing with the physical therapy?" she asks, staring at his tie as if to decipher its meaning. Michael chose his single-lane highway tie this morning, black with a dotted white line up the centre and receding into the distance.

"Psychokinetic therapy," he clarifies.

"Oh. She'll be happy to know that her father's condition is stable and that he's coming home from the hospital in a couple of days."

"Was she aware he was in the hospital?"

"I'm not sure now what I've told her, to tell the truth."

"Well, we just don't want her to have to deal with any more bad news at present."

"I understand." Mrs. Taylor smiles happily and Michael has to wonder if she does understand.

"She has enough to process at this point," he adds, for good measure. "Now, Kerry is not responding in our sessions as I would have expected. Apparently her responses are stable with the other staff but I put her to sleep."

Mrs. Taylor snickers at this for some reason. "Perhaps she's just very relaxed around you," she says. "I'll tell her you're the doctor and she needs to pay more attention."

A simplistic approach, it's Michael's turn to snicker. "Well, you're her mother. Go right ahead."

"Darn it, I meant to bring that journal of hers that I mentioned."

"Next time," he says, meeting her eye for a fleeting second. Her unfettered enthusiasm reminds him of the bright metal ring of music triangles.

WHEN MICHAEL enters the room for his afternoon session with Kerry, the change in her appearance is dramatic. Her head and shoulders are erect, alert even. Her cheeks and lips are so rosy with colour, he'd almost swear she was wearing makeup. Her hair is swept clean off her face and woven into a braided concoction that curves around the upturned collar of a pale yellow shirt-dress.

"Nice to see you again," he says, a smile threatening his lips. "Looks like we're finally getting some much-needed rain." He thought he'd try a lighter approach to help keep her interest. He arranges a chair opposite hers. "I hear you get a lot of thunderstorm activity around here. They're a rare occurrence where I come from."

He was about to mention the ad he saw for The Joffrey Ballet performing at Wolftrap, but in the minute it takes to settle himself in a chair opposite, her palms have turned upward on her armrests. He stops, glances at her eyes, which stare dull and unblinking at a point between his feet. She begins to breathe in a more pronounced way, as if she's waiting for him to hurry up and begin. Michael shakes his head. This extreme contrast between her face and body is something he's never encountered before. He can sense her impatience and has to remind himself not to react but to find his breath, take his time and settle himself.

Michael begins by mirroring Kerry's hurried breathing and finds he is easily able to manipulate it and slow it down. He parts his lips to allow the breath to circulate through both his nose and mouth and, despite the fact that Kerry's not looking at him, her lips have also eased apart. He has a sudden impulse to place his palms onto her upturned ones, but remembers that physical contact is not recommended before Stage II. Since these are his own recommendations and subject to change, he writes an addendum in his head: Instinctive or spontaneous responses are trustworthy when holding the welfare of the patient in mind.

Kerry's hands are surprisingly cold as he lays his over hers. There is a slight resistance upon contact, a push upward to meet his weight. He looks once to her barren face and continues. Fingers extending to the insides of her wrists, he feels her pulse against his fingertips. A steady urgency. Planting his feet on either side of her wheelchair, he pictures the foundation of the clinic embedded in the earth and grounds his awareness in his feet, legs and in the weight of his torso on the chair. Squaring his head and shoulders, he visualizes the immensity of the sky beyond the clinic's roof and allows his thoughts to disperse like clouds torn apart by the wind. He draws his inhaled breath up to his head and exhales back down to his belly in a circular fashion, gradually synchronizing his body and mind. Senses uncluttered, ripe with receptivity, he begins.

Several minutes pass and the rest of his body begins to numb slightly as if all his blood is pooling in their hands. Hands. Kerry's hands feel as though they're vacuuming in his warmth. His blood, red and vital, seems to leak out through his hands to mix purple with the cooler, watery blue of hers. Now a curious sensation of their hands being two not four, wrists like twisted roots, fingers earnest purple shoots. For a second he considers pulling away but has a vivid image of their blood spurting wildly onto the floor, staining their clean clothes. Shaken but curious, he allows his eyelids to close, capturing both him and his patient under a soft blanket of awareness. Outside, the rain taps at the windows as if to be let in.

MICHAEL HAS lost all track of time when Frieda enters without knocking.

"Oh, I didn't expect you in here, Doctor," she says without apology.

Michael reluctantly opens his eyes. "What time is it?"

"Three-twenty, your session was to end at three. She'll be late for physio."

"The time got away from me. Please give me a minute to wrap up."

Frieda appears loathe to move, concern in one lifted eyebrow as she takes in the proximity of patient and therapist, how his legs straddle hers, how their hands touch.

"Just one minute ... Frieda," he adds with effort. He does not want to finish such a promising session in an abrupt manner. She closes the door but Michael can tell she stands stationed on the other side, ears yawning.

Michael slowly removes his hands from Kerry's. He waits, then gently places her hands palm down in her lap. He looks to her static face, which appears softer to him, more vulnerable. After letting Frieda wheel her away, he remembers that he forgot to say parting words to confirm the session. Perhaps it wasn't necessary this once.

MIND AS FRESH as the paper in front of him, Michael takes up his pen:

unexpected

Well-being

a windless lake fed from an underground Spring

cool beams of fish slipping through the shady Deep

hello down there

Washing his face and hands, Michael skips the soap and douses with cold water only. As he makes a cup of tea in the empty staff room, he considers inviting Terese out for a glass of wine after work. It's last minute but maybe she's not doing anything. He could use some company. A little flirtation. It is Friday night, after all. This is the most relaxed he's felt since being posted to the prestigious Rosewood and, all in all, this week has proved encouraging.

Back at his desk, Michael begins dividing one stack of files into two. Having completed the orientation sessions with all eight resident patients, he's reached his decision about how to proceed: two are not yet stable enough to begin Stage 1. It will take at least another month before they're weaned off their pharmaceuticals. Two others have sustained serious physical injuries and will require extensive rehab to unearth their pre-accident physiology. He reads the names on the remaining files: Marcus Novakowski, Norma Daily, Johnny Bourne and Kerry Taylor. These four will determine his program's success. He swivels around and looks out at the river beyond the clinic walls. The sun stains the water an olive-green and the wind whips up tiny whitecaps that aren't quite white but a pale brown. With a little luck and a lot of work, these four should help to launch what he hopes will be a long and distinguished career. No one can say he's not making good time.

MICHAEL STANDS behind the front desk where Terese faces away from him typing into her computer. He can see his reflection in the screen, suspects she knows he's there, but she continues typing, forcing him to address her first.

"Will you join me, Terese, for a glass of something after work? Or maybe you already have plans." Michael pronounces this to her back, makes his tone hopeful, a touch apologetic.

"It's only Friday, Michael. Thought I wasn't scheduled in until Saturday." Terese swivels around slowly, crosses her arms under her breasts making them bloom brilliant out the open neck of her shirt. "You're not being spontaneous by any chance?"

He lifts his eyes to her face, then back to her cleavage. "Even the dedicated need to loosen up occasionally." Terese smiles, keeping her arms where they are. "You're buying," she says.

He removes his glasses, knowing she'll be reminded of the one and only time she's seen him without them, and then smiles what he thinks is an arresting smile. "Of course."

"And I pick the place."

Terese seems to need to have the last word. Michael is happy to oblige.

MICHAEL PICKS up some Greek food on his way home, starving after three drinks, a few pretzels and a sweaty romp on his office rug. He's pretty sure she came this time, manhandling herself like she did, her face distorting into someone unrecognizable. Orgasm, he thinks, is not always pretty. After all that wine, he'd stupidly forgotten that she was a noisemaker and kept having to cover her mouth. It was a reckless thing to do, what with patients just down the next hall, and not something he'd risk again.

Michael had dropped a pickled Terese off at her apartment and begged off dinner, saying he had loads of reading in preparation for next week, hoping to imply that tomorrow's picnic at the Smithsonian might not happen.

"Look at me," she'd scolded, her words slurring. "You, Michael Paul Myatt, have to learn to live a little."

She may have said "love a little," he wasn't sure and didn't ask.

BEFORE SITTING down with his dinner, lamb sausages, rice and salad, Michael showers and puts on his bathrobe. A blue-and-white-striped terry cloth thing, Michael has had this robe since he was sixteen, the cotton soft, almost satiny, with age. The robe provides a satisfying weight across his shoulders and its oversized, monkish hood is nice on cool mornings after a shower. Michael imagines it carries the accumulated smell of all the places he's ever lived and has begun to think of the robe as an old friend with shared memories. Twice he's sewn up a hole in the seam of the collar.

Michael eats his sausages in front of the sports channel, glad to see the Mariners are doing well. He enjoys watching the Japanese player, Ichiro Suzuki, who's as dogged as a metronome's beat. Each time Ichiro's up at bat, preparing for a pitch, he performs what resembles a Zen archery manoeuvre. With perfect posture and his eyes locked on the pitcher, he holds the bat vertically in the air in front of him and circles the other hand as if pulling an invisible string across his chest. Michael thinks of it as a grace-filled moment. He also loves how Ichiro will swing at anything, lunging into the ball already on his way to first base. And sure enough the wiry Asian beats the throw more often than not.

After dinner Michael pours himself a Jamesons and sits outside on the small deck off his bedroom. Jameson Irish Whiskey was what his father drank in the evenings after dinner as he sat in the chintz armchair in the living room, hidden behind the paper. The day Michael realized his father was gone for good, he'd taken the half-empty bottle, a twenty-sixer left behind in the liquor cabinet, and drank it by himself. It was the first and last time he drank to the point of vomiting. Yet oddly, the experience secured rather than severed his allegiance to the stuff. The wind picks up and leaves fly chaotically in the darkness beyond the deck. He recalls his session earlier today with patient Taylor, the odd frozen colour of her eyes. It's been a long time since those trips north with his father. How old was he was he stopped going with him. Eleven was it? Twelve?

"To nurture the nature in him," his father would chide his mother, who was predictably sullen at their leaving. Her hardened hands would roughly adjust Michael's hat and coat in a semblance of goodbye, almost as if she knew what was waiting for them on the other end. *Who* was waiting. His sister, Isabelle, always tearful at their going, would whine pathetically, begging to come along. She and Michael, not much more than a year apart, had once been the closest of friends.

"It's for men only, I'm afraid, not little girls," their father would say, though Isabelle was older than Michael.

Michael was maybe five on that first trip to Lake Bernard, to the newly purchased cabin at the end of what seemed like miles upon miles of bumpy dirt roads. Upon their return, Michael watched his father embrace and kiss his tall, high-heeled mother hello, just as he'd watched him embrace and kiss the shorter and younger woman of the woods goodbye. His father had given him curt, precise instructions never to mention Eden to anyone.

"Why, Daddy?" he'd asked, perfectly content that his father was loved by another woman, a quiet one who never complained or yelled like his mother and who didn't mind playing with him.

"You heard me, Michael, not one word. I'm trusting you."

This warning was spoken with such uncharacteristic passion that Michael felt bound to honour it at all costs. His father's lie became his, planting itself in the pit of his stomach to sit undigested alongside the venison and gingerbread Eden had cooked in the big cast iron stove. It was a burden that made his child's mind suddenly cautious and self-aware, and Isabelle instinctively began to mistrust him. With each trip north, she withdrew her affections more.

Now he tries to picture Eden's face, but all he manages is the black snake-like braid that wound down her shoulder. Obviously First Nations, she was probably from one of the local bands his father spent time with. "Why reinvent the wheel," his father once said, "when the First Nations people have been experimenting with these plants for thousands of years?"

Michael had to assume his father met Eden on one of his fact-finding trips.

He knows that his parents had met at the University of Washington shortly after his father began teaching in the biology department. Michael's mother was an art history major, sophisticated, fiery, pretty. She had ambition, something his father must have shared in those early years. But his father proved to be a stubborn man with simple tastes and, over time, became nothing more than a circle of stones to contain Michael's mother's fire and smoulder.

Michael worked through his youthful confusion over his father's infidelity and, to a satisfactory degree, has released his anger over the man abandoning his family. Indeed, this very directive sits on page one of his award-winning thesis: "An effective therapist must acknowledge and comprehend his own inner conflicts in order to recognize, without bias or projections, the confused emotions of others. One must develop the ability to become a clean, unclouded vessel ..."

Michael tosses back the last swirl of whiskey and makes a mental note to visit Isabelle next time he's in Seattle. He's probably seen her less than a handful of times in the past dozen years. Made it to her wedding to the draftsman guy with the ears, but missed the births of both her sons. He can't keep track of everyone's birthdays but does manage to send a package at Christmas. In an ongoing joke between them, Isabelle sends him a tie on his birthday and another tie at Christmas. By now he has quite a collection. "A man can never have enough ties," she says, insisting "it's the one way a guy is allowed to be creative in his dress." Her ties are never plain; they're abstract or conceptual, "ties with something to say." For the most part, he likes them — the M. C. Escher with stairways leading back on themselves, the Dali with clocks bent over branches and table edges, the highway one he wore today and the paisley one with a hundred-and-eight hidden yin-yang symbols. The West Coast conference is coming up in December. He'll tack on a day, take Isabelle and her brood out to dinner, be sure to wear one of her ties.

Inside, he washes his glass, dries it and replaces it mouth down in its row in the cupboard. Then he goes to his closet and picks out what he'll wear tomorrow. He considers his appearance part of the environment that affects his patients, and for this reason makes sure his clothes are of a good quality, cleaned and well-pressed. With the exception of his tie, he wears only solid colours in neutral earth tones. He moves a pair of brown pants and a purple-heather shirt to the front of his closet and picks out one of Isabelle's ties. Why not wear the Wile E. Coyote? His patients might get a kick out it. The tie shows Wile E. hurtling from a cliff, anvil gaining, the familiar look of defeat dragging down the corners of his mouth while Road Runner stands innocently mute on the clifftop, beaming his satisfied smile. No, he meets with Scarlet Roth tomorrow, a young woman who crushed her pelvis and her windpipe in a drunken flip off a third-floor balcony. He chooses the Van Gogh, then heads for the bathroom. After washing his hands and face, brushing and flossing his teeth, he wipes away stray droplets starring the mirror or faucet, then flushes the tissue down the toilet to keep the wastebasket trash free. Uncluttered surroundings equal an uncluttered mind.

In his bedroom, he drops to the floor and does forty push-ups, rolls over and does the same number of sit-ups. As he climbs into bed with this month's *American Psychiatric Journal*, he hears an explosion outside. A gunshot or a car backfiring? It makes him wonder about the crime level in the area. He's heard that D.C. has surpassed Detroit as the world's murder capital, but Alexandria is across the pond, so to speak, in Virginia. Though rumour has it, Virginia is trying to change state law to allow its citizens to carry handguns. A scary notion. He turns his attention to an article on craniosacral manipulations and precognitive memory. At half past eleven, he presses the button on his alarm clock and turns out the light. He's asleep in a matter of minutes.

Later that night, Michael dreams of a woman with translucent blue skin, her insides non-existent. She floats above him, legs hidden under the colourful swirl of her skirt, her long black hair pressed to her back like the pelt of an animal. She is as big as the sky. When she reaches down to scratch his tanned young back, he groans with the desire for it never to stop. He tries but is unable to turn his head far enough to see up to her face, but he knows it is strangely wondrous.

∽○∾

ARLENE LIES awake in her bed while the adjoining bed, Beresford's, is flat and neatly made. Nightly she tests herself, imagines him gone from her life and gauges her reaction to being without her partner of forty years. Shopping for one, no longer saving the other half of banana, making a single cup of decaf, not two, not having to share the morning paper, utter the daily greetings and partings. No male arm to escort her into a roomful of people, to open the door for her, to signal the waiter at a restaurant or pick up the tab. All those little gestures and formalities that make her feel cared for and esteemed. She'll have to learn to pay the bills and be aware of her cash flow, be responsible for the transactions of their scarf business. She'll be dependent on friends and her children for sharing life's details and making them matter. There'll be two widows in the family then. Not that Kerry and Allan's eight-year marriage came close to what she and Beresford have.

The single sound of Arlene's breathing dissipates too quickly into the quiet. Without Beresford's palpable presence, a solid sense of herself is hard to locate. Her thoughts arise without echo and pass quickly. The darkness feels too dark and when she turns on the bedside lamp, the colour peach lifts off the walls and invades the room. She painted these walls herself, thrilled to have found a shade that accented the mums on the bedspread. She had the bedspread professionally done but made the valance, drapes and throw pillows herself, out of the same deep green, gold and peach flowered fabric. Beresford always there to encourage her, commending her on her efforts and good taste.

All these lovely things they have accumulated over the years will outlast the living, thinks Arlene, and she is vaguely comforted by the idea. Her heart will most certainly stop beating, her body will run out of breath, yet these rooms will be still here — her legacy, her authored work, the acquired caches from wandering the globe with Beresford. Treasures that were cooed over and disputed, all carefully chosen to create a whole, to express who they were then and who they are now. Paintings, carpets, sculptures, her Nyloc pottery collection, glass-blown plates that hold hand-picked rocks from their trips to Crete and Monaco. There's her carousel horse, which was something she'd hunted for, in an appropriate colour, for years. Without Arlene's knowledge, Beresford had kept in contact with local antique and novelty dealers and finally tracked a horse down in rust and gold to match the decor. Beresford, who could be relied on for surprises, had saved the unveiling of Sir Cinnamon for Arlene's sixtieth birthday.

Arlene picks up her Len Deighton book but puts it face down on her chest. Kerry-Ann has lost it all, she thinks sadly. Her sense of place, her roles in life, even the simplest of satisfactions. Her most prized possession, Thomas, buried six feet under. Allan wasn't quite right for Kerry in Arlene's opinion. He was too flighty and selfish. He had the attitude that the world owed him something, which always bothered Arlene. She knows that it was the pregnancy that made Kerry marry before she was ready. Allan was a good father, Arlene'll give him that, but Kerry-Ann will get over Allan. A callous thought, but that's what she believes. Thomas, on the other hand, her daughter will never stop mourning. We'll all never stop mourning.

Arlene had arranged for Kerry's possessions to be boxed away in a friend's garage in Metchosin. She'd left the furniture, they owned nothing fancy, and arranged for the house to be rented out. Kerry's neighbours were kind enough to oversee the rental and find a home for the dog. What was that animal's name? Flapjack?

Arlene puts her book back on the night table and gets out of bed. She wants to see the few items, tucked under the chaise longue, that she'd brought from Kerry's home. These particular objects had stood out for Arlene, offered her solace when she'd walked the silenced rooms of Kerry and Allan's modest cottage, rooms expectant with shopping lists, laundry, herbs and flowers hung upside down to dry, cookie sheets marked with crumbly circles where cookies had recently been. Sliding the tin box along the carpet, she pries up a corner and lifts out each object tenderly, as if it might be sensitive to pain. The sculpted mahogany burl, fist-sized, of a muscular figure curled in on itself with its head in its hands; the collection of angels made from straw, ceramic, glass, even paper — some

of them gifts from Arlene; the framed crayon-drawing a six-year-old
Thomas did of his family, the heads far too big for their bodies, bright red
smiles spanning noseless faces; and the white satin pointe shoes signed
by Balanchine and Stravinsky. Arlene runs her finger over the tip where
the satin has been cut away, then over the leather soles that had been
cross-hatched with a knife. These defacements provided traction where
there was none. Arlene can't count the number of times she'd watch
these beautifully crafted, very expensive shoes be half-destroyed before
they were even worn. The toe boxes smashed with a hammer, the insoles
held over the stove burner to soften the arch, elastic and ribbon stitched on.
At the tins' bottom lies the leather-bound book Hugo gave Kerry as a
retirement gift. Arlene had found it tucked inside the upstairs window seat,
beneath the one window in the place that afforded a view. An extraordinary
view really, of the strait of Juan de Fuca across to the Olympic mountains
in Washington State. Kerry-Ann had told her that on a clear day you
could even see Mount Baker. Arlene had read Hugo's inscription that
day back on Vancouver Island, but was unwilling to pry further. It didn't
seem fair. Maybe she didn't want to know. Again she ventures as far as
the inscription.

> *In hopes that you'll be able to translate your magic into words, so I can*
> *figure out how you do what you do, sell it and retire in the decadence*
> *I deserve. If you get fed up with country dancing, Frankfurt awaits.*
> *In love and awe, Hugo Ego*

Something slips out from between the book's pages and hits the floor.
She picks up the small bundle of folded papers she'd come across in
Kerry's dresser drawer. Arlene had recognized the stationery Beresford
bought the girls one Christmas way back when. He'd ordered it in their
favourite colours, blue for Kerry-Ann and violet for Patricia. Arlene opens
three creased sheets to reveal her daughter's slanted left-handed script,
writing that looks like its trying to catch up with itself. From scissors
and gearshifts, to can openers and the placement of doorknobs, Arlene
always felt that being left-handed was a disadvantage in this world.

How sorry she used to feel, watching her youngest child's frustrated attempts at using the can opener or scissoring a straight line. When left-handed scissors finally came on the market, Arlene went straight out and bought a pair, then mailed them to New York. Arlene hadn't taken the time to read these back in July and now she shifts herself into the light to read the top sheet.

Wishes
1. To dance with the New York City Ballet.
2. To marry a man like Dad, except with more hair, and have one baby, maybe two, probably just one.
3. To eat whatever I want and never gain weight.
4. To have dimples.

Kerry, age 10

My sweet child, Arlene thinks, almost hearing her daughter's lost voice. I'll have to show this to Beresford. She turns the page.

The teacher teaches my body the vocabulary, practice teaches my body to make sentences, the music teaches my body to sing and the audience teaches my body to disappear. Kerry, 13

Interesting, though Arlene doesn't begin to understand the last part. She settles her back against the foot of the chaise longue and turns to the last page.

Muscle distorting bone
the hunger for approval makes my body neon loud.
Dress me up and shine down the light
Inflated with music I take thoughtless flight
Accept this human offering, silent gods of beauty.

Blistering pain transmutes to bliss
self-hatred absolved by the external kiss

of applause
which staves off the hollowness
of satisfying everyone
but my self

Arlene's stomach drops. She instinctively turns to Beresford's bed for assurance before remembering his absence. The poem doesn't state an age but, judging from her handwriting, Kerry was probably sixteen or so. Always nose-bent on her goals, Kerry never expressed any problems at the time, never complained about being unhappy. Then again her youngest did tend toward histrionics, Arlene tells herself. Kerry had to dredge up emotions for the stage no doubt, and it was a very transitional time, leaving school early like she did. She couldn't have worked that hard at something and been unhappy. Arlene tucks the papers into the bottom of the box and carefully replaces the other objects over top. She leaves out the journal to remember to bring to Dr. Myatt, places it on the dresser in front of the numerous photos of her family captured in their best clothes and polished smiles. She had put Kerry and Allan's wedding photo, along with Thomas' school picture face down in the top drawer, worried that seeing those young faces that are now gone might have triggered Beresford's heart attack. An old heart can take only so much.

Arlene picks up the picture of Kerry, nineteen-years-old, balanced on one toe-tip, her other leg suspended weightless in the air behind her in what's called an arabesque. How does one's spine bend like that? Kerry-Ann's head is thrown back, bent inhumanly at the top of her swan-like neck, her palms pressed together at her chest as if engaged in violent prayer. It's a rehearsal shot and her lithe figure is voraciously exposed in pink bodysuit and tights. Her eyes are closed, her mouth open. A moan of ecstasy no one can hear, but for all the world to see, thinks Arlene. At least Arlene used to think of it as ecstasy.

She was proud to have a professional ballet dancer in the family, her friends impressed, even a little intimidated by so refined an art, an art so difficult to succeed in. But she was also embarrassed by her daughter's lack of inhibition. Moving in the way she did lacked a modesty that made

Arlene uncomfortable. She recalls one reviewer, a man, describe Kerry's performance as "lush abandon." "A performer that sheds her skin," said another. Arlene always felt that her daughter's relationship to her body was too trusting, too intimate. It was as if Kerry had no sense of distinction between it and herself. And despite Kerry's present unresponsiveness, that suspicion hasn't changed.

It strikes Arlene that she and Kerry haven't had a chance to grieve together over the loss of Allan and Thomas. She hopes that time will come, sooner rather than later, as she replaces the box beneath the chaise longue and returns to bed.

∽∘∾

WALTZ MUSIC lifts and falls, lifts and falls, quieting her fearful thoughts and pulling her feet forward toward the light. Eyes in her feet, easy knees, arms moving from the fingers and beyond. Breathe with the music, as the music, and turn and turn, eyes bringing the body around, quicker and quicker. Chassé relevé and balance, heel forward, pull the leg up into the waist, hold it … hold it … until … her partner's steadying hand is there, to hold her, hearts thrumming chest to chest before he's gone. And she's falling, the music stops, her toes bleeding and bleeding and bleeding. The falling curtain lops off the end of the stage and the lights go out. No one watching. Nothing to applaud now.

Maintaining a respectful distance, each night secured in her presence, the anger lodged in Johnny's throat melts anew, oozing downward to coat his insides with sticky warmth. He glides to sleep on the rise and fall of her breath until a rough hand shakes him awake, wrenches him up by his elbow and leads him back to his bed.

THE WILL TO THRIVE

Once a basis for trust and communication has been established between therapist and patient, the kinetic patterning exercises are introduced. Prepare the patient as much as possible to "welcome" or be open to a surfacing of memories both rational and irrational. These memories may be experienced as brief flashes, dreams or subconscious reenactments of the developmental stage being simulated. The practitioner must assess the patient's integration of these flashbacks or "re-experiences" in such cases where an early childhood trauma is recovered.

The program is divided into five stages, which denote the progressive stages of human physiological development. This first developmental stage includes in utero, birth and the newborn experiences. The psychological counterpart to these kinetic experiences is the struggle for survival or the will to thrive.

I acknowledge the following for their influence in this specific phase of my work: Leonard Orr's rebirthing techniques, Dr. Frederick Leboyer's **BIRTH WITHOUT VIOLENCE** and Dr. John Lilly's **FLOTATION TANK THERAPY**.

Dear Hugo, Is my son the most handsome boy in the universe or what? He's got long hair now, well, down to his shoulders. Apparently it's back in. It reminds me of when he was a baby. We never cut his hair those first four years (it simply didn't occur to us), and it had these beautiful soft gold curls. Strangers would stop and coo, "such a pretty little girl."

I was on tour in South America when Thomas got gum stuck in his hair and Allan took him to this ancient barber shop around the corner from our apartment. Remember that place on Sixty-Ninth and Columbus with the spinning barber pole? Anyway, the guy cut off all Thomas' curls and gave him a classic fifties cut; shaved up the back with bangs swept back and over to one side. I cried when I saw him. He looked like a little man, looked masculinized (is that a word?) and I was furious at Allan for not keeping a lock of his baby hair. My mother kept a lock of each of her kids' baby hair that I have to this day.

As if in protest, Thomas' hair grew in straight as a bone. But now, even though his hair's straight, the way it frames his big, hangdog eyes takes me back to those baby years. I can picture him first learning to walk, toddling around our cramped apartment, tipping side to side like a circus bear, and I just want to squeeze his face in my hands and eat it.

He's growing up so fast I can hardly believe it. I can't forgive myself for missing so much of his early life. I saw his first steps, his first words on videotape because I was working. He learned to swim with Allan, he learned to ride a bike with Allan. It's my own fault, I guess, for wanting to have a career and all. But, on the other hand, someone had to pay the bills. Even after Allan finally got his green card, I couldn't trust he'd stick to one job long enough to make ends meet. I mean I was glad Thomas had a parent at home with him and wasn't being raised by a stranger or having to compete for attention at a daycare. And Allan was probably more patient than I would have been, less of a worrier. I used to worry all the time that Allan would forget to feed him or bathe him, or wander off and leave him at the playground, forgetting he even had a son. But Thomas helped Allan focus. Even as a baby — no, especially as baby — Thomas had a way of doing that. He's very one-pointed, perhaps a little obsessive like his mother.

I have to admit, though, that I'm jealous of Allan and Thomas' closeness. They have such an easy rapport, understand each other with just a few primal grunts and tossing of eyes. I watch them at the computer together, in front of the TV together, playing cards or banging away at some carpentry project, and feel on the outside looking in. In truth I'm a little self-conscious around Thomas. I'm a little unsure if he likes me. I know he loves me but I'm not sure he likes me. He is self-contained and tends to keep his thoughts to himself. Practical Allan tells me it's just a boy thing and says "what's to talk about?" But then I don't know if Allan has deep thoughts. I don't want to force the issue with Thomas, but sometimes I'm desperate to know what he's thinking, deep down. For once, I wish he'd confide in me. I can tell he's a bit of a brooder and want him to know how good it can feel to talk about stuff that's bugging you. I should know.

For now, I have to settle for hugging him and cuddling him as often as possible. He seems to like it, he's a great hugger, and it satisfies a place in me that words might not reach anyway.

I'm thrilled he's signed up for breakdance. I'm hoping I can give him pointers, help him figure things out. I'm teaching him how to do the moonwalk, which he's almost caught on to. And remember that cool hand thing we used to do in Rhett Dennis' jazz class, the Luigi move with the East Indian flair? It's really simple but has that optical illusion thing going on. Thomas has been practising it but I think his hands are too small yet to create the effect.

I can picture him at school dances in the not-too-distant future, doing his dance moves, his long hair getting in his baby blues, the girls all over him. Or, if he takes after his "Uncle" Hugo, the boys all over him. I don't think he's got

the gay gene but I am glad that he's not very macho and that, unlike his father,
he seems sensitive to how others are feeling. Though Thomas may not say
much, I can tell by the way he smiles at me or by the tone of his voice that he
knows when I'm down or frustrated. Once, after I'd tossed my cookies, he gave
me this weird, sad look that made me think he knew what I'd just done. Not
that he knew I was bulimic exactly, but that he knew I'd hurt myself in some
way. The look was enough to cure me for six months.

I can see Thomas being a real friend someday. I imagine the three of us —
Thomas maybe eighteen, you and me complaining about our arthritic hips —
knocking around Manhattan together, showing off our old haunts. We could
take him to our favourite comedy club in the Village, to a concert in Central
Park, to a musical if there's a good one and to a Yankees game. Notice I didn't
say we'd take him to the ballet, though, unlike you, I like what Peter's done
with the company.

We could take him up to the turret at the top of the Waldorf-Astoria and
dive bomb paper airplanes. I sure hope we never blinded anybody with those.
What an awful thought.

⟨∽0∾⟩

THE TANK water is set precisely to body temperature, as is the room's
thermostat. Michael designed the flotation pool for maximum mobil-
ity and experimented for days to find salt levels that allowed for both
easy flotation and ordinary standing. Today, Michael sits outside the
ten-by-eight by four-foot-deep pool, a clipboard balanced on his lap.
In one hand he holds a pen. In the other he holds the hand of Norma
Daily, to which he applies a soft but confident pressure. This is intended
to give the patient a sense of security yet still allow for a feeling of inde-
pendence and unrestricted movement. Norma, who has refused to put
on the hospital issue bathing suit, floats in a pool of turquoise green
surgeon pants and gown, her five-foot, two-hundred-plus figure a green
island, perfectly buoyed. Despite floating weightless in a pool of body-
temperature water with her ears comfortably plugged, Norma is unable
to remain silent.

"Am I still here, Dr. Mike, honey?" she asks for the tenth time, tapping a nervous thumb on the top of his hand. Because of the earplugs, she is almost yelling.

"Still here," he calls back with a squeeze of her hand.

A sweet and unpretentious fifty-year-old, Norma has a maternal nature and joviality that Michael instantly liked. He thinks of her personality as warm cornbread spread thick with butter and honey.

"I can feel the hand that's in yours," says Norma. "And I can feel my mouth. But it's as if the rest of me's up and disappeared and I'm just a hand and a hole."

"That's good. Try and stay with the sensations."

"A hole's a pretty empty thing, Dr. Mike." Her southern accent makes the word "hole" onomatopoeic.

"You're all here, Norma. Just let yourself relax now. I've got you."

"What's that?" she yells.

"I've got you."

She squeezes his hand and he squeezes back.

"Singing helps me relax," she says. "Mind if I sing?"

"Go right ahead."

"It's okay?" Unable to turn her head without wetting her face, her eyes twist to the side and up to locate his.

He nods, mouthing "Yes."

"But now she's gone even though I hold her tight, I lost my love, my li-ife that night." Norma's loud crooning song seems to come from deep in her belly. Her voice isn't bad, although the earplugs rock her slightly off-key. She stops. "Are we still here?"

"Still here," Michael reassures her, deliberately not squeezing her hand this time. A subtle weaning.

She launches into the song again, beginning exactly where she left off, then abruptly stops again.

"My daughter, Courtney, would have liked me to buy her a hot tub like this. She's none too happy about this clinic idea. It was Joce who kept telling me, 'Momma, take care of *yourself* for a change. Momma, do something just for you.' That same voice, clear as bells, nagging me for days after my poor girl …" Norma cuts back to the song. "Oh where, oh where can my baby be? The Lord took her away from me. She's gone to heaven so I've got to be good, so I can see my baby when I leeeave this world."

Michael doesn't recognize the song — he never listens to country music — but jots down the words. He knows Norma's youngest daughter died of an aggressive breast cancer a year-and-a-half ago and that Norma's gained close to a hundred pounds since.

"We still here, Dr. Honey?"

She squeezes his hand and though Michael meant not to, he squeezes back.

AS SOON AS Johnny enters the flotation pool, he vacuums his pinky finger into his mouth, the rest of his hand a fist against his cheek. As if he'd punched himself in the face, the moment frozen in time. His drumstick knees jerk randomly and his eyes, which Michael realizes match his hair colour, dart side to side like he's watching a ping-pong match. Gradually, he pulls his hand free of Michael's and snakes it into his swim trunks, hooking his thumb just under the waistband. When the hour is over, Johnny refuses to get out of the water. When Michael is firm with him, Johnny goes rigid and comes close to tears. Rejecting lunch, he stays in his room after the session and sleeps for four hours straight. A concerned Frieda brings this to Michael's attention and Michael can't help but allow himself a smug smile, which he fails to explain. She'll just have to learn to trust him, Michael tells himself. He's the doctor around here, after all.

DURING HIS first two sessions, Marcus Novakowski had refused to enter the pool. At the third session, he got in, but insisted on standing up, complaining about the lack of room service in this place and all the looney tunes in the cafeteria. Today, day four, Marcus finally lets the water support his compact frame and Michael is hopeful that he's making progress at last. For the first time Marcus is wearing an earring in one ear — two dangling socks, the Red Sox team symbol — which bobs on the surface of the water, gently tugging at his earlobe. Must be a fan, thinks Michael. Perhaps he was a ballplayer? He's certainly built for it. Michael debates whether or not to ask, but decides against it. He doesn't want to interrupt this heartening development.

Five minutes later, Marcus' earringed head lifts forward out of the water and he starts yammering at Michael. "What moron came up with bathtub therapy? Gee, I'm an amoeba, clean and lame, connecting with my ocean roots. Dividing and dividing into more and more of me, until there's so goddamn many of me, we all puke our little green guts out. Hey, those diapered crazies haven't pissed in here, have they? They did, I'm out of here. Never catch me in fuckin' monster diapers. Rather be shot or gassed or set fire to."

Michael manages to settle him down but five minutes later, Marcus is hustling toward the steps of the pool, complaining. "Fucking salt is eating my fucking skin off!"

A CALMLY dying swan, Kerry Taylor floats motionless, her eyelids closing dreamily over her unfocused gaze as her muscles appear to let go, one by one. Her hand grows limp in Michael's and finally slips away. Her breathing, however, remains calculated, so Michael knows she's not asleep. Lost in sensation, perhaps, but awake. Scanning her dancer's form, he follows the defined musculature of her lean thighs down to pronounced calves and well-arched feet. He does a double-take when he reaches her toes. Utterly mismatched to the rest of her, floating above the waterline are the gnarled toes of an old warrior—joints lumped with scar tissue, missing parts of nails, big toes swinging inward above bunions like ancient stones. Michael stifles his revulsion. What kind of relationship must this patient of his have to pain?

Michael is making a written note about the sad state of her feet when he realizes that Kerry is moving. The compression of her limbs is almost imperceptible. Her legs are ever-so-slowly folding in to her torso. Her head, too, he realizes, is curling inward. The whole package of her body is contracting, as if being gathered by a force at its centre. He wishes he could rise above her for an aerial view, take in her entire body at one glance as her long legs fold up in equal force to the downward curl of her head. As she slowly accomplishes the fetal position, the redistribution of weight forces her body over onto its side. It's like watching the slow noble capsize of an iceberg or ship.

Bravo, thinks Michael, writing on his pad. When he looks back up, he sees that Kerry's unresisting face is two-thirds submerged in the salty water, one eye underwater, open and staring mutely downward. It takes another second before Michael realizes she is calmly choking on the water she's inhaled.

He jumps over the pool's edge, heaves Kerry up on his shoulder and strikes her solidly between the shoulder blades with the heel of his hand. She coughs two hard coughs, then belches warm water down the back of his shirt. His heart knocks at his ribcage. Jesus, she could have drowned, he thinks and only when her lungs seem fully clear and her breath normalizes, does he feel his heart begin to slow. He's breathing heavily as she manoeuvres downward and inward to nestle into the wet shirt and tie of his chest. Like a nursing child, he thinks, pleased.

Looking down at her closed eyes and undisturbed face, he can feel the pointed curve of her backbone along his arms and is aware of the contrasting shape of his own spine, tall and straight, a stick in the water. Suddenly he remembers his made-to-order, leather Birkenstocks stuck fast to his submerged feet. Damn it. His leather wallet, too, in his back pocket. He thinks of trying to remove them but doesn't want to disturb his patient. At least his watch is waterproof, he thinks, and bends his knees, lowering himself into the buoyant water until his entire chest is submerged. Kerry is weightless in his arms, and he rocks her back and forth in a careful motion. He tries to refocus on his patient's responses but finds it difficult to move beyond an awareness of his own softening muscles under clothes that now cling to him like a second skin.

Kerry remains in a state of seeming tranquility for the rest of the session. Michael becomes so relaxed that when the timer buzzes, it startles him.

"Good work," he whispers as much to himself as to his patient. "Time to get out."

He carries Kerry up the stairs, unforgiving gravity hardening his muscles one by one as they emerge from the water. As he reaches the top step, his foot slips over the wet edge and the hand supporting Kerry's legs lunges for the stair rail. Her reaction is instant: Her arms spring out to wrap around his neck and primate-like legs clasp round his waist, her scarred toes splayed in readiness. Forced off balance, Michael falls backward, lands on his bum on the top step and catches Kerry's weight in his lap. If he is astounded by the strength of her startle reflex, he is further amazed by the utter deadpan of her face.

Frieda enters on schedule.

"Good grief," Michael says under his breath, seeing what she's seeing: him sitting in clingy wet clothes on a pool's edge with a bathing-suit-clad patient straddling his lap. What is with this woman's timing?

"I don't normally get in the pool myself," Michael begins to explain. "The patient was experiencing difficulties."

He rises and continues down the steps, Kerry's limbs wrapped around his waist, monkey-like. It would be a suggestive pose, if it weren't for the patient's white-flour face. He places her gently into her chair, tugging away the resistance in her arms and legs more forcefully than he would have if Frieda weren't there. He decides not to buy into the nurse's accusatory frown and, saying nothing more, walks away, clothes dripping, his ruined shoes creaking.

AFTER A QUICK taxi ride home to change, Michael reports in Kerry Taylor's official file: *Kerry accomplished in one session what I would expect after three to seven sessions: womb-like visceral relaxation, fetal positioning, bonding, and grasping reflex. Because she exhibits such acute kinetic receptivity, I expect her mental health to be restored much more quickly than anticipated.*

He goes on to describe the details of each response, then adds the one conflicting note: *The patient ensured her physical welfare when confronted with falling, yet she appeared willing to drown without a struggle.*

THAT EVENING, alone in his apartment, Michael makes lasagna for dinner, his mother's recipe. This is one of four recipes he learned to cook when first on his own, along with a decent lamb curry, tuna casserole and chicken fajitas. While he eats, he reads an article on how posture influences the reptilian brain. Realizing he's hunched over his food, barely tasting anything, he adjusts himself upright and mindfully raises his fork to his mouth. After washing and putting away his dishes, he refines a section on his website and answers two e-mail inquiries posted at his mailbox. His work done for the day, he pours himself an Irish whiskey and watches the evening news: more casualties in Afghanistan, the revival of local poppy production, concerns about Iraq secretly harbouring nuclear weapons. Entire generations in the Middle East could be labelled PTSD by now, thinks Michael. How does one begin to address such mass injury? At ten, he tunes into *Sports Desk* to catch the baseball highlights, see if Seattle's still in the running. The phone rings, the sound so intrusive he hesitates to answer it. After three rings, he's out of his chair. It's Terese.

"I just wanted to say that I have this great leftover casserole from Bagga Pasta that I thought you might like for lunch tomorrow. It's a kind of spinach pie thing with black olives, ricotta, lots of garlic."

Sounds to him like she's scraped the rest of her fork-contaminated dinner into a doggy bag.

"Thanks, but I really shouldn't eat garlic during a workday. Why don't you freeze it."

"Okay, but it's your loss."

Terese keeps it short and sweet — so short that, after they hang up, Michael wishes he'd thought of something more to say. Maybe he could have asked if she likes baseball. They could go to an Orioles game someday. In any case, now he knows the ringer on the phone works.

Sometime in the early hours of the morning, Michael dreams that he is underwater, suckling like a baby on heroic-sized breasts. The nipple suddenly draws away from him and, desperate to latch on again, he swims after it. He is painfully awakened with his face on the hardwood floor.

⋙०⋘

"MRS. TAYLOR, come in."

"Hello Dr. Myatt, nice to see you," Arlene says before noticing his face. The young doctor's bottom lip is split and swollen, his chin bruised or smudged with dirt, she can't tell which. "Oh, what happened?" She touches her own face, tries to imagine this contained young man getting into a fight.

"Fell out of bed, if you can believe that," Dr. Myatt says, fingering the sore lip.

"It's not a regular occurrence, I hope."

"No, no. Please, sit down."

"Kerry-Ann is looking well cared for. The nurse said she's gained six pounds?" Arlene tries not to look concerned.

"That's good news," says Dr. Myatt, as he opens the file on his desk.

She's already spoken to Mrs. Carter to ask if she might join Kerry for lunch in the cafeteria after this meeting. She'd like to see not just where she's taking her meals now, but how much they're feeding her.

"Actually, Kerry is responding quite well since you spoke to her last week."

"So glad to hear that." Arlene is happy to accept the credit.

"She shows a good deal of visceral, or deep physical response," says the doctor. "I'm looking forward to engaging her on a more conscious level. But that should come."

"She is the dancer in the family," Arlene sighs.

"Yes, and I couldn't help but notice her feet in the pool the other —"

"Unsightly things. I've encouraged her to see a podiatrist about her bunions but there was really no point when she was still dancing. I'm hoping toenails and things will … grow back now. She started on pointe at the age of ten and never once complained about pain. It's when most kids quit. Some of the blisters were dreadful, her tights were always bloodied at the toes." Arlene flinches. "Sometimes she'd bleed through the shoe's layers and right through the satin covering. It's not a block of wood in there like some people think, but cardboard and glue.

Nowadays I think they might use some kind of plastic but Kerry preferred the old-fashioned kind. Anyway, she didn't bandage up her toes like I saw her classmates doing. When I asked her about it, she said that pain helped her focus."

"Like a Christian hair shirt."

"Mmm …" Arlene has no idea what the doctor is talking about, but continues nonetheless. Best to hold up her side of the conversation. "She had lots of perseverance, which I suppose is what got her to the top. I can remember her in the corner of the living room, sewing ribbons on pointe shoes. Terribly pricey, those shoes. Her sore calves would be wrapped in my old hand towels, which were soaked with castor oil, and the skin around her toes painted bright red with Mercurochrome. The oil was supposed to keep the muscles supple and the other was to toughen the skin. Her dad used to massage her feet …"

Dr. Myatt cuts her off — somewhat urgently, thinks Arlene.

"Actually, today, I was hoping to gain some insight into Kerry's birth. I was curious if there were any complications or unusual circumstances. If you don't mind my asking?"

Despite his limited capacity for conversation and eye contact, Arlene is warming to this young man. A cougar, she thinks happily. His reserve, his build and his careful movements remind her of a cougar. A scholarly cougar with funny glasses. This has been a game Arlene has played for as long as she can remember: if this person were an animal, what animal would they be? She herself is an emu, Kerry-Ann a gazelle, Beresford with his slicked-back hair an otter, her son, Richard, with his Roman nose and outspokenness, a blue jay …

"Forceps deliveries were popular then." Arlene shifts in her seat. "I was put to sleep, of course, for the actual birth, but the waking memories are as clear as glass." She sits upright on the edge of the chair. "I was happily propped up in my hospital bed, smoking a cigarette, as we were allowed to do in those days — hard to imagine such a thing nowadays — and then the pain hit. With my other babies, I was knocked out before experiencing any great discomfort, but this one had other ideas. Well, the pain was so severe I couldn't made a sound to call the nurse. I dropped my cigarette, which luckily landed on the floor and not on the bedsheet. Then somehow I got my hand to that call button." Her hand slaps down on Dr. Myatt's desk, causing him to look up from his papers. "It took two nurses to pry my fingers off that button before they could wheel me down to delivery." Arlene laughs gaily.

"I see," Dr. Myatt says with a polite smile. "Any complications with the birth itself?"

"Oh. Well, I was asleep, like I said. Didn't see her until whenever it was that I woke up. But the nurse told me that she swallowed quite a bit of fluid and they had to suction her lungs or some such thing."

"Good, good," he says more to himself, than to her. He scribbles something down.

"But she was fine, really, seven pounds, one ounce," Arlene continues. "Of course, in those days the husband stayed out in the waiting room, smoking heavily, along with the next guy. I still think one's partner should be spared witnessing the gory details. I mean, who needs it?" Arlene settles back into her seat.

"Yes, well, thank you, that was very helpful." Dr. Myatt looks up from his notes, appearing not to have heard her last comment. "And Kerry's journal, did you — ?"

"Oh, that book is sitting right there on my dresser where I forgot it. I'll get my son to drop it off. I apologize."

The doctor rises from his chair. Arlene reluctantly gathers up her purse, disappointed at the rather abrupt ending to their chat. It's always fun to tell one's stories to new ears.

"Oh, I did remember to bring this." Reaching into her purse, she pulls out a signature scarf. "It was a business idea of my husband's but I take credit for the design."

She spreads it out over his desk.

"It has the signatures of all the presidents. It wasn't easy to track some of them down and don't tell anyone, now, but we couldn't find Zachary Taylor's signature anywhere. We got my son to create one." She tries to catch his eye with this shared secret but he's somberly studying the scarf. "Sells in all the gift shops. You may have seen it in the Holiday Inn, just up King Street? Or Gifts and Garb?"

"No, I haven't. And thank you," he says, his eyes alighting briefly on hers.

Definitely a cougar, she thinks, with those flecks of gold in his eyes.

THE CAFETERIA smells of garlic and cleaning ammonia, and a steady din of conversation hangs in the air like low-lying fog. "Italian Day" reads the chalkboard above the service area. Arlene walks past tables filled with plates of spaghetti and meatballs, garlic bread and salad. She sees a middle-aged man in a black T-shirt and army pants, his ears pierced with two gold loops. Arlene got used to men wearing the one earring, but the new style of two still shocks her. Makes them look like grandmothers, in her opinion. She wonders why he has a table all to himself until he lifts his chin, opens his mouth and belches long and loud like a proud ten-year-old.

An unsmiling older man, wearing a bright-yellow bucket hat, is waving her over to his table. Arlene gives him a dismissive wave and finally spies Kerry at a table in the corner. She's sitting with the spunky receptionist with the dimples, Terese, and the boy — what's his name? — Johnny. Johnny's chair is pulled so close to Kerry's that the seats touch, and he's leaning into her as if to head-butt her shoulder. Moving closer, Arlene is relieved to see that the boy is simply studying the signature scarf she'd tied on the handle of Kerry's wheelchair this morning. Hopefully he'll move his chair back when he's done. She's been led to believe that Mrs. Carter oversees Kerry's feeding and is surprised to see a male nurse, a burly black fellow at that, gently urging her daughter's lips open with a spoon.

"Mrs. Taylor, hi," exclaims Terese. "Are you having some lunch? Best spaghetti in town."

Arlene had been hungry, but has inexplicably lost her appetite. She shakes her head. "No, I was just going to join Kerry-Ann for a bit." The chairs next to Kerry are taken, so she sits opposite her daughter, beside Terese.

"Have you met Bryson?" asks Terese.

Arlene smiles and nods at the man feeding Kerry. "We haven't been introduced, but I've noticed you in the halls," she offers.

"She's eating well," Bryson says, as Kerry mechanically opens her lips to accept a spoon mounded with pale glop. Ground up spaghetti? A bit falls onto Kerry's chin, quivering precariously. Arlene waits, desperate for Bryson to wipe it off.

"And you've met Johnny?" Terese continues. Arlene would rather skip the introductions but what can she say?

Johnny is still peering over Kerry's inert shoulder at the scarf.

"Johnny," scolds Terese. "Say hello to Kerry's mother?"

"Hello, Johnny," says Arlene and he stares back at her. Like a rabid squirrel, she thinks, then notices that the boy has three oranges on his lunch tray.

"Eat, Johnny, your food's getting cold." Terese takes an enormous mouthful of twirled noodles, then stabs a meatball on the end of her fork as if to show him how to do it.

Johnny squints. He looks revolted.

"I was expecting to see Mrs. Carter here," Arlene says to the table at large.

"Secret meeting," Johnny whispers to his plate. "With the president."

George Bush? wonders Arlene.

"Yes, she's meeting with Dr. Scully." Terese talks with her mouth full and Arlene has to lean in to catch everything. "He's president of the board."

The mole of noodles stuck to Kerry's chin is elongating toward her bibbed front. Wipe it off, Arlene thinks loudly, hoping the nurse will hear. He catches it just before it falls.

"She's lovely, your daughter," says Terese, an edge in her tone that confuses Arlene.

"Lovely," echoes Johnny to the single noodle strand now dangling from his fork.

"Thank you."

"Did Kerry go to school around here?" Terese has so much Caesar salad stabbed onto her fork Arlene is just waiting to see how she's going to fit it into her mouth. "I went to Abington myself, and then Wakefield High."

"Kerry-Ann went to private school."

"Oh, of course."

Arlene detects disdain in the young woman's voice. She watches as Terese fits the explosion of greens into her mouth. A small miracle.

"I saw the *Nutcracker Suite* on TV when I was six and was desperate to take ballet lessons," says Terese, lettuce blackening a front tooth.

"And did you?"

"My mother told me I didn't have what it takes and enrolled me in tenpin bowling instead." Terese's laugh isn't happy.

"Bowling's a graceful sport," responds Arlene, trying to say something nice, a peace offering. She doesn't want her daughter to have any enemies in a place like this.

Terese smiles ruefully and stabs up more salad.

A short and uncomfortably overweight woman walks past with a tray of pudding and Jell-O.

"I'll have one of those, Norma," says Terese. The fat woman smiles, her eyes disappearing behind her bunchy cheeks.

"Who else?" asks Norma, her words tumbling out. "Bryson? Johnny you need to put some meat on those bones. The dancer? She can eat pudding, it's easy eating, nice and smooth. What do you figure she likes? Butterscotch or vanilla. She doesn't look like chocolate to me."

"She doesn't eat dessert, thanks," interjects Arlene. Somebody has to watch out for her daughter's figure.

Norma looks at her, shamefaced, as if Arlene had just slapped her. "Yes, okay, good," she mutters and shuffles away without having given anyone anything.

"Kerry-Ann was never a dessert eater," Arlene explains to Terese and Bryson. "I must have failed to mention it to Mrs. Carter."

"Kerry-Ann," Johnny mutters.

It's time to leave, thinks Arlene, although she still has a good two hours before picking up Beresford. She makes a point of looking at her watch and excuses herself. Walking around the table to kiss Kerry on the top of her head, she can smell Johnny's sour body odour. He has yet to

move his chair over and she is about to say something about it when he
�꜀ꜱᵖᵉᵃᵏˢ first.

"I like handwriting," Johnny says, more to himself than to her. It seems
rhetorical enough, so Arlene leaves it alone.

As she walks away from the table, she hears Bryson say to Terese, "So
I understand Dr. Myatt's making house calls." She glances back to see
Terese's chewing face flush pink. She's a chipmunk, thinks Arlene, or
maybe a beaver. Odd combination with a cougar.

ARLENE can't sleep. She listens to Beresford's arrhythmic breathing
and anticipates the next one and the next, afraid that if she stops, so
will he. The ticking of the bedside clock resounds in the gaps and she
almost misses the simpler silence of being alone. There is some relief
when the air conditioning kicks on and fills the room with its steady
white *whirr*. Her thoughts begin to drift in the dark and a song seeps in.
Sinatra? Darin? The memory of her younger days, hers and Beresford's
together, wafts around the room like pale chiffon. She is thirty-three
again, he forty-five, his strong arm supporting her back as she follows
his lead, her feet not having to think. She can almost hear Beresford's
soft vibrato tickling her ear as he joins in the refrain. They are stylish,
successful, with three beautiful children. They are in control, admired
by friends, making their goals a reality. As the music comes to an end,
they kiss on springy lips.

In her mind's eye, she is forever thirty-three. She is always surprised
by the loose skin and grooved lines she sees in the hard-hearted mirror.
She read just the other day that thirty-three, Christ's age when he died,
is the age of all the inhabitants of heaven. Another motivation to be
good. She says a prayer and sends out her angels to watch over Beresford,
Kerry-Ann and the rest of her precious family. This has become a nightly
ritual, a passing of a loving torch, before she can surrender herself
to sleep.

⌘

KERRY IS curled up on her side, her knees pulled into her chest, her ear pressed against the dry pillowcase. Her wings are folded into her sides, her mouth an open eye. She is an underworld creature all in black, Wagner's music crashing in her head. Orpheo and Eurydice have been torn apart. Kerry is alone on the stage with him, Orpheo. Her grey wings are frayed with burn holes and tug at her wrists and ankles. A headpiece of black snakes. Orpheo's wife, Eurydice, is dead. She is not allowed to leave this place. No one must speak to her or touch her. Wings full span, Kerry rushes at Orpheo, hurls her black pointed feet at his head, wraps her legs around him and rides him like a scared horse. He is dripping wet. She must block his way, keep him from passing, from entering the deep. He smells of life above and she doesn't want to let him go but he pries off her arms and legs, like cat's claws off a screen door. She runs in circles around him, but knows that nothing can keep Orpheo from Eurydice. Keep your eyes ahead, Kerry tells him. Don't look back. Don't look down. Don't open the tin of bombs. Must wait for the swans at the lake. The swans who know how to tuck their heads under their arms and go to sleep. Who know about dying.

Nothing can keep Orpheo from Eurydice. Keep your eyes ahead. Don't look back or she will be lost to you.

Dear Hugo, When I think of the air I used to breathe, how you still breathe it, day in and day out, my lungs cringe. Remember that heat wave in New York when so many elderly people died? The only relief was the turrets of the Waldorf-Astoria, the air surprisingly and delightfully cool up that high. We were house-sitting Suzanne Merril's loft that week — how you loved those white satin sheets — and spent that worst of the worst day sitting in a cold bath in our underwear, holding the shower head over each other's mouths and drinking what seemed like gallon upon gallons of water. God, was I bloated. I remember Copland's Appalachian Spring playing in the background and you telling me about your first and last girlfriend. You were in eighth grade. She had a great name, but what was it? All I can think of is Agatha Christie but that's not it. I remember you saying the girl, whatever her name is, put her hand on your crotch and you screamed and she ran off. Oh, we had some gay days together, pun intended, before you were lost to the Continent.

Hugo, you may not believe it, but I'm glad to be retired from the business. It's great being here for Thomas, for the everyday routine stuff that I missed out on for most of his life. I'm getting to see the tiny seeds I planted in May become real edible plants and watching our puppy learn new words and commands. Did you know dogs can learn up to one hundred words? I'm doing stuff I haven't done since I was a kid, like bike riding and throwing a ball — no Vanessa around to tell me it'll "ruin my line." She once told me I shouldn't even walk to the studio, but should always take a cab. I actually worried that walking was going to undermine my career, so I took the bus for a while. Couldn't afford a cab.

You should see this funky cottage. We (yes, I helped) have finally finished one room, the upstairs office/family room. This girl has learned how to strip wallpaper, spackle, sand and paint. Sounds like a movement combination. I even refinished an oak desk, the classic schoolteacher kind, that I found at a yard sale. Me, who didn't know how to hammer a nail to hang a picture. Did you know that you have to use a stud finder? I thought you'd appreciate one for your birthday.

The view from the upstairs window seat (that I painted Tuscany orange) would blow your mind. I'm sitting here now. There's the ocean, which is spectacular enough, but then across the strait in Washington State there's the snow-capped, cloud-wrapped Olympics and, on a clear day, Hugomongous Mount Baker. It's like having an audience of gods in your backyard.

I never thought of mountains as changeable scenery but every day I wake up and they've changed costumes. White headdresses one day, pink peek-a-boo scarves the next, stiff blue tutus another, then long white Sylphide skirts. And then for days on end they're gone, poof, hidden behind a solid curtain of cloud, as if mountains have mood swings, too. And I swear they're constantly shrinking and growing, which I guess has something to do with the way the light hits them. It's disorienting.

I don't miss bunion hell, shin splints and that recurring stress fracture in my fibula. And teaching kids is more satisfying than I thought. When I get totally absorbed in demonstrating a combination, the passionate ones in the class seem to get it, which is really exciting. I leave the technical side to the professional teachers and they let me transmit "the sex," as you call it.

You'd be proud to hear that I've gained twelve pounds and have regular periods for the first time in my life. I'm even sporting what Allan calls breastlets. It's adolescence all over again. Three more pounds and I'll be up to my full-term pregnancy weight. A miracle Thomas turned out all right. In fact, his teacher told me the other day she thinks he's got a brain for math.

⌒⌒

ALTHOUGH Kerry Taylor has already accomplished in one session everything that Michael expected from Stage 1, three is the minimum number of sessions Michael's set for this exercise. The second session was unremarkable, but today — the final session — is proving different.

At first he thinks he's imagining things. He sits up attentively, straining to confirm movement in Kerry's feet. With exquisite control, Kerry is slowly elongating her scarred toes to a pointed position, like a cat luxuriously stretching its body after a nap. As her sculpted feet arch unnaturally high, Michael assumes that's it, her yawn's finished. But then the movement continues. Now her toes are peeking up out of the water as her feet reverse their motion, equally luxuriously, into a flex. As they reach, what looks to Michael to be a hyper-flexed, Achilles-snapping position, the pattern starts over. The action of her feet dictates what is happening to the rest of her leg. Under Kerry's pale skin, her calf muscles inflate on the flexed position, then ride higher up the back of her leg when the toes are pointed. Her flattened kneecaps and bulging thighs make more subtle shifts. Michael tries not to notice how the lean muscles of her bum appear as mere extensions of her leg muscles.

To Michael's amazement, over the next ten minutes, the flexing and pointing pattern gradually involves Kerry's entire body. As her toes sharpen to a point, her back arches and expands her chest, her head pushing back against the water to expose the white bridge of her throat. Michael notes with a feeling of gratification, that such audacious posturing implies an extreme level of trust. Then, just as the arching motion reaches its sumptuous peak, Kerry's chin begins a smooth retreat into a tuck. Her chest and abdomen contract, pulling toward her now-upturned toes and feet. All the while Kerry's knee and hip joints remain locked straight, keeping her body balanced in the water.

After another few minutes, even Kerry's floating palms are laid out in the extended position before being fisted up tight in the flexed position. This perfectly controlled, subtle water ballet is mesmerizing. His patient is playing with the water, thinks Michael, moulding herself against it, testing its limits as partner. The whole display makes him want to get up out of his chair, touch his toes, then reach for the sky. He spontaneously performs a yawning stretch, the pleasurable morning kind that sets his spine tingling and leaves him wanting more.

Turning his attention to Kerry's face, Michael is perplexed once again. Nothing's registering, not an ounce of effort or pleasure, yet it's obvious to him that what she's doing is pleasurable. The skin of her closed eyelids is perfectly smooth, her mouth relaxed. How can a body be so completely and fully engaged, yet leave out the face? He's never seen anything like it. Other catatonics he's encountered over the years have worn a fixed expression, but at least it's an expression.

The more Michael watches the control Kerry has over her body, the harder it is for him to believe that she isn't in conscious control of her facial muscles, too. The notion taunts him and, in the last few minutes of the session, he decides to try a little experiment. Leaning over the pool's edge, he places one hand on Kerry's chin and one on her forehead. Slowly he pushes down and eases her face into the salty water. Water rushes into the depressions of her closed eyes and blocks her open nostrils. Kerry offers no resistance as the salty water cascades through her slightly parted lips and into her mouth. Only her hands and feet protest, twitching and causing small splashes. He doubts her a second longer before coming to her aid and lifting her into the air.

AFTER THE session, he writes in his personal file: *I sometimes think she's faking, like a stubborn child refusing to cooperate. Hearing and comprehending, but choosing to remain comatose. Those dead eyes coupled with such an alive torso defy the inseparable nature of mind and body. Catalepsy from the neck up.*

Michael puts this sheet aside and picks up a black pencil. On a second sheet of paper he draws a side view of a horizontal Kerry Taylor. First he executes her musculature in its fully flexed position and then overlays, in the style of da Vinci's anatomical drawings, the extended body arch. He then draws a third body holding a position between the two extremes. Now the drawing has an illusion of movement. And, like da Vinci, he renders Kerry's figure naked, complete with details, and though in reality her hair was clipped back, in the drawing her long hair fans out over and under the single line that denotes the water. Drawing was a skill he inherited from his father; he would practise it more often if he had the time. As he places the pages in his personal file, he recognizes voices below his opened window. Swivelling his chair around, he leans on the windowsill and removes his glasses to chew on one rubberized end.

"And how are you feeling today, Norma?"

"I'm hungry, Mrs. Carter, all the time hungry. I think the portions the cook serves up are a bit small or else he cooks with Pam. I should ask if he's using Pam instead of butter. Nothing cooks like butter. Food of the divine, as my mama called it. My stomach is always singing songs of desire, which is why I chew so much gum. Trident, no sugar because I respect my teeth. I sure could use my radio from home, though. Can't seem to get hold of my daughter, Courtney. Off gallivanting with who knows and whatnots, most likely have-nots. Takes after her daddy, that one —"

"Yes, I understand, Norma," Frieda says in a measured tone that contrasts with Norma's nervous speech. "I can loan you a radio of my own until your daughter brings yours. Now, you should try drinking more water in-between meals, it's healthy and will fill you up. Chewing gum stimulates the flow of digestive juices, which will only encourage hunger pains."

"Is that true? I don't know if I could give up gum. I stopped smoking twenty-seven years ago pregnant with my Joce ..." Her voice hesitates. "Gave me some fierce hallucinations it did. I'd see spidery things scrabbling over the walls, sure they were going to fall in my hair, or in my food or —"

"Maybe just cut back on the gum a little."

Michael is impressed by Frieda's practical advice. She extends a generosity toward the patients that Michael has yet to experience himself.

"How are you finding Dr. Myatt's therapy sessions, Norma?"

Michael moves his ear closer to the window.

"Dr. Mike? He's a quiet one, he is. Doesn't say too much, but he can make you go all jelly-like inside and kind of blank in the head. Now that I think of it, I'm more hungry than ever since my first sessions with him sitting there staring at my legs."

"Oh?"

"Set my gut to growling something fierce."

"He doesn't talk to you?"

Michael hears the barb in the question and shakes his head.

"Not much. I like that he doesn't go on like my last doctor, always telling me it's all in my head and to stop feeling sorry for myself. As if I enjoy being miserable, sheesh. Dr. Michael just tells me to relax and let the exercises do the work. 'To stay with the sensations' or some such thing. I don't know what to make of it but at least he doesn't make me feel crazy. Maybe because the things he has me doing seem crazier than I could ever be." Norma laughs, a quick nervous laugh. "That pool stuff, stroking my cheeks like that something about a rooting reflex ... Even had me sucking my thumb! Made me miss my mama, I tell you, and my stomach was rumbling fierce that day, come to think of it. I never did learn to swim but floating's awful nice. Do you offer swimming lessons here? In the big pool? I never learned as a youngster and —"

"No, but I'll see what I can do for you, Norma." Frieda sounds weary now, ready to go. "You let me know if you need anything else and I'll bring you that radio. Keep drinking water and go a little lighter on the gum." Frieda's voice grows fainter as she moves off.

"Thank you, Mrs. Carter," Norma calls after her. "I'll try. I do miss my music and there's that new singer who sings like my Elvis ... what is his name ... Hell's Bells ... Oh, it's going to bother me ... What's his name ..."

Michael replaces his glasses, pleased with Norma's answers and glad to know that Frieda reserves her ornery side for him. He can abide her criticism if she's decent to his patients. Norma, especially, deserves to be treated with kindness. He imagines it's not what she's used to.

He turns to the patient files on his desk and suddenly realizes who Frieda reminds him of. His mother. Always finding fault with him, yet patient and loving with his sister. Maybe this recognition will help him keep his perspective and undermine any knee-jerk reactions. His eyes alight on his father's photograph. Though his father was never verbally harsh like his mother, Michael couldn't help feel his father was partly to blame. Never once did his father interrupt his mother's attacks on Michael, or even suggest she be a little less fault-finding. Isabelle was the one who came to Michael's rescue. His mother calming down just to please Isabelle. What hurt Michael the most about his mother's rants was that his father was unwilling to stand up for him.

Michael removes his glasses to rub the bridge of his nose. The man's still not willing to fight for him, thinks Michael. And it still hurts.

SITTING IN a bar called "The Nuts," Michael takes a long sip of his ice-cold Corona and loosens his tie. Terese has cajoled him into having a quick drink: "Free peanuts, chesty waitresses and me."

"So, how is it going with your patients? Progress?" Terese asks.

She leans into him across the table and Michael leans back against his chair. She corrects herself and he's embarrassed at his overt body language. He compromises with an elbow on the table.

"Progress is often anything but linear. But, all in all, I'm feeling pretty positive."

"Mrs. Carter says she doesn't know how you get patients to do the things you want them to do," she says, squeezing a peanut into her mouth and tossing the empty shell on the floor. An open trunk of peanuts stands against one wall and patrons help themselves, scooping the nuts into baskets to take back to their table and then tossing the shells. The floor is a sea of crushed shells that Michael finds disturbing.

"Well, she's of the old school where talk and more talk is everything. I don't judge my patients and they relax accordingly."

"I guess." Terese pops another peanut into her mouth, hurls the shell over her shoulder and smiles coyly at Michael. "Mrs. Carter told me that her youngest son, you know the one in the army, sucked his thumb until he was fourteen. She blamed herself for it. Said she'd come to work at Rosewood when he was just a baby and wasn't there for him like she was for the older ones. Something about her husband being out of work. Anyway, I bet that's why she's taken such a shine to finger-sucking Johnny. Lets him play on her computer, sneaks him extra oranges from the kitchen. Apparently he loves oranges. And she's the one who bought him all those white socks. He arrived without a sock to his name, you know, and I heard his shoes were so rank they had to be thrown out.

She bought him an old pair of runners from Salvation Army."

"I hope it wasn't out of her own pocket."

"I'm not altogether sure how his funding works. I don't do the money."

Michael cracks open a peanut and leaves the shell on the edge of the table. Terese sweeps it onto the floor.

"Mrs. Carter's miffed at your refusing to attend Wednesday socials."

Michael snorts derisively.

"What exactly did you say to her?" asks Terese.

Yesterday was Frieda's third attempt, this time in person instead of with a memo, to invite Michael to the Wednesday "mingling" sessions. He probably should have explained his motives better than he had.

We at the clinic, Frieda said, as if speaking for every last employee, *view this as a time to deepen the bonds between patient and staff. All of the other doctors make time for it. Surely you feel that trust is the foothold of counselling.*

"I told her that I don't consider my therapy in any way, shape or form as counselling, which is the term she used, and that I'm old enough to decide what's most effective for me and my patients."

"Ooh, that would piss her off."

He'd been blunt, a little too blunt perhaps, still reacting to that slap-hand edge in Frieda's voice. He drains his beer.

"You need another beer." Terese signals the waitress to bring two, then slips a soft hand over his. "Ever spoken with Mrs. Novakowski, Marcus' wife?" she asks, toying with his fingers.

"Never had the pleasure."

"Yeah, she's a pleasure. If you think Marcus is loud, try telling his wife that she isn't on the visitor list."

Michael pulls his hand away to pay the waitress for the second round, then places his non-drinking hand out of reach on his lap.

"Is that man angry or what?"

"In my experience, the truly angry tend to be on the quiet side." Michael feels something nosing under his pant leg and jerks his leg away.

"It's just me," says Terese, incredulous.

"Sorry. Thought it was a spider or something."

"You were saying," she says.

"Oh, just that I find chronic talkers aren't angry so much as trying to hide something, often a low self-esteem. They're terrified of being denuded by silence." Michael thinks of Norma before he feels Terese's foot nudging down the top of his sock. He doesn't especially like the feeling but holds his foot steady.

"I have a girlfriend whose mouth never stops. I try to listen to her but go blank after the first sixty seconds."

"Which is probably how she's feeling inside. Blank."

Terese leans forward and lowers her voice. "Is it true that Marcus beat up two guys on his tour bus for talking during his spiel?" She sits up and cracks open a peanut between her teeth. "Hard to picture him as a tour guide, except that he was probably never short of things to say."

Michael points an accusing finger at Terese. "Do you sit out there reading everyone's files?"

She slaps his hand away. "Actually, his mother told me. Said it was a choice between jail and Rosewood. Let's see." Terese taps a finger against her lips. "What would I choose?"

A beer on an empty stomach helps Michael to laugh along with her.

"I understand things started to break down after his father died," he confides, feeling himself relax. "Technically he's more manic depressive than PTSD, but we had the extra bed."

"'My Marcus,' his mother said. Does she call him that when she talks to you? 'My Marcus' has never been the same since marrying the B-I-T-C-H. She actually spelled it."

Michael's laughing again. Talking about work over a beer makes him realize how isolated he's felt these past two months. The only contact he's had with doctors at the clinic has been at staff meetings, where the discussions centre around policy, liability, fundraising or griping. No one else works in his field, so ostensibly he's the director of his own program. He corresponds with his old supervisor via e-mail, but it's hardly the same as talking face-to-face. Theoretically, he and Frieda might be having these discussions.

Terese's stockinged foot, now resting against his ankle, feels almost pleasant. He flashes on her naked breast under his hand, their shared hard breathing, her noises.

"I get to know a lot about patients through their relatives," Terese continues. "Norma Daily's daughter calls every third day to ask how mum's doing. Like we're sisters. Then she gives me her excuse for not visiting. Like I care. Fluorescent lights, that was her latest. She can't stand to be around fluorescent lights. They set off her hormones or some such," Terese lowers her voice. "Bullshit. Now, Mrs. Roth, Scarlet's mom, from what I can tell, is a healthy drunk, and stinking rich I understand. And poor Johnny's as alone as it gets."

"Dad is long gone if he ever existed," Michael confirms, in spite of himself, "and his mom, well, she ..."

"Killed herself.

"You do read files."

"I sort them." Terese takes a slug of her beer. "Kerry Taylor's family seems normal enough, from what I can tell."

"I've only met Mrs. Taylor, but yeah, she's a healthy product of the fifties."

"Mrs. Cleaver or Lucy?"

"More Lauren Bacall mixed with wannabe Jackie Kennedy."

"Yeah, she is elegant, always so well-dressed. My mother somehow missed out on the panache of that generation. She loved bowling, horror flicks and Montgomery Ward. Still does. Oh, while I think of it, a Richard Taylor dropped off a package for you. Kerry's brother, I think. He wasn't too shoddy himself." She waggles her eyebrows. "I forgot to put it in your box so it's sitting on my desk. Sorry."

"That's okay, I have some work to finish up. I'll pick it up on my way home. By the way, I noticed that the bottom was torn off a letter in my outbox. Do you have any idea who —"

"Johnny B."

"Johnny?"

"For your autograph. Mrs. Carter told me he finds meaning in people's signatures."

"I guess that explains it, though it doesn't explain what he was doing in my office."

Terese turns the talk to a TV movie she saw last night, and her toe starts tickling up Michael's pants again. He takes this as his cue to down the last third of his beer and leave.

"You're leaving me?" Terese glances down at her half-full glass.

"Sorry, but I'm off to that conference in Boston early in the morning and still haven't packed or had a chance to look over my talk. But thanks for getting me out." He leans down and tilts her chin up for a kiss on the lips, knowing this public affection will please her.

"When are you back?"

"Late Sunday, sometime. Hope you enjoy your weekend."

"Not nearly as much as I would if you were around." She reaches out and strokes his arm as he walks away. Michael turns back and waves, catching sight of her shoeless foot dangling, aimless, under the table.

ALONE IN his office, Michael finishes the day's progress reports and opens his correspondence drawer to file some letters. He sees the scarf Mrs. Taylor gave him, folds it carefully and tucks it in the last file folder, the one marked "Superfluous."

As he turns out his light and locks his door, he remembers the package at the front desk.

"Quiet tonight?" he inquires of the night nurse as he slips the parcel into his briefcase.

"All quiet at the front," she says, without looking up from her paperwork. "Most of your litter's either watching television or in the games room. Marcus apparently thinks he's a pool shark but Bryson's put him in his place."

"No betting, I hope." Michael smiles.

"I'll check Bryson's pockets before he goes home."

He takes the stairs at a trot. Hootie opens the front doors as he sees Michael approach. "Out with the ladies tonight, Dr. Myatt? All right band at the Holiday Inn."

Hootie's voice sounds like dog food, muses Michael. "Nope, headed home with a good book." Michael pats the briefcase under his arm.

"To each their own," quotes Hootie with a shake of his shorn head.

LISTENING TO Handel's *Water Music* on the radio, Michael slides two frozen burritos into the oven. The piece comes to an end and the radio news comes on and reports five drive-by murders in the past twenty-four hours in Montgomery County, Maryland. "A suspect white van has been observed at the scene of these seemingly random slayings. The bullets confirm that the same weapon, a high-powered rifle, was used in each case. Maryland schools in the Montgomery County area will be closed tomorrow and people are being asked to keep their children indoors." Michael shakes his head. Maryland is only a half-hour's drive from here. How is it that people are allowed to buy high-powered rifles? What are they used for beside killing humans? He dresses his cucumber and tomato salad with balsamic vinegar, olive oil and garlic and puts it in the refrigerator to marinate. After pouring himself a whiskey, he tears open the manila envelope with his name on it. Inside he finds a leather-bound journal, in mint condition. He flips through to find it two-thirds empty, then returns to the inscribed page at the front. A gift from someone named Hugo, obviously also in the dance scene. A small world, Michael imagines, not unlike psychology. He recalls the two times in his life that he's been to the ballet — once as a boy and once in grad school. His Sicilian mother loved both the opera and the ballet and had seasons tickets to the Seattle Opera House. His father would accompany his mother at first, until he decided the performing arts were synonymous with vanity and stopped. Isabelle became her escort then. She brought Michael along only once, begrudgingly, when Michael's father was away at a botany conference and she couldn't get a sitter.

Drink in one hand, book in the other, Michael goes and sits in the armchair in the living room. He was only eight or nine when he saw that first ballet performance, but has a strong memory of dancers clad in dark bodysuits, marking out the pattern of the sounds against the wooden floor of the stage like personified musical notes. It wasn't until the end of the evening that he realized that the dancers' changing shapes also reflected the mood of the music. It was as if he could see what he was hearing. Perhaps that was his first notion of synesthesia. He sips his drink and leans his head against the chair back. What he remembers most about that night was turning to his mother to ask to go to the bathroom and receiving a distracted little slap on the cheek.

"How I hated you," Michael says aloud. He raises his glass and drinks to his honesty. He flips to a random page of Kerry's journal and reads one line. "God, it was nerve-wracking having you as a partner." This fellow Hugo? Michael assumes.

The other time he went to the ballet was in L.A. Some girl insisted on taking him. What was her name? She'd purchased the tickets herself so he felt obligated to go even though he was in the thick of finishing a section of his doctoral thesis: "Redefining the Patient/Therapist Relationship in the Psycho-Therapeutic Dynamic." He remembers digging out his father's cashmere dress coat for the occasion. Michael takes a long sip of whiskey and the memory comes rushing back.

The program was dedicated to the great George Balanchine, who had died earlier that same year. Michael remembers even now that a few oddities stood out in the Russian master's brief bio — that he was married six times to various prima ballerinas and that he used to buy perfume for all his favoured dancers so he could identify them by their scent and detect which ones were in the theatre at any given time. The program included two quotes from the master that stuck with Michael:

"Dance is visual music."

"Dance is woman."

The childhood trip to the ballet had affirmed the truth of the first quote. The second, Michael figured, was mere indulgence. He gave Mr. Balanchine a quick diagnosis: obsessive-compulsive, with a heightened Oedipal period.

"Conductors always have such great hair," he recalls his date commenting as the conductor took his place at the head of the orchestra pit. The first piece, "Allegro Brilliante," was a spirited dance with an equal number of men and women, all costumed in airy blues. Michael observed the men staying behind to lift, balance and turn the women, their movements mere echoes of those of the females. Was a man's role to present the women, show them off? Is that all Balanchine meant? She's prettier looking and better smelling, so keep her down front? The piece seemed an exacting demarcation of the music, echoing the musical counterpoint as well as accents, sustains and rests. He noticed that when the music shifted over to a minor key, the dancers' shapes became more angular — a flexed foot here, a turned-in knee there.

It was the second piece, though, that caused him not only to appreciate Balanchine's sexist blurt, "Dance is woman," but to call into question a supposition to his thesis, making the evening indeed worthwhile after all. "Valse Fantasie," choreographed to foreboding waltz music, began with four female chiffon-draped dancers moving in graceful unison diagonally across the stage. He wondered what they saw, heads held high, looking so intently into the black space of the audience. Were they indulging some beauty-pageant fantasy or completely blinded by stage lights, their eyes merely another artificially placed muscle?

Bored, Michael had conjured up the section of his thesis that refuted the widely held notion that the mind governed the body. Then a flash of magenta snared his attention. Sitting up straighter, he found his hearing had shifted. As if they'd become enlarged, his ears were being assailed by sound. Suddenly he could clearly distinguish violin from viola, cello from bass, each alternating peel of the harpist's hands. Every crystalline note melded his ears with his eyes and with the sweeping limbs and timed steps of the principal dancer. His senses had ballooned into the vaulted ceiling. In a flash, he understood that he was somehow sharing the sensory perceptions of the woman presently commanding both stage and audience.

His date leaned over and hissed something inaudible in his ear, puncturing his blissful absorption. He dismissed her with a nod, then with fresh distance, again studied the lead dancer. She seemed oblivious to everything except the poignant urgency of the music, as if the music's will, not her own, shaped her body to its liking. Michael was struck by how much this dancer stood out among the self-conscious flourish of the four other females. Meanwhile her partner, though moving right along with her, had faded into the backdrop.

That dancer's performance had caused him to embrace the theory of an enteric nervous system. He'd found data suggesting that the digestive system was packed with millions of neurons and neurotransmitters that mirrored forebrain activity. And he'd read the work of scientists, not only here in North America, but in Japan and France as well, who had reported that being in touch with one's "stomach brain" elicited a sympathetic emotional response from others. Those scientists specifically cited performing artists and athletes as examples of people who could spontaneously access this other brain.

Michael flips the pages of Kerry's journal back to the beginning. The word "Favourites" is written across the top. Judging from the handwriting, the categories appear to have been supplied by Hugo, the friend who gave Kerry the book. This could be helpful for future sessions, Michael thinks, tracing down the list.

Colour — *grey-blue*
Classical music — *Bach's Double Violin Concerto in E-Minor*
Place — *Shingle Beach, Metchosin*
Animal — *Blackjack*
Character role — *Julie*
Body part — *shoulder*
Book — Mists of Avalon
Sauce — *red curry coconut*
Movie — The Piano
Choreographer — *Mr. B*

Balanchine?
He skips the rest and flips through to the final entry. It's undated. He wonders how close to the day of the Kerry Taylor accident this was recorded.

Dear Hugo, It's Sunday in July, West Coast perfection — heat plus the built-in air-conditioning of the sea. The air here is so breathable. I'm in a good mood after days of being mad at Allan. I know what you'd say. Allan is too adaptable to bother getting mad at, and you're right, but that doesn't stop me. After leaving me stranded at the studio for an hour and a half — because he lost track of time while watching a baseball game — probably watching two games plus a fishing show, because he can never watch one thing at a time — I didn't speak to him for days. He was too self-absorbed to notice, though, which kind of defeats the purpose and makes the whole cold shoulder process even lonelier. So I finally broke down and told him what an insensitive jerk he was, forgetting me like that. And then was doubly hurt that he didn't notice how hurt I was. Of course, Allan was his seductively apologetic self, all an act, no doubt, but very effective, and we ended up in bed.

Sex, the great catharsis, makes me feel human again. Sometimes it seems to be the only thing that works, the only thing that can release my pent-up, angry energy. Well, that and puking. But sex, if Allan's around, is a lot nicer than puking. After making love I'm all forgiveness and can accept and love Allan for what he is and accept and love myself for what I am. I can even feel love for spiders and I hate spiders. There are these spiders here called wolf spiders. They're everywhere and they're hairy and huge and move disgustingly fast. Ew, I don't love them quite as much today. But it strikes me that making love does just what it says — makes more love.

Today we're off to an area called Swan Lake to birdwatch and picnic. That's the actual name, I swear. I've made a picnic, got the capers and dill in the tuna salad like you taught me, and I made double fudge cookies (chocolate bombs I call them) rivalling Famous Amos. Remember those? A whole bag in one end and out the same. Only the most expensive binge food for this sick-chick.

Time to round up the boys. The dog's beside himself with anticipation. He lives for car rides. Remember our old VW Bug? Well, it's still running and Allan's repainted it for the third time and it's no longer fuchsia colour but lemon-chiffon. A less loud colour, which is nice, especially since the car's noisier than ever. I really have to learn to drive if I'm going to be living out here and working in town. Not many checkered cabs drive by our dirt road. First step,

though, is to pass a driver's test. I've been studying and taking mock tests on
the Young Driver's website. Am planning to take it Monday before I teach

"There is a person in there," Michael says quietly. He closes the
journal, gets up to put on some music and check on his dinner.

He'll have to question Mrs. Taylor about the bulimia — when it started,
if Kerry ever needed hospitalization. He traces his finger along the rows
of CDs neatly organized both alphabetically and by genre, finds the piece
Kerry Taylor listed as her favourite classical piece and pops it on. The
impassioned precision of Bach's double violin concerto makes the small
living room seem much bigger. When the oven timer buzzes angrily on
the stove, the feeling is lost, and the world shrinks back to the familiar.

∽o∾

ARLENE SITS at her dressing table and checks her roots to see if it's
time for a rinse. No man wants to be married to someone who looks like
his mother, she tells herself, fussing her short ash-blonde curls over her
ears and forehead. Since Liz Taylor's scare she does worry about the
cancer connection and hair dye but, if it was that clear a connection,
would Liz have gone dark again?

Tonight is Saturday and two of her three children will be here for
dinner, along with their families, to help celebrate Beresford's seventy-
ninth. Arlene has placed sixteen red candles in the shape of a seventy-nine
around the top of a blue-flowered cake with white icing. Red, white and
blue. Arlene talks herself through the evening's details. "We'll open gifts
first with some champagne, then skedaddle everyone out of the den for
awhile, give Beresford some respite before dinner. I'll use the gold placemats and the good paper napkins, seat the kids at the table and the adults
can buffet it."

Locating the placemats, Arlene spots a miniature American flag in the
back of the cupboard and remembers the family reunion two summers
ago. She'd used the flag as part of a centrepiece for the Fourth of July picnic
at Richard's place. Kerry and family had come out from Vancouver and,

after lunch was over, Thomas had asked Arlene if he could borrow the flag for a game. He had his mother's single-mindedness and she can picture his serious little face, the intent eyes. Thomas had organized the kids and any willing adults into a game of capture the flag. He was the cousin in the middle, younger than the twins by two years, but older than both Marshall and Evan. Marshall, only a year younger than Thomas, looked up to his keen-eyed cousin with all the ideas, and had insisted on being on the same team. Allan had joined in, along with Patricia's husband Bill. Arlene remembers how Allan, eager as any kid, had lost himself in the game. When his team captured the flag, he'd made such a show of winning that poor little Evan, who was on the losing team, had burst into tears. Peter Pan was how Arlene had thought of Allan after first meeting him in New York and, sure enough, he'd never held what she'd considered a real job and, she considers sadly, never had a chance to grow old.

Richard, Leslie, the twins, Sarah and Sydney, and Marshall arrive first, followed by Patricia, Bill and their boy, Evan. Leslie is wearing a fabulous pair of silk pants and a fitted shirt that call attention to her great figure, while Richard, still in his work clothes, is wearing the Armani suit Arlene likes so much. Patricia's blonde curls are clipped on top of her head and shower down her back in a fountain of near-ringlets. She's wearing a lilac blouse over black capris, which to Arlene's dismay, look awfully tight around the backside. She doesn't dwell on Bill, her daughter's husband, in fact tries not to look at him because his odd proportions bother her nerves.

Beresford sits in his swivel chair in the den, his shiny dress shoes looking cumbersome as they shuffle sideways to aim his body at his well-wishers.

"Cheers, Dad," says Patricia in her sympathetic tone. She lifts her champagne glass in the air to bend over and plant a kiss on his speckled forehead. Arlene hasn't been able to figure out just what kind of spots those are. Sun spots? Age spots? Liver spots? Can you get liver spots on the head?

"Happy birthday, Beresford, Dad, Granddad" — the names mesh into one choppy metre as everyone gathers in the den, deposits gifts on the coffee table and finds a place to sit or stand.

"To seventy-nine years and counting," Richard officiates. "We're looking forward to ninety-nine."

"Don't hold your breath," Beresford says with a forced laugh.

"Or you'll turn red, then blue," says five-year-old Evan. "Right mama?"

Patricia nods at Beresford, who's about to open his gifts. She ushers Evan forward to stand by the arm of his grandfather's chair opposite Marshall, who is already posted on the other arm. Arlene encourages Richard and Bill to take the loveseat, while the three women remain ringed behind Beresford's chair. The twins kneel at their grandfather's feet and take turns passing him his gifts.

Beresford accepts each present with much ado. "Mmm, mmm. My favourite, Russell Stouffer's milk chocolates. And all for me." He hugs the box to his chest.

"Mom, Granddad's not sharing," whines Evan softly, testing the air.

"He's joking," Patricia assures him. "But no sweets until after dinner."

Arlene has given him a new silk robe. "Nice, very nice. Feel that, Marshall? That's silk, one-hundred percent. You, too, Evan. Feel good? Spun from the backsides of worms. Thank you, sweetheart," he says, reaching his hand blindly over one shoulder for Arlene to grab hold. He reels her in for a peck on the cheek. Arlene smiles fondly, knowing that, despite his perpetual headache, fatigue and the chill in his spine, Beresford will always rise to the occasion.

"Check out the quality of that robe," he gloats as his shaky hand extends the opened box over the heads of the twins to the men on the couch.

What about the girls? Arlene wants to point out, but doesn't.

He opens a pair of pajamas from Patricia, then a bottle of good port and Len Deighton's latest from Richard. Sarah and Sydney's gift is a glass terrarium filled with layers of dirt and coloured sand and three phallic-shaped cacti. Each cactus has a different colour dried mum glued to the tip.

"We made it," they chime together.

"The girls spent all day on that," says Leslie, her Louisiana drawl making "all day" sound like an eternity.

Marshall has made a card in the shape of a football with a picture of him inside dressed in his football gear. "That's me," he said. "I'm number ten."

Sarah passes Evan his card to give to Granddad but he knocks it out of her hand to the carpet. "Mine doesn't have a picture," he grumbles.

"It's okay, Evan." Patricia bends to get it and whispers loud enough for every ear in the room, "you're giving him slippers, remember?" She gives Arlene a helpless smile.

After the last gift is exclaimed over, Evan cranks his face up to his mom. "Can Marshall and I go wrestle?"

"Sure, sweetie."

"Come on, Marshall," Evan says, tugging at his cousin's shirt.

"No way, you're boring." Marshall rips his shirt out of Evan's small grip.

"Marshall." His mother's mint-julep scold sounds noncommittal.

Evan hits high whine and Arlene sees Beresford's neck stiffen.

"Marshall," Richard takes over, "you apologize to your cousin. Now."

"I'm not," says Marshall, running out of the den and down to his grandparents' room. He slams the door behind him.

"Sorry, Mom, I'll get him." Richard starts from the couch.

"No, I want to talk to him," says Arlene. "You stay with your father and the rest of you can go into the living room. Girls, you can start bringing the food to the table. It's all in the fridge ready to go."

Arlene finds her grandson standing in front of the family photos on the dresser.

"I want to see Thomas," he grumbles, his arms crossed and head hanging down.

Arlene's heart squeezes in her chest. "Oh, sweetheart, you know you can't see Thomas."

"He used to be here."

Marshall is scanning the photographs and it dawns on her that he's looking for Thomas' school photo. She receives an updated school photo of each grandchild every year and replaces the new one over the old. Before she can reply, Marshall squints up at her in the mirror. "If I die, will you throw my picture away?"

"Marshall." Arlene bends down, tucking his smallness under her chin. She inhales the powdery smell of his young skin. "Thomas is right in here, sweetheart. We'd never throw your pictures away." She opens a drawer and lifts out the face-down frame. "Granddad and I were just so sad about the accident that it was hard for us to look ..."

"I was going to show him the card trick I'd learned," Marshall interrupts, taking the picture from his grandmother. "Thomas didn't know this one." Arlene feels her eyes growing wet and holds Marshall tighter. She takes a breath to help blow away the emotion. They sit in silence, staring down at Thomas' eternally smiling face.

There's a knock at the door and Richard sticks his head in. "Okay, Marshall, you still have an apology to make, big guy."

Marshall hands the photo back to Arlene and leaves, the moment past.

Arlene looks at the bright-eyed boy in her hands, steadying herself as the sadness drags through her once again. He had Beresford's bedroom eyes, she thinks, except for the colour, that odd bleached-blue of his mother's. She makes room, then places the frame carefully on the dresser in front of the others. She takes one more look, then straightens her shoulders and leaves, gently shutting the door behind her.

The adults sit in the living room with plates on their laps, while the kids eat up at the table. Beresford has requested that he be left to eat alone in the den. The energy of the grandchildren wears on him.

"Another shooting today, did you hear?" says Richard, settling on the sofa beside his wife. "In Virginia this time."

"No," says Patricia, as if denying it would make it not true.

"Down near Fredericksburg."

"Oh," says Patricia, sounding relieved. "That's quite a bit south, isn't it?"

"Woman was loading her shopping bags into her trunk. She's in critical condition but they think she'll make it."

"And they still have no leads?" asks Arlene.

"The white van lead didn't pan out, so, no," says Richard. "The bullets come out of nowhere. And the sniper has a silencer on his gun."

"They have police patrolling the streets corners in our neighbourhood," says Leslie with a shiver. "It's eerie. People are saying the sniper's probably part of a terrorist cell."

"I don't know about that," says Richard.

"How's Kerry doing?" Patricia asks Arlene, changing the subject.

"Any progress?" The emotional member of the family, Patricia can hardly mention her sister's name without becoming weepy.

"The doctor says she's responding well to treatment and he's very positive. She's eating well but, no, still not a word out of her, or a glance for that matter."

"God, it's too sad." Patricia stares blankly at her roast-beef sandwich.

"Kerry was not very talkative at the best of times," says Richard. "Being a dancer and all."

"Maybe she should have dance therapy," Bill says, making everyone look. He dabs the corners of his mouth with his napkin and innocently stares back. No one has a clue if he's serious or joking. "Good horseradish," he says. "What brand?"

Bill is a gourmet cook, a dedicated father and successful CPA. But the fact that he is proportioned like an overgrown three-year-old, his head noticeably larger than the rest of him, makes it difficult for Arlene to look at him. She knows it's irrational, but there it is. He's also two inches shorter than her perfectly formed daughter and, as Patricia's once-lovely figure begins to soften, Bill is now thinner too. They couldn't look more mismatched in her eyes. A standard poodle with a chihuahua.

"Well," Richard says, picking up the thread, "this doctor takes a physical approach. Mom has some information about it and I researched him on the Net. His therapy sounds pretty space age to me, but he's had results. At those prices, he'd better." Richard has directed this last comment to his wife beside him on the couch. "You like him, don't you, Mom?"

"In some way, I think Kerry-Ann and he are similar animals."

"Our science teacher," pipes up Sydney from the dining room, "calls us human animals."

"The animal with opinions," finishes Sarah.

Thunder booms in the distance and the children all pause in their eating and look toward the doors to the deck.

"We're supposed to get rain to—" Arlene starts to say before Richard continues where he left off.

"I had to drop off a package at Rosewood on my way home from work," says Richard, "and was given a little tour. You should see the place.

Indoor pool with a track around it, fully equipped gym, a games room with card tables, Ping-Pong and a beautiful mahogany pool table. Every patient has a private room and bath. It reminds me of a resort Leslie and I stayed at in Maui," he laughs.

"Why do they call them shrinks?" Bill poses this question to the room at large, his head looming enormous.

The room is hushed, brains scrambling for answers.

"Maybe the term came from the days of shock therapy," offers Leslie. "Destroyed brain cells sort of shrinking the brain." She ends her answer with a shrug.

"Or maybe it refers to the psychiatrist's focusing in," Patricia starts, "narrowing in on the patient's problem. So shrinking the focus ..." She looks unsure and leaves off.

Richard interjects with authority. "I assume it must have to do with analyzing a personality into a neat bundle with obvious handles. Compacting the mess." He has mastered the art of being convincing even if he hasn't a clue what he's talking about, thinks Arlene proudly.

"Like a garbage compactor," says Bill. "Well, a few beers and watching the game is what I call therapy."

People laugh politely as Bill raises his empty beer glass and heads to the kitchen.

"Now, this fellow working with Kerry-Ann is a psychologist, not a psychiatrist," Arlene says, attempting to join in the conversation, but people are rising to replenish their plates, the topic abandoned. She takes a sip of her champagne. "Save room for cake," she calls out.

AS HER FAMILY is leaving, Arlene gives each grandchild a lingering hug, moulding her chest against theirs. Marshall hugs her back, quick and fierce, and she can feel his hammering heart through his shirt. She kisses her children, cheek to cheek, their spouses, too, even Bill, relishing eye contact as she pulls away. "Drive carefully," used to be included in her parting words. Now she calls out, "Be good."

UNSTEADY ON his depleted legs, Beresford lets Arlene help him stand and urinate, wash up at the sink and then get into bed.

"Happy birthday, Darling," Arlene says, imparting a kiss from fingertips to forehead.

"This getting older business was fun once upon a time," Beresford says, collapsing into his pillow. "Now it's hell. Plain and simple. End of story."

"Well, it's an excuse to get the gang together."

"That whine of Evan's will be the death of me."

"At least he's still around to listen to," Arlene shoots back, miffed at Beresford's lack of appreciation for all her efforts tonight on his behalf.

"Touché, I apologize. Goodnight, dear. The robe is a beauty."

This last remark drains her resentment. She went all the way downtown hunting for one in the colours he likes. "Glad you like it. Good night, Beresford."

∾o∾

IN HER ROOM, in the dark hum of silence, Kerry's right hand twitches, restless. Her wrist transmits a message to her forearm, which informs her elbow to command her shoulder to move just enough to slip her hand through the steel bars and reach toward the masked head … the bandaged head? … left behind … over there. Her thoughts call out to him, *Come. I'll hold you. Make it better.*

Pinky finger in place, the man-child rolls silently across the floor, his rubberneck leading his body, white towel whipping along behind him. He stops just under her hand, which now dangles above his head. The red light on the intercom beside her bed projects a pink almond-shaped light onto her palm. A palm that sees, fingers that speak.

Johnny's finger is extricated from its hole with a sigh of wonder, his abandoned tongue a small hairless mammal tucking itself in behind his front teeth. Still damp, his little finger reaches skyward to be enclosed in the warm tunnel of her palm. Johnny and Kerry remain in this odd embrace, even after sleep claims them.

The tinkling sound of the bells on the doorknob catapults Johnny under Kerry's bed. Kerry wakes, but her eyes refuse to open. *Shh …* her thoughts whisper, *or they'll take you away. Shh …*

A circle of light shines around the room and then around Kerry's bed before the door closes again. Johnny's knee stings from where it scraped the edge of the box spring and he fingers the torn cloth of his pajamas, feeling for blood. There's just a little blood, but that's enough. He's been told, time and again, never ever to touch another patient. Never disturb her. Never disturb or touch. That would be very, very bad. Only mommy can touch. Only mommy. Never tell or you know what'll happen. They'll take you away. And it will be your fault, Johnny. And who will love you then? Because you're a bad, bad boy. My bad, bad boy.

Kerry is being rocked now, remembering being in the borrowed car-top boat out in the strait, being knocked up and down by a bigger boat's wake. Up, down, up, down, hold on tight. From below the boat, a violin screeches off-key. A seagull's cry. Or maybe a baby seal. Hurt? Injured? Her teeth imagine they're grinding away to nothing before the rusty smell of blood hits her nose and the world is racing away from her, racing away from her. Before it is gone, she must keep her head up, look ahead, move her hand toward the red light on her bedside table. Her fingers find the button and press for help.

Soon beams of light roam the room, the beacon from the lighthouse signalling the way back.

"Do you think she could have …"

"Oh, sweet Jesus. Call for help. Hurry."

Kerry is being lifted into the air, long gown trailing, to be seated on her throne.

"We lift the bed on three and you, Bryson, pull him out. One, two, three."

"Get the towel out of his mouth."

Dual violins are shrieking now, Tibault's death spilling onto the floor.

"It's going to be all right, Johnny, I promise you." It's the big nurse's voice. "You're a good boy, Johnny Bourne. Understand me? And I'm telling you it's going to be all right."

Her good boy is being taken away on a flatbed, the violins fading to nothing.

The princess sits upright on her throne, breathing hard, staring at the floor where Cinderella creates thin red swirling circles with a white towel. The rusty smell is coming closer. She is lifted again, gown and all, into the lights and returned to the boat, the water perfectly calm now, perfectly calm.

"Sleep now, girl. You sleep. Everything's going to be all right."

THE WILL TO WONDER

As infants, we experience our senses as inseparable from the world around us. The olfactory sense and the odour of a rose are one and the same, as are taste and the thin sweetness of mothers' milk; sight and the colour red; touch and the silky fur of a kitten; hearing and the sound of a mother's heartbeat. The infant experiences its senses and sensory phenomena simultaneously and dwells in a kind of mindful stupor.

Freed from conceptual bias, the experience of pain is no more nor less desirable than the experience of pleasure. Crying and laughing are merely different responses to different stimuli. Because the infant has no conceptual labels of preference, such as good versus bad, he has no capacity to screen or filter out potentially harmful experiences. All experiences, however positive or negative, are imprinted equally.

At this highly vulnerable precognitive juncture, the infant's internal experience and his experience of the external world of phenomena are inextricably linked in a state of pure wonderment.

STAGE II: THE PATTERNING EXERCISES

As the infant is squeezed through the birth canal, the connective tissue, glands and organs receive a deep and thorough massage. This active compression forces cerebral spinal fluid along the channels of the spine, which in turn stimulates the endocrine system. The birthing pattern, initiated at the crown of the head, stimulates each endocrine gland and an associate sense perception, in sequence, beginning with the pituitary gland and sight. This awakening of the autonomic nervous system is the cause of an infant's alertness and receptivity during its first hour of life outside the womb.

Babies born by caesarian section miss this vital soft tissue stimulation, and are therefore less wakeful post delivery. They should receive hands-on stimulation and appropriate massage therapy to fully activate their body systems. Because a vaginal birth releases the necessary hormones to ensure bonding, care should be taken after a traumatic birth, such as a caesarian, to ensure that bonding occurs. Nursing within the first hour of birth is one such insurance.

This vital transition from womb to life outside the womb will affect, for the rest of an individual's life, how he responds to life transitions and how well he is able to cope with change.

Dear Hugo, It's raining like thunder, no gardening, Thomas at school, Allan on a carpentry job and I have no classes today. My mountainous audience has been hidden behind a curtain of cloud for at least a week now and Blackjack's my lone companion. I've started scratching behind my ear with my foot and thinking in single words. "Food? Walk? Food?"

Speaking of food, these long days bring out my restlessness. Today I've made chewy ginger cookies, the crinkly kind with sugar tops, and I've already had six. Uh-oh, when the cat's away, the mouse will ... eat the pantry and regurgitate in the garden.

Sometimes it's weird teaching kids ballet and trying to square the beauty of the art with the neurosis that seems to bump up against it. It's masochistic, really, to distort our bodies like we do. Ballet hurts not just a lot, it hurts like hell. What's wrong with us? I grossed out the beginner pointe students the other day by showing off my toes and destroying, I hope, their Sugar Plum fantasies. Trying to save a few souls before it's too late. And then there are all the rampant eating disorders, which I see now as just another form of self-mutilation. Can't afford to slice up our pretty outsides, so we slice up our insides instead. How discreet.

We've got this amazingly talented ten-year-old here at the school who's gone anorexic. AWOL as we used to call it. Ten! You always said that I was one of the lucky ones. That it was the ones who stopped eating that you had to worry about. It's so true. We bulimics just lose our stomach contents and our self-respect while the AWOLs lose their muscle tissue and their minds. Remember poor Dasha and that super talented girl at the Academy. Jennifer? At least she was twelve, not ten.

I really have to credit you for my having a career at all. You with your amoral, guilt-free approach to everything. I remember you saying that every-one was addicted to something and I should be grateful I could satisfy mine without breaking any laws. Speaking of which, I can smell those chewy morsels of ginger, molasses and butter calling me downstairs. Their cartoon waves of scent are floating upstairs and zig zagging their way up my nose ...

I don't know why, Hugo, but I still do it. God, I'm thirty-three years old and I'm prolonging a fifteen-year-old's habit. It's as if I'm taken over by some demonic force that can't think of anything else but food. But before I'm reduced to stuffing my face, it always starts with the same feeling: there's this internal pressure that builds in my stomach, like yeasted bile, and the only relief is to stuff down enough food to have something to throw up. Puking feels like the only way to release whatever it is that's compressed in there. I've come to think it's anger, mostly, that I can't get a handle on. I don't know if I'm angry at myself for being a wimp, or angry at all those people I let insult me while I just stood there and smiled pretty. That's a directive my dad used to give me and my sister. "Smile pretty," he'd say with a chuck to our chins, as if that simple gesture would aid mankind, wipe out hunger, stop war. But he'd say it with such love in his eyes. Who was I to question it? And not to put the blame on him, but that's what I tend to do in the face of insult and injury: smile and take it because my brain freezes and I can't think. So I resort to niceness, even though deep down I'm seething. And I'm sure I look like an idiot. Only later, when I'm alone, do I think about all the clever, biting comebacks I might have said if only I'd stood up for myself. If only I wasn't such a traitor. How I've envied you with your quick comebacks.

Purging feels like finally talking back, roaring out all those belated words I could have, should have said. It's like I'm drowning out my niceness, my femininity, and I'm not afraid of being ugly. Ugly mad. Puking ugly mad. Mad ugly puke. Puke ugly.

Too bad that after my glorious proclamation of ugly, I'm weak as a kitten with dehydration and a raw throat, apologizing to God and everyone else for being a self-destructive wimp. And then, of course, I go back to my disciplined good-girl self, smiling pretty and waiting for the cycle to repeat itself.

The books say bulimia's a perfectionist's game, an inability to relax with how "perfectly imperfect" we are. And I worry that I'm projecting that criti-calness on others, Allan for example, and poor Thomas, too, though I try not to. It feels as if my inner and outer selves are disjointed, two images flipping back and forth like a hologram. One side is obliging and nice and the other is stubbornly ambitious and proud. And if I could only bring the two images together in some sort of balance, I wouldn't keep tripping up and falling blind into that same hole where the bile builds up.

I'd say it's really only onstage and, I guess, in making love that my two selves seem to come (pardon the pun) together and I feel "heard." Feel strong, even dominant. But now that the curtain's come down, it's like I have to learn another language to bridge the gap. One can only have so much sex. You being the exception. But then you were never short of words in any case. I think I need to be more outwardly aggressive, less of a people pleaser. I need to toughen up in a way without being hard on myself. Oh, I don't know. It feels like a Catch-22.

You know, to this day I still can't mention a thing about my bulimia to my parents. Even after good ole Jane Fonda and Princess Di confessed to the entire planet. My dad is so proud of his kids and to disappoint him always feels like disappointing God. I'm afraid he'll feel my neurosis was some personal failing on his part. But there I go, trying to please people again. I hide my bingeing from Allan for the same reason and then get mad at him for not intuiting when I'm in that head space so that he'll do something to stop me. I think if I told Mom, she'd just be momentarily grossed out, then happily ignore it.

I will say, that over nearly two decades of closet-tossing my cookies, I've mastered the art of the silent puke, not to mention of cleaning toilet bowls.

∽o∾

MICHAEL ADMIRES the shapely calves of the airline hostess as she wheels the drink trolley up the narrow aisle. Sipping his ginger ale, he pictures the woman who sidled up to him in yesterday's brunch line after his morning lecture. Beneath her short skirt, her legs were long and well-muscled. She had dark hair and eyes, and smooth white skin, a sensual mouth. She looked like how white chocolate smells, was a verifiable knockout among the heady world of psychologists. A fact she seemed well aware of.

"Dr. Myatt, explain to me, what makes these simple-sounding therapies so effective?" The tilt of her head made him think she was more interested in his reaction to her than an answer to her question.

"Your name?" he asked, ignoring the sticker nametag.

"Dr. Sheila Morag," she said and extended her hand. Her nails were long and painted a pale orange.

Michael decided to play it cool.

"Well, to answer your question, Dr. Morag. First the patient is taken out of his or her habitual environment and placed in a neutral zone, a safe place. Then, as I described in my talk, because the exercises I employ mirror human physiological development they feel natural to the patient, non-invasive, and therefore short-circuit resistance. And in reconnecting to pre-traumatic physiology, the patient finds the means to move through the places he's emotionally stuck or frozen. But foremost in importance for the treatment's success is the ability of the facilitator to break down barriers by bringing genuine sympathy to the exchange."

"Yes, but can you really step into someone else's skin?" Dr. Morag challenged. "And how do you discriminate your own projection, or dare I suggest, your own imagination, from a genuine sympathetic exchange, as you call it?"

"You feel it. It's no more or less remarkable than picking up on the vibe in a room or being influenced by someone else's mood. When someone you care for is depressed, you start to feel down. When that same person is happy, you perk up. It's like catching someone's germs, only these are physiological germs."

Michael smiled and then yawned, a full-fledged, open-mouthed yawn, barely hiding it behind his hand. Sheila Morag yawned, too, a small yawn at first. She turned her head to the side as it grew bigger.

"See," said Michael, "it's as natural as catching someone's yawn."

"You tricked me." Dr. Morag batted his shoulder.

"I did." He smiled, flirting back. "So it comes down to a question of training to become aware of these intuitive exchanges, which in reality are taking place all the time. And the next step is learning to recognize where the sympathetic energy locates in the body. There's no need to manufacture anything."

"Thanks, that answers my question," she said, then turned back to her spot in line.

She's playing coy, he thought, listening to her ask the man in front of her what was on the menu. A minute later she shot him a fleeting smile, a smile that quivered at its edges and he was surprised to feel a cool, slightly hollow feeling in his stomach. She wasn't trying to seduce him, he thought, she was just insecure and using his attentions to buoy her self-image. His stomach growled audibly. Sheila Morag turned around, armed with a new question, but Michael excused himself to the washroom.

He realizes now, thirty-thousand feet above the Atlantic, that he has never devoted much thought to why this visceral sympathy comes easy to him. Maybe he should be more grateful for having had emotionally distant parents. Perhaps the primal longing that tooled in his gut those early years taunted his enteric nerves to stay alert. Thinking of his parents, he feels an emotional neutrality settle over him. His father, engrossed as he was with his work, was never unkind, just not there, while his mother was a foreign land to which Michael was denied all access. His earliest memories are of wanting to be held by her, squished against the cushion of her chest and kissed just once, in private, with spontaneous affection. Her kisses were rare but he was always sure of getting one in front of an audience of dinner guests. His mother liked to throw parties, and would invite important people from the museum where she worked, or the deans and professors from his father's biology department. He remembers one dinner party when, after his good-night kiss, he hooked his arms around her perfumed neck and hung on.

"Enough," came her terse whisper as she discreetly wrested apart his hands. Turning back to her guests with a martyr's smile, she'd given him a firm shove. "Off you go, Michael." It was never Mike or Mikey, or the endearments his friends' mothers used, like Honey or Dear. Isabelle, was Belle or Bella, but Michael was always Michael. His father sometimes called him "Son," as if qualifying his relative genus.

In bed, Michael would concentrate on luring his mother to his side and, failing this, on drawing the warmth out of her body, up the stairs and into what felt like the cold, empty tunnel of his own body. He was afraid when the sun went down, the dark minutes passing like hours before he'd fall asleep each night. He would have liked to sleep in his sister's room, but that was strictly forbidden. Once, he couldn't have been more than four or five, he snuck his pillow and blanket across the hall and slept on Isabelle's hard floor. His mother was livid when she found him the next morning and the thrashing he received didn't warrant the risk.

As the plane banks, Michael looks over to see the solid rectangle of the Kennedy Center along the tree-lined Potomac, the curves of Watergate next door. The box that Watergate came in, as the joke goes, or so Terese told him. It suddenly occurs to Michael that pain, not pleasure, is the medium of his therapeutic exchange. Pleasure is something he doesn't even think to look for. But then, he's never been moved by optimists. Optimists seem to be racing up a mountain only to career down the other side. A forced cheer destined for a downslope. His talent as a psychologist appears to be his ability to bring patients to a neutral place, a plateau somewhere between the extremes of pain and pleasure, a limbo of sorts, where life becomes manageable again and expectations are lowered. Perhaps Freud was right when he said: "The task of therapy is to transform neurotic misery into ordinary unhappiness." But should he, as a therapist, consider this good enough?

Michael recalls with a wince how he's failed to swell to orgasm at the same time as any of his various lovers. Failed at sharing the ultimate pleasure.

The stewardess with the shapely calves walks past, checking that all seat backs are raised for landing. The engine throttles down noisily and the young woman in the seat beside him startles, her hand clutching the armrest between them. Michael envies her for being so attached to the living.

ARRIVING HOME to his apartment, Michael sees that all signs of life have been tidied away by the cleaning service he's hired. They come in every second week, but he's never yet laid eyes on them. He pictures a group of tiny elves in green suits, red boots with curled up toes. As he sorts through the mail, bills and flyers, the smell of ammonia causes the back of his throat to fill. His territorial scents have been overruled by chemicals and he has an irrational urge to piss in a hard-to-get-to corner, like behind the armoire. The cleaners have turned off the radio, again, assuming he'd absently left it on. Of course, he's never told them otherwise. Michael flips the switch on the radio and welcomes the laconic pillow voice of the classical music expert introducing a Bartok concerto.

AS SOON AS his foot hits the top step of the landing, Terese is waving him over to reception.

"Welcome back. Did you bring me anything from Boston?" she says.

"Uh ... I didn't think ..."

"I'm only kidding. How was the conference?" She says this quickly, as if to get it out of the way.

Michael shrugs as he reaches for his mail. "It's hard to get mental health professionals to think below the neck."

"I'm sure the right ears heard the right things. But I have to tell you," her tone turns solemn, then she pauses until Michael looks up from his mail.

"Just waiting for you to look at me while I'm talking."

"Oh," he says, keeping his eyes from reading the envelope in his hand, a bill from the flotation pool people.

"Johnny got into trouble while you were away. Self-inflicted lacerations to both his knees. They found him under Kerry Taylor's bed and apparently he scraped his knees ..." she winces, her shoulders rising, "along the exposed edge of one of the metal springs. Right down to the ..." she can't seem to say it.

"Bone?"

She nods and then shakes her head. "He was taken to emergency.

Twelve stitches in one knee, sixteen in the other. A nasty infection, apparently."

"And Frieda?" Michael has to ask.

"She's waiting for you in her office," says Terese, giving him a flat smile.

"Thanks, Terese. And I hope you had a nice weekend," he adds, in lieu of a souvenir box of Boston tea.

"I stayed in and listened to the shootings on the news. A thirteen-year-old this time. Luckily he survived." Michael had read about it in the *Post* but Terese is on a roll. "The shooter left behind a tarot card, the death card, and wrote on it "I am God. It's nuttier out there than in here." Then Terese makes some sort of sideways leap and adds, "Hey, I missed you."

Michael smiles. He needs to go see Johnny. "Yeah, it's good to be back."

Before answering to Frieda, Michael will visit Johnny and assess where he's at. He's sorry to hear the news but considers Johnny's actions to be neither good nor bad. They simply indicate emotional movement. Whether the movement is forward or backward doesn't apply at this stage of therapy.

He knocks once on Johnny's door before entering. "Hello, Johnny."

Stretched out on top of his bedspread, Johnny glances up from his magazine. The magazine, a computer game manual, slowly rises, as if on its own accord, until it covers Johnny's face. Dressed in shorts, his pale wishbone legs are dissected by bulky, white bandages. As Michael pulls a chair up beside the bed, Johnny pulls the magazine closer.

Michael sighs loudly, then proceeds to talk to the magazine's cover. "Hurting yourself can distract you from the real pain for only so long," he says bluntly. "A few days. A few weeks, maybe."

Johnny reaches for the towel beside him on the bed, expertly interlocking it with his thumb and forefinger.

"I believe you know what I'm saying. Johnny?"

Johnny slowly brings the towel up behind the magazine.

"We've got a lot of good work left to do, you and me. This is only the beginning and what's happened here is not an obstacle. You understand?"

Johnny quietly turns the page.

"There are other ways besides hurting yourself to get relief. And I'm going to prove it to you over time. Johnny, can you look at me please?"

Johnny lowers the magazine to the bridge of his nose, his long bangs brushing his eyelids.

"No more injuries then?"

A quick nod.

"Would you like to talk about it?"

Johnny shakes his head tightly.

"That's all right. A shame we'll have to delay the patterning exercises, though, until the infection's cleared. Then again," Michael says, thinking aloud, "I could use the manual manipulation I employ with disabled patients." He nods to himself.

Johnny's magazine has slipped back up to cover his face.

"Good. I think we can keep things moving."

MICHAEL DECIDES against going to see Frieda in her office and goes to his own office instead and rings Terese.

"Terese, tell Frieda that I'll see her in my office whenever she has a minute."

"Your office? Ooh," says Terese.

He hangs up. I am the doctor, he tells himself. Frieda should come to him.

Minutes later, he hears two terse raps at his door. Refusing his offer of a chair, Frieda stands just inside the door.

"I saw Johnny," Michael begins and picks up his pen. He realizes too late that he has nothing to write on. He'd meant to take out Johnny's file.

"Will you be postponing treatment?" Frieda's tone is terse.

"I hadn't thought it nec —"

"Until his knees have healed?"

Her superior tone galls him. "There are ways to work around his knees. To halt therapy now is to halt his progress and perhaps even reverse it. Self-mutilation is a common phenomenon as trauma begins to edge into consciousness. But I'm sure you're well aware of that." He glances up into her unforgiving eyes. "And don't we have round-the-clock nursing care to prevent patients from acting out such extremes?"

Michael knows this last remark is a low blow. Frieda is the type to blame herself for any oversight on the part of her staff. He almost feels guilty as Frieda's eyes flicker toward the floor. Almost.

"It won't happen again," she says, momentarily beaten.

"Excellent," says Michael, not meeting her eyes. He leans over to pull out Johnny's file and she leaves, closing the door behind her with a quiet click.

Somebody has to get a rein on that woman, he tells himself, flipping open Johnny's file. I don't care how long she's been here.

MICHAEL MAKES a recommendation that for the next ten nights, an extra nurse be put on night shift and posted inside Johnny's room. Frieda offers no argument. For the following ten days, she leaves a night-time report on his desk. The only unusual note in the report is the observation that Johnny, while seemingly sound asleep, removes his finger (or fingers) from his mouth, extends his arm to the ceiling and presses said finger (or fingers) upward like he's trying to push in a tack. As if perfectly balanced in its socket, the arm remains suspended there for up to forty minutes, swaying ever so slightly

THE MAKESHIFT room-within-a-room is soundproof and entirely dark, with the exception of opaque light from a small circular window at floor level. Michael guides an uncertain Norma down on all fours, into the hands-and-knees position, so that the small window is directly behind her.

"Trust me now, Norma," Michael cajoles. "You are doing exceptionally well."

"Trust you, now," she repeats. "It's awfully dark. Can't we turn on some sort of light?" Her big voice fills up the small space.

"I know it's dark," Michael lowers his voice, "but if you place your forehead to the mat on the floor you'll see, between your legs, the window behind you."

"Between my legs … I'm not sure my figure's fit for such stuff, Dr. Honey."

"Just like I demonstrated before, Norma." Michael ignores her protests and eases her forward with his hand. "Now place your hands on either side of your head. Yes, that's right, and bend your elbows almost to the floor."

"But all the blood will rush to my head." She tries to sit back up, but his hand prevents it.

"Very easy now. We won't stay in the position for long. Here …" Michael places both his hands on the back of her fleshy neck and guides her head to the floor. Norma moans unabashedly at his touch, her resistance forgotten as her forehead contacts the mat. Catching her just under the base of her skull, Michael gently rolls her head up to its thin-haired crown and then back to her forehead.

"See, you can do it. Just a gentle tuck of the chin and roll up and back."

Norma's momentarily quiet.

They repeat this motion several times until the whole of her body joins in, her spine gliding forward, from neck to tailbone and back again. Norma is oddly graceful as she settles into a slow rhythm.

"I feel like one of those glide rockers," she says "You know the kind I mean?"

"I do." His voice is hushed, pulling her focus back to the exercise. "Now, eyes open. Just watch the window and relax. That's it. Eyes open and relax."

"Eyes open, just relax, eyes open, just relax," she repeats.

One of Michael's hands remains on Norma's neck while the other hovers just above her tail bone. As he places his attention in his hands, Norma's cranial rhythm becomes clear to him. There's a subtle but distinct squeeze and release of the skull every one and a half seconds. He allows the pulsing motion to synchronize with his own. With each contractive beat cerebral spinal fluid washes up into his brain and splashes like warm light behind his eyes.

"Ooh, that light is bright," says Norma, the uncertainty in her voice gone. "And look at that, it's moving, too."

"Shh, don't tell me, just stay with the sensation, keeping your eyes open." Michael's voice is liquid smooth.

Maintaining her rhythmic glide forward and back, Norma begins a chant-like hum. Gradually, Michael eases his hands away from her body and she continues on her own.

After several minutes, he has her rest.

"We'll repeat the movement for three minutes, then rest for two. After each sequence, I'll light the window with a new colour."

"I'll be getting my exercise for the day, I will. Joce was always after me to sign up at one of those fancy indoor gyms, but somehow ..."

"Let's try to stay on track, Norma. I just want you to keep listening to your body."

Norma does as she's told and Michael slips a coloured gel over the soft-lit window, changing it to a vivid blue.

"That's a pretty colour," says Norma, then catches herself. "Oh, sorry. I'll shut up."

They begin again and Michael's hand is there to help her refocus and ensure the proper speed and flow of movement, both inside and out. Soon Norma quiets and Michael knows that the colour has burned into her retina. Her attention is being reduced to a single sense.

"SO, THAT wasn't so tough, was it?" Michael asks Norma on her way out.

"You're a little wizard," she hisses. Her smile bunches her cheeks into her eyes.

"It's not me. Your own body is where the magic lies," he says.

"Aw," says Norma slapping at the air. She throws her arms around his waist and gives him an enthused squeeze. Michael pats her padded back tentatively in return.

"It's all right," Norma says, releasing him. "It's a hug."

MICHAEL'S EVERY attempt at manually directing Marcus in the visual stimulation exercise fails. Marcus keeps knocking Michael's hand off and accusing him of being a "frigging faggot."

It is Day 3 before Marcus finally surrenders enough to experience the proper body motion and pituitary stimulation.

"It's heaven's light at the end of the fuckin' tunnel," Marcus remarks. "Moonlight reflecting off the fuckin' river."

Today, Michael is introducing Marcus to the audio stimulation exercises.

"What you got for us today, Doc? Primal fuckin' screaming? Dressing up in diapers? Tarzan calls?" Marcus drums his fist on his chest and yodels.

He is wearing gold rings in his ears. Michael looks at them twice. Didn't the patient have only one ear pierced when he arrived?

"So today we're adding to the movement learned yesterday." Michael gently encourages Marcus to sit down on the mat. "You repeat the single rolling motion from the crown of your head back to the forehead, then slowly lift your face up to see in front of you," Michael explains. "At which point I may touch your skull lightly, just behind your ears."

Marcus freezes like a wary animal and Michael gives him a moment to digest this possibility.

"Show me yesterday's movement a couple of times please, Marcus, before we begin."

Marcus' stocky body drops to the floor. He does three energetic push-ups with a clap in between, then springs into a rigid hands and knees position. "Alrighty." He performs the rocking motion up to the balding crown of his head, once, twice, and on the third execution Michael's hands are there, fingertips brushing the jawbone stubble, to dip Marcus' head downward slightly before the subtle curve upward to face the wall.

"Like surfacing out of a dive," Michael says gently. "Clear?"

"Clear as the mud on my butt," Marcus rumbles, then snorts out a laugh. "No, no, really, I think I've got it. Boy, you think of some weird shit. You're making this up as we go along, aren't you?"

"And I want you to wear this mask over your eyes, please."

"Sure, why not. Got some bunny ears for me, too? Or a cape?"

Marcus laughs his grim laugh, pops up to his knees and obediently flips on the eye mask. He extends his arms stiffly out in front of him and wiggles his stubby fingers. "Where'd you go? I can't *see* you," he sings.

Under his black T-shirt, the broad muscles of Marcus' chest remind Michael of a Rottweiler. Marcus' hand brushes Michael's shirt near the collar, then catches the knot of his tie. Michael tenses his neck muscles. Marcus hesitates.

"Gotcha by the silky," he says smoothly.

Michael deliberately releases his muscles so as to exude nothing but calm. Marcus runs his fingers the length of the tie, hesitates at the tip, then lets it drop away.

"Shall we begin?" says Michael flatly.

"Nurse, this man needs an enema," Marcus calls out before dropping back onto all fours. "Let's get this freak show on the road."

Michael breathes a sigh of relief and kneels beside his patient.

"I'm now going to put on a soundscape that's been engineered to induce something called an alpha state."

"Whatever."

An ethereal, synthesized monotone leaks from hidden speakers to fill the small room. Marcus sits back on his haunches and, with his face moving in a blind man's exaggerated figure eight, starts singing, "When a ma-an loves a woman. Ain't got his mind on nothing else ..."

He stops and turns to Michael. "Now that's a song. I'm not sorry to say your taste in music sucks big time. Can you adjust that friggin' dial?"

A gentle hand on Marcus' shoulder instantly halts the show.

"Just focus on your ears. Now, let's begin the movement sequence. I'll guide you."

"Yeah, yeah. Hands stay above the waist, Doc."

It takes two repetitions of the exercise before Marcus stops the flippant remarks and relaxes enough to let the sounds penetrate. A few minutes into the third repetition, an involuntary groan bubbles past Marcus' lips.

"That's it," Michael confirms.

"Umm ..." Marcus groans again.

"That's it, let the sound enter. Let it work with you."

Michael is impressed with the full minute of silence that ensues before he signals Marcus to rest. He feels a sudden warmth toward his patient. It must take a lot of energy for Marcus to keep up this tough-guy persona.

Marcus abruptly sits up and flips off the eye patches. His intense green eyes are rodent quick in the dimmed light, his voice tight with emotion.

"My wife does nothing but insult me, push me around and threaten to leave. When I start to push back, the bitch turns around and says it turns her on. You know, when I'm raging." He shakes his head.

Michael says nothing, just gives Marcus the moment.

"But it doesn't do it for me. I just get depressed, leaving her high and dry, and cussing me out again." Marcus looks down at his hands.

Michael notices tension draining from the muscles of his own arms and chest.

"Shit, my life sucks." Marcus' jaw visibly tightens. Michael can see that he's bordering on a rant and does not want this important epiphany to become buried under more cynicism.

"Let's continue, Marcus. Let the thoughts go, for now. You're doing great. Let's start the movement pattern again."

Marcus shakes his head. "Yeah ... What the fuck else do I have to do?" He flips the patches back down over his eyes.

After the session, as a calmer Marcus is about to leave, Michael attempts ordinary conversation.

"Did you do that yourself?" he asks, tugging at his own ear.

"What?" Marcus crosses his arms over his formidable chest.

"The second earring?" Michael says, keeping his body language non-defensive.

"You got a problem with it?"

This isn't really working. "Nope. You a baseball fan?" he asks, remembering the Sox earring.

"No. Why?"

That's enough, thinks Michael. "Just asking."

MICHAEL SITS at his clean desk, the back of his shirt striped with the sunlight that streams through the blinds.

> *Defences quiet … self is heard*
> *brute strength fighting off Brutal longing*
> *for what?*
> *gold and silky*

Just as he's finishing up, the phone rings. It's Terese informing him that Tia Long isn't coming in this week. "She says she's not leaving her house until the war's over, as she put it," says Terese. There's been another sniper attack. A woman her exact age, dead. "I'm thinking of buying a bulletproof vest."

"You can buy such a thing?"

"On eBay."

TODAY, AS soon as he guides Kerry out of her wheelchair and into the makeshift room — "the big box" as Frieda insists on calling it — without being told and with her face dull as dirt, she takes up the hands and knees position on the floor mats then lowers her forehead into the starting position. In two previous sessions, she executed the movement sequence with true dancer precision. During the visual-stimulation session, Michael simply sat back in wonder, watching her flawless performance and feeling the intended stimulation of gland and sensory nerves under his own skin. After the audio-stimulation exercise, he found himself substituting coffee for his afternoon herbal tea in order to shake off the alpha waves flattening his intellect.

"All right," says Michael. "Today we'll be adding another move to the sequencing pattern to stimulate the olfactory sense. After performing the rocking motion a few times forward and back …" as he talks, his docile patient demonstrates his words … "then forward to dip the head down and lift the face to see the wall in front …" He purposefully slips in the word "see" but notes that, though Kerry's face points to the wall, her eyes lag behind, fixed as always toward the floor. "Now, the upper body will drop downward onto the ..." Michael stops as Kerry does exactly what he was about to describe. Her arms straighten, causing her torso to arc back as her hips lower to the floor. Her face is now offered to the ceiling and she holds this posture for the length of a snapshot, then pushes up on her hands, lifts her hips and folds back onto her haunches. She returns to the initial pose of her forehead to the mat.

"Yeah," Michael says, barely hiding his amazement, "very good." He can only assume that since the movement sequence is modelled on the birthing pattern, some sort of primal muscle-memory has been triggered. Satisfied with his explanation, he continues.

"I'll tap your shoulder once to begin the sequence and another tap to stop the sequence and rest. I may manually guide you, if necessary. I'll be releasing aromas into the air, which may bring certain images or memories to mind. But first I want to fit you with these earplugs."

Michael plugs Kerry's ears with soft wax and again places the blindfold over her eyes.

"You may continue," he says with a flourish of his hand, then lightly taps her shoulder. Reaching for the first vial, he twists open the cork, releasing an aromatic concentrate into the room. After a few minutes, the aroma will be just as quickly eradicated by a switch of the ventilation system. Normally, Michael tells his patients that they are free to associate out loud if they desire, but he doesn't bother saying this to Kerry.

The first aroma is a female musk. Michael recalls how, in this morning's session, Norma began whimpering, "Mama." This was followed by a detailed description of her mother's home cooking.

On the opposite end of the spectrum was Marcus' reaction: "Who let the bitch in?"

Michael watches Kerry closely as the scent permeates the contained space. The dumb, continuous flow of her movement, so effortlessly executed, lulls him into reverie. An image comes to mind: a woman laughing, a toothy smile bordered by walls of dark hair, her pupils black bottomless wells, urging him to fall in. Michael checks his watch, then signals Kerry to stop with another tap of the shoulder. He flips on the ventilation switch.

Kerry rests, folded over her bent knees, head down, long arms stretched out in front of her like a cat. After a couple of minutes, he signals her to begin again and picks up a second vial. The aroma of burning wood wafts into his nostrils. As he watches his silent patient, he's reminded of the cabin at Lake Bernard, the winter embers in the fireplace sprouting orange faces, arms wrapping his knees into his chest. A deep, childlike contentment fills his belly. He thinks of his mother's house, and how she didn't allow fires in the fireplace because she was afraid it wasn't safe. He chides himself to bring his attention back to his patient. Kerry, perfectly at ease, looks to be enjoying the physicality. If nothing else, thinks Michael, the exercise is good for her.

He opens the third vial: tidal smells of ocean, fish and seaweed. He taps Kerry's shoulder but she doesn't move. He checks her face: nothing. He taps her again, firmer. This is all the prompting she needs as she starts the movement pattern with hypnotic precision, but Michael makes note of her hesitation. She lived by the ocean most recently, he recalls, and the car accident took place close to home. His thoughts soon drift to Seattle's Pike Place Market, where his mother used to shop every Saturday, dragging him and Isabelle along. He remembers the tang of fish in air, the vendors' mishmash of accents, legs moving past in both directions, crystal hills of ice, a rock cod's jelly-eyed stare. A hot hand encasing his, yanking his shoulder forward making the fish head disappear. Michael's attention jerks back to his patient. His jaw has tensed, his molars pressed together. He checks Kerry's face to see if it's her tension he's picking up on, but her jaw is so slack that her mouth hangs open.

The next vial, a sweet vanilla aroma, gives Michael a temporary stomachache and as he watches Kerry's agile performance, he considers the possibility that she's playing them all for stupid. If she can do these exercises, it's ridiculous that she's pushed about in a wheelchair, he thinks, suddenly irritated. That chair's a convenience for everybody else, is all. Force her to walk and maybe she'll start watching where she's going.

When he unleashes the last scent, a male musk, Kerry's speed increases, as if she's adding challenge to an already mastered movement. After the allotted time Michael taps her shoulder but she keeps going, strong and steady, and it takes two firm hands on either shoulder to bring her to rest.

He removes her earplugs, then the blindfold. "You can stop now. That's fine, Kerry, excellent."

Michael helps Kerry to her feet, her firm grip is so alive on his arm that he looks, optimistically, over at her face. Meeting her familiar deadpan stare, he sighs and leads her out to the nurse, who will wheel her down to physical therapy.

"She *can* walk, you know," he says to the nurse, unable to hide his irritation, and pulls the wheelchair off to one side. Something soft caresses his hand. He looks down and sees, tied to the handle, a scarf like the one Mrs. Taylor gave him.

The nurse hesitates, looks from the patient to Michael and back to her charge.

"But Mrs. Carter told me —"

"I'm the doctor here. Got it?" The nurse just looks at him, wide-eyed. "Hold her by the arm or by the hand and guide her down to physio or wherever she needs to go," he says, struggling to fold up the wheelchair. "Physio, she needs that about as much as this chair," he mutters under his breath.

"Pardon me, Dr. Myatt?"

"Just take her."

Unable to figure out how the damn chair collapses, he leaves it as is and watches them walk away, the nurse in her thick crepe-soled nursing shoes and Kerry in worn ballet slippers. With each step, Kerry stretches a long leg forward as if pulled by the toe, the ball of her foot contacting the floor an instant before her heel. It looks like she's verifying the floor in front of her before daring to step, as if any minute it might give way to space. The farther down the hall they go, the more Kerry's toe-first walk looks like a glide, or a slow motion skate. Next to the thick-footed step of the nurse beside her, Kerry appears to be floating a hair above the linoleum.

⁓⦵⁓

ARLENE HAS brought Kerry two new sweaters, one black and one periwinkle blue, that she'd found on sale at Fanny's Warehouse. Short-sleeved, mock turtlenecks with buttons up the back, their retro look reminded Arlene of the sweaters she and her girlfriends wore back in college. Now those sweaters used to turn a head or two. The best part about these is the buttons. Forcing sweaters over her grown daughter's silent head leaves her cold.

She tries the blue one on Kerry first, then the black. Her daughter's limbs are more helpful these days, not the dead weights they were for awhile. As she finishes buttoning up the black one, Arlene takes a few steps back.

"The blue brings out your eyes but the black looks so dramatic with those black pants. Now, a high ponytail would give you a fun, beatnik look."

Arlene removes a hairbrush from Kerry's dresser and rummages in her top drawer for a black hair elastic. "Talked to Hugo today," she tells Kerry. "Said he's got a long weekend coming up and wants to fly in to see you. I told him I didn't think Dr. Myatt would allow a non-family member to visit. Not just yet. He wasn't too pleased and asked for the clinic's phone number. I wonder if he'll give the doctor a call. It would be great to see him, but then your father's really not up for visitors right now. Your father's doing fine, though," Arlene is quick to add. "So hopefully Hugo will delay coming until you're ... feeling more outgoing."

Kerry-Ann does look heartier, thinks Arlene, as if there's not only more flesh but new strength to her body. She understands Kerry is out of the wheelchair and being led around, which is some exercise in any case. And her face no longer appears morose, just still, as if biding time, as if she's waiting for a bus. As Arlene leaves for her meeting with Dr. Myatt, she sees the wheelchair parked in the corner of the room. The signature scarf she'd tied onto one of the handles is gone. That unattractive young man with the pimples has probably taken it. Ah well, she'll just have to bring another one.

⌖

JOHNNY IS wheeled back to his room after playing "Starcraft" on Frieda's computer. He learned how to build barricades today, discovering that the more he focused on defence, the better chance he had of winning, or at least of not dying so soon. His mood is fine when he sees the orange on his nightstand, the colour a lesson in contrast to the grey walls and white sheets. He knows Mrs. Carter must have left it, but chooses to imagine it's from Kerry Taylor. A secret gift.

"Have a rest now, Johnny," says the nurse. She helps him to his feet and onto the bed. "Here's the TV remote and I see you have a new magazine." She bends to pick it up off the floor, then gives his thigh a pat. He stiffens. "I'll check up on you shortly."

Johnny doesn't hear her. He's thinking of how the orange in his room reminds him of those black and white ads on TV with the single punch of colour, like the blue beads of sweat bleeding down the basketball player's forehead. He picks up the orange, digs out the stem with his thumbnail, then peels off the skin. Turning the rind inside out he proceeds to chew off the lining of white pulp. A teacher at school once said it was good for you and he likes the rubbery texture against his teeth. He sections the orange and places each piece on the nightstand, one curved inside the next until they form a circle. A flower orange.

"She loves me," he says aloud, raising the first piece to his mouth to puncture the taut skin with his front teeth. Tiny explosions of juice sweeten his tongue. "She loves me not," Johnny says and tears open the tip of the next. He places the raw end lightly between his teeth and his pimpled cheeks indent like a fish as he sucks out as much juice as possible before chewing up the pulpy sack. He eyes the splayed orange on the table and nervously counts off the remaining sections. "Yes, no, yes, no, yes, no, yes." He nods to nobody and decides to leave the rest of his fruit flower intact, a testament to unspoken love. Maybe he and Kerry can be wheeled side by side again this afternoon at fresh air time.

He opens the drawer of his night table and rummages around. He takes out Dr. Michael Myatt's signature and again studies its tight vertical 'M's, the closed-up loops of its 'H' and 'L,' the tiny, near-invisible cross over the double 'T's. He wonders what his ambitious doctor is holding onto so tightly, what it is he's afraid of losing. His musing is interrupted when he sees Kerry, assisted by a nurse, walk by his door.

"Wait," he calls out from his bed and the nurse stops and peers in. "Where's her wheelchair?"

"Miss Taylor's?"

He frowns and nods.

"The doctor ordered it taken away for now," the nurse says with a little shrug. "She's doing just fine, though."

Johnny looks at his own wheelchair and, with one hand, shoves it across the room.

"TIME TO go the bathroom," says a nasal voice. Karinska?

The belt across her lap is undone and Kerry rises on cue, like a sleepwalker, to be escorted to the toilet. Practised hands brush her teeth, rub her hands and face with a washcloth, remove her clothes and pin on new ones. Karinska is muttering for her to stand still as she yanks in the zippered back of the tutu. She comes around to the front and pushes up her breasts. "No breasts," she barks, a nasal Russian accent. She pulls down each layer of tulle to see where it touches Kerry's thigh, grunting in complaint. "Bend," she commands. "Lift arm. Can breathe okay?" Satisfied, she unzips the back. "Not eat in my confection or I'll bludgeon you."

In her white Clara nightgown, Kerry lies strapped in bed, every pore an ear listening for mice and for the Nutcracker's return. She listens for another breath echoing hers, another voice in the dark, the snoring hiccup that sometimes woke her, the touch of a hand, a mouth. Where has he gone? Her prince, her lover. She must keep looking. There are no more Nutcrackers and therefore no more princesses. No more magic lands or dancing flowers. No more there and no more here. Her hands ache with emptiness. Where have they taken you? Mustn't stop looking ahead.

Here's an incident from my childhood that I don't know if I ever told you, Hugo. It's another precursor to my becoming a stage slut. The apartment I grew up in was on the garden level, and Patricia and I shared a room that had two large picture windows on adjacent walls. It was morning and we were getting dressed for school. As usual, my more modest sister was getting dressed in the walk-in closet while I was standing smack in front of the window, still trying to wake up. Even as a kid I had trouble falling asleep, so was always deep in dreamland when my mother barged in each morning, flipped on the overhead light, opened the window blinds and kicked us out of the beds so she could make them while they were still warm. I hate mornings to this day. On this particular morning, as I stood yawning in the middle of the room, I noticed a man outside tucked up against the corner of the window. He had a cap on. Not a baseball cap but an old-fashioned wool cap that shaded half his face. I saw him an instant before my mother came up behind me, muttered "hurry up" and peeled my flannel nightgown up and off. I didn't stop her nor did I say anything about the man in the hat. It didn't register in my sleepy mind that a strange man at the window was a bad thing. It was just different, like waking up in a new play. I stood there watching him scrutinize my nine-year-old nakedness. And then I did a sutenu turn, which was something we had just learned in my last ballet class. Yes, sir, I went up on my toes and shamelessly twirled naked for him to show him my backside, too. After a perfectly executed (if I do say so) sutenu, it dawned on me that the man was probably bad and scary and I screamed and fled to the closet.

My clear-headed mother went for the blinds, then called the police.

"Peeping Tom," she said into the phone. I hadn't heard that word before and assumed, at first, that my mother somehow knew this guy and his name was Tom.

After that, Mom kept the blinds down each morning until we were dressed. Sometimes, though, blinds up and no Mom around, I would undress down to my underwear, glance over at the window, then leap into the closet. If it was night, I'd admire my reflection in the window first, then search the window's depth for Tom's peeping eyes, expecting them to glow in the dark like a cat's. I guess I was mixing my toms.

I realized two things from that incident: I didn't own an ounce of modesty and I loved being watched. So who was the desperate one in this story?

Allan and Thomas are away at a Boy Scout jamboree for two nights, so I've got Peeping Toms and psychos on my mind. Tonight will be my first time sleeping alone in this house and my imagination is running on the reckless side of gory. One always thinks of the country as so safe and the city as dangerous, but it feels just the opposite to me. In the city you're so crammed together that people can't help but hear you scream. We only have half an acre here but still I'd have to scream pretty darn loud to be heard over the neighbours' TV. I do have Blackjack to protect me, though. He's big and has an intimidating bark despite being a spectacular wimp who steps over slugs.

I wish you were here, Hugo, braiding my hair and telling me the story of your first and last girlfriend. I've got to remember her name, it was something ugly but sparkling . . . I know . . . Agnes Marvel. That was it. A great name. Or did you make it up? You probably made the whole story up. God, I'm a sucker.

Well, I've got to go do something physical to ground myself, fight off "the hole that must be filled" feeling. Maybe I'll go plant something in the garden, — like my feet up to my knees.

∽o∾

BEFORE BEGINNING today's taste-stimulation exercise, Michael reviews Johnny's file.

Reactions within normal range for both visual and audial.

As for the olfactory, female musk scent: patient Bourne makes an electronic bleep sound at three second intervals as if censoring thoughts or mental imagery.

Male musk: patient exhibits contracted feelings of anger. Mutters the old-fashioned chant, "She loves me. She loves me not."

Instead of Johnny performing the movement sequence like the other patients, Michael has used craniosacral therapy to manually stimulate the flow of Johnny's cerebral spinal fluid. Today, Johnny lies face up on the floor mat and Michael gently rolls Johnny's head backward, flexing his neck. He instructs Johnny to stick out his tongue. Johnny thrusts out his tongue and quickly pulls it back in.

"I'm going to need you to keep it out for about a minute," says Michael, "so I can spray different tastes on different parts of your tongue."

Johnny tries again. His pointy tongue quivers in his attempt to hold it.

"Fine, relax," says Michael. "Now we'll cover your eyes and plug your ears, and when I arch your neck, you'll please stick out your tongue. After you taste the spray, I'll lower your head and you are free to say whatever that taste brings to mind."

Blindfolded, ears plugged, Johnny crosses his hands over his chest like a corpse. His right pinky can't keep still but brushes back and forth over the exposed skin of his clavicle.

"Okay, let's begin."

Michael gently tips back his patient's head and Johnny stabs out his tongue. He sprays one of the four tastes onto the surface, beginning with sweet. As soon as Johnny feels the fine spray, he snatches back his tongue. As Michael slowly releases Johnny's head to the mat, he can hear the squishy sounds of violent tongue sucking.

"Num, num, num, num, num, ah," Johnny exclaims in a rapid-fire sliding scale.

Michael tries not to laugh.

He administers the sweet spray twice more and each time Johnny reacts with the same babyish sounds. With each new taste his reaction changes only minutely.

"Num, num, num, num, num, ooh," after the sour.

"Num, num, num, num, num, eh," after the salty.

"Num, num, num, num, num, ugh," after the bitter.

Without analyzing his motive for doing so, Michael deviates from normal procedure and sprays the pinky finger of Johnny's sucking hand with the bitter spray, then invites him to try it. Johnny tentatively puts his finger in his mouth, then bolts upright and rips at his eye patches, on the verge of tears. Michael quickly and sheepishly ends the session.

IN PREPARATION for the final sensory exercise of Stage II, Michael has covered the entire orientation room floor in five-by-five mats whose surfaces display a variety of textures: wool carpet, soft rabbit fur, wood, satin and suede. To activate tactile awareness, the sequential movement pattern culminates in a cross-lateral belly crawl. Over the days that follow, this "infantile creeping" is accomplished by each patient with varying degrees of success.

Norma's stomach prevents the contact between the mat and her knees and big toes needed for forward locomotion. She ends up worming slug-like across a mat or two, then rolling onto her back to catch her breath and berating herself for being "a fatso."

In contrast, Marcus moves like a man in the trenches under enemy fire and has to be repeatedly calmed. The heightened tactile stimulation makes Marcus unusually silent, his muscles tense. A human landmine, thinks Michael. Ten minutes into watching Marcus, Michael begins to feel a hollowing-out sensation behind his sternum, an intent, purposeful burrowing. Michael breathes in this sensation of retreat until he can sense the quality of the hollow as one of containment and stillness. Qualities so unlike Marcus' normal persona.

Back in his office after the session, Michael looks up a section of his thesis. "As the infant howls louder to be put down, the well-intentioned, albeit over-attentive, mother continues to hold and coddle the child in her attempts to soothe him, in a fashion similar to a child over-handling a much-loved pet. And just as the animal will seek solitude when it manages to escape, the non-ambulatory infant either gives up in sleep or cries to the point of exhaustion."

Marcus the infant was not of the sleepy variety, Michael muses as he pictures Marcus' frantic crawling pace. He writes in his report: *Most likely, Marcus, who is naturally endowed with a strong tactile sensibility, was over-handled as an infant by a well-meaning but unperceptive mother.*

JOHNNY'S KNEE infections have cleared and the skin almost healed by the time he's scheduled to begin the tactile exercise. His knees cushioned with knee pads, each time Johnny does the belly crawl, he covers no more than a few yards, performs two abrupt sideways rolls and ends up in the fetal position, a finger or two magnetized into his mouth. Although Michael knows that many infants prefer rolling or even scooting on their behinds as their first mode of locomotion, he finds his own body bristling each time Johnny performs this near-flip out of the crawl position. Such marked flinching from a heightened sense of touch makes Michael assume that Johnny is a victim of some form of physical abuse. Most likely, it took place at a young age, he notes, when the need for touch is primal and indiscriminate. And, if it was of a sexual nature, then Johnny is going to be longer at Rosewood than anyone expected.

KERRY TAYLOR is Michael's last patient of the day. Despite her monotone expression, Michael discerns that all of Kerry's senses are fully operative as she manoeuvres with ease across the mats. She crosses each texture with the same even, rhythmic pace, a relaxed gravity to her body. The first time she approaches the far wall, Michael restrains his impulse to warn her, curious to know just how accurate her vision may or may not be. But it is as if invisible antennae protrude from her head; she pauses mere inches from the wall, backs up, expertly reverses the cross-lateral belly crawl just enough to turn and then continues forward again.

It occurs to Michael that Kerry is reducing the psychokinetic exercises he's taken years to develop to mere repetitive movement, flawlessly executed. This thought not only nags at him but fills him with self-doubt.

Halfway into the session, he is merely going through the motions with her. All the resentment he's contained over the years toward certain know-it-all teachers, combative fellow students, jealous colleagues, clingy girlfriends, his mother and his father insidiously rises in his consciousness like scum to the surface of pond. With each passing minute, his mood becomes increasingly foul. After Kerry's rest period, he decides to make things more difficult for her. As he instructs her to belly crawl forward, he plants himself in front of her, blocking her way. She knocks her head on his shin. When she attempts to back up, he steps behind her. Her bare foot jams against his shoe. Barking out directives, he allows her to move only enough to trap her again.

"Stop."

"Go backward."

"Turn."

"Faster."

"Slower."

"Again."

Like some sort of circus animal, she obeys every command without the slightest noticeable reaction. *Where is your will?* thinks Michael, quickening the pace. Despite his frustration, he can't help but marvel at the control she has over her body, able to halt or shift at a moment's notice. Like a boy with a remote control car, he roughly manipulates Kerry's motion — even after sensing her fatigue.

"Backward. Stop. Turn. Go forward. Quicker …"

He knows there's a person in there with passions, humour, intelligence, because it's all there in her journal. *Show me something in your face, Kerry.* He gets down on the floor to mirror her crawl position.

"Come here," he commands.

Kerry comes directly toward him and stops inches from his head, her mannequin-like face flushed and freely sweating, her hard and fast breath blowing against his face.

Look at me.

"Look at me," he says aloud, urging her, willing her to glance up at him, just once.

She doesn't bat an eyelash.

"Jesus." The word sprays saliva on her face. Michael stands up and brushes off his pants. As he turns back to his chair, Kerry collapses to the floor and crumples into the fetal position. A thin line of sweat has bled along the spine of her cotton shirt and an air of what feels to him like grief rises with each heaving breath.

"I'm sorry," Michael says, as if Kerry had finally answered him. But he's mostly sorry that he can't find the key to open up that impassive face. If only she'd quack, squeak, bark, anything, he'd feel they were getting somewhere. "It's all good and trustworthy," he adds mechanically, as he helps her to stand.

She is breathing hard and leaning against him for support when he opens the door to signal the duty nurse.

Frieda is standing there, clipboard in hand, concern spreading over her face.

"Is something wrong with Miss Taylor? She's overheated."

"It was an energetic session," he says simply. Only as he turns away does he realize how inappropriate that sounds.

TERESE SLIPS into the elevator just as Michael's reaching for the down button, the doors closing. He had worked late tonight and is surprised Terese is still here. They have the elevator to themselves.

"Up for a walk?" she asks. "It's a beautiful night, no wind off the river."

"What about snipers?" he teases.

"Oh, God. With any luck, no snipers." She tips her chin, smiles hopefully. "So?"

"Why not?" he says, feeling a need for a little frivolity. In his current mood he doesn't really care if he's taking advantage of Terese. Her attachments are ultimately her problem, not his, he tells himself. "Maybe we could even hold hands?" he offers and Terese's eyes light up.

"Maybe."

"Maybe I'll buy a nice Merlot at the corner and we can share it out of the bottle."

"Maybe keep it in the bag. We don't want to get arrested."

"It's in the bag." Michael pulls her to him with one arm and, nosing under her hair, kisses her on the neck, soft, feathery kisses. He feels her shiver and pulls her closer.

Terese pushes him against the elevator wall and kisses him long and slow on the mouth. His hands roam over her breasts and down her back. He forces her hips forward against him. When Terese presses the stop button and the elevator jerks to a halt, Michael is too recklessly horny to think about consequences.

∽о∾

ARLENE HAS just returned from filling up the car and going to the drugstore. She's had another prescription filled to add to her husband's cornucopia of pills.

"If you can believe it," says Arlene, pulling the orange pill jar from its bag, "the Texaco station has a big tarp up to shield their customers from the road."

"A smart precaution," says Beresford. "Don't want people to be sitting ducks."

There's been more shootings by the serial sniper. One in Manassas, another near Fredericksburg, both men were pumping gas and both are dead. A more recent shooting has taken place not ten minutes from Arlene's home, in the parking lot of a Home Depot store. A woman who worked for the FBI was shot in the head.

"I wish you'd just stay in for a change," says Beresford. "Wait until this sniper business is over."

"Oh, I don't think I'm special enough to die in a random shooting," says Arlene, looking at the time. She wants to have a quick visit with Kerry before meeting with Dr. Myatt.

"Is that what it takes?" Beresford shakes his head. "Being special?"

"Last chance for the bathroom," she chirps, and helps Beresford out of his chair.

She's arranged a wicker TV tray with cookies, tea, the newspaper, the remote, his nitroglycerin tablets and all the other pills whose names she can't begin to pronounce. She sets it down beside his chair, making sure everything's within reach.

"I'll be two and a half hours max," she says, and kisses his cheek just above the Band-Aid. She'd shaved him again this morning — his hands are too unsteady now — and nicked him along the jawline. *I'll get better with practice*, she tells herself.

She hates leaving him alone, but Beresford is too private and proud a man to want a hired nurse, a stranger in his home, babysitting. He's been shunning all visitors of late, doesn't care for friends to witness him in his "less-than-dignified" condition.

"You go on. I'll survive," says Beresford, lifting up his chin like a stalwart child. "So, it's almost three. I'll see you by five-thirty?" His eyes can't hide his anxiety.

Odd, she thinks, how the man who used to feel like her protector now needs her protection.

"Yes, Beresford. *Wheel of Fortune* is on at five-thirty and again at six. I'll be back to watch them with you. I think the golf channel has a tourney on."

He nods obediently and picks up the remote.

"That Tiger Woods is a gracious winner, but when he's losing he's a petulant child," she says as a golf green appears on the screen.

"It's a lot of pressure," says Beresford, being his diplomatic self.

She kisses him again, this time on his head through the thin strands of greying hair. "Are we out of Grecian Formula? Shall I pick up some?" she asks.

A knowing smile lifts the sides of his mouth. "You never give up, do you?"

"Well, you can't blame a girl for trying."

Beresford laughs weakly and, though the joke's on her, Arlene laughs along. It's not easy to get a smile out of her husband these days.

LOOKING LIKE a boy with too much responsibility, Dr. Myatt swings his swivel chair side to side and thrums his fingers along its arms as he tells Arlene of Kerry's progress. Arlene, meanwhile, wants to ask where Dr. Myatt gets his hair done. It's a good cut, short on the sides and back with longer layers on top, and balances his squarish face. Richard could use a new hairdresser. She didn't think much of his last cut, though apparently he paid an arm and a leg for it.

"I'm just waiting for that first glimmer of response," continues Dr. Myatt.

"Aren't we all?" Arlene replies.

The doctor does the asking today for a change, wanting to hear more about Kerry's childhood. Arlene senses he could use a little cheering up. She searches her brain for a humorous anecdote. "Well, Kerry-Ann was always very expressive. It was almost comical at times how she'd literally leap with joy, spin with confusion, pound her fists in frustration. She was a good three, three-and-a-half before she began talking."

"Was it a refusal to speak or just a difficulty grasping the tenets of language?"

He's so serious behind those little glasses, thinks Arlene. She's only storytelling.

"No idea," she continues, "but with Kerry-Ann being our third child, we weren't particularly concerned. It was a relief, actually. Once kids start talking, they don't stop." She gestures with her hand beside her mouth, fingers quacking. "My son, Richard, talked enough for all three. Still does." Dr. Myatt's pen receives a polite smile. "When Kerry-Ann did begin talking, I couldn't understand a thing she was saying. Richard had to interpret for me."

Arlene laughs at the memory as glum Dr. Myatt removes a string from his shirt sleeve. She perseveres.

"At lunch one day, I asked what everyone wanted and Kerry-Ann said, 'Cream ween the wonder dough. So white, no browns. And swimming words.' Well, what in heaven's name is that? But Richard piped right up with, 'She wants a mayonnaise sandwich and letter soup. No crust on the sandwich.'"

Dr. Myatt is looking at the orange painting. She detects a hint of a smile, though, and is encouraged to continue.

"And then there was that neighbour, a retiree two patios down from ours who never had enough to do with himself. A Mr. Sumner. Well, one day Kerry-Ann was showing him some little bird she'd rescued. She had it in a shoebox; it had hurt its wing or some such thing. She was always bringing home these animals." She shakes her head. "I was sure she was going to catch something awful, but anyway, after this neighbour had been talking with my daughter — who was maybe four or five — he made the unsolicited suggestion to me that she needed speech therapy." Arlene sits up straighter in her chair. "Any child of mine, I said, who's clever enough to make up her own language, certainly doesn't need therapy. And that was the last advice I heard out of him."

Dr. Myatt has started scribbling on his pad. Perhaps she's said something helpful.

"But, yes, she was forever bringing home these animals some cat had probably gotten hold of. I'm surprised she never got bitten. For all I knew they carried rabies or —"

"I'd like to ask you about Kerry's eating habits when she was dancing," Michael interrupts. He puts down his pen, folds his hands on his desk.

"Oh?" Arlene takes a breath to regroup. "Well, she was always watching her weight, of course, never would touch dessert or even bread for that matter. Admirable willpower." She pats her stomach while sucking it flat. "We were a little worried when she was a teen and attending the ballet academy because she lost an awful lot of weight one summer. I ended up taking her to the doctor that fall because," she hesitates, "her menstruation had stopped. He assured me this was common among athletes. That they had more muscle than body fat and that a woman needs a certain amount of body fat for the hormones to do their business."

"She suffer any eating disorders? Also common among young athletes."

"Heavens no," Arlene says, wincing. "Her father would never have tolerated such a thing."

Dr. Myatt looks directly at Arlene and it's her turn to look away.

"We were all surprised when she got pregnant. I think she was, too."

Arlene's voice trails off. "By the way, I wanted to ask where you get your haircut?"

On her way to the elevator, Arlene passes a stocky fellow dressed in army pants and a black T-shirt. She recognizes him as the burper from the cafeteria. She does a double take. He's wearing one of her signature scarves around his neck, knotted like an ascot.

ARLENE TAKES a roundabout route home to avoid rush hour traffic and save time. It's probably six of one, half a dozen of the other, but to keep moving *feels* faster. Her stomach churns with hunger pains and with concern over leaving Beresford on his own so long. It's after six and she can feel him waiting. She shouldn't have stopped in at the Torpedo Factory, but wanted to see where they'd hung her painting. She found it hung under the staircase where the lighting was terrible. No wonder it hasn't sold. She couldn't leave without saying something. Now it's hung on a well-lit pillar just inside the entrance.

She pulls up to a red light. Seems like she's catching all the lights today. Always happens when you're in a hurry. Why, she asks herself, was Dr. Myatt so interested in Kerry-Ann's eating habits? That's in the past now, and so unattractive. She remembers finding telltale signs of vomit around the inside of the toilet bowl, after Kerry-Ann was up late by herself the night before. Fifteen, was she? But she'd told Beresford about it and he threatened to take Kerry-Ann out of the Academy if she ever made herself throw up again. End of discussion. She'd never noticed any signs after that. In truth she tried not to look.

With a measured increase of pressure on the gas pedal, Arlene just barely beats out the next light. A small victory against time, she thinks, eyeing the clock. At that moment, a policeman on a motorcycle appears in her rearview mirror. He's pointing and gesturing for her to pull over.

"Damn it to hell!" she says pulling over along the curb. She starts to do a habitual check in the visor mirror to assess her makeup, catches herself and slaps the visor back up. "Who am I trying to impress?"

In the side mirror she watches the slow approach of baby-blue belly.

It stops and provides support for a ticket book, which is flipped through at a luxurious pace. Glad one of us isn't in a hurry, she fumes, foot tapping the gas pedal.

She rolls down her window and looks up at the white-helmeted head, only to see her own reflection in the officer's mirrored sunglasses. Rude, not to remove the glasses. She'll write a letter of complaint.

"Yes, officer?" she says to her steering wheel.

"Are you aware of why I've pulled you over?" His voice is languid.

"To my eyes the light was yellow, officer, and I have a husband who's not well and needed me home half an hour ago."

"Yes, it was yellow when you loaded your foot on the gas. And then it was red when you sped through it. So I could add speeding to the first charge of running a light."

Her shoulder blades pinch. Now he's playing her to beg down an extra violation? He should be pulling over snipers, not old women in a hurry.

"You are obviously right." She bites off each word. "And I'm obviously confused. Now," she pauses for a breath, "if you could please take the information quickly and allow me to get home to my husband." She reaches for the glove compartment.

"Just watch it next time. Accidents don't save time."

Arlene's mouth remains open as the large man walks off, his thighs audibly chafing in his snug black pants. She waits for him and his motorcycle to pull out and go around her before restarting the car. Who teaches these policemen their intimidating game playing? Taking a deep breath and letting it out, she shakes off the experience and pushes the speed limit the rest of the way home.

NINE, TEN, eleven, twelve, fourteen ... The numbers lazily light up across the elevator panel as Arlene ascends to the seventeenth floor. Her watch says nearly six thirty — an hour past the time she promised Beresford she'd be home. The phone — she forgot to place the phone within his reach. The kids are always calling to check up on him, and his crib buddy, Arthur, calls every evening around five. As number seventeen lights up, she punches at the button for the doors to open.

"He might have tried to get to the bathroom," Arlene mutters, hurrying off the elevator, around the corner and down the hall. "We should invest in a walker so I don't have worry so much. If he weren't so proud ..." She feels around in her purse for the mini tennis racket that holds her house keys. It takes forever to find them. After fumbling the keys in their respective locks, she finally manages to open the door.

"I'm home," Arlene calls out. She listens for Beresford's greeting over the beer commercial blaring from the den. It's too quiet. Something's wrong, she can feel it.

"Beresford?" she calls again, rushing forward, kicking off her shoes.

Something's happened. She knew it when she gunned that light. She rushes into the den and the smell of defecation blasts her nostrils. Beresford is on the floor, inches from the swivel chair, moaning into the carpet between hard choppy breaths. He looks only semi-conscious, and in agony.

"I'm here, sweetheart," she says, grabbing for the phone. "Hold on just a little longer."

She dials for an ambulance, then calls Richard, who agrees to meet her at the hospital. She kneels beside her husband and caresses several fallen strings of hair carefully back into place. His skin is a sickly white and cold to the touch.

"Hang on, my love, they're coming, help is coming," Arlene manages, her strong voice wavering.

She grabs the blanket folded over the back of the couch and covers him. The foul smell burns her eyes and they film over. Glancing up at a blurred TV puzzle, a wobbly Vanna White turns over three 'E's. *French Lieutenant's Woman*, Arlene decodes, then averts her gaze. She cannot bring herself to turn off the familiar company of the television. For both their sakes.

∽∘∾

JOHNNY LIES on his side, away from the nurse sitting by the door. She's reading by flashlight and every time she turns the page, light bounces around the walls. It's keeping him awake. He knows who took Kerry's name scarf and needs to tell Frieda. But Frieda has gone home. He can hear Kerry wanting her scarf back, wanting him back. Soon, he tells her. Soon. He closes his eyes and lifts his pinky in the air, reaching for her, touching her, feeling her touching him.

Kerry's hand dangles out between the bars again, ears attuned to the faint click of the door. It doesn't come. She has been waiting so many nights for the soft big-boy hand, the fruity smell of clean hair. Her thoughts spin out into the dark. Where is he? The bombs are done. Still warm. One between my teeth. Falling, falling. Is he hiding his head? Her muscles, no longer sore, are primed and ready.

She manoeuvres over onto her stomach and begins to crawl forward, wriggling herself out from under the restraining belt and up onto her pillow. She eases herself over the edge of the bed, squeezing between the guard rail and side table. The floor is farther away than her body estimates and Kerry falls with a thud onto her side. The pain radiates through her hip and screeches to a peak out the top of her head. Feeling her way in the dark, she crawls bug-like around the cold linoleum, searching for the warmth her body once knew, things lost that must be found. The bombs are in the tin with the flower duets. *Lakmé's* flowers falling from the sky, bleeding all over the seat. Engine humming, humming, a single wrong note. No one can dance in this small a space. Head up, cheek to the light. Too much light, the ceiling now the sky. Where has the roof gone?

The next morning, she awakes to someone pulling her nightgown over her back side. Her bum is cold, her knees are on fire. Her bed has turned to stone. There are voices. Dim light streams through the opened blinds.

"Who was on last night and failed to belt the patient in?" she hears.

"Do you want me to check the roster, Mrs. Carter?"

"Strange. It's fastened. I don't think she could have gotten out of bed and re-fastened the belt behind her. Do you?"

"No, ma'am."

"Johnny was in his room all night?"

"Yes, he was."

"She must have been crawling around the floor on her belly the way Dr. Myatt taught her yesterday. Unless these knee burns are from yesterday."

"Should I record it on her —"

"No. I'll take care of it. Just help me get her off the floor and into her chair."

She is being pulled by her arms. Heaved to her feet. Her knees are flames licking the cool air. A ripping sound and sunlight stains the floor a blinding white. Stravinsky, *The Rite of Spring*.

THE WILL TO KNOW

Beginning at approximately nine months of age, the child makes the painful discovery that he is a physically separate entity from his mother. This leap in perception, and the subsequent feelings of uncertainty and insecurity, is termed "separation anxiety." In frantic search of a new reference point now that the old one has deteriorated, the child's shift in perception gives rise to a sense of an individual self or ego, the concept referred to as "me" or "I." With this self-identification as his new reference point, the child will now begin to differentiate the perceiver (meaning himself) from the object perceived; i.e., himself from his mother, his hand from the rattle he's holding, his hearing from the barking dog. In this way, the infant's amorphous and unified experience is shattered and replaced by an active discrimination, which is considered to be the beginnings of critical thinking or the intellect.

After the perceptual adjustment is made, the child will learn to take delight in differentiating himself from the things around him. The amorphous sounds of language now begin to make sense and soon each person and object in his environment will be ascribed a name. Soon after, they will be ascribed discriminating modifiers: mother, my; ducks, two; tree, big; bug, ugly. And on it goes.

The child's critical intellect continues to evolve in sophistication with the addition of the trio of personal preferences: "I like," I hate," or "I am indifferent toward." At this all-important self-defining juncture, predilections, belief systems and patterns of reactivity are being established.

As the momentum to define oneself in relation to phenomena takes precedence over the pure experience of sensory perception, the formerly uncensored personality and feelings of the infant recede into the storehouse of consciousness. The self-defining process will come to be questioned in the future identity crisis of adolescence and again in mid-life.

Dear Hugo, I just went to see Les Grands Ballet perform this amazing work by Israeli choreographer Ohad Naharin called Minus One. The choreography was clever, fairly original, even great in some parts, but the piece went beyond clever. In fact it touched me to the core. I wept uncontrollably. I also laughed, was frightened, was embarrassed, thrilled and whatever other human emotions one can experience. In short, you'd be jealous as hell. A must-see. Or I should say a must-experience, because it's way beyond mere visual spectacle. Naharin not only completely bulldozed the fourth wall but actually invited the audience onstage. But I will try and begin at the beginning, which actually started before the beginning.

As we (me and a neighbour friend, Felice) walked into the theatre to find our seats, full house lights on and people gabbing and making noise as usual, there was already a dancer onstage in front of the curtain doing this strange little dance-for-one in silence. He was dressed in classic black pants, vest, white shirt and black tie with a bowler hat. It was as if we were all late for the show. We were all a little embarrassed for ourselves as well as for him because he was so alone up there, sweating away with no lighting, music, no real audience. Nobody was sure if they should be talking or simply watching. The dancer didn't seem especially concerned either way, though he was definitely trying to get our attention. His movements were vigorous, often humorous, yet full of longing as if, bereft of a partner, he was trying hard to fill the gap, to dance for two. Here and there he even danced with a pretend partner. He was making eye contact with people, and with us (we were in the second row, the cheap seats) in a candid, straightforward way that was engaging yet not intrusive. Honest, not contrived.

So nobody knew if this was part of the performance or just some sort of little prelude joke, a cartoon before the main feature. Then the lights went down, music and curtain came up and this guy's energetic dance-for-one stopped and he took one of the seats in the horseshoe of chairs set around the stage. Each seat, minus one, was inhabited by men and women dressed identical to the pre-show dancer. This chair dance involved lots of cleverly timed throwing of various pieces of clothes and hats, and was a wonderful visual. Its repetitive sequence kept ending with one person left out and scrambling for a seat. This left-outness was an ongoing theme within each dance.

Anyway I'm not going to describe the whole damn thing because I can't remember the whole damn thing but what I will try and describe is what blew me away. It started with each dancer telling his or her story. A particular dancer would separate from the group in a downstage solo and there'd be this voice-over — but in that dancer's voice and in that dancer's own words. Now this could be really stilted, obvious stuff but it wasn't. It connected you with the person behind the dancer. Not behind, it was more stark than that, less divided. You could tell by the raw and real quality of their voices that the choreographer had made each dancer examine who they were and where they'd come from. He had brought each person to a difficult place, an honest place, and helped them understand the deeper reasons behind choosing to become a dancer. Some stories were funny, some bland, some tragic, some cheeky (which reminded me of you) but all were powerful. Even the girl who couldn't say anything but clichés — "I wanted to use my body to create something of beauty and to push myself to the limit" — came across as brave because her pride and self-protectiveness was so exposed, along with her inability to articulate in front of people. This would probably have been me.

One girl told about a younger sister who had wanted to be a dancer but died of cancer at age sixteen. So this girl, who wasn't as committed, dances in her sister's place, with her sister's spirit. Her voice and our hearts were cracking with emotion. One of the guys told of this strange disease he has, of being unable to sweat, and how being a dancer is a life-threatening occupation, but it's the only time he feels alive. You could taste the ambition and desire in his voice, and the fear. He had to drink ridiculous amounts of water and pee a lot to do what he did. There was, of course, the bulimic shame tale that had me squirming in my seat. There's one in every group, if not ten. The cliché girl was one for sure.

There were lots of stories, but it was in the telling — the honest and very lonely place each person got to — that gave them meaning. And as we met each dancer, in name and body and in honesty, they not only became just like you and me, but individuals you couldn't help but feel for and love. They weren't just a group of precious athletes with perfect bodies, caged on the stage for others to admire while sucking their Mentos. That great divide was crossed, like I'd never seen it crossed before, with simple honest humanity.

Near the end, each dancer walked into the audience to find themselves a partner to bring up onstage. You could feel the audience's collective self-consciousness, their fear of being chosen, of being exposed, and you could feel the shyness of the dancers, too, which made it doubly real and oh so human. I was terrified and suddenly all confused about who I would be if they picked me — an actual dancer. Would I pretend to be an ordinary Joe or try and match the other dancer move for move? I was quickly passed over in any case, which made me feel even more stupid and full of myself. The audience members that ended up onstage were young, old, fat, thin, shy, flamboyant. With their personalities written in their movements and on their faces, each person started dancing with their dancer partner. A couple of people got right into it and became completely uninhibited; most were more tentative, repetitive in their movements and laughing at themselves, embarrassed but having fun. And with each person exposed up there on the stage, we in the audience knew that they were also us. We had all gone on this journey together and we too were exposed, sitting there wishing we'd been chosen or relieved not to have been or, like me, imagining what we might have done. It created this tremendous softness toward people, this love like I said, and I was laughing and weeping at the same time, my heart overfull.

Gradually the dancers released their partners back into the audience, except for the guy who started out the show alone in front of the curtain. He kept his partner onstage the longest. She was a slender older woman in her late fifties, elegant but lively. He began flirting with her and she played right along. It was this wonderful tête-à-tête, each challenging the other to be that *much braver, that much more spontaneous and true. They hugged at the end and we all felt that hug.*

I've never been so affected by a dance piece before. Even when I'd lose myself in a performance, I never felt for people. I felt with people in a sensorial way, but never took that extra step of really caring for the strangers in the audience, and understanding that they are just like me.

If I was prodded and kneaded to honestly say why I became a dancer, what would I say? Ten years ago I might have said, besides the clichés, that I'm obsessive and once I get my teeth into something I can't let go until I've conquered it or it conquers me. But now, with a more "mature" perspective, I'd say it was the only means that I'd come across to express my longing. I longed to meet minds with other people, truly connect heart to heart, probably because I instinctively felt so separate. But it's funny how much heart got covered up in the process of training so hard to be a dancer with a capital 'D.' A far more direct path seems to be realizing one's utter ordinariness — which is how I felt watching Minus One. *Like just another struggling human missing the point.*

∽o∾

THE SKY is lit with the promise of winter. Michael, on his walk to work, exults in the wakeful bite chilling the morning air. The trees ignite the landscape with fantastic shades of orange, red and gold and, as Michael draws the dry air into his lungs, he feels he's being given permission to turn his mind inward. Fall's promise of winter with its contained vitality makes him feel like he might actually belong on this earth.

There's a noticeable increase of people on the streets since the terror team has caught what they're now calling "The Beltway Snipers." Two Jamaicans, a man in his forties and a teenager. They had outfitted a Chevrolet Caprice with a tripod and sniper platform, drilled two holes in the trunk for a rifle and scope, and therefore could pick off people at will. Like a live shooting gallery. The man, John Mohammad, is a Gulf War veteran, a demolition expert and decorated marksman. Once a mind is trained for war, thinks Michael, there's a need for an enemy. Peace can become disconcerting; peace can become the enemy. Mohammad had given himself away, calling the police with a tip that allowed them to easily track him down. Some people, thinks Michael, are so far gone they're beyond human reach. He kicks apart leaves. He doesn't believe in the death penalty, though, which the state of the Virginia seems to be clamouring for. That just adds up to another murder, in his calculation, reduces everyone's humanity. Virginia, he recently discovered, has put more criminals to death than any other state, including Texas. He's not so sure he fits in here.

Michael's eyes pick out the yet-to-be-carved pumpkins that decorate the stoops of homes, the dried Indian corn hung from door knockers, the black cats and dancing bones of skeletons taped to the inside of windows. Halloween is his favourite holiday by far — the night when humans of all ages, under the thin guise of darkness, willingly display their unconscious, liberate their alter egos.

As a boy, Michael found Halloween to be kind of confirmation because he finally got to see people as he guessed they might be under the surface. Take Mr. Bremmer, a neighbour full of false humility in Michael's eyes, who on Halloween always wore a rubber mask of the president. "Trick or treat, Mr. President, sir," he'd insist the children say before handing over any candy. If Michael's father were in town, he would invariably dress up in a white ghost sheet with black egg-shaped eyes cut from an old pair of Michael's mother's stockings. The eyes were angled in slightly at the top, which made them look more sad than scary. And though outwardly Michael's sister, Isabelle, was practical-minded and caught up in doing the expected, her costumes never failed to have wings. She was a fairy, a ladybug, an angel, anything that might release her from being earthbound. Most of the boys at school chose to be werewolves, vampires or the Grim Reaper, exposing the innate brutality their parents worked so hard to discredit. Michael's own choice of costume always involved some sort of tool. He was a pirate with a shovel, an archaeologist with a dental pick, a surgeon with a scalpel or Sherlock Holmes with a magnifying glass. His was a sly violence against the known, each tool a weapon for getting beneath the obvious. His birthday happened to be the first of

November and Michael would awaken the day after Halloween a year older (maybe smarter? taller?), as if truly transformed by the previous night's magic.

This morning, Michael's mailbox had held, along with a phone bill and November's issue of *The American Psychiatric Journal*, a pastel blue envelope containing the single birthday card that arrived in the mail each year a couple of weeks before the fact. Inside was a Hallmark card from Eden with the usual sentimental rhyme about friendship. But this year, instead of just a plain signature, the card contained another plea for Michael to come west:

"It will not be long now. For your peace and his. Please come."

Michael can't really be mad at Eden. She was Michael's father's pawn before and apparently she still is. She was nothing except kind to Michael on those clandestine visits north — almost overly so at times, as if to make up for her crime. His father's crime, really, but his father was too slippery, too ghostly, for the notion of guilt to take hold. His father indulged the ultimate male fantasy Michael thinks now: a younger woman waiting for you in a rustic cabin in the woods, willing to pluck the feathers off the ducks you shot. Willing to cook for you, to wash your underwear. Never complaining about that wife in the city. He steps on a crack in the sidewalk. Why has she stuck by him? Couldn't be love. Money, maybe.

For your peace and his. He struggles to believe that, after all this time, his father gives a shit about him. But it would provide closure, if he were to visit. He's seen what happens when people don't get a chance to say goodbye in the flesh. As he rounds the corner, he smells cinnamon and spice coming from the bakery over on King Street and remembers the gingerbread Eden used to make each Christmas, dark as chocolate, moist and plugged with bits of crystallized ginger. There was something peculiar about her smile, but he can't remember what. He recalls how she'd shyly offer to scratch his back at night, which at first made him tense and uncomfortable but then felt so good that he wouldn't let her stop, demanding she keep it up until he fell asleep. What the hell is Eden's last name? Why doesn't he know that? Was it written on the return address on the envelope? No, he remembers seeing only a rural route number.

He passes the converted torpedo factory and the restaurant in behind where he and Terese had dinner last Friday. She had warned him about the annual Halloween party coming up in two weeks time.

"Another one of Mrs. Carter's social institutions, it's a time for staff, patients and patients' families to come together. Costumes are encouraged, as is dancing. She invites the whole third floor, so we get to party with the Alzheimer's patients." Terese had whooped a finger in the air. "They're a lively bunch. Last year this old guy insisted I was his dead wife and wouldn't let me dance with anybody else. Any day," she warned him, "Mrs. Carter will be asking you to screen the family guest list." The nurses always had punch in the staff room, Terese told him, identical in colour to the generic punch in the cafeteria but spiked with gin. The party usually continued afterward at the pub.

Hoping to appease Frieda about the Wednesday tea business, Michael has decided to attend the Halloween party. He has already located the names of two high-end costume shops in downtown Washington. But what he really wants to find is a makeup artist, someone who can transform his face.

He punches in his code at Rosewood's front gate and enjoys its delayed, spooky opening.

AS MICHAEL brews his mid-morning cup of tea between patients, he finds Terese in the staff room pouring coffee into her mug. She seems to have her timing, or his timing, down to an art. It's okay, though; he can use a little female energy after enduring another angry session with Marcus.

"Did you decide how you're dressing up for the big night?" asks Terese, sidling up to him at the kitchen counter.

"Maybe," he teases.

"So tell me."

"Revealing your costume before Halloween is as taboo as the groom seeing the bride's gown before the wedding."

Terese slaps at his arm, clearly thrilled by his choice of simile. "People are planning to hit Duck's Inn post party."

"Sounds like a plan." He knows she's eager for their relationship to go public and can't help but feel like a cad for the way he's kept it in check.

"Great ... good ..."

"Do you like baseball?" he asks just as Frieda strides through the door.

"Terese, the phone is ringing off the hook out there," says Frieda curtly.

"Sorry, Mrs. Carter, just getting a coffee." Terese lifts her cup. "We'll talk later," she says quickly to Michael, a smile lighting up her face.

"A budding romance in our midst?" Frieda asks Michael as she washes out her stainless steel mug.

"Just making friends with the staff," replies Michael, hoping she'll get his innuendo.

"Oh, isn't that nice." Frieda presses her lips into something resembling a smile. "I trust you've been informed of the Halloween party?"

"Already at work on my costume," he says, smiling.

As Frieda dries her cup, a self-satisfied look crosses her face. Michael is content to let her think his coming to the party is some measure of victory on her part.

NORMA LIES on her back on a padded mat on the floor. Michael speaks to her with a heavy voice.

"The weight of your torso ... melts into the floor. Every muscle in your face ... drops away from your skull ... dripping with gravity's pull. Organs sag against a long, flattened backbone. Your breath expands each cell with oxygen ... and each cell sighs in comfort as that breath is released ... and dissolves into the atmosphere ..."

After ten minutes of Michael's guided relaxation, Norma looks lulled to near-sleep and almost ready, he thinks, for him to flip the instruction around. "Okay, Norma, that's good. Feel the outline of your body, where the sides and front stop and the air begins. Feel your insides. You should have a full three-dimensional feeling."

"It's a big feeling," mumbles Norma.

"That's right. Now stay with me, please, and we're going to reverse things around."

"Okay, Dr. Honey."

"Begin to imagine that the space surrounding your body is getting denser. As if the air is gelling, compacting. Where it presses along the outline of your clothes and exposed skin, the air is becoming thick like molasses."

"Mmm," says Norma.

"Like tar," Michael substitutes, "slowly hardening. As the tar is laid on thicker, you must start tensing your muscles to protect yourself from this external pressure that's gradually increasing. Now it's pressing against your body, like hard foam."

He pulls down one of Norma's toes. "Don't let me move it, Norma. Use your muscles to hold it in place."

"Ooch," she says, concentrating.

He pulls her arm away from her side. "Hold it still."

"Now that tar is becoming as rigid as the floor beneath you, Norma." His voice gains urgency. "It's as if that very floor has risen up and wrapped itself around you like a stiff cocoon, threatening to squash and crush every square inch of your body. Growing tighter and more and more solid." He pushes on the side of Norma's head but her neck muscles hold strong. "Your face muscles harden in self-protection. Your neck, shoulders, back, stomach, arms and legs … resist the pressure, every muscle pushes out against the crushing force threatening your body."

Her body stiffens, eyes wide.

"You need to protect the front, sides and back of your skull," he continues, pressing down on her face. "Push out against the mass suffocating your nostrils, indenting your eyeballs, forcing its way between closed lips."

Norma screws her eyes shut, scrunches up her face.

"Continue to breathe, Norma. Just push outward with your muscles. Chest muscles, stomach muscles, back muscles all clench to protect the soft, vulnerable organs beneath. Feel the hard outline of your body claiming its space."

He presses down against the fleshy mound of her belly to engage the muscles. She turns her head as if in embarrassment and he quickly lifts his hand away.

When Norma reaches the point where her face is turning red and every contracted muscle is visibly shaking against the imagined force, Michael switches back to relaxation.

"The hard cocoon begins to soften, to thin, allowing room for your lungs to breathe ... let your face muscles go ... all your muscles slowly release ... melting into the floor ... organs sink against your backbone ... your jaw is slack with ease ..."

Norma collapses with a huff. "Oh, my," she says, catching her breath. "I've never —"

"Shh ... just stay with the sensations."

The guided sequence of tension and relaxation is repeated three times to increase Norma's awareness of her body and its relationship to the space around her. After the last set, Michael guides Norma back to a balanced state before asking her to walk around the room. As he assists Norma to her feet, she sways side to side.

"It feels like my feet are being asked to hold up far too much weight," she says, shaking her head. "God, I've got to lose some of this fat. Food's been my comfort since I lost Joce. That's no substitute, I know, but it helps fill up the empty feeling."

"I know, Norma. Now let's have a walk around."

She starts to walk across the room in a straight line, holding her arms out as if any wrong move will send her falling to her death.

"Boy, are my feet flat. Like two pancakes they are. I wonder when that happened."

AT THE END of Johnny's first body-awareness session, he walks around the room, slapping blindly at his back.

"Something's on me," he says to Michael in whiney desperation. "Is something on me? What's on my back? Is something touching me?" He hikes up his shirt, exposing his pimpled back. "You see anything?"

MARCUS' REACTION after the spatial awareness exercise is to execute a dozen high-flung jumping jacks. Then he plunges to the floor for fifty push-ups, a manic grin aimed up at Michael. Rebounding back to his feet, he proceeds to take boxing jabs at an invisible opponent, feet prancing back and forth, jerking around to throw a punch behind him, dodging an imagined high one with a duck to the right. His usual black T-shirt has been replaced by what looks to be a brand new shirt; his mother must have brought it when she visited on Sunday, thinks Michael. It too is black and short sleeved, but tailored, with a collar and buttons. Michael notes the heavy silky material, how its soft folds whip around Marcus' torso as he prances back and forth.

"How 'bout it, Doc? Take on your sorry white ass? Well, it's not so white, now, is it? Bit of Spic? Dego?" Marcus coughs out a laugh. "Should I smash your *spectacles* into those smart-ass eyes? We're about the same weight class. My width makes up for the height thing." He gestures with what looks to be the sign of the cross.

Marcus' tactile sensibility is on overload again. "I'm in prime shape, you know," he continues. "Been doing the bike thing." He wheels his fists in little circles. "Swimming laps." He does the breast stroke, then jabs, one-two, at the ceiling, his soft shirt dancing. "Come on, Doc."

Michael decides this may be an opportune moment to call Marcus' macho bluff.

"You'd like to smack me good, would you, Marcus?" Michael steps toward him, arms limp at his sides, his palms turned out—the body language of surrender. "Knock loose some of my teeth, rip my shirt in half …" Michael moves closer and Marcus prances backward. "Like you did to those guys on the bus …"

Marcus twitches as if suddenly itchy. "I didn't really hurt them," he protests.

"You were just trying to mess with their heads?" Michael's voice is soft and seductive.

"Get away from me." Marcus' feet stop moving and his fists fall to his sides. He moves toward the door. Hand on the door, he turns back and squints at Michael. "But I could put you down like putty, buddy."

"How far down?" Michael taunts in his soft tone, taking more slow steps toward Marcus but maintaining his still defenceless posturing.

"Aw, shit, fuck off." Marcus swings open the door and leaves.

Michael watches him move down the hall and erupt into boxing jabs every few feet.

"I could take you," Marcus yells and springs around, jabbing right, then left in Michael's direction. "I could have been a boxer like my old man," he calls out, punching at ghosts. "If only you didn't have to wear that codpiece in your fuckin' mouth. How're you supposed to talk with that thing in?"

Michael pictures a young Marcus yelling at his opponent with a mouthguard in place and tries not to laugh out loud. He has ordered that Marcus be allowed on the cycles only in the exercise facility, and absolutely no weights. Nothing to compress his energy. He has also encouraged Marcus to swim daily in the heated pool. Apparently Marcus is closing in on eighty laps a day.

Back in his office, Michael writes in Marcus' unofficial file:

Putting down the megaphone and putting up his fists. Grounding his frustration in bodily ownership. He is starting to listen, to hear. Excellent progress! Ask his mother if she knows what the guys on the bus were wearing.

P.S. He's got no timing. I could take him.

FROM THE neck down, Kerry's body is so rigid that every inch is shuddering. Michael continues, in vain, to talk at the disowned head. It's as if all the nerves to her head are somehow severed.

"The minutest facial muscle must twitch and fight against the oppressive crushing weight of rock-solid space. Your nose must resist being flattened like a pancake, your lips squeezed tight before your breathing passages are entirely closed off. Your eyelids scrunch in protection of the tender spheres beneath ..."

He wants to press his palm over her mouth, pinch her nose closed and he's disturbed by the level of his impatience, knows it would be pointless, that she'd pass out before fighting back.

Afraid the rest of her body will become one big muscle spasm, he gives in and switches back to the relaxation instruction.

AFTER HIS less than gratifying session with Kerry Taylor, Michael wolfs down his lunch. He's eager to update the backlog of his patients' progress reports. He's two weeks behind and Frieda is on his case. He's asked Terese to hold his calls and is not amused when the phone rings.

"I'm sorry to interrupt," says Terese, "but there's an overseas call for you."

Overseas? The nurse he met in Kosovo? Elena something? He hopes she's not coming here. "Who is it?"

"A Hugo Brooks. Apparently a close friend of Kerry Taylor's."

"I told you to hold —"

"He insists on talking to you. I've tried to tell him ..."

Michael drops back in his chair. "Fine, Terese, put him through."

"Michael Myatt here," he says when he hears the line click over.

"Michael, hello," comes a cheery voice. "Name's Hugo Brooks. I've heard a lot of nice things about you from Kerry's mother, the inimitable Mrs. Taylor. I look forward to meeting you."

Michael doesn't have time for chumminess. "Yes, can I help you?" he says.

"You may. I'm planning on coming to see Kerry, my poor darling girl. I've wrangled some time off —"

"Clinic policy doesn't allow for non-familial visits."

"Non what?" Hugo's voice is incredulous.

"Non-family members."

"I understood the first time, but you need to understand that I *am* family, in the true sense of the word. We're brother and sister. Well, maybe more like sisters. We go back to the apes, went to the same cave school —"

"Mr. Brooks —"

"Hugo."

"Hugo, I'm very busy at the moment. I'm sure Mrs. Taylor will let you know when Ms. Taylor is functional and back at home —"

Hugo's voice turns soft, almost into a whisper. "Do you know what it's like to lose the reason you live? She needs me now, while she's in so much hell she can't even speak."

"I'm sorry, but it's for the benefit of the patient."

"Do I have to kidnap her in order to give her a hug?" Hugo's joviality now has an edge.

"Please trust that we are taking excellent care of the patient. We're doing everything we can —"

"'The patient' has a name — or do you guys use numbers?"

Michael's not up for this right now. He says nothing, lets this Hugo person get it out and over with.

"It's people she needs around her, people with blood running through their veins."

There's a gap on the line.

"Are you a stick person, Michael? Five lines and a big head? Hello?"

Michael puts Hugo on hold and buzzes Terese.

"Tell this guy in no uncertain terms that the answer is no, he'll just have to wait. And no more interruptions, please, Terese."

He returns to the file open on his desk, but the words on the page run together. He wonders if anyone would be so insistent to see *him*, if he fell into a hole the size of Kerry's. His sister? Certainly not his father. He recalls the rich baritone of his father's voice, a sumptuous sound, like loamy soil. Once a person dies, that's it, he muses. Their voice is gone forever. Swallowed up into the abyss. Or maybe it's out there somewhere in irretrievable space, a last word, a last breath pushing out the limits of the universe.

Thinking of lost voices, Michael returns to the task at hand.

MICHAEL'S NEXT exercise, a right brain, left brain exercise, involves using mirrors to remove five featherweight balls placed behind the patient's head. Each ball is a different colour. Standing between two mirrors in order to view the back of the head, the patient is asked to remove each coloured ball, first with one hand then the other. Norma has such trouble with her left hand that she quits in tears, while Johnny's right hand ends up flailing wildly at his head and still he finds only three balls out of five.

Marcus has little trouble with the exercise and Kerry makes it look like child's play. With her fixed stare well below mirror level, a robotic Kerry directly plucks off each ball, in the order they were placed, using touch only. Michael wants to shake her.

MICHAEL'S FINAL exercise for this stage of treatment begins to engage the patient on a verbal level using word association. He starts with Norma, who sits in front of him dressed in a muumuu of turquoise tulips and orange tangerines. With her upright posture and her hands clasped under her expansive belly, she looks like a Hawaiian Buddha.

"Norma, favourite colour."

"Lime green."

"Favourite animal."

"Horse."

"Favourite number."

"Eight."

"Favourite shape."

"Circle."

"Favourite food."

"Cream horns."

"Favourite season."

"Autumn."

Michael pauses, struck by the choice of the word "autumn" instead of "fall." It strikes him that the word "autumn" captures the lush quality of the season, while "fall" describes merely endings, the death of summer and trees shedding their fruit and leaves.

JOHNNY is next.

"How are the knees, Johnny?"

"Better."

"I'm glad to hear that."

"Scabby."

"Don't pick at them, right?"

"Right."

Michael is pleased that Johnny answers him directly and makes intermittent but solid eye contact. He seems to be practising better hygiene of late — his red hair is fluffy clean, his blemishes markedly less noticeable. Michael wonders if this is Frieda's doing.

"Please try to answer my questions with the first thought that comes to mind. Certain images may remind you of painful things." Michael catches Johnny's eye. "But we won't linger. Are you ready?"

Johnny nods once and blinks hard. His hands are jammed under his thighs and Michael imagines fingers struggling to escape.

"Favourite colour."

"Blue."

"Favourite animal."

"Eagle. Oh, that's a bird."

"It's fine, good. Don't edit yourself. Let's continue."

"Favourite number."

"One."

"Favourite shape."

"Triangle."

"Favourite food."

"Mother's milk."

"Favourite season."

"Winter."

"Favourite element."

"Rock. Is that all right?" Johnny is staring at Michael, making sure *all* his answers are understood.

MARCUS BOUNCES in his chair, as if testing it for purchase. He's got another new shirt on today. It's another softie and Michael notes that it's grey and not black. This feels like progress of some kind.

"What's the deal today, Doc? Arm wrestling? Pie eating? Snivelling contest?"

"Simple word games I'm afraid."

"I gotta ask. Are you looking at me or is there a leprechaun sitting on my head? It's as if your eyes are always, like, looking at ghosts and it drives me nuts."

"Sorry about that. It distracts me from my other senses to look in people's eyes," Michael explains.

Marcus just grunts. "Okay, whatever. I don't really care. Sock it to me, Doc."

"All right then."

"Not that I'd mind a lucky green man on my head."

"Yes."

"Green knickers, a ruffled shirt, a gold fuckin' necklace …"

"Let's focus on the exercise now. Just respond freely —"

"I always do."

"And say the first answer that pops into your head —"

"I'm geared, vroom, vroom." Marcus plants his hands on his knees and leans forward toward Michael. "Go!" he shouts.

"Favourite colour," Michael says calmly.

"Liver," Marcus says, nodding for more.

"Favourite animal."

"Bullfrog. I almost said bullshit." Marcus croaks out a laugh and then abruptly cuts it off. "Hit me."

"Favourite number."

"Double zero."

"Favourite shape."

"Liver."

"Favourite food."

"Liver."

"Favourite season."

"Springtime." Marcus smiles.

"Favourite element."

"What the fuck does that mean?"

"Like fire, water, air, metal, earth …"

"Spit. Go on."

"Favourite day of the week."

"Thursday, and I don't know why I said it, but come to think of it, it's true: Thursday."

"Just one word will do."

"One word, my ass. Sorry, that's two words. 'My' and 'ass,' which has two parts, sorry, one part and two cheeks …"

"Let's focus, Marcus, you're doing great so far."

"Great, all right, I'm with you. Fire away, jackass," he says with a smirk.

"Favourite material." This is not on the list.

"Satin."

"Favourite month of the year."

"May."

"Do you like poetry?" Michael slips in.

"What?"

"Poetry. Ever read any?"

"No. Can I leave now?" Marcus says in a tired voice. It's as if something's been punctured, his hyper energy drained out. "I really want to have a swim."

"I ordered some poetry books for the library. You're a word man, thought you might find a few of them interesting."

"Yeah, sure. Father knows best." Marcus shoots him an acid look. "Fuck, are you dull."

MICHAEL SITS across the table from Kerry. He has placed in front of her a large pad of white art paper and twelve fat coloured markers.

"Kerry, I know you understand me and I respect your choice not to speak." Michael pauses for a possible reaction to his use of the word "choice." Not a blink. "So, I've brought along pens and paper for today's exercise. I'd like you to try and answer me by choosing a marker and writing or drawing on the paper."

Kerry's otherwise arbitrary gaze appears directly aimed at the paper on the table.

"Pick out your favourite colour, please."

Michael leans back in his chair and waits. He noted from her journal that her favourite colour is blue-grey and has included three markers of that colour, two of them arranged closest to her.

Kerry is motionless and Michael waits as patiently as he can. In the strength of her physical presence, he can't shake the feeling of being duped. He scratches his shoulder.

"You can do it," he says, as gently as he can, knowing the pointlessness of rushing. He waits two minutes, five, six.

"Here," he says unable to wait any longer. He gets up and moves around to Kerry's side of the table. He uncaps the blue-grey marker and, standing behind her wheelchair, lifts an unresisting arm and begins to shape the fingers of her right hand around the pen's shaft. Focused on how to arrange the proper grip, he does a double-take when her left hand is suddenly there, easing the marker out from between her right hand and Michael's fumblings.

"You're left-handed?" he asks, turning expectantly and encountering the wooden face. Duped again. He watches Kerry place the marker against the paper, where it pauses, poised and ready. Michael follows her lead.

"Your favourite shape, Kerry."

The marker starts to move, taking the paper with it. Michael quickly reaches down to hold the paper in place, his arms straddling Kerry's torso, his face now alongside hers. He should move back to his seat but does not want to interrupt. The marker continues in a circle that fails to close but spirals into itself, around and around until space has run out. A non-static open-ended shape suggestive of movement, thinks Michael. Or of a rose. He's aware of the breath releasing from Kerry's nostrils, then from his, their shoulders lifting lightly in unison as they inhale.

"Excellent," he says quietly, removing the top piece of paper to uncover a new sheet beneath.

"Favourite number."

A one followed by the two loops of an eight smoothly form on the paper. Her hair smells of some exotic flower or fruit he can't quite place.

"Eighteen," he reads aloud. "Favourite season."

She draws a circle on the next page, painstakingly adding lines radiating outward, every second line shorter than the first. A child's rendition of the sun.

"Summer," Michael states and thinks *papaya*. That's the smell.

"Favourite food."

She draws a circle with one wide stroke, then colours in the centre.

"Pizza?" he guesses. "A cookie?" He removes the paper to reveal another sheet, thrilled at this new level of communication. Will writing words be next? He can feel the heat rising off the long curve of her neck.

"Favourite animal."

The blue-grey marker clatters off the edge of the table and onto the floor. Kerry's hand lands on the table with a thud, as if slapped down from above. Startled, Michael straightens up. It takes him a few seconds before he thinks to change the topic.

"Uh, favourite time of day."

But the game is over.

IN THE BATHROOM, Michael stands in front of the sink smelling his hands. Suddenly aware of what he's doing, he quickly turns on the water and picks up the soap to wash. He remembers the mention of a Blackjack in Kerry's diary — the family dog by the sounds of it — and makes a mental note to inquire about Blackjack at his next meeting with Mrs. Taylor.

✂

FITTING THE hospital bed into the den has meant moving Arlene's drafting table and painting materials into storage. Bedridden since fracturing his hip, Beresford has visits from hospice for a few hours every other afternoon but Arlene does the bulk of the nursing. For the time being, she's arranged permanent substitutes for tennis and excused herself from lunch with the girls. Dorothy will come here to the apartment, so at least Tuesday's Scrabble games can continue.

Arlene pulls open the drapes. Through the thick plate glass doors, fall colours warm the scenery. Imagining the cool air, she takes a deep breath only to inhale a urine smell from her husband's catheter.

Over the last week, Beresford's feet have swelled to three times their normal size. The puffed white skin is covered with a fine webbing of broken capillaries and dotted with red spots, some of which have matured into blistering domes. His legs, no longer functioning as such, are cylindrical weights stuck to his torso. At least breaking the other hip is unlikely, Arlene muses, as she helps her husband roll onto his side so she can remove the bedpan. Arlene never had a moment's desire to be a nurse, but things present themselves and must be dealt with. Both parties look in opposite directions as Arlene quickly administers the Wet Naps and talks steadily about other things.

"Dorothy's boy, Garth, and his cousin broke it off, couldn't stand the stigma … June discovered another lump, hopefully this one's benign like the last … Nancy Wolff's new baby's a whopping ten pounds …"

Beresford says nothing. It's only after Arlene's through and Beresford's pajama bottoms are back in place that he comments on her news.

"Nice that Nancy finally had a baby, she's been trying for an awfully long time. What is she, forty, forty-one?"

"Forty-two."

"Dini called this morning from Wisconsin and guess what?"

Beresford waits for Arlene to continue.

"There was an anthrax scare at her granddaughter's high school. Dini was just beside herself when the child arrived home with the news. Just some kid's prank, of course, but I said, imagine that, Dini, even in small-town Wisconsin. And then, like every phone call, she replays that damn plane crashing into the Pentagon. As if it happened yesterday. Time to move forward, I want to say, but just change the subject instead. Says she misses all her old friends but is enjoying getting to know her grandkids."

Arlene cranks up the head of the hospital bed and hands Beresford the remote. With feigned purpose, his tired eyes fix on *Jeopardy*. Arlene covers his legs and feet with extra blankets, hoping they can both forget about what's happening to his body, at least for a brief period of time. Kerry-Ann is feeding herself now with only a minimal amount of prodding, thinks Arlene as she directs a straw between Beresford's lips. Beresford hasn't any appetite these days. He says he can't taste anything and eating feels like work so Arlene feeds him high-protein milkshakes, which he sips through a straw. Arlene imagines Kerry-Ann getting stronger while Beresford's strength dwindles. A passing of the torch.

"Oh, and did I tell you that Kerry-Ann's nurse at Rosewood, Mrs. Carter, has a son over in Afghanistan and that he was one of the boys in that jeep that got blown up the other day. Apparently he's all right but his buddy is now permanently blind. She usually looks so energetic, but I must say she looked tired yesterday. Her job's tough enough without having a boy over there. It's got to take it out of you."

"It's a crying shame," says Beresford. "They're all so young."

She knows he speaks from experience. She strokes his head back on his pillow.

"Remember I told you I saw one of the patients wearing the scarf I'd left with Kerry-Ann? Well, it made its way back to her chair somehow. I think I'll give it a wash in the sink next time I'm there. Who knows where else it's been. I'll be right back, I'm just going to get your medications."

"Wait," he says. "Come here."

Momentarily shy, Arlene takes his extended hand. With a strong hand he pulls her down while his other grip cups the back of her head and brings her face toward his. She smells his stale breath and closes her eyes. He kisses her lips and she his. And then he releases her and it's over, her eyes opening to see his tender smile, his eyes full of gratitude. She smiles back, embarrassed by such a blatant show of sentiment and kisses him again on the forehead.

"I'll get your medicine," she says, and goes out to the kitchen. As she fills a glass with water she tries to recalls the last time she and Beresford had sex. Five years ago now? Six? If only she'd understood then that it was the last time.

∽o∾

WITH THE night-duty nurse no longer assigned to his room, Johnny stuffs his extra pillow under the blanket on his bed and drapes a towel over the rolled up pants he used to make a mock head. Once again he imagines he's invisible and makes his way to be near his angel. With an achingly slow turn of the doorknob, so as not to disturb the bells, he peeks out, grabs the knob on the outside, slips into the light and closes the door, slowly turning the knob back the other way. Johnny doesn't exist, he tells himself, emptying his breath into thin air, a phantom that makes no sound and brings no attention. This is a game he's practised almost every day of his life. Here at Rosewood, at the hospital, at school, at home. Especially at home. He imagines he blends into the wall beside him as he moves along. He stops at his angel's door. They can see through me, thinks Johnny, and there is only her door. Visualizing Kerry's string of gold bells hung on the other side in a perfect motionless line, his invisible hand turns the knob with soundless care. He reaches around to the inside knob, grabs it with a frozen hand and slips inside. The door is closed with the faintest of clicks.

In the near dark, he sees her hand is already sticking out through the bars, waiting. She hasn't forgotten, he thinks, his heart alive again in his chest. She has waited for him. He crawls across the floor to kneel alongside the long graceful fingers singing his name. As he nuzzles the top of his head against the hand, her perfect fingers fondle his hair, the hair he has vowed to wash daily, for her. Small explosions of pleasure ride his spine. He turns his face upward and her fingers lovingly trace the outline of his eyes, nose, his lips, the face he scrubs with Frieda's special soap. All for her. His tongue extends its length to lick between her fingers like a dog. Then, starting at her perfectly plump thumb, he sucks each finger in turn, saving the best one for last.

People think being a ballet dancer is some sort of exalted, romantic thing. And maybe it does feel a little like that off stage, but certainly not on. Besides the pain and sweat, performing is just plain humbling. A kind of surrendering to any magic that might be waiting out there, whether it's in the music, the choreography or in the fantasies of the audience. I was pretty trusting, now that I think of it, believing that the audience would be there to catch me if I fell, buoy me up with their own desires for escape. But then again, it was such a relief not to be in control for that little while. I'm such a driven mess, as you know, Hugo.

When I think of it, my best performances were not when my mind was in my feet, but when it felt like it was in my stomach. Figure that one out.

∾∘∾

MICHAEL SITS at his desk examining the sandwich Terese insisted he try. Grilled eggplant, red peppers and hummus. He takes a bite and tastes nothing but garlic, sees the wilted parsley sprig crushed in the bottom of the bag. Terese claims parsley counteracts garlic breath. He'll find out if it's true. While he eats, he studies patient responses from the abstract word association sessions. He finds the individual answers more revealing when comparing them to each other.

Black:

White — Norma

Night — Johnny

Shoes — Marcus

White:
Knight, the kind on a horse — Norma
Angel — Johnny, eyes closed
Shoes — Marcus

Love:
Heart — Norma
Beep, beep, beep, beep, beep — Johnny goes off like an alarm
Lie — Marcus

Mother:
Dear — Norma
Killed — Then Johnny adds a quick, "beep, beep." Sounds like the
roadrunner in the cartoon
May I? — Marcus folds his hands together at heart level, fingers
thrumming along knuckles

Father:
Camel, as in cigarettes — Norma
No — Johnny presses his lips closed
Prick — Marcus

Name:
Me? — Norma
Mr. Wiggles — Johnny mumbles, starts rubbing hands on thighs
Farkus — Marcus yells, beats his chest Tarzan-style

Truth:
Unkind — Norma
Beeeeeeeeeeeeeep — Johnny's single syllable escalates to a ridicu-
lously high note, before he whips his head away. Remarkably, fingers
have stayed out of his mouth
Ain't pretty — Marcus

Michael twirls the tiny bouquet of parsley between his thumb and forefinger before popping it into his mouth. He glances at his watch. Almost time for his session with Kerry. Unsure how to approach the abstract word association exercise with his catatonic patient, he's decided to have paper and markers available again. Who knows? She drew shapes, she just might write words. But even without a decipherable response, Michael tells himself, the trigger words should still mobilize subconscious imagery.

He tosses his sandwich bag in the garbage and heads to the bathroom to brush the parsley out of his teeth.

HAVING SETTLED himself across the table from Kerry, an uncapped marker on the left side of the paper, Michael explains the exercise. Then he takes a few minutes to breathe in the shared space between them, to open himself to the subtlest of his patient's reactions.

"Black." Michael allows several seconds to pass between words.

Stars litter the sky outside the attic window.

"White."

Blinding spotlight, a thousand invisible hands like waves pounding the shore.

"Love."

Baby at the breast, asleep, soft gurglings.

"Mother."

Strong hands, brushing my hair too hard.

"Father."

Distant longing.

Michael watches as Kerry takes a deep breath in. She holds it for a long time before slowly releasing it.

"Truth."

The roof is gone, blood pooling in her seat, soaking her pants as she turns her impossibly heavy head to see Blackjack licking the unthinkable.

Kerry's head hits the table with a harsh crack, lifts back up and hurls forward again to smack dully against Michael's forearm. He quickly turns the legs of her chair away from the table and kneels to catch the next blow against his chest. Working his arms around her, he gradually closes the gap by coaxing her rigid torso into his. Astounding him with her strength, she heaves back and forth in the confined space between his arms and chest.

"It's over now. It's okay. You're extremely brave," Michael says softly.

Stealing a look at her face, he sees her eyes are dry, not one facial muscle out of order. How is it possible? Her forehead has reddened from where it struck the table and her nose has been scraped and sprouts tiny beads of blood. He continues to hold her until her body gives way and falls limp against his. He strokes her long hair and says nothing, aware of a weighted grief now droning along his nerves, a heaviness to his muscles. Even his eyelids feel fatigued.

"It is all good and trustworthy," he says to the top of Kerry's head. "That's enough for today."

AT THIS point in Stage III, Michael is able to deduce a great deal from his patients' responses. He's convinced that the root source of Norma Daily's trauma stems from her adult years, Johnny Bourne's from his childhood and Marcus Novakowski's from his teen years. This helps Michael to confirm Norma's case history — divorce, loss of a daughter to cancer, problematic relationship with her other daughter — as the actual causes for her breakdown. Michael has added this diagnosis: "a loss of purpose coinciding with perimenopause."

On the other hand, Michael is convinced that Johnny's emotional and social delay originates from long before his mother's death, truly from the early finger-sucking years. And Marcus' responses point to the identity-forming teenage years and not job stress, a bad marriage and his father's passing. Whatever's happened in Marcus' adult life, thinks Michael, is just icing on an already-baked cake.

Outpatient Tia Long is in for her weekly visit. She takes a seat in the wingback chair farthest from where Michael sits behind his desk. She's dressed in thick corduroy pants cinched at the waist by a wide leather belt, a high-collared shirt and a buttoned-up vest with a matching jacket over top. Her permed hair, now greying at the roots, is tidied into a knot at the nape of her neck. Her legs are crossed and her hands clutch the purse on her lap as if gripping a building ledge. In the past few meetings Michael has provided Tia with techniques to stay grounded in the present moment and free herself from obsessive thinking and she's responded well. But today's prim outfit and posturing has him concerned.

"I'm feeling much better recently, more self-contained and more in control." Tia takes a deep breath in through her nose and blows it out through pursed lips. "Still doing the relaxation exercises you showed me," she says with a dutiful, good-girl smile. "The big news is that I have a steady beau." The pinky finger of one hand starts rhythmically stroking the edge of the purse. "He's a little older than me, a little … balding." Her head winds to the side and she winks with both eyes. "His name's Wallace, Wallace Beard. I call him Bearrrr," she growls. "He's in insurance, a very stable influence, extremely *handy* around the house." She sends Michael another sidelong smile and Michael quickly looks away. "Now, that's not what I meant," she says, wagging her finger, "but he's satisfactory in that regard." One of Tia's hands fiddles with the clasp of the purse; the other runs the loop of the strap between thumb and forefinger.

"How about if we do the deep breathing exercise together," suggests Michael, sitting even more upright in his chair. Without looking at her, he waits. He hears her sigh and, out of the corner of his eye, sees her follow his lead.

"Using good strong posture, allow your thought stream to quiet and come back to feeling your feet on the floor and the seat beneath you." He chooses his words carefully.

They breathe in and out together, Michael counting. "One. Two." After the third breath, he can see that her hands have stopped moving. He counts to seven and then instructs her to count to herself.

"Let your weight settle into the chair. Nice and easy," directs Michael. "Relax the area between your eyes. Good. And continue to bring your attention back to being present with your body and breath. Then another nourishing breath in and let any thoughts dissolve as you exhale."

After a couple more minutes of this, he signals her to stop, leans back and sips his tea.

Tia reaches for her own cup of tea.

"Like you, Wallace is very good at keeping me … focused. When my appetites are at high tide, he gets me out jogging and eating things made of tofu. That's soybean curd and it's supposed to do hormonal wonders for us middle-aged women. And yams. He makes a wonderful yam pudding." She starts fanning her face with her hand. "Is it hot in here or is it me? Would you mind, doctor, if I take off my jacket? I think I'm a little overdressed or having one of those heat flashes. I know," she says, gesturing with both hands, "breathe it out —" She's interrupted by three urgent raps at the door followed by Terese's dimpled face. Michael's reminded of the movie he's promised to go see with Terese tonight. And dinner. He'd almost forgot.

"I'm sorry to disturb you, Michael, but Frieda asked if you would come right away." Terese tucks herself in behind the door, out of Tia's view, grits her teeth and jerks her thumb over her shoulder.

"Excuse me, Tia. Sit tight," Michael says coming round his desk. "You could practise your breathing, have more tea. A cookie." He pats her shoulder on his way past and Tia's hand darts up in time to stroke the retreating tips of his fingers. "I'll be right back."

Out in the hall, Michael can already hear the distant racket of raised voices. Terese grabs his arm and pulls him along. "It's Norma. Hurry."

Norma's door is open and Nurse Bryson — who Michael understands played college football — has his arms around Norma's waist, pinning her arms to her sides. Her plump cheeks are bright red and streaked with tears. Frieda has Norma's daughter Courtney in something resembling a choke hold. Mother and daughter are screaming at each other.

"Get those clothes off that imposter. Those are my Jocelyn's, my sweet baby's—"

"She's dead, Mother. Remember?"

"Get her out of here," Michael orders Frieda.

Frieda artfully shuffles Courtney's short but solid frame toward the door.

"I gave those earrings to my Joce for her last ... Christmas," Norma sobs, her nose running freely.

"What should I do, throw them away?" Courtney flings her words at Norma.

"Just don't touch them."

"Ever think, Mother, that I might miss her, too?" Courtney doesn't so much say this as screech it. As she's pulled through the doorway, she breaks into a wailing sob and Terese quickly draws the door shut behind her. Courtney's crying grows fainter as she's taken into another room. Norma's face is frozen as she stares at the closed door.

"Bryson, you can leave us alone now," Michael tells the nurse.

The nurse slowly releases his hold and Norma's eyes close before she sinks to the floor in a heap.

"Bryson," Michael calls after him, "could you have Frieda reschedule my outpatient? She's still in my office."

Norma's wide back heaves in jerky sobs and Michael kneels on the floor beside her and takes her hand in his. After awhile, Norma's crying eases off and she starts to rock back and forth.

"I, I, I wasn't there, you know, when Joce died." She lifts her swollen eyes up to Michael.

Michael nods, eyes focused on Norma's hand in his. He feels she needs room to say what she needs to say and tells himself to breathe and stay out of it.

"I had to go home to feed the dogs, because Courtney ..." her voice wavers somewhere between anger and grief, "was too busy." Norma brings his hand to her bobbing cheek. "My Joce died alone in some stranger's arms ... because I, I, I stopped on the way back to the hospital ..." she hesitates before sobbing, "at Rye's Deli for a Reuben." Norma collapses in on herself, burying Michael's arm in the convulsing ball of her body. "Worthless fat woman," she says, between hiccupping cries.

Michael shifts his weight in order to cradle Norma against his chest. They rock back and forth together, his birthday tie from Isabelle (depicting a boy taming an ox), becomes a convenient handkerchief.

BEFORE LEAVING for his evening with Terese, Michael receives a message from Gerald Scully, third-floor program coordinator and president of the board. Michael is to stop in and see him. He checks his appearance in the washroom mirror, cleans his glasses and heads upstairs. On his way, he passes Johnny in the hall and is happily surprised to see him sporting a haircut.

"Nice hair," offers Michael, and Johnny quickly covers his newly exposed forehead and several ferocious-looking pimples with his hand. Michael can't decide if his looks have been improved or not. It's definitely an improvement in hygiene, though. "I'll see you tomorrow, Johnny."

"Okay." Johnny hurries down the hall to the lounge.

Michael realizes that Johnny's not carting his towel around anymore. He allows himself a congratulatory moment as he takes the stairs to Gerald's office.

"Michael, good to see you again. Please, sit. How are you?"

"I'm fine, thank you, Dr. Scully."

"We're all colleagues here. So please, call me Gerald."

"Gerald."

To Michael's eyes, Gerald Scully is bureaucracy incarnate: he has a face that looks like a thousand others, prematurely white hair and a practised neutral manner. Michael recalls teachers of this ilk, distinguished by his never being able to remember their names. Michael compares the appropriately bigger size of his boss's office to his own, and suddenly worries if he could turn into a Gerald Scully some day.

"Enjoying a little East Coast colour? Don't get this in Seattle." Gerald's voice sounds like vanilla ice cream tastes, plain yet pleasant.

"No, we don't, not by a long shot."

"Well, you're probably curious as to why the head honcho called you in today. I trust your research is progressing well? We're all very excited about the new therapies you're bringing to the clinic."

Michael notes the hint of gravity in Gerald's voice. "Yes, so far so good. Patients seem to be responding well. I have four progressed to the halfway mark and, in another few weeks, all my patients will have begun the program."

"Yes, good, moving them along. Well, I'm needing to clarify an incident that was brought to my attention by our Frieda Carter."

"Oh?"

"Devoted nurse, bit of a mother hen, I know. I worked the floors once, too." Gerald peers at Michael over his glasses. It's a practised look, serious yet supportive. "But, here, one of your patients," he fumbles among the chaos of his desk for the right folder, "Tia Long, yes, was found uh … unclothed this afternoon … in your office?"

Michael can't help but snicker. "Really? Now, I don't know why I wasn't informed, but trust me, Ms. Long was fully clothed when I left to attend to another patient in crisis. Of course, you've read the woman's file?"

"Ah yes, right here." He waves the folder reassuringly.

"So you know what I'm up against." Michael leans back in his chair. "Frieda should be well aware, too."

"Yes, yes, and did you tell the patient in question to, what does it say here," he lifts his head and peers down his glasses at a sheet of paper clipped to the outside of the folder, "to enjoy her libido while she still can?"

"Yes, I gave an affirmative slant to her disorder. A common enough device to loosen the guilt that solidifies neurotic patterns."

"I understand."

"Frieda Carter isn't my biggest fan, Gerald, though I have nothing but compliments for how she runs the wing."

"She's always looking out for the patients' and the clinic's best interests. And, uh, you're a handsome young man, so perhaps it would be best if Ms. Long was reassigned to, say, Janet Powers in Obsessive-Compulsive." This is a statement not a question. The look in Gerald's eye reveals a shrewdness, some gristle, Michael hadn't given him credit for before now.

"Well, I have no problem with working with her and feel we're making progress, but I respect your decision —"

"Very good, then. Thanks for coming in." Gerald Scully stands up, all smiling ease again, and extends his pale hand. "And you really should take a drive some weekend, out to Mount Vernon or down to Charlottesville, see the Virginia countryside while the leaves are blooming."

∽o∾

"CAN YOU fix these pillows, Arl? Or does the bed raise any higher?" Beresford pats around the covers for the bed's remote control.

Arlene takes off her reading glasses and rises out of her chair. "It's as high as it goes and I don't think any more pillows can fit behind you." She pushes him forward, reaches behind his back and folds a pillow in half. "Try that."

"No, it does nothing. When you pushed on my back, it felt good, though," he says. "I'm having trouble breathing."

This has been Beresford's complaint for several days now. He can't get a good breath, his lungs feel hard and tight as if they're drying up, withering inside his chest.

Arlene picks up a throw pillow from her chair.

"No, not another pillow. I want you to use your hands and push underneath my shoulder blades." His voice is pleading now, hinged with anxiety.

"Okay, I'll try."

She sets herself beside him on the edge of the bed and heaves him forward, amazed how heavy a bag of bones can be. She holds him forward with one hand and pushes the other between his shoulder blades.

"Two hands," he moans. "Under the shoulder blades."

"Well, I can't really use two hands unless I get on the bed behind—"

"Please."

He sounds so pathetic that Arlene slips off her shoes and, planting one knee on the bed, starts heaving all his bed pillows, save one, onto the nearby loveseat. He coughs again, the sound weak and watery, and she climbs onto the bed, carefully wedging herself between him and the raised back of the bed. Sitting on a pillow, she plants a hand under each of his shoulder blades.

"Okay, I'm going to push now."

"Good."

She starts pushing and his head falls heavily onto his chest. For a second she thinks he's passed out or maybe even died.

"Beresford?"

"Hmm."

"You okay?"

"Push."

She pushes.

"Hurts right there," he wheezes.

"Where?"

"Under your right hand."

Arlene pushes with her right.

"Can you push harder?"

Bending him forward over his legs like this, she's afraid he'll break in half, pull a muscle at the very least.

"Not unless I use my feet," she jokes.

"Okay. Let's do it."

She wasn't serious, but if it can relieve his discomfort and panic, it will relieve her own. She hopes the watery sound in his cough isn't pneumonia. That's all they need. She wiggles off her knees and onto her backside, then, letting go with her hands, catches Beresford's weight with her knees. She leans back against the raised bed and grabs the sides of the mattress to steady herself. "I'm getting there."

He coughs feebly as she walks her feet up his back, one, then the other. She can feel the soft rattle of his breath vibrating under her soles. Knees bent nearly to her chest, her hamstrings feel awfully taut up the back of her legs. She pictures a teenage Kerry sitting in the living room stretching one long leg, foot in hand, vertically up by her opposite ear.

"Okay, I'm going to push now."

She can make out the broad triangular bones of his shoulder blades despite pajama top and skin. She pushes and he groans.

"Too much?" she asks.

"No. More."

She pushes harder and he coughs again. A dryer sounding cough.

"Any better?" Something's pinching in her left hip joint.

"It feels good. Just like this." He sounds relieved. Against her feet, his back lifts in a breath and releases. He does it again. And again.

Does he expect her to stay in this position? Arlene tries to adjust her position a little to relieve her hip and turns her head to catch sight of their pose in the glass doors. They look like some sort of human machine, with levers and pistons. Both, she might add, in serious need of new parts.

∾o∾

KERRY FEELS for the buttons on the front of her nightgown. The fingers ease aside the cloth and push the plastic circles through. One, two, three, four, five, six ... and her small breasts receive the cooler air, the thirty-four-year-old nipples liberated and eager. The child is welcomed along her body, knees folded up, tucked warm against her. Instinctively she turns on her side, offers her breast to pacify his hunger, soothe his sore gums or simply keep his tide of fears from rising. She sighs when she feels the vigorous workings of his tongue and cheeks. Such a strong suck. She feeds love into her child in order for him to flourish, to live anew. He is only a baby, so there is no Swan Lake, no picnic, no flatbed truck. There are no thimble-sized pears. Her hand reaches out to stroke the downy head. The hair, electrified, rises to greet her. She will take care of him, watch out for him, keep him safe.

Johnny is well hidden under the blanket when the night nurse tinkles the bells, making her rounds. A flashlight passes briefly over Kerry's closed face. Then they are free to fall asleep as one and, by the time dawn slides through the cracks in the blinds, Johnny is gone.

Dear Hugo, I heard an old man speaking in Haida at Thomas' school yesterday. I'd have sworn that he was speaking in the elements. Sometimes the words sounded like water rushing over rocks or like the clatter of rain on a roof, sometimes like the cluck and caw of a raven or like wind rustling branches. Listening to him was a visceral experience, as if his voice wasn't merely coming from his mouth but from his hands, too, or even his organs. It was so satisfying, like listening to the weather. I wouldn't call Haida lyrical, musical with all its staccato beats, but it's rich and colourful. I can't quite describe it, only to say that the sounds were soothing and that the words communicated to me despite my not knowing their literal meaning. The speaker wasn't calling water by the single word of "water" but by the hundred-thousand different sounds water makes. Or so it seemed. From listening to him, I imagined the Haida people didn't try to name the world like we do, but that it was the other way around. The world told them what it was and, consequently, who they were.

As I was walking home from the school afterward, I found myself stopping along the way to listen to the "voices" around me. At first, I couldn't hear anything but distant trucks on the Trans Canada. But then the more I listened, the noisier it got. It reminded me of the musical build in Ravel's Bolero. By the time I got home, birds seemed to be screaming at me, the wind was a constant soft buffeting noise and, though I could have been imagining it, I thought I could hear the sun overhead, humming this straightforward unchanging note — a middle C. And just like the ending in Bejart's version of Bolero, I was waiting for the "music" to come to a sudden stop and the surrounding trees —

*starting from the centre and moving out — to collapse to the ground. And then
on that last dramatic tumble of notes, I, as the centre, would fall. That was one
ballet I always wanted to do. You gay choreographers create the sexiest work.*

At dinner Allan told me that the Haida were hardly the peaceful nature-
lover artists people like to imagine. He says they were imperious and aggressive and that they slaughtered other "inferior" tribes and captured their
women and children as slaves. He told me a horrific story of how the Haida
would break the women and children's wills by decapitating their loved ones
and placing the severed heads in the bottom of the boats to roll around at their
feet as they were being taken to their new home in the Queen Charlotte
Islands. Supposedly it's because the Haida had slaves that they found the
leisure time to become such fabulous artists.

*Allan's stories have made me aware of a persistent feeling I've had about
the West Coast. I've never really felt the spirit of this place as "laid back" as
you often hear it described. Though maybe the rest of the First Nations tribes
here were and are placid cowards, British Columbia has always held an edge
for me. I often feel as though it's poking me with a sharp finger, telling me to
keep my eyes open, be more astute. Be more cunning even. I don't have a
cunning bone in my body. As you know, I can't even tell a white lie without
blushing. Maybe after ten years of living out here, I'll have become a shrewd
businesswoman type, ha ha. Just imagine.*

ഗ≈ീ

AFTER THE incident with her daughter, Norma refuses to eat and refuses
to leave her room. Michael makes a point of sitting with her each morning and before he leaves for the day, holding her hand and listening to a
mother's guilt and a woman's self-loathing. He asks no questions, just
offers the occasional affirmation of her personal insights with a squeeze
of the hand.

The nurses report that Norma spends most of the day sleeping, a
deep, unshakable sleep. After a week without touching her food trays,
she has lost over twenty pounds and is hooked up to an intravenous drip.

A few days later, without warning, she awakens one morning, takes a long-overdue shower, drinks a glass of orange juice and proceeds to the indoor track. She jogs breathless around it once, then walks around it twice. Donning a life jacket and gripping a flutter board, she does ten grunting laps in the pool, gets dressed and ends up in Michael's office.

"I just wanted to tell you, Dr. Mike, honey, that I'm ready to get back on the horse. But first," she stretches the elastic on her pants well away from her waist, "I'm going to need some new clothes." She smiles proudly. A sadness has settled in her eyes, lending a warm dignity to her round face.

"I say something in a muted lavender would compliment your green eyes," says Michael thoughtfully as he chews his pencil eraser.

"Oh, you," says Norma, turning to go. She looks back over her shoulder, smirks, then waves him off with a flap of her hand.

MICHAEL'S NEXT exercise is to try and elicit from his patients descriptions of the physical space they grew up in. When Michael first asks Johnny to describe his and his mother's home, he refuses to cooperate. After three unsuccessful tries, Michael leaves it alone. Instead, he instructs the staff to place wooden construction blocks and a bucket of Lego in Johnny's room. After three days, Michael is informed by Frieda that the nurses are fed up with stepping on the sharp bits of Lego invariably strewn across the floor each morning.

"You should know, Dr. Myatt, that Bryson slipped on a piece just this morning, badly bruising his tailbone and last night the janitor dislodged several blocks from a backed-up toilet. I'd like permission to take them out of his room since he apparently spends more time bashing than building," she says, exasperated.

"So Johnny has been constructing things?" Michael asks.

"He builds little houses —"

"How many rooms?"

"Pardon?"

"How many rooms do the buildings have?"

"Just the one."

"Any doors or windows?"

"Well, no —"

"Roof?"

"I think it's the roof that's causing the frustration."

"Thank you, Frieda. The building materials can be removed."

"Fine," she says, clearly unsure as to whether her request has just been granted or rendered irrelevant.

AT MICHAEL'S next session with him, Johnny is willing to talk. He insists that the apartment, or apartments, he grew up in were bachelors, with no separate bedrooms. He describes the Formica table with the one wobbly leg, how he'd use it to tap out rhythms by tipping it back and forth in time with the dripping faucet on the sink. He says that he wasn't allowed to open the blinds, but there was one slat that wouldn't bend back into place. Through this slanted eye, he'd watch the kids race their bikes up and down the street, set up jumps for their skateboards.

"The TV had a skip," he says, "but if I blinked in time with it, I didn't really notice."

In the following session, while rubbing his pinky on his cheek and twisting his head awkwardly to one side, he describes the intricacies of the spaceship motif on the curtains. "They were shaped like fried eggs with bubbles on top with little green Martians inside. The Martians' eyes were stuck up on stems. They were always flying over my head, bumping into me. Beep, beep, they said, beep, beep."

Johnny eyes suddenly blink furiously. "Get out of my bedroom," he hisses before his pinky and ring fingers are sucked into his mouth.

Whether he had a separate bedroom or not, writes Michael after the session, *Johnny's privacy was likely violated on a regular basis. No place to hide.*

MARCUS IS uncharacteristically focused as he depicts the garden in his parents' backyard. Apparently, he had helped his mother design it. He's wearing his grey shirt again, but has replaced the gold hoops with diamond studs. Matches his shirt better, thinks Michael, trying not to smile. The studs look real, even antique, as if he'd raided his mother's jewelry box. Michael knows better than to say anything.

"Hydrangeas in progressive shades of pink to blue, a whole range of maroons and purples in between. It takes just a minor adjustment of the acidity of the soil. One section we devoted to varieties of lilies bordered by sweet william. Then we planted rings of violets around the weeping willows." Marcus is thoughtful, absorbed. "I wanted to build a small pool, put in a couple of carp, but that idea was killed." His voice starts to tighten.

"What about the house, Marcus?" asks Michael.

"My mother's house?" Marcus ponders the question. Michael takes note of the fact that there's no mention of the house also belonging to Marcus or his father.

"We had this orange and olive-green flowered couch, which just about says it all. My room was all done up in plaid. Another woman on the planet with too much money and not enough taste. Shit."

MICHAEL LEARNS that Norma grew up in the country on her parents' three-hundred-and-eighty-eight-acre farm. Details of the family's kitchen take up the full forty-five minutes. It was the room the Dailys lived in, "the only warm room in the cold months. The cast iron stove was the centre of our lives." The kitchen table was where meals were prepared and eaten, clothes washed and dried, schoolwork done, letters written and lives shared. "That table was a four-inch-thick slab resting on legs three-foot round. Daddy made it from an old tree that fell out back during a wind storm. It missed the house by inches. Solid oak," she adds, knocking a fisted hand on her knee.

Norma describes each household appliance, the original ones and then each modernized replacement. She recalls the cookware, favourite wooden spoons (all homemade), the chip in the big yellow mixing bowl used for breadmaking. Then she details the family's meal regime, one for each day of the week. Michael simply leans back and listens. The same meals in the same order are served week after week. Apparently their dog Bosco, whose diet consisted of supper leftovers, fasted one day each week, refusing Friday's cornbread and baked beans.

"Sweetest dog alive until a raccoon crossed its path. Ooo-wee, you should have seen him go."

"Sunday's surprise desserts" receive great elaboration and bring colour to Norma's ample cheeks. Michael has never seen her enjoying herself more. He makes a note to arrange for her to be allowed to assist in the cafeteria kitchen. Perhaps, he thinks, she can be responsible for making cookies for afternoon tea.

SINCE KERRY is unlikely to talk and her childhood home is in the area, Michael arranges to take her around to the apartment complex where she was raised. He had hoped Mrs. Taylor would accompany them, but because her husband has suffered a recent fall, she is unavailable. When he'd spoken with her yesterday by phone, he'd asked about a possible dog Kerry may have owned by the name of Blackjack.

"Blackjack, yes, that was the name of their dog. He was black, you see, and Allan, Kerry-Ann's husband, liked to play poker. Taught Thomas all sorts of games. Anyway, the dog more or less came with the house because the neighbours' dog had umpteen pups and they accepted one as a welcome-to-the-neighbourhood gift. A casserole would have done just fine in my books. He turned out to be an awfully big dog."

"And where is the dog now?"

"The neighbours were kind enough to find him a home. You know he was with them, in the car that is, when it went out of control and they ran under the flatbed. I was told they found Kerry-Ann and Blackjack, both on all fours, her poor hands and knees bleeding from the glass and metal bits scattered on the grass. Witnesses said it was broad daylight but she was crawling around with her head down, feeling with her hands as though she couldn't see. They figured she was looking for the … apparently Allan's head was cleanly severed and Thomas' well, partly …"

"Yes, that was all in the hospital report."

"My poor child," Mrs. Taylor said quietly.

FALLEN LEAVES blow around their feet as Michael guides Kerry into the passenger side of his silver Saab. Frieda had reminded him at least three times that taking a patient off the premises would make him personally liable if anything happened. And, each time, he assured her that he had Mrs. Taylor's written permission and more insurance than he knew what to do with. In truth, he didn't know what sort of coverage he had, but he refused to give Frieda the satisfaction of knowing that. Unsure how Kerry might respond to car rides, he eyes her carefully as he turns the key in the ignition. After several minutes pass with no discernable stress, Michael slowly drives out of the parking lot. At a low volume, he puts Vivaldi's *Four Seasons* on the CD player. Kerry appears relaxed, her breath even and full. Michael attributes this to her appreciation of the music and turns up the volume.

They head north on King Street and turn right on Duke Street. He recalls Mrs. Taylor's commentary when he'd asked for directions. "At the top of the hill, on your right, you'll pass Kerry-Ann's old school, Blessed Sacrament, which is where she went before the dance academy."

As he pulls up to a red light, Michael notices a man giving Kerry the once-over, her proud profile looking lost in reverie, perhaps, rather than simply lost. It seems unfair to Michael that she be helplessly observed like that, and he pulls the car ahead a foot.

They park in front of a three-storey, white brick building, number 4527, one of many in a complex called the Park Shirlington Apartments. Considering Mrs. Taylor's style and bearing, Michael is somewhat surprised by the humble setting. He recalls her mentioning that Mr. Taylor was in the retail business before he retired — rattan furniture. Must have spent their money on private schools instead.

Like any number of such suburban developments built during the baby boom, Park Shirlington has a used feel, as if one too many families have left their fingerprints on the windows, their scuff marks on the floors.

"It was nice in its day, lots of ethnic families now," Mrs. Taylor had qualified over the phone. Hers was not a politically correct generation, Michael reminded himself. He assists Kerry from the car and, remembering the liability issue, holds her hand firmly in his. Her palm is lightly moist and he senses a faint excitement, an anticipation.

He glances at the note in his hand: *Corner apartment, garden level, on left as you face the building. Number 10B, first patio around back.*

He walks his patient up the sidewalk to the entrance of the building and pauses, allowing time for her to subliminally register the place. Since leaving her wheelchair, Kerry has become a more assured walker and Michael finds he can keep a normal pace. Hand in hand, they move down the inside stairwell to the grey metal door of apartment 10B. The hallways are stone quiet and Michael can't be sure if the faint sound of children's laughter is imagined or coming from behind one of the doors. Walking back upstairs and outside, he guides Kerry around to the back of the building and down a small hill. Dry leaves litter the ground and crackle underfoot as he and Kerry approach a patio bordered by laurel bushes. Cheap outdoor furniture is piled in one corner of the patio and a picture window is decorated with a string of pumpkin lights. Pruned rose vines flank the fence that edges the yard and there is a towering locust tree just inside the fence, a round picnic table beneath. Michael pictures family barbeques, badminton games, sledding journeys down the hill.

There is a large window to the right of the patio and, with seemingly sightless eyes, Kerry moves to the window, pulling Michael's hand in hers.

"Someone may be home," he warns her, imagining the tenant promptly on the phone to the police.

But Kerry continues until her face is set in the corner of the window, barely a foot from the glass. Michael sees a double bed adorned with stuffed animals, a pile of clothes in the centre of the floor, and gently tries to lead Kerry away, but she resists. He's holding his breath waiting for someone to walk into the room when suddenly Kerry turns away, pulling him with her to stand under the locust tree, its yellowed striated leaves scattered over the grass. Hand in hand with his silent patient, he's beginning to feel like an awkward teen on a first date, neither person knowing what to say. A sudden wind blows stray hairs across Kerry's face, one dissecting an eye. He waits to see if she'll remove the hairs, and when she doesn't he takes the liberty of brushing them back. With the familiarity of the blind, she leads him on again, down the grass slopes behind the buildings, ducking the low-slung branches of crabapple trees, the wine-coloured fruit browned and rotting under their feet. He plucks a lone crabapple still on its branch, having read about but never seen this type of apple before. Taking a cautious bite of the bitter fruit, he quickly spits it back out. It's nice to be outdoors, see the flora up close, he thinks, and tells himself he should do it more. A series of small hills gives way to a flat stretch of dying grass where the buildings end. Behind a chain-link fence sit the bleached white cauldrons of a large rectangular pool. Long emptied after the summer months, leaves darken the deepest end. A deserted playground with a slide and swings sits alongside the pool's parking lot. One of the rubber U-shaped swings has been torn or sliced in half and hangs from its chains like idle black hands. He can almost hear the summer chaos of water play, the singsong of an ice cream truck, the chafing squeak of swings, of scolding mothers.

She's showing me her past, he thinks, feeling the soft pulse in Kerry's small fingers against the back of his hand. Or is it his own pulse? He can't quite tell.

ON THE DAY of the Halloween party, Michael sits in the windowless backroom of a unisex hair salon, watching in the mirror as a feral-eyed woman named Penelope blends putty over his forehead to conceal the line of the skullcap. Sitting to his right, on the end of the counter, is a dummy dressed in a plaid shirt and jeans whose stuffing of garbage bags leaves a glassy black hole where a head should be. With dirty garden gloves sewn on to the ends of its shirt sleeves, the dummy holds its carved pumpkin head in its lap. Its pant legs are stuffed into faded red cowboy boots. The detached head's toothy grin has strings of pulp hanging off it and its eyes tip inward to look sinister. In the confined warmth of the small room, it gives off a gamey smell.

With abrupt jerks of her head, the makeup artist looks from Michael to the pencil drawing taped high on her mirror and back to Michael. He'd brought in the photo of his father and from this Penelope has drawn an aged likeness, like police departments do for children missing for many years. His father would be in his mid-seventies, Michael told Penelope, and was grateful she didn't ask any questions. He watches the picture watching him, recalls an unhurried, distractible man so readily absorbed in nature's obscurest details that his attention seemed to be continually leaking outdoors. Michael's fondest memories are of the hikes they used to take, just the two of them, packs of food and water on their backs, his father stopping to sit in front of a wildflower, a mushroom or lichen, Michael watching in awe as the long-knuckled fingers rendered its perfect likeness on paper. They'd be gone all day, heading home only when it was becoming hard to see, the sun having disappeared when they weren't looking.

"Wonder what *he* thinks of my likeness?" Penelope says, indicating the dummy with a toss of her head. She has a voice like a horizontal line.

Michael looks at the pumpkin head. "He's smiling, sort of."

"I'm just finishing up but, before you disappear, I want the guys out front to see," she says, patting on a last layer of powder. She wipes her hands across her apron. "Be right back."

Left alone with his new face, his new head, Michael tries not to analyze what his choice of mask means. It's not a bad likeness, really, he thinks, assessing his face in the mirror. Penelope had used shading to elongate his chin, lift his cheekbones and hollow his cheeks. The receding hairline lifts his forehead. His nose is similar enough to his father's to need no work, as are their eyes, discounting the colour. The detached pumpkin head in the corner seems to mock him, asking Michael to admit he wants to see his father again, in the flesh.

Michael wonders if the dummy's body could support its big head and wants to set the head on its neck where it belongs. He flashes on Kerry Taylor and the car accident that took the lives of her husband and son. Pictures her on her knees in the grass searching for the parts to piece her family back together. Not unlike Jackie Kennedy in Dallas, he muses. Then the insight hits him so suddenly and so clearly, his temples ache. Of course. What took him so long? Sympathy exchange on an acute symbiotic level, Kerry's own head psychically severed in sympathetic transference. It's so obvious. How could he not have figured that out?

His revelation makes him restless. Where's Penelope? Knowing what Kerry is doing means understanding how she's stuck. He knows how to talk to her now, how to be with her. He'll have to wait until tomorrow, though, schedule a meeting first thing, get Terese to juggle his schedule. If there wasn't this damn party ... Michael rips the plastic cape from around his neck. He needs to get out of here, pay the bill and leave, but as he moves toward the doorway a bevy of effusive, hair-damaged young men and women are blocking his way. He can't tell if they are dressed for Halloween or always look like this. The ones with the torn shirts and patched pants look like hobos and those with coal-lined eyes and greased, directionless hair look like ghouls or vampires.

"Amazing, Penelope," one coos.

"Believable," says another.

"Couldn't not tell he wasn't a real old man." This string of negatives from a guy with a tiny chicken leg bone piercing his septum. Or is he a she?

On the way out of the salon, Michael notices the vintage music store on the corner. He adjusts the spring in his step to a more feeble key and enters the store. A young clerk is ready to assist the old man and, after misspelling "Darrin" three times on the computer, finally locates the CD he is looking for.

BACK AT his apartment, Michael digs out his father's brown corduroy sports coat, the one with the patched elbows. In his father's era, this was the cliché, the fashion-challenged professor's uniform. He remembers his father wearing it more often than anything else. His mother hated it, called it his pauper's coat. Michael can picture him under the spotlight of the standing lamp, reading in the armchair in the living room, pipe jutting out the side of his mouth.

Fit's fine, Michael thinks, smoothing his hands down the lapels. A lump in a hip pocket reveals one of his father's pipes. It's like finding an unexpected twenty, only better. Michael places the bowl carefully under his powdered nose, smells the stale hint of tobacco. He slips the tapered end between his pale lips and feels his father's persona settle his spine into a soft curve. Then, as if peeling off a fresh scab, he remembers his eagerness to please this man: the high marks in school, the swimming medals, the memorization of hundreds of species of flora and fauna — all wasted efforts. Fits of mischief and temper were equally overlooked. Or should he say "treated with the same equanimity, the same innocuous distance."

At some point, thinks Michael with his own practised detachment, a child gives up expecting more than nothing.

NOBODY NOTICES Michael — just another anonymous family member — as he makes his way to the pumpkin-coloured punch. The cafeteria has been transformed for the occasion. The tables have been pushed to the sides of the room and are covered in white tablecloths decorated with miniature pumpkins on beds of coloured leaves. A dancing area has been created under vines of orange and black streamers. He's glad, for Kerry's sake, that there are no carved pumpkin heads and wonders if Frieda was the one who had such foresight. He takes a chair against a far wall to watch the gathering crowd and play his childhood game of matching personalities with choice of costume. He spies Terese dressed in the uniform white lab coat of a doctor (perhaps a psychologist?), black-rimmed glasses, pens and pad protruding from her breast pocket. She's scanning the room, probably for him, but her eyes don't even pause as they pass him over, a grey-haired, pale-faced man with retreating hairline. He recognizes Norma's voice from under an authentic-looking, horned Viking helmet. She's dressed in a floor-length lavender caftan (seems like all she wears is lavender since he made the suggestion) covered with plastic silver breast and abdominal plates. It's something you'd see on Xena, the Warrior Princess, or maybe Madonna, thinks Michael.

The cone-like breasts ride a good six inches above Norma's own. She is noticeably trimmer these days, despite spending a couple of hours every afternoon baking in the kitchen, and is considerably more cheerful. She's even asked if he'd be willing to meet together with her and her daughter Courtney sometime.

Frieda, strikingly colourful, wears a flowery gypsy skirt, white peasant blouse, yellow bandana and big hoop earrings. An armful of gold bracelets and a belt of coins around her ample hips jingle loudly as she fusses and arranges the food table. Over in the corner, Johnny appears to be costumeless, but on closer inspection Michael sees a large question mark drawn in the middle of his newly exposed forehead. Michael almost laughs out loud, pleased to see some humour in this most dour of patients. Then he sees something else, a red paper heart taped to Johnny's shirt.

He ponders the symbolism. A heartfelt question? A question of love? At that moment, Kerry is being wheeled in by an unusually tired-looking Mrs. Taylor, who struggles to manoeuvre around a gaggle of patients from the Alzheimer's wing, each of whom is wearing an old-fashioned hat of some kind. Thought we did away with that chair, he thinks, shaking his head. Kerry and her mother are flanked by two adults and a young boy. Michael feels a flash of annoyance — he had specifically told Mrs. Taylor no children. He guesses the pretty blonde with the dewy eyes is the sister, Patricia, and the man in the expensive-looking suit, the brother, the famous Richard. Richard is looking alarmed as he dodges the unreliable motion of a grinning man in top hat and tails, who seems to purposefully block his way. Patricia is holding the boy protectively by her side. Only the boy and Kerry are in costume. Kerry's hair has been piled on top of her head in a doughnut-size bun ringed by a glittering tiara. Over a white, loose-fitting Indian cotton dress, she wears a bolero jacket made entirely of rhinestones and, on her feet, sparkly silver shoes. Her face is obviously made-up and a smudge of mascara blackens her right eye. She looks ridiculous.

Mrs. Taylor claims a table and Michael studies his patient as she's wheeled up to it, her head held stiffly as if to keep the tiara from slipping.

Any frustration Michael's felt over her lack of responsiveness has dissolved with today's revelation and he finds himself watching Kerry with a sympathy bordering on respect. Amazing, really, that she could identify so acutely, so passionately with another's physical condition. He can see it so clearly now. She disowned her head, left it behind with her loved ones. And just like her husband and son, the rest of Kerry's body is undamaged and, in her case, functioning as well as can be expected without a head. Michael can see how all these months, suffering in silence, she's been waiting for someone to understand how it is she's had to cope. It pains him to see this and, if it weren't for this damn party, he could be working with her right now. But she's waited this long, he tells himself, another day isn't going to make a hell of a difference. Besides, he muses, once she wakes up, the real work will begin.

Mrs. Taylor is pointing, urging her grandson toward the food table. The boy, dressed as a miniature Charlie Chaplin, shuffles out of his grandmother's reach to stand at Kerry's elbow. Staring in earnest at his aunt's face, he leans sideways to line up his gaze inches from her deadpan stare, then starts making goofy faces. Richard notices and pulls him aside, then Patricia takes him by the hand and heads toward the punch.

Terese's eyes alight briefly on Michael's again before moving on. If there was a prize for best costume, Michael thinks, he'd be taking it home. He notices Dr. Scully over by the punch, wearing the proverbial large nose and black glasses, bushy eyebrows and mustache of Groucho Marx. He holds an unlit cigar between his fingers. An aspiring funny guy.

"Is this chair taken?" An elderly lady, primly dressed in a grey suit, is gesturing to Michael.

"No, no, please," he says, then recognizes Mrs. Novakowski, Marcus' mother. Marcus and his mother look so much alike, the same bulldog features, the same short stature. From their meetings, Michael discovered that Mrs. Novakowski also tends toward dramatics. Marcus is her only child, a blameless victim she defends at every turn.

"I'm here for my boy," she tells Michael. This is followed by a huff. "He's a good boy. A bit of a temper but I blame that on his wife. Nasty piece of work, that woman. Of course, he probably never would have married her if his father, rest his soul," she flutters her eyelids heaven-ward, "hadn't kept badgering him. But you see, they have no children." She places her hand over her chest. "A sure sign of a loveless marriage."

She reaches into her handbag and removes two paper party hats, one folded flat inside the other. "I've great expectations of this clinic." She pops one hat open at the base, places the polka-dotted cone over her white perm and stretches her chin upward to pull the thin elastic under-neath. Angling herself toward Michael, she offers the other hat.

"No, thank you," Michael says politely.

"And you, do you have a loved one here?"

"Me? Oh, well, my son works here. One of the doctors," he says with an old man's quiet pride. "I'm just along for the punch."

Mrs. Novakowski's attention is suddenly arcing past him across the room, her head gesturing a slow no. Michael follows her gaze to where an unattractive woman wearing a blonde Marilyn Monroe wig and mauve satin gown is squeaking out greetings at an attention-grabbing volume. The dress is stretched so tight it shows off a muscled six-pack. The woman hooks one muscular arm around an Alzheimer's patient, who smiles proudly under his fedora. It takes Michael another second before he recognizes Marcus in drag.

"That's my dress," mutters Mrs. Novakowski.

His assumptions about Marcus' cross-dressing proclivities confirmed, Michael makes a mental note to research Dr. Weber's dress-up therapy. "Excuse me," he says, rising. "Nice to have spoken with you and I'm sure your son is in good hands."

Mrs. Novakowski sighs, despairing eyes fixed on her blonde-wigged son.

A tinkling Frieda has now placed herself in charge of the music and "Saturday Night Fever" is playing at a moderate to low volume. Michael approaches her and asks in a low voice if he may interrupt the present music to play an old favourite he brought just for the occasion. Frieda smiles her helpful smile and offers to take the CD from him.

"Oh, I can manage," he quavers.

He inserts the disc and nudges up the volume. Without waiting for the music to begin, he works his way over to the Taylor table. As the opening notes of "Mack the Knife" cream the air, he asks an uncertain Mrs. Taylor for this dance. She looks at him as if he's crazy.

"It's Michael Myatt under all this goop," he says.

"Dr. Myatt, really, that is a good disguise." Arlene's lips purse as she gives him closer scrutiny. "There was something familiar about you, I just couldn't put my finger on it. I'm a little rusty at this dancing business, but I do love this old song."

Without missing a beat, Marcus has swung a young female nurse onto the dance floor while several other costumed figures also slide into available space. Viking Princess Norma leads a bug-eyed Johnny out of his corner and stamps around his motionless figure, staring at him like she'll be roasting him later. Michael sees Terese craning her psychologist's neck before sifting through people and heading in the direction of his office.

As Michael does his best to do some simple jive movements with Mrs. Taylor, he observes that her weary eyes house an innocence, a game curiosity, even after all these years.

"And they called him," Marcus booms over the music.

"Mack the Knife!" the room rejoins before erupting in laughter.

Michael can tell Mrs. Taylor's not up for this. "Mind if I see what the dancer can do?" He nods in Kerry's direction.

"Certainly." Mrs. Taylor sounds relieved.

Michael escorts her back to the table, where Kerry sits passive in her wheelchair. As he takes Kerry's hand in his, it appears to be shaking slightly. With excitement? Nerves?

"It's me, Dr. Myatt," he says close to her ear. "Shall we dance?"

Kerry rises at his urging and moves mechanically beside him. The tremulous energy in her hand seems to move up Michael's arm and reverberate, along with the music, in the cave of his chest. When they reach the dance floor, he reaches for her other hand but it's already moving toward his. Her eyes are downcast in the direction of his feet. Michael starts moving halftime to the music, in small steps side to side. Compassion fuels his thoughts as he regards the slack face atop the vital body.

He closely studies her face, swaying her arms along with his, back and forth. He knows he shouldn't say anything, not here, not now, but he simply can't resist.

"Come on," he says quietly, "let's have a look behind that mask, shall we?"

Over Kerry's shoulder, Michael sees Johnny glaring at him. *I'm dancing with his girl*, he thinks, before his attention is brought back to Kerry, her knees now bobbing tentatively to the beat.

"Yes," whispers Michael. "That's it."

Her arms offer a hint of resistance against his hands, then one silver shoe steps to the side, in careful mimicry of his own feet.

"That's it, Kerry, right together, left together," Michael says louder, eyes probing her face. "You can kick off your shoes," he quotes from her journal.

She's stepping in time with him now, side to side with the fluid ease of a dancer. Michael smiles and picks up the pace and Kerry's feet instantly adapt.

"That's it," Michael says encouragingly, eyes riveted to her lowered lids. "You're dancing." He tries to dampen his enthusiasm. This is *not* the time or place, he reminds himself. How might he address her in tomorrow's session? *You've lost your husband and your son, but you're still here, whole and intact. And, you know they'd both want nothing more than for you to carry on living your life. And, no one is doing this to you, Kerry. You are doing this to yourself.*

He tries to forget being a doctor for a minute and just enjoy the music, suddenly wanting to do something he and his sister used to do as kids. He moves his head toward Kerry's until their foreheads meet. He gently presses his skull against hers until she pushes back with just enough pressure. Her breath quickens and he can feel warm air forcing its way in and out of her nostrils. Slowly he raises their joined arms out to the sides and then higher. Head pressed against hers, he begins to turn his body under and around. Their linked hands force Kerry to turn with him. Grinding their heads together, hair against scalp, they reach the peak of the turn, then whisk back around to face each other again.

Michael can't help but laugh at accomplishing this small feat and lifts his head away, smiling. The music begins to fade just as two pale-blue irises, like dual moons, rise to meet his eyes. Michael startles and lets her hands drop. The alert eyes before him falter and begin a slow fade back to the floor.

"Sorry ... no." He reaches for her hands. "Again," he calls over his shoulder to Frieda standing by the music. "No, don't," he says, changing his mind. The room has gone quiet. "We need to get the patient out of here." He says this too loudly, directing his words to a very confused looking Frieda.

"Dr. Myatt?"

People have ceased moving, all eyes on the crazy old guy holding hands with Sleeping Beauty.

Michael can see the effort in Kerry's facial muscles as her lips press together, fall away then press together again. Michael's head feels immensely heavy on his neck.

"That's it," says Michael. "But ..." But *just wait* is what he wants to say. *Wait until we're out of here and someplace private, someplace appropriate.* His head is feeling lighter and his pulse is beginning to race. Frieda has gone for the wheelchair.

Kerry's eyes rise again to meet his, brilliant with determination, her sudden full-blown presence demanding acknowledgement. Everything he has projected onto the blank face falls away. Michael suddenly feels like a ridiculous fraud in this mask. He wants to look down, look away, but her eyes are holding onto his for support. His scalp is suddenly itching mercilessly under the edge of the skullcap and, when a bead of sweat slips into his left eye, causing a single violent blink, it's a relief to turn away. He has never been happier to see Frieda standing beside him.

"Take her someplace quiet, please, Frieda. I'll be right along."

The quiet is mercifully interrupted by the next song on the CD. Michael watches Frieda wheel Kerry away and sees the Taylor family hurrying after. Kerry shouldn't have to deal with family members right now, he thinks, and is about to go stop them when he feels a hand slip into his. Terese.

"I've been looking for you, and you've been here all along," exclaims Terese. "I thought you were Kerry Taylor's uncle or something. What was she doing that got you all riled up? I couldn't see."

"She was just ... I really should go see how —"

The music stops abruptly, slicing a lyric in half, and Michael sees Viking Norma proudly hoisting a candlelit, orange-frosted cake. She leads a chorus of "Happy Birthday" as a crowd of patients and staff falls in behind her. She's aimed directly toward him. Since she started helping in the kitchen, she's made a point of finding out the date of everyone's birthday, along with their favourite type of cake. Michael watches the gawdy faces, a mosaic of madness and fantasy, lurch toward him, pinning him against a table. It would be rude to leave now and he just hopes Frieda has the sense to keep Kerry's family at bay.

The battery of voices trails off to a squeaky end, and Norma calls out, "Make a wish, Dr. Michael. Big breath now."

"You can do it," Terese encourages in his ear, releasing his hand.

He mindlessly obeys and all the candles go out but one.

"Means you have one girlfriend," Norma teases before blowing out the remaining candle herself and initiating applause. Michael feels Terese give his leg a soft kick.

"Touch blue so your wish will come true," comes Marcus' mocking voice. Michael looks over and Marcus grabs hold of one dangling earring and wiggles it at him, sneering.

Terese offers Michael the blue wristband of her watch, which he touches even though he hasn't yet thought of a wish. He cranes his neck to see if any of Kerry's family have returned to the party, but can't see past the tall bobby hat of one of the Alzheimer's patients. When he tries to look past the hat, the patient moves his own head in a game of mirror. *Why did I dance with her?* he berates himself. *Where was my head?*

"First cut's by Dr. Mike," Norma yells over conversations starting to reseed themselves. He feels Terese's hand stroke the small of his back under the corduroy jacket and is hit with a wave of claustrophobia. Norma ceremoniously hands him a plastic knife. It feels ridiculously small and useless in his hand but he raises it dutifully before bringing it down through the inch-thick icing. It stops short of the cake beneath, which he saws through, thoroughly icing his knuckles in the process. Norma nudges Michael aside, his function finished, so she can cut, serve and feed her creation to the hungry hoard.

"Gingerbread," she says to him smiling. "Low-fat. But don't worry, it doesn't taste like it. I used applesauce instead of butter and low-fat cream cheese in the icing."

"You know, I thought maybe you'd decided not to come. I even called your apartment," says Terese, now pulling on his sleeve. She smells like she's been into the staff room punch.

"Nope," he says distractedly, looking for a napkin to wipe the icing from his hand and the sweat from the back of his neck. "Terese, will you excuse me for a minute?" he says. "I really need to check up on Kerry Taylor."

"But the party's just started." Terese sounds peevish.

"Save me some cake," he says, signalling with an index finger that he'll be right back. "Fat chance," he hears her grumble as he pushes through the crowd.

AS MICHAEL rounds the corner, he sees Frieda coming out of Kerry Taylor's room.

"Dr. Myatt?" she says, sounding unsure. "I was just coming to find you."

"And I was coming to check up on the patient. She's still communicating?"

"Yes, yes, perfectly awake, but not saying much." Frieda lowers her voice. "Her family's doing all the talking for her."

"Let's get them out of there," he says moving toward Kerry's door before Frieda stops him.

"I'll do that. You should probably, uh ..." She circles her face with her hand.

"Get rid of the mask. Absolutely. I'll go do that first."

"I'll send the family back to the party, with the exception of Mrs. Taylor, maybe?"

"Yeah, sure."

"It's a lot of attention for Kerry, all at once. Though she seems to be handling it."

"I'll be five minutes," Michael says, distractedly moving down the hall.

"Are you worried about something?" she says in a rhetorical tone, but when he turns to ask what she means, her back is to him.

He washes the icing off his hand, pulls off putty and skullcap, and scrubs the makeup off his face as best he can. As he emerges from the washroom, his hair is still powder grey and traces of foundation brighten the skin around his ears and his neck. Johnny's head appears and disappears around the corner.

"Johnny?"

Johnny's question-marked face emerges from behind the wall.

"You okay?"

Johnny disappears again.

"Were you hoping to talk with Kerry?"

Johnny's head pokes out again, nods once, then looks away.

"I understand. But she probably needs a little time just now, don't you think?"

Johnny's eyes narrow and look past him at Kerry's door. Michael notices that the paper heart's no longer on his chest, just a stub of scotch tape.

"Have you had some cake?"

"Cake," he says, his hands closing into fists as he turns on his heel and leaves.

Johnny's become possessive of Kerry over these past months, muses Michael. At some point, he'll have to consider how to wean the boy off her.

MICHAEL KNOCKS twice, then opens the door to Kerry's room. Frieda has stationed herself just inside the door. A guard? Or is she a witness?

"Mrs. Taylor," he says, ignoring Frieda.

"Michael, come in, it's a relief to see your real face again. That was quite a mask. Kerry-Ann was a little confused, thinking that maybe her father was here. Not that you look anything alike, really. Perhaps it was the combination of the music and all. I've told her that her father is doing fine, just waiting for her to come see him." She catches his eye. Michael has instructed her not to mention Beresford's ill health in front of Kerry. "He's not quite up for the commotion of parties yet."

"Yes, it was getting a bit rowdy for my taste, too."

"Her father will be thrilled to hear Kerry-Ann's ... responding again. Richard is on the phone to him right now. We have you to thank, Michael."

Michael is nodding but not fully hearing her. His attention is focused on Kerry, who comes to stand by her mother. There's an expression of embarrassment on her face, despite her proud posture.

"Hi," she says and Michael stifles the urge to shake her hand, introduce himself as if meeting her for the first time.

Kerry is still in costume, but the crown is gone, her hair freed down her back. Her words come slowly and with effort. "I ap ... preciate all you've done for me."

Her voice is deeper than he's imagined. She is studying his face, as if finally putting a face to the voice. He finds the odd brightness of her eyes hard to look at and remembers the time he pushed her face underwater.

"It's nothing," he says, feeling like an idiot. "You've been doing the work yourself, whether you know it or not." He can feel Frieda's eyes on him.

"Did you want to do an assessment, Dr. Myatt?" suggests Frieda.

"An assessment. Yes," Michael says, turning to scope out two chairs. What does an assessment *mean*? "Shall we sit?" His voice sounds weirdly formal to him. "I'd like to ask you a few questions. Please." He gestures for Kerry to sit down.

Kerry settles soundlessly into a chair. Michael sits and straightens his posture, reminding himself of his role here. He's the therapist, the one in charge. Arlene sits on the bed, eyeing the pillow as if she'd like to lie down. Frieda remains standing by the door. It feels to Michael as if she's doing her own assessment. He takes a calming breath in an attempt to slow his adrenaline and justifies his uneasiness with the fact that Kerry's coming around is possibly the most dramatic therapeutic moment of his career. He proceeds with what he knows are meaningless questions, mostly to satisfy Frieda. He focuses his gaze just past Kerry's left ear. Tomorrow, he tells himself, he'll have a proper session with her.

"So, how do you feel?"

‿‿o‿‿

"I WISH YOU could have seen your daughter," says Arlene, putting down the leisure section of the *Post*. She skips the front page section these days because she's so tired of reading about how many people hate Americans. She doesn't know what she, personally, can do for these people short of being happy herself. And reading about their grief is not happy making. "She didn't have much to say, but to see her beautiful eyes brought back to life after wishing for it for so long ... well, it was incredible."

"Couldn't be happier," says Beresford from his bed, his voice nothing more than a hoarse whisper.

"Though you'd think, after three-and-a-half months, she'd be talking a blue streak. I know I would."

"She needs time," says Beresford, his eyes closing.

"And you, Mr. Taylor, have to hang on until Christmas, when she's strong enough to see you."

"Hmm ..." he murmurs, then presses on the morphine patch that is taped to his upper arm.

At first, after the Halloween party, Arlene thought Kerry would be able to come right home but Dr. Myatt assured her that would not be in Kerry's best interest.

"There are still issues your daughter needs to address before we can be sure her condition has stabilized," Dr. Myatt told her. "The signs of grieving should increase now that she's fully cognitive. There comes a point in the healing process when the traumatic event crystallizes and is, in essence, relived. With the aid of the therapy we've already undergone, and with distance from the actual event, this painful 'revisiting' can be met without any regression on the patient's part but with renewed conviction that life is still a worthwhile journey. Then the physiological experience of the trauma can integrate into the individual's conscious fabric."

Arlene was surprised that she was able to understand most of what Dr. Myatt was saying. And, considering Beresford's present debilitated state, she was almost grateful to have Kerry-Ann in the clinic for a few more weeks yet. One invalid under her roof was enough.

Over the past month, Arlene has learned how to change and clean a catheter, replace an intravenous needle, monitor blood oxygen levels and shave a man's face without nicks. By now, she can do all of this in her sleep and lately it seems as if that's just when she's doing it. Her tennis elbow is acting up, not from tennis, but from lifting her husband's dead weight forward to readjust his pillows every hour on the hour. She scrubs oddly orange urine stains from the beige carpet when he forgets why a tube is inserted where it doesn't rightfully belong. He calls her name, day and night, always hers, only she will do. He is short with the home care nurses, complains whenever Patricia or Leslie come to relieve her. He's embarrassed, Arlene tells the girls, to be nursed by those who looked up to him, who depended on him for so much.

Like a slow fading of light, Beresford sleeps much of the time now. He has stopped eating and lives off air, sips of watered-down juice, a glucose drip. For short respites, Arlene escapes the smell of alcohol and latex that has burned into the apartment walls. She goes downstairs to help decorate the games room for Hawaiian Night, down to the mall to get her hair done, saves a manicure for another day. She shops for the smallest treat — a chocolate bar perhaps — for the half hour each day she has to herself, alone in her bed at night, reading a sleuth novel full of beautiful people. In the night, she hears his laboured breathing through their opened doors and doesn't budge when he first whispers, "Arlene." When she hears the pained wheeze of him saying it a second time, she is out of bed and pulling on another pair of surgical gloves. Every time she steps back out of the den turned sickroom, she wants to sprout wings and fly away.

It's only in her morning shower that she allows herself to shed a tear or two, tears that are quickly washed away, rushed down her strong body and down the drain. Putting in her blue-tinted contacts has become more difficult, as if fatigue has shrunk her eyes, but each day she puts her face on — mascara, powder, lipstick, a smile for her man. Thinking of the mess it makes when mixed with tears, mascara is her first line of defence against her emotions.

∽◡∾

KERRY WALKS around her room, finally left alone by the night nurse, who kept asking if she could help with anything. To think that all these people have undressed her, washed her and brushed her teeth is so embarrassing, she thinks, as she strokes the petals of the yellow tiger lilies in a vase on her dresser. She puts her nose to one. It smells cold. She's used to controlling her own body, she told Dr. Myatt in their session yesterday. He smirked, then assured her that her condition showed she has perfect control over her body, such perfect control that she could function while denying the most vital part, he said.

She knows he goes by "Michael" and not "Dr. Myatt" but she can't bring herself to call him by his first name. It just doesn't fit. He feels too distant and he never looks at her when she talks. Perhaps this has some psychological purpose, but it doesn't change her feeling that he seems uncomfortable around her.

When Dr. Myatt had asked her how much she remembers of the past two-and-a-half months, she didn't know quite how to answer. "Things are blurry," she said. "People feel mixed up with other people."

She told him that she could remember all the movements he'd had her do in his exercises, just like she could remember the choreography to any piece she'd ever learned. But she felt a dullness, an emotional wall she couldn't get past, didn't *want* to get past.

He'd got up and opened a window then, as if something she'd said bothered him. It made the room way too cold but she didn't say anything.

"Are you aware of having lost your husband and son?" he asked and her mind went more or less blank.

Yes, she knew they were dead but couldn't recall any of the details of

the accident. He assured her this was perfectly natural and fine. As she
felt stronger, he told her, she'd be able to handle remembering and the
memories would surface. She missed Allan and Thomas, she said, but it
was a familiar kind of missing, as if she was just away on tour and would
see them soon, could call if she needed to hear their voices. Yet she felt
anxious, worried about being so far away. The way she felt when she first
went back to work and leaving Thomas, who was just three months old.

"Understandable," was all he'd said, which was hardly satisfying.

What she didn't say is how clear her memories are of snuggling her
son's small angular body in bed, the bony knobs on the tops of his shoulders, the dip in his waist, the arms and legs that were all elbows and knees.
And how she can even remember what it felt like to nurse him. Most of all
she missed human touch, she wanted to say, but couldn't because she felt
as though Dr. Myatt would somehow be embarrassed by this.

"I MISS our walks." Johnny distinctly heard Kerry say this to him.

They were standing in the hall. He could hardly look up, he was so
excited, but when he did there were two silhouettes of his face reflected
in her cloud-like eyes. He's been too shy to approach her, his angel, who
now has eyes and a tongue that speaks in the ordinary way. He had kept
away, like the doctor told him, but here she was inviting him to come
back. *She loves me*, he thinks, *not him. Not the old doctor.*

Since the Halloween party, Johnny has spent each night in his own
room, focusing on the clean smell of his towel jammed under his nose
and the contours of the roof of his mouth under his probing fingers. He's
been working fiercely to forget the taste and smell of her and how her
nipple moulded itself so perfectly in the cradle of his tongue. So much
better than even his little pinky. He'd stayed away, like his mother had,
when she chose the man over her boy. She took her hands and tongue
and nipples away to give to someone else. Her cigarette breath huffing its
sour rhythm above another, her eyes winched tight, hissing at him to stay
still as she drained the life from his body. Did she always cry afterward,
with the man, in her bigger bed? Was the man also not allowed to tell?

"If you tell anyone, Johnny, I'll kill myself," repeats the little mouse that runs around his brain.

AFTER THE night nurse has made her rounds, Johnny listens at his door. When he can tell the hall is clear, he slips through and eases it closed behind him without even a tinkle. He turns off his thoughts — stop time — causing no ripples as he moves along the wall, down around the corner to the door at the end of the hall. His steady hand turns her handle in one smooth curve. There she waits, his earth angel, who greets him now by name.

"Johnny?"

Her bedside lamp comes on with a click, illuminating her perfect face. He waits.

"What are you doing here? Are you all right?"

She sits up and moves over, touching the space on the bed beside her. She wears a blue T-shirt, her white angel dress gone. *You asked me to come*, he thinks, as he sits against the lump of her legs. He wonders what a real man would do now.

"I wasn't asleep. It takes me forever to —"

His nervous hands stumble over themselves, then lunge for her breasts.

"Johnny!" her voice breaks as she bats him away. "What are you doing?"

He snatches back his hands, horrified at upsetting her, at seeing fear narrow her eyes as she yanks the covers over her chest.

"I'm sorry," whimpers Johnny, clenching his hands into fists. "I thought —" He punches his fists against his forehead. "Bad Johnny," he repeats under his breath, punching harder. "Bad, bad Johnny." But then her hands are there, pulling his down.

"I've let you touch me before, haven't I?" Her voice is hushed.

Johnny nods timidly, his fingers aching toward his mouth.

"I remember now." Her eyes stray past him. There's an unsettling pain in her voice. "I confused you with him ... with them both ..." Her words fade away.

Did I hurt her?

Tears are falling fast down her cheeks. *Bad Johnny*, he thinks, grinding his teeth together.

"I didn't mean to …" he starts to apologize, but her chest slumps, startling him. Then her head breaks backward and sideways on her neck and, eyes closed, she is falling toward him. Johnny grabs her.

"I'm so sorry," he says as her body convulses against his chest. He wraps his arms as far around her as they can go, trying to still her jerking body and hide his own contorting face in her hair. She is crying now, grasping his shirt in closed fists, her gaping mouth crushed against his shirt. His head feels overfull and then he too is crying. They muffle their cries so no one will hear, so no one will come, no doctor or nurse with their smart ways and sleep-needles. But the bed rattles, noisy with their grief. Under his hands, Johnny grips two knobby protuberances that bob up and down on Kerry's back. He holds her closer. His fallen angel is growing new wings.

THE WILL TO LOVE

The human psyche develops to the point of an acute self-referential awareness, traditionally known as the ego. This ego, or "I," can exist only in relationship to its opposite "other," another person or thing outside of the self. To whatever degree we are concerned with self-confirmation, we become equally obsessed with concretizing the "other."

At this stage, the child develops a covetous attachment to the parent of the opposing sex, which Freud termed the Oedipal complex. How this attachment is played out between parent and child becomes the underpinning for the child's future relationships with the opposite sex. We generally refer to this attachment as "love." As this love is felt by the child, he attempts to secure the object of his love by temporarily rejecting the same-sex parent, who represents the child's rival.

The prospect of not securing or of losing the object of one's love is completely destabilizing to the ego. It naturally follows that when feelings of attachment or love are threatened by a third party, such as the other parent, aggressive tendencies arise. Depending on the child's personality, this hostility will be directed inward toward "I" or outward toward "other."

At this stage in the process, group therapy is introduced.

MICHAEL CLEARS his throat and looks around at his circle of patients. He is pleased to see that all four have progressed to this stage — especially knowing Kerry would have been left behind if not for the breakthrough at the party. Four's a good number, he tells himself. Even numbers in group therapy are always more amenable than odd.

Marcus sits to his right, Norma to his left and Johnny and Kerry across from him.

"Although we already know each other to various degrees, I'd like to begin very simply, with each of us giving our names and saying something about ourselves. I'll start. My name is Michael Myatt. I'm originally from Seattle, the other Washington, and I'm a doctor of psychology and work at the Rosewood Clinic. Marcus, maybe you could go next."

Hands planted on his knees, Marcus leans forward, as if in a huddle, and addresses the empty centre of the circle. "Hi, I'm Marcus, worked as a monument tour guide for eleven years. I'm from Baltimore originally … Oh, and I was middleweight boxing champ in my high school." This last bit of information brings colour to his cheeks and he looks up defiantly at Michael.

"Thanks, Marcus. Kerry?" Michael gestures to her with one hand. She's wearing silky wide-legged pants and a halter top. Her hair is pulled up in a ponytail that looks messy on purpose, soft tendrils falling around her face and neck. Beaded bracelets in muted colours line one arm. He saw her making them in the lounge.

"I'm Kerry Taylor. I'm from around here originally, Arlington actually, and spent most of my life in dance." Kerry has acknowledged each face in turn and now she looks down at her hands. "I was married and we had a nine-year-old son but I lost them both in a car accident." Michael had told her in their last session that it would be therapeutic to acknowledge this last fact aloud and he feels an odd pride that she's followed through on his suggestion.

"What kind of dance?" Marcus demands.

"Ballet."

"Oh, nice." Marcus bunches his lips and nods his approval. "I like your pants."

"Thanks."

"Johnny?" Michael gives Johnny an encouraging smile.

Arms and legs crossed, Johnny begins to rock in his chair. He doesn't meet Michael's eye.

"Johnny Bourne, Fairfax. I like computers." The words stop but the rocking continues until Norma pipes up, unprompted.

"I'm Norma Daily," she says cheerfully. "I'm originally from a small town outside St. Louis. Missouri that is, but raised my two daughters here in Falls Church, Virginia. I too lost a child, my youngest, last year to cancer." She addresses this information to Kerry. "I'm a terrific cook. I've been the one responsible for the tea-time goodies." Norma leaves pause for acknowledgement before clapping a hand to her thigh. "And I'm single," she adds.

Michael chuckles and sees Marcus grimacing.

"Thank you, and nice to re-meet you all," says Michael. "Today, I'd like each of you to take a moment to think of an object or pet from your childhood that you were personally attached to. And then, when you're ready, to share that relationship with the group. You are free to stand and move around the room if need be. Anyone can simply raise a hand when ready. There's no pressure here to share this out loud. If you prefer just to think about this privately, you may."

Marcus and Johnny both lift their hands at the same moment. A glance from Marcus, and Johnny tucks his hand back into his elbow. Marcus stands and flips his chair around in front of him.

His protective shield, thinks Michael.

"Yeah, well," Marcus begins, "we had a dog. A beagle. Named Sonny. Good-natured pup, kinda brought the family together. We all liked her, anyway. I used to close my eyes," Marcus says, closing his eyes, "and she'd lick my eyelids trying to reopen them. She slept in my room. I was in high school when she died. She was ten. Had nothing in common with my folks after that."

"Yes," Norma says, her eyes welling up. "Our Bosco was the same, just another member of the family. Even ate what we did. Except on Fridays." She sniffs back her tears with one ample snort. "No way would he eat my mama's homemade beans or the cornbread she made with bacon and bits of real corn ..."

Michael passes Norma the box of tissues and glances at Kerry, wondering if the talk of pet dogs might be disconcerting.

"We had a white Persian cat named Bloom," says Kerry in an even voice. "Sadly, my mother had her declawed because she scratched the furniture. I loved to watch her leap. It was so effortless. Like flying." Kerry looks at Michael, eyebrows raised as if she'd just asked a question.

He had been absorbed in the line of her neck as she spoke and didn't catch all her words. He nods and smiles for her to continue, hoping she didn't just ask something requiring an answer.

"I imagined she liked me more than cats probably do. She died a year or two after I left home."

"Never had a pet," Johnny jumps in, grabbing Michael's attention. "But one day, she found mouse turds under the sink."

"She?" Marcus says bluntly.

"My mother," Johnny mumbles, looking down at the floor.

"Please Johnny, continue," says Michael.

"I'd leave crumbs from the kitchen to my bed." Johnny's hand has escaped from his elbow and his fingers make scurrying motions over his thigh. "When they were in my room, I'd shut the door. She," Johnny glances hard at Marcus, "didn't like mice."

Marcus raises his face to the ceiling and mouths the word, "Freak."

"One had a black circle around his eye. I named him Pirate." Johnny looks to Kerry, who smiles kindly.

"How 'bout you, Doc. Pet?" Marcus asks from behind his chair.

"No pets allowed in my mother's house. Never a one, though I used to sneak in toads and snakes behind her back," Michael says with a smile, before his eyes drift out the window, caught by a memory. "There was a dog, come to think of it, a mixed breed, at my father's cabin. Raven, she was called. Nice dog. Yeah, she was all black and loved to chase ravens. The birds would play right along with her, dipping down low to give chase before flying out of reach. And she'd bark and then they'd caw back, taunting her before dropping down again to continue the game. Every afternoon." He suddenly remembers Eden saying once that Raven was known as the trickster. *See how both dog and bird pretend the game is not a game.* "Boy, I must have been just small ..."

The room has become still, all ears attuned to the man behind the pen and paper, suddenly telling them something about himself for a change.

THE NEXT morning, Michael is hoping to quickly retrieve his mail and get down to work, when Terese stops him to talk.

"Just thought you might like to know that you're not the only one with a November birthday around here."

"Oh?" He peruses the mail in his hand. "Who else is a November brat?"

"Me."

"Really," he says, unsure what she expects from him. He'll have to buy her something since she gave him a shirt for his birthday. It was a cotton and synthetic wrinkle-free shirt in a salmon pink. She said she was tired of seeing him dress in the same bland colours all the time, adding, "bright colours can change your life." He didn't bother to explain why he dressed as he did and why he still hasn't worn her shirt to work. "Sounds like an occasion to wear my new shirt," he thinks to say.

"Yes, I'm waiting to see it on you."

He's ready to retreat to his office but Terese is not finished.

"Aren't you going to ask when it is?" She purses her lips, waiting.

"When is it?"

"November 16."

"We'll have to ... celebrate."

"There is this place I've always wanted to go to," she says, the words finally spilling out. "It's in town, Massachusetts Avenue, just on the edge of Georgetown. It's quite famous, maybe you've heard of it? It's called La Niçoise. Don't know if I'm pronouncing it right or what it means, but I know there's a salad that goes by the same name."

Michael has stopped listening. Wearing a shortish flared skirt that swings as she walks, Kerry Taylor is coming toward him on long articulate legs. An olive-green shirt just meets the black skirt's low waistline and a sliver of pale skin appears and disappears with every second step. Since waking up, she's been dressing more youthfully.

"Hi, Dr. Myatt," she says, not slowing her pace.

"How are you today?" he asks, failing to notice that the magazine he's holding between two letters is slipping.

"I'm okay, thanks." She nods, tilting her chin, Michael notes, in the self-effacing way she has.

"Good. Will see you later in group —"

"Ouch!" Terese has stood up from behind her desk, lifting her skirt away from her legs. "Michael, you've knocked over my hot coffee."

"Oh, sorry." As Michael stands there helplessly, Terese looks at him, then at Kerry's disappearing back, then back at him. "Now that she's gone, do you mind getting me some paper towels or a cloth from the staff room?"

"Yeah, sure." He wants to tell her that it's not what she thinks. That he's not attracted to Kerry Taylor but he's affected by her in some way he can't quite figure out. And it's because he can't quite figure it out that he's attracted to her. Not *attracted*, affected. He dumbly goes to fetch something.

"TODAY, CLASS," Michael mocks a teacher's tone, "I would like you to share the name of a favourite playmate from your childhood and something that you enjoyed doing together. I'm talking about a human, now.

However long or brief the relationship doesn't matter. Just someone you enjoyed being with and what your favourite activity might have been. First, I want you to visualize yourself as the child you once were. Let's keep it to age eight and under, which is a time when we can recognize our purity of intention, our innocence and our guiltlessness."

"You mean, before we started to hate ourselves," drones Marcus.

"More or less," says Michael. He sees Kerry and Norma nodding their agreement, their understanding. Johnny rubs his hands back and forth on his thighs and watches Kerry.

"So, to help nurture that memory, try and imagine what you might be wearing, what your friend would be wearing, your hairstyles, the places you played, the smells of that place. We'll just take a few minutes and —"

"I'm ready, I'll go," Marcus interrupts, slouched in his chair. "My best friend was my cousin Stacey, who lived next door. She was my mother's sister's kid and we were the same age. We'd play dress-up in her mouldy basement. The end."

Norma bristles at Marcus' dismissive tone but Michael pays no attention. He is impressed that today Marcus hasn't removed himself from the circle.

"That's fine for starters, Marcus. Anyone else ready?"

Hand up, Norma is waving her fingers. She looks ready to talk the wax out of everybody's ears.

"My best friend in the whole universe, my bosom buddy and blood sister, was Louise, who lived down the lane and over the crick," she begins.

"Crick?" Marcus says to the ceiling.

"You know, it's a —" Norma starts to explain.

"I know, it's a creek. Say creek."

"Oh, pshaw," Norma dismisses him with a wave. "Down at the creek," Norma says, enunciating the word, "Louise and I would spend hours floating homemade boats that we made out of just about anything. Corn husks, cauliflower leaves, zucchini rinds, onion skin —"

"We get the idea," Marcus says, a fake smile widening his wide face. "How delightful."

"And the other thing we'd lose our little selves in," continues Norma, "was making mud pies in her Easy-Bake. What a toy that was. That child had all the latest gizmos, being an only child and having rich grandparents. I wasn't jealous since I got to play with all of it anyway. Well, those mud pies, cooked up hard and cracked, dry as a desert in a drought, would stink to high heaven." Norma laughs heartily. "Then came the saddest day of my young life when my Louise was sent to the fancy Catholic school in town instead of the public up the road with the rest of us. She didn't want much to do with the likes of me after that, I tell you." Norma pushes her nose into the air with her finger. "So I wrote that girl off then and there. Norma, I said to myself, that's no friend of yours. Let's you and I go make some truer, bluer friends and start learning the difference between the two." She punctuates this with a sharp nod.

"Is this the moral of the story?" Marcus yawns noisily.

Norma turns to Marcus. "It may mean nothing to you, Smartie Pants, but it's a lesson that I'm still learning after my husband left me and ..." Norma stops talking, closes her eyes and breathes deeply.

"Norma, you have an excellent memory for details," Michael says. "Thank you for sharing that personal story with us. Don't mind Marcus, who will try his best not to interrupt when it's someone else's turn."

"Yes, sir," Marcus says with a salute.

"Johnny?"

Rubbing the back of his neck, Johnny angles his head down at the floor as he speaks. "I had a friend in this one building. He was younger than me. He liked me. We'd bounce balls off the stairwell steps or see how high a step we could jump from. We'd sit in the cave under the stairs and eat pretzels. I don't know his name." Johnny stuffs his hands under his thighs.

"Thank you, Johnny. Kerry?"

"My closest friend was, believe it or not ... deaf and dumb." Kerry smiles at the irony. "Her name was Debbie Tomer."

Marcus turns his face away as if trying not to laugh.

"Mostly I recall playing Barbies in her basement and climbing the tree in her front yard. We'd make up elaborate stories for the dolls, yet I don't remember ever having to explain myself much. As if the story in

my head was somehow in hers, too. If I couldn't communicate something, I'd use sign language. She taught me the alphabet and the colours.
She was always happy, as I remember it. Good-natured."

Kerry looks up to Michael for permission to stop.

"Fine," he says, glancing down to his notepad. He still feels thrown
by the directness of her gaze.

The exercise continues with physical descriptions of the aforemen-
tioned friend and then Michael asks everyone to describe something bothersome or irritating about the friend. Afterward, Michael passes out pens,
paper and clipboards and instructs the group to write a storyline about
what they imagine has happened to this friend since childhood, the chal-
lenges they've faced, their accomplishments, joys and hardships. Clipboard
in hand, Marcus leaves the circle and wanders over by the windows.

"I know what happened to my cousin, Stacey," he says over his shoulder. "She married asshole number two, has two teenage brats, and works
at the Stuporstore. The rest of her time she wards off death by shopping.
Can I go now?"

"Marcus, maybe use your paper to write a letter to Stacey, tell her
something she might not know about your life. And don't worry, I won't
be reading any of it. We'll burn all the paper before you leave this room."

Marcus pulls over a metal wastebasket and holds up a yellow lighter
as proof. Catching Kerry's eye, he suddenly feels guilty. He still has her
journal, and now that she's no longer catatonic, having her private
thoughts on paper, feels sneaky, dishonest. When Mrs. Taylor recently
asked about the book, he'd said he was still finding it a valuable resource
and asked that she not mention to Kerry that he had it. What bothers
Michael now is how contained Kerry remains in conversation with
him when he knows there's so much more depth and dimension to her.
It almost makes him jealous of this Hugo person.

"Yeah, okay." Marcus seems suddenly caught by the idea of writing a
letter. He takes up his pen and clipboard and perches on the window ledge.

Five minutes in, Marcus starts to hoot with laughter. "Oh, shit, it's
too much, Doc, I gotta burn this letter and go for a cold swim." More
hooting ricochets off the walls. "Shit, I gotta get out of this nut house,"

he says, tears of mirth filling his eyes, "get myself divorced." Marcus laughs to the point of holding his stomach.

Michael, Kerry and even Johnny can't help but smile at the sound and sight of him. Norma, however, looks concerned. "I'm divorced," she says.

Marcus laughs even harder. "I gotta get divorced like you."

Michael doesn't comment and, when Marcus hands over the paper, Michael holds it over the metal trash can and flicks on the lighter. The flames seem to lick off the paper's white coating to reveal its grey flaky insides before the ashes fall into the can. Marcus heads for the door, still chuckling.

"Marcus." Norma's voice stops him in the doorway.

He turns, grinning like a little boy, tears staining his cheeks.

"I just wanted to say that I don't think you're as mean as you make out to be."

"And," he says, still smiling, "you talk too much but I liked that one muumuu with the purple azaleas."

He salutes with two fingers and leaves with the air of a man who isn't ever coming back. Norma frowns over at Michael, but Michael shrugs good-naturedly and a subdued Norma returns to her writing assignment.

∽ం∾

KERRY continues to write her letter:

Debbie Tomer married a tall, quiet man, a city planner, had three hearing kids who now speak two languages fluently, English and Sign. She is an avid mystery reader and volunteers at the local library. A happy ending for a happy person.

I'd rather write about Dr. Myatt. He's impossible to talk to. Kind of funny, eh? A psychologist you can't talk to. Or perhaps it's just me. He holds his head in an alert, doggish sort of way and has an endearing split-toothed smile. I can't tell if he's arrogant or shy but he always seems two steps back and one to the right. He's got an intensity, though. I can feel it colliding with my own at times, which reminds me of catching the reverb off an audience and trying to resonate with it. Kind of like a human tuning fork.

Looks lonely being that smart. I wonder what he does for fun. Understand he's dating the daytime receptionist, who gives me the evil eye every time I walk by. Don't know what I did to make her hate me, but she does. Maybe I did something to her earlier on that I'm not aware of.

Writing her thoughts down makes Kerry remember her journal — the retirement gift from Hugo that became her private catharsis. Where could that book be? She sees the attic room in their cottage in Metchosin, the window seat where she used to stare at the view and write while she waited for ... her stomach tightens and she shuts the image down, brings her mind back to this ordered room, this simple structured Mozart-ish world, telling herself that if she just stays focused on the here and now, it's all workable, doable. Thinking of being present makes her think of Hugo. A moment-to-moment guy, Hugo never fails to bring her into her skin. He helps her forget the past and the future, too, for that matter. And because he feels outside of what's happened to her, he reminds her of a life before the accident.

She's finished her letter and wants to go for a walk in the garden, maybe play some rummy with Johnny. As she takes her letter to Dr. Myatt, his vibration hits her at chest level. She moves against it, willing him to peer up over his glasses and watch her approach. When he does, his eye contact is guarded and short-lived.

"I find it easier to formulate my thoughts when writing," she says as she hands over the letter, offering a kind of excuse for herself, maybe for him, too.

"Yes, writing can be helpful," he says in his professional doctor tone.

"I'd starting keeping a journal of sorts a little while back," she says with a shrug, and he doesn't respond, just flicks on the lighter.

Together they watch the paper ignite and descend flaming into the wastebasket.

"Thank you," he says, not looking up, and she walks out feeling lonelier than ever.

⌒oᴖ⌒

MICHAEL LIFTS his glass of champagne. "Let me be the first to wish you an early happy birthday. To my, I'd have to say, best friend on the East Coast."

"Is that all I am, a friend?" Terese keeps her glass on the table, peers up at him with an impish smile.

"No, of course not. But friendship is at the root of all important relationships, don't you think?" He hopes that doesn't sound too clinical.

"I guess so," she concedes. They clink glasses and she takes such a gulping sip, Michael wonders if she even tasted it. It's a seventy-dollar bottle, smooth with just a hint of tart sweetness. Blackberry?

Dressed in penguin black and whites, complete with bow tie and tails, the same waiter who'd brought their champagne sails over on Rollerblades with a basket of steaming rolls and an appetizer of escargot.

Michael had offered to take Terese to the restaurant of her choice for her birthday dinner. La Niçoise, according to Terese, was a famous D.C. institution and *the* dining choice for anybody famous who came to town.

"I've always wanted to come here," she says, gazing at the signed photograph of Sinatra and Mia Farrow on the wall beside their table. "I won't forget this, Michael Myatt."

"Any celebs here tonight?" she playfully asks the waiter.

"I was sure you were a celebrity, Miss," the waiter teases in his French accent. "An actress, perhaps, or the dictator of a small country?" Terese laughs loudly and a few grey heads turn their way. "Or is it Madame?" He looks to Michael, who shakes his head.

Michael can feel Terese staring at him.

"But today happens to be this young and single dictator's birthday," he tells the waiter.

"Very good, sir," says the waiter with just the right balance of formality and personableness.

"It's tomorrow, really," Terese says as the waiter rolls away.

"Close enough."

"Have I told you, Michael Myatt, how collegiate you look in those loafers."

"Two or three times. The Birkenstocks I ordered are taking too long. They said six weeks but it's already been seven. My feet are killing me by the end of the day."

"I'll rub them later," she says. "But what you really need are some good runners. New Balance gives loads of arch support."

"I prefer looking collegiate to athletic."

"So suffer, then, Michael Paul Myatt."

He wonders if his name's going to keep getting longer. "Is serving on skates a tradition or is this something new?" As Michael watches the waiters gliding around the scratched oak floors, he feels as if the whole restaurant is in motion.

"It's how it's always been. Only they used to wear roller skates instead of Rollerblades."

He pries a snail from its house, dips it into the butter sauce and Terese grabs his hand and guides the fork into her mouth. She holds his hand there while she groans and chews. "I never knew slugs could taste this good."

"Snails."

"Aren't slugs just snails without their house?"

"Not exactly." He extricates his hand.

"I have another birthday desire," Terese says, ripping apart a roll and dunking it in the butter sauce.

"We have yet to eat your first desire. Waiter?" Michael pretends to gesture. "This woman is getting ahead of herself, or is it ahead of me?"

"I just want to get this out of the way, so I can enjoy the food."

"Shoot," Michael says, feeling a tad less jovial.

"Tomorrow being the actual day, I'd kind of like to see the morning sun from your bedroom window. Find out if you're as horrific a snorer as my Aunt Gladys."

Michael had managed to avoid spending an entire night with Terese. He's careful not to pause too long. "I snore like a lumberjack, but that's a minor concern."

"Oh?"

"I shun sleepovers because I have to shave my face each morning."

"Yeah, so."

"My entire face." He turns his face toward the ceiling and mimes a howling wolf.

"Sounds rather exciting. So is that a yes, Dr. Jekyll?"

He can tell she's holding her breath. "I guess it is." Her smile is worth it, he tells himself. It's only one night. He'll make sure she doesn't leave her toothbrush behind.

When the waiter arrives with a bottle of Italian Massey, Terese asks him in a low voice about the couple who were just seated at the table in the window.

"The National Ballet of Canada is in town. It's two of their premier dancers, I believe. I can find out their names if you'd like."

"No, that's okay," Terese says, her excitement fading. "I thought they were actors."

As the waiter finishes filling their glasses, Terese blurts, "Mrs. Taylor thinks you're pretty amazing, bringing her daughter around like you have."

"It's nice to have your work confirmed in overt ways." Michael taps his fork on the table, tries to remember the Morse code he once taught himself as a kid.

"Since Kerry Taylor's come around, Mrs. Carter thinks she's underestimated you."

"She said that?"

"Yesterday. Anybody can see that whatever it is you do is helping. I mean Norma's load is a lot lighter, so to speak, and Johnny's way more sanitary, if nothing else. Haircut's a little short but I think the barber was thinking maybe it was a one shot deal. Even Marcus isn't quite as scary as he was."

"To Mrs. Carter," he says, lifting his glass.

"No, to you, Dr. Michael Paul Myatt," Terese says, clinking their glasses dangerously hard. She doesn't actually drink but lowers her glass thoughtfully, as if she hasn't quite got around to her point. "It's interesting how Kerry's speech doesn't seem to have suffered. You'd think something would have atrophied in there."

278 · *Dede Crane*

"Hmm …"

"I have to say, I find it so pretentious how she wears ballet slippers all the time. As if she's going to start twirling down the hall or something" Terese slugs back her wine and spills some down her chin. "Oh, shit."

Michael knows from experience that Terese is a little tipsy now and will proceed to let off some steam. Namely her angst for Kerry, by the sounds of it.

"I don't know how Kerry Taylor's supposed to get back on her toes, pardon the pun, the way everybody coddles her. Especially you men. Bryson turns into this big teddy bear around her and I heard Hootie calling her 'darlin' the other day. God, it's like a lace hanky drops out of her skinny ass wherever she goes."

Crude but funny, thinks Michael, smiling.

"And you, Mister, were so distracted by her the other day, you spilled coffee all over me."

His great long name has been reduced to Mister.

"She's a patient I'm still trying to unlock, is all. And now that her father is dying, I'm rather concerned that —"

"Is he really?" Terese slaps her hand down on the table, just missing the edge of her bread plate.

As Michael hoped, this news causes her to switch tracks.

"God, to lose her father now, on top of everything else …"

"Absolutely. She doesn't know, by the way, how ill he is. So you have to promise to keep it under your hat." He spears an escargot and holds up his fork. "Another slug?" This one he puts into her mouth all on his own.

"Look at me, Michael," Terese says while chewing her snail. "I think," she starts, then stops, eyes moony and swimming slightly. "I think I might could fall in love with a man like you."

Might could? He's both flattered and afraid. And he is not about to feed this fantasy. To lighten things up, he quietly howls at the ceiling again. "Don't tell me I didn't warn you," he says and quickly changes the subject.

AFTER DINNER, because he's got a whole night ahead of him yet, Michael orders cognac for himself and Terese. As he swirls the amber liquid around his bowed crystal, Terese does the same. Once again, she takes too big a sip, and is coughing into her napkin when a trio of waiters appears behind her and the first harmonized notes of "Happy Birthday" float over the table. She looks at Michael with tears in her eyes and he can only hope they're from coughing. The prettiest pink and beige marzipan cake is set before her, its single tall sparkler burning so brightly, Terese's shining eyes momentarily disappear across the table.

∽o∾

AT SEVEN THIRTY this morning, Arlene had called Richard. As she waited for him to arrive she got dressed, put on her face and made coffee. When she answers the door, they don't speak, only hold each other's gaze for the few extra seconds it takes to make both of them appreciate that they're not alone. As she leads the way to the den, Arlene can feel the stoop of her shoulders, her mother's shoulders, and she tries in vain to stand up straighter. The room had smelled so "off" that she'd touched Beresford up with some of his Old Spice cologne — a little much, she thinks now, seeing her son squint. But she had to disguise that god-awful smell.

"I'm pretty sure he's dead," she says, and Richard looks at her, confused.

"Did you check his pulse?"

"I tried, but couldn't tell for sure."

"Get me a mirror," says Richard and Arlene hurries to her bathroom for her hand mirror.

He places it under his father's mouth and nose, checks it for moisture, then searches his neck for a pulse.

"He's gone, Mom," confirms Richard.

Arlene sighs, a large breathy sigh. Maybe it's not appropriate, but she can't help it. Right now all she can feel is relief. Another week of this and she would have had a nervous breakdown. Together they look at Beresford's lifeless face, the smooth lines of skull clearly outlined underneath the slack grey skin. His mouth is parted, his eyelids half drawn, and Richard uses two fingers of one hand to gingerly close the lids shut. Like they do in the movies, she thinks, watching her son's face. He's breathing through his mouth, his eyes more inquisitive than sad. They stand there in the quiet, the faint sound of a toilet flushing overhead.

"Know what he said to me last week?" Richard says, not waiting for her answer. "It's been a good run." He smiles and Arlene looks up to see his eyes filming over. She feels herself stiffen, preparing herself. "Told me to ..." Richard's strong voice rises and cracks, "take care of his girls." Arlene takes her son in her arms, presses her cheek against his shoulder. The touch becomes an embrace and she lets him cry next to her ear. She breathes deeply, willing her own tears away, thinking of the mess her mascara would make on his pressed white shirt.

"Have you called the funeral home?" Richard asks, straightening up and wiping his eyes.

"I haven't. I only called you."

Arlene feels suddenly restless and full of energy, like she could run a marathon. It's as if someone's just untied heavy ropes from her arms and legs, ropes binding her to a sinking ship. No, not just someone, Beresford. He's finally let her go and, at least momentarily, she's extremely grateful.

"Do you mind staying with your father and calling the funeral director for me?" she asks.

"Sure, Mom. You go ahead and lie down, get some sleep."

"Well, I made an appointment to get my hair done."

She can see Richard struggle to hide his amazement.

"But it's not until nine, so let me make us some coffee," she says, not wanting to seem in too much of a hurry.

Over coffee and toast, they talk about anything except the dead body in the room twenty feet from them. They talk about Leslie's upcoming business trip to Connecticut, Marshall getting his orange belt in karate, the Beltway Snipers' upcoming trial, the possibility of a war with Iraq despite the UN's lack of support.

"How many of the hijackers were Iraqis?" asks Arlene.

"None," says Richard and Arlene is surprised to hear it. "In fact, Hussein and bin Laden are known to hate everything the other stands for. But no matter, Hussein's a monster, is no doubt harbouring weapons and we need a secure foothold in the Middle East if Israel is to survive."

"Israel should move itself to New Jersey," says Arlene irritably.

Richard smiles. "That might actually solve a few things."

Arlene abruptly gets up from her chair, her coffee mug still half full. She simply can't sit still any longer. "I've got a letter to mail and a few groceries to pick up before my appointment. I'll need you to write up an announcement for the paper, Richard."

"Sure, Mom." He sounds honoured.

"And can I leave it to you to call Patricia and your Aunt Mary with the news? Before telling Kerry-Ann, we'll have to talk to her doctor and see if he feels she's strong enough yet. Maybe you could call him, too."

The thought of more grief being served up to her youngest child makes her stomach hurt. She grabs up her purse and, embarrassed by her need to flee, turns and kisses Richard on the head. "Sit in there with your father, please," she says, not knowing why it feels important for someone to physically be near him, but it does. "I'll be back by ten."

∽◦∾

THE SOUND of footsteps comes down the hall. Kerry urges Johnny to duck behind the bed. The steps pass by and fade away.

"It's all right," she whispers and Johnny's head reappears.

They have timed this meeting for the interval between bed checks because Kerry could tell from the way Johnny was after dinner that he needed to talk. Away from prying eyes, a doctor's agenda, away from open-door policies and schedules. Lying side by side, they hold hands, she under the covers, he outside the covers, his hand tense and fidgety in hers. He'd been starting to tell her something all week, but then someone walks by and he shuts down.

She squeezes his hand and suddenly his throat begins to make a low gurgling sound like a baby before needing to belch. Kerry feels a wave of nausea lift her stomach, then drop it down low.

"It's not your fault," she hears herself say, turning to stroke the hair back from his staring eyes.

His face is contorted as if he's revolted by the pictures playing in his head. He'd already told her that his mother had killed herself, that he never knew his father. That his mother drank and invited strangers in the apartment. He shakes his head spasmodically before the words escape with a light spray on her face.

"She was still alive."

Kerry focuses on the neutral colour of the ceiling, squeezing his hand harder in hers, silently urging him to lower his voice.

"I could have ... her lips were all dusty. Jittery like she was talking, but there wasn't anything coming out." He speaks fast, his voice constricted and high-pitched. "She'd had her bottle, too, and was deep, deep gone somewhere else. I didn't tell anybody then, like I never told anyone before, because that's what she always said. Don't tell, Johnny. Don't tell." He coughs, clearing his throat and the struggle in his body suddenly ceases. She feels his hand go limp in hers but she doesn't let go. She glances over and his eyes are empty and unseeing. He speaks slow and methodically now, overcome with a strange calm. Kerry feels a shudder race up her back but sends him all her strength to keep going, because she knows he needs to keep going.

"I laid down beside her and pulled her arm over me. It was cold, bluish-white. I pulled the blanket over us and thought of how she used to love me. I liked it and hated it." He hesitates, but Kerry will not ask what he means by love. "I called 911 later, after the convulsing stopped and her last breath blew past my ear, all hot and rotten. I didn't call when I should have. I waited ... until I was sure she was dead."

Johnny's hand squeezes around Kerry's too hard and it hurts. His whole body has hardened.

"I hate her," spouts from twisted lips, his jaw muscles bulging, teeth grimacing. It's a face Kerry doesn't recognize and she feels sick to her stomach again. "She would force my pe—"

"I know Johnny," Kerry rips free of his hand and, turning onto her knees, grabs his face between her hands, looks him in the eyes. "I know already." She won't hear it said out loud, can't allow herself to imagine what his horrors were. "It was wrong," she says firmly. "She was your mother and supposed to take care of you and protect you. It was not your fault."

Her own words whisk her away and she is gone from this steel bed and concrete room, her bottom couched in the saggy passenger seat of an ancient VW Bug, spiriting along familiar roads. *She was your mother and supposed to take care of you, protect you.* Allan is driving too fast, as usual. The chocolate cookie smell is too much to take. She hasn't had one yet, hasn't allowed herself even a smidgen of the dough, the best part, but doesn't know how much longer she can hold out. Allan pours over the map, his lips mouthing the words "Swan Lake." Thomas, whom *she's vowed to protect*, sits in the back next to Blackjack, intent on his Game Boy. It's the ideal day for a picnic, sunny, sweet newborn air. For the moment she thinks she knows what it is to be happy.

"Delibes, *Lakmé's* 'Flower Duet'," she says, matching the weather to a piece of music. An old game of hers and Allan's.

"Beach Boys, 'California Girls'."

"No way, the sun's not high enough or hot enough."

There's a flatbed truck up ahead, parked on the left side of the road in front of the Henry's, its back angled out onto the road. It's facing the wrong direction. In the city, you'd get a ticket for that, or get towed, she thinks, before bending down to locate the cookie tin in the picnic things at her feet. Just one before lunch. That's all she'll have. So much for her famous discipline.

"Found it," Allan says, a second before the car explodes to a stop.

Kerry's head thuds against the glove compartment, pain ringing her neck before time turns to sludge. The engine rumbles merrily, intent on continuing when forward no longer exists. A breeze has entered the car and the cookie caught between her teeth is heavy as a gold bar. She opens her mouth and it falls in slow motion to the floor. She places one hand to her hair to catch the drips of warm liquid running off her forehead onto the flowered cookie tin with a dribbly banging. Red rosettes bloom on the blue-checked tablecloth. Something, no someone, is wedged behind her in the seat as she struggles to manoeuvre upright, the air a mountain of wet sand weighing her down. Half the car, their half, is hidden under the flatbed. Where is the roof? It takes hours, a lifetime, to lift her head and see blood erupting in jerks from a hole where Allan's head should be. Her pants are sopping. Blackjack whines in a chant-like rhythm, an insane singing. With the most effort she's ever exerted, she turns her head around to see an unending pink tongue licking the grotesque wound that was her son's face.

She plants her hands on Johnny's shoulders as blood surges against her skull. The contents of her stomach heaves into her throat and is regurgitated over the grown-up boy she wants to hold and not hold. Again her stomach roars its denial, acid burning the lining of her throat, the truth searing her raw.

THE WILL TO CHOOSE

The pinnacle of the development of ego is the child's recognition of and acceptance of his own physical autonomy. At this stage, the child grasps the concept of the loss of other. Now is when he asks about death, becomes afraid of the dark and worries excessively over the potential disappearance of his caretakers and loved ones. The concept of his own death is more abstract and therefore secondary to the fear of being abandoned by those he loves. He will imagine what it would mean to be alone in the world and will wrestle with the idea until he has some emotional grip on this worst of all scenarios. In this way, he prepares himself to make the instinctive and vital choice to psychologically reject the parent as integral to his personal survival. This is a necessary step toward establishing his autonomous will

This self-assertion marks the transition from physical and emotional dependence on parental figures to self-reliance and independent thinking. Coming to terms with his physical autonomy, the child will begin to own his perceptions, thoughts and emotions. By taking ownership in this way, the child will try and shape the world around him to his liking, gradually discovering and developing strategies to secure his personal wants and needs. This gives rise to the monumental power of choice, otherwise known as free will.

MICHAEL PUNCHES the alarm clock to stop its grating buzz. Half past seven. Beside him, Terese is splayed on her back with her mouth open, snoring as if she's kidding. The sound kept him awake most of the night. He pushes himself up on his elbows and blinks tired eyes at the French doors to the deck. They are veiled in a white lace curtain that wasn't there last night. He reaches for his glasses, puts them on and the curtain is gone, each squared pane of glass now a frame for the dizzying fall of fat white snowflakes. He gets out of bed, goes over to the doors and looks up at the white sky. If he thought it wouldn't wake Terese, he'd open the doors to watch the flakes melt against his hand, catch one on his tongue. Seattle too temperate, his only childhood experience of snow was over Christmastime at Lake Bernard. He remembers the time he skated way out in the middle of the lake, Eden watching from the shore, waving at him to come closer. Alone, pushing off his edges and swinging his elbows, he reached a speed he knew was faster than humans were supposed to go. With the sky perfectly upside down on the ice, his crunching feet loud as rockets, it was the freest feeling in the world. Every year, Eden would knit him two new pairs of mittens, one set always hanging to dry by the kitchen stove. Funny, he thinks, to remember that.

Terese rolls onto her side and her snoring gears down to a nasal whine. A trail of freckles dots her pale back from her shoulder to the opposite hip in a near-perfect diagonal. He looks back outside to where the floor of the deck is now completely obscured by snow.

"Are you up already?" Terese yawns from the bed.

"And I have another birthday gift for you."

"Really?"

Michael points to the deck. "Look."

"Snow!" she exclaims like a schoolgirl, then turns a raised eyebrow on Michael. "Who does that make you? God?"

He laughs. "It has a certain ring to it."

"Come here," she demands.

She pulls him onto the bed, straddles his chest, pins his arms over his head. Her breasts jiggle above his face like happy clowns.

"I think maybe you need to be brought down a notch or two, Dr. God," she says.

"If you, a mere mortal and descendant of Eve, say so. But God is not afraid."

"Are you underestimating the fairer sex?"

The gentle thrumming sound of the kitchen telephone makes them both look toward the door.

"Don't go picking any fruit or donning big leaves," Michael says, shoving her over on the bed. "I'll be right back."

WHEN HE RETURNS, a cozy Terese has confiscated both pillows, the sheet and comforter into one cloudy lump. "Anybody I know?"

"It was Frieda," says Michael, his playful mood gone. "Marcus is gone."

"What do you mean gone?"

"Slipped out this morning sometime. Maybe during the kitchen deliveries."

"No one signed a consent form?" Terese asks like a good receptionist.

"Nope."

"He's not supposed to leave without either your consent or his family's consent. And he was sort of on parole in the first place, wasn't he?"

Michael runs a hand through his hair. He's disappointed at losing a patient at this late stage and worried how this will reflect on his reputation.

"Are you going to call the cops to track him down?" Terese insists.

"It's not exactly a prison we're running. If he wants to leave, he can leave."

"I guess." She runs a nail down his back. "Well, you shouldn't take it personally, Michael."

He wishes she would just stop talking.

"If you ask me, Marcus is a guy who needs his meds. For life."

Michael doesn't reply. He takes socks from his dresser and moves toward the closet.

"Ooh, you can't go. It's my actual birthday and I've got my party suit on." She kicks off the covers with a naughty smile, as if thinking the sight of a naked woman will turn him into a drooling idiot.

"Terese, this is not a great start to my day. What's happening with Marcus is important."

"And I'm not?" She tugs up the covers with a pout.

"Sorry, I'll have to make it up to you."

"But you're going away tomorrow," she protests.

He disappears into his closet, cutting the conversation short.

MICHAEL WRAPS his loafers in plastic bags and walks to work through six inches of snow. Since Terese isn't due in to work until noon — clinic policy for birthdays — he's left her in his bed, told her to help herself to whatever she can find for breakfast. He left a wrapped box on the counter, trusts this little gift will cheer her up and make her forgive him for leaving so abruptly. Inside is a silver bracelet, an original designed by a silversmith in the Torpedo Factory. He'd meant to give it to her at dinner last night but forgot and left it at home.

As Michael walks through the cold, he doesn't quite know how he feels about someone roaming his apartment, touching his things, rummaging in his fridge. Does he feel violated or comforted? If only his enthusiasm for the relationship was as heated as hers. A mere mortal, he'd called her in jest, but that pretty much expressed it. What is it that keeps him from feeling something more, keeps him from buying the fantasy of intimacy? Of love?

By the time he arrives at the clinic, the bags on his shoes are ripped and his shoes are so wet that his socks are soaked through. Another pair of shoes down the drain. He'll have to start driving to work or invest in some snow boots.

FRIEDA IS surprisingly civilized over the matter of Marcus' disappearance, but this doesn't really make Michael feel any better about it. He doesn't like to end the therapeutic relationship until he can honestly visualize the patient with prospects for a decent life. He's jump-started something in Marcus but it's too soon to tell just where that something might lead. For Marcus to stop treatment now is like a person with a bacterial infection stopping an antibiotic prescription halfway through. One doesn't know what new form of microbe might be encouraged to flourish. Michael pictures an aggressive, flamboyantly dressed Marcus picking a fight with the wrong kind of men.

He decides to call Marcus' mother and wife to break the news, and to see if they've heard anything, although his gut feeling is that no one will be seeing Marcus for a long time. He checks his voice mail first and finds a message from Richard Taylor, Kerry's brother, informing him that Mr. Taylor has passed away in the night. When it rains, it … snows, he thinks, swiveling around to the window. The falling flakes now look menacing.

After speaking with Marcus' family, he calls Mrs. Taylor to offer his condolences. Richard answers the phone; his mother is out on an errand. After expressing how sorry he is, Michael asks Richard to pass on a message: he'd like to keep the news from Kerry until he's back from Seattle.

"A conference, yes," Michael offers in response to Richard's query. "Yes, and I have a sister who still lives there. And … my father." He feels suddenly guilty, not because he has a father and this man on the phone doesn't, but because it may not be true anymore.

After he hangs up, Michael rings Dr. Scully to ask if he can add a few extra days to his trip to Seattle tomorrow. "It's my father," he says. "He's dying."

IT'S A long flight, non-stop D.C. to Seattle. The movie, a romantic comedy with this year's young stars, is of no interest to Michael. He sips his scotch on the rocks and reaches into his briefcase for his conference notes. His hand knocks a book he doesn't remember packing and he pulls out Kerry Taylor's journal. He'd forgotten to remove it before the trip. Though by now he's read the scant twenty-three pages several times over, he adjusts his reading light, then flips to a passage that stands out in his mind as a turning point in her pre-patient life. Perhaps, in a year or two, Kerry will be able to continue where she left off:

"Big Daddy's Girl," you used to call me. I didn't really know what you meant until now. Between my dad, Catholic school and Balanchine, I guess I pretty much let men control my life. Maybe I fell for Allan because he wasn't outwardly controlling and this allowed me to feel in charge. Now I realize he's a passive-aggressive type and, though the control isn't as blatant, I'm still letting myself be yanked around. I know I've depended on you, Hugo, an awful lot to get me through life, but I'd like to say that you never made me feel weaker or lesser in any way. You were very empowering in your own demented way. So, thank you.

You know, all my life I've been rewarded for being attractive and body-smart and never gave myself credit that I might have the brains to do other things. Not that there was time for other things. But I've realized I don't have a clue about all these things regular folk know how to do. Like make a decent white sauce, prune a plum tree, refinish a table, read the newspaper and know what's going on in the world. I've been so sheltered, blissfully ignorant of lives other than my own. I know it's a depressing time to start keeping up with world affairs, and I have a hard time understanding how anyone can think war will lead to peace, but I'd like to try to grasp what's going on in this complicated world of ours, and why.

A neighbour, Felice Henry, really nice, who's become my gardening guru, is taking an English course at the University of Victoria this fall — "Woman Authors of the Nineteenth Century." She hates driving alone at night and asked me if I might want to take it, too. I read about one novel every three years but in the past two months I've read all the Brontë sisters' books and am starting in on Jane Austen — writers most normal people would have read back in high school or college. God, our education sucked. I remember my father saying that one year at the Academy cost more than putting both my brother and sister through four years at University of Virginia. You would have thought at those prices we'd have come away with more than a memorized stanza of Hamlet. Anyway, I'm completely into these books and am thinking of saying yes to Felice. I'm not much of a critical thinker but maybe this course will nurture the other side of my brain. The left side, I think it is.

Hey, Wuthering Heights would make a gorgeous ballet or better still, Jane Eyre, which has fewer characters. You could do some fantastic interactive dances with the crazy wife haunting Jane and attacking her husband. You probably haven't read it, so I'll send you the book for your birthday. Thomas is trying to teach me to make friends with the computer, which would come in handy if I took the course. It takes me forever to type, though. Why the hell didn't the Academy teach typing when they knew we'd all be out of work by the time we were thirty-five?

I do love dance, Hugo, but it really feels like time to move on. Time to do something entirely different. I'm still young enough to learn new tricks, I think. Got a few million left-sided brain cells that have yet to be exercised. Felice has also offered to give me driving lessons since Allan and I can't seem to coordinate time to do it. She's great, funny and down-to-earth, very big-hearted. I think you and her would hit it off.

Blackjack's barking rabidly out there. We had a cougar sighting up the road last week. Maybe he's back. Is that wild, or what? Cougars. I have a fantasy of coming across an orphan cub and raising it as a pet. A playmate for Blackjack. Do you think a cougar would eat cat food? Could you train it not to sharpen its claws on the furniture?

Michael closes the journal, making a mental note to return it to Mrs. Taylor when they next meet. He tucks the journal away and takes out his conference notes.

∾o∾

LINGERING IN the walk-in closet, Arlene fingers the milky-brown cotton and silk weave of one of Beresford's sweaters. It's her favourite. They bought it in Myrtle Beach after crabs and beer at the Blue Dolphin. An entire wardrobe, up-to-date and well-maintained, fills the rack and shelves in front of her. A dozen shoes line up in gleaming pairs along the floor. Beresford insisted on good Italian leather, the kind that needed to be polished and buffed.

None of his father's things will fit Richard, who is that much broader, or Patricia's husband, who is that much smaller. Arlene tries to ignore the fact that Kerry-Ann's Allan would have been able to wear almost everything, hand-me-downs more than welcome in that make-do family. Now, Beresford's likeness will be dispersed among strangers, who may or may not appreciate the good taste, the weight and quality of the fabric. Will the shirts be properly cleaned, even hung on hangers? Who knows? Arlene acknowledges each familiar item, bids it an unspoken farewell, inhales his smell still lingering in the cloth, imagines it being absorbed through her hands and scenting her blood, scenting her memories. She rubs a sleeve of his new robe against her cheek. This is too new to give away, she decides, and hangs it on her side for now.

An hour later, five boxes filled, Beresford's side of the closet is bare save for the hollow swing of hangers. Stacking the boxes by the front door, Arlene puts on a pair of leftover surgical gloves and scrubs the shelves clean, tweaking grey corners white again. After vacuuming, she mists the closet with lemon air freshener. Her goal is to have the house in order for the Christmas holidays, to transform it into a widow's home with space for family or an out-of-town friend. She got rid of the hospital bed in the den right away, but will keep the extra bed in her room for now. Kerry-Ann will need someplace to stay when she leaves Rosewood as an outpatient. And who knows how long that might go on for. Besides, why would Kerry-Ann go back to Canada now? Arlene's angry stomach tells her it's lunchtime. Two widows living together, she thinks, heading toward the kitchen, one much too young and naive for such a sentence.

Arlene makes herself a sandwich, then calls Blessed Sacrament Church, where Beresford's service will be held. Her favourite priest, Father McLeod, is out of town but she can't put it off. While cleaning her lunch dishes — a single plate and glass — Arlene receives a call from Patricia. Such an emotional child, thinks Arlene, as a tearful Patricia goes on about wanting to put together a collage for the reception after the funeral.

"Fine, fine, I've got loads of pictures in the albums you can use. But I'm in the middle of cleaning out your father's things ..." Arlene stops as Patricia sobs anew into the phone.

"You can come by after dinner and pick out any items you think you might want," says Arlene. "And you can help me decide which dress to wear to the funeral. I think I'm going to go navy. Let everyone else wear black."

After hanging up, Arlene starts filling another box with her husband's carefully sorted socks, his Italian undershirts, silk boxers and pajamas. Then she sorts his leather jewellery case: ancient rings, watches old and new, expensive cufflinks and a collector's assortment of pins. She puts on his gold band, his wedding ring, pleased with how well it fits her middle finger. She takes out Beresford's onyx pinky ring with the diamond border, bought on credit the day he arrived in Washington, D.C. from Moose Jaw, Saskatchewan. He said the ring symbolized his expectations of his adopted country. It took him three years to pay it off. She'll pass it on to Richard. Though there's no way it will fit around her small wrist, Patricia said she wanted her father's watch because he taught her to tell time or some such sentimental nonsense. And what about Kerry-Ann? Arlene picks up the jewellery case and pictures her as a child of six sitting on the floor, enjoying how it snapped sharply open and (watch your fingers) clapped shut. She was forever emptying it out, mulling over the cufflinks and pins, then replacing the items in a fresh order. Kerry-Ann's never been one to wear much jewellery. A hangover from her performing days, perhaps she'll get over it now. That long neck would look awfully elegant with a thin chain, some matching gold hoops in her ears. Arlene decides to give Kerry-Ann the emptied case. She sets it aside and turns to the dresser.

Arlene struggles to open the bottom drawer of Beresford's dresser, which is weighted down with sixty-odd years of official papers, news clippings, photos and correspondence. Her cleaning mission comes to a halt when, after managing to slide open the drawer partway, she sees an envelope lying across the top of the yellowed files, her name written in wavy letters across its front. She sits back on the bed to open it. The envelope isn't sealed, the flap just tucked neatly inside. Arlene can see her husband at his desk, his shaky hand wielding the pen. When did he write this? He was always one for surprises. As she reads, she hears his voice for the last time. *You will always be my home, Beresford.*

She needs to read it only once and she is thirty-three again, beautiful and beloved by her man, the one she wanted, the one with the bedroom eyes and smooth confidence, the father of her children.

"I miss you," she whispers through a smile, pressing the page to her chest.

Arlene tucks the letter back in its envelope, dabs at her eyes and gets back to business.

∽o∾

KERRY HEARS Johnny knock softly on the opened door and looks up from her boots. He waits for her permission to enter.

"Come in," Kerry says, struggling with zippers on the snowboots her mother brought over yesterday. It's snowed again last night and the grounds are blanketed under a foot of snow, if not more.

Johnny enters tentatively, looking around nervously as if to make sure they're alone. On this afternoon, like every afternoon, Kerry and he are going for a walk together before tea. After tea there's art therapy, then dinner, then gin rummy in the games room. Kerry has started working out each morning, using the barre and mirrors in the gym, while Johnny, her one-man audience, sits on a red, rubber exercise ball and watches. He claps when she does things that surprise, like grandes battements or turns. He says "Whoa," at the fast footwork. Kerry finds the familiar barre work soothing, reassuring. Today, Johnny asked why she scrunches her nose when she watches herself in the mirror. She hadn't even known she did that. She works out until sweat is streaming down the sides of her face and then she and Johnny go for a swim. She spent her childhood summers in a pool or at the ocean and water calms her. She feels the need to keep busy and, for this reason, she encourages Johnny's desire to follow her around like a puppy. Whenever she's alone she thinks too much, remembers too much. The images of the accident hound her, and she is filled with survivor's guilt.

"You don't have any boots?" she asks Johnny.

He stands just inside the door, hands stuffed in the pockets of his windbreaker. "No."

"Your runners'll get wet."

"Oh?"

Kerry smiles sadly. Poor Johnny. She'll ask her mom if Dad has any old boots he doesn't wear anymore. "Have a seat, I can't get the zippers up. These boots must be fifty years old, at least."

Johnny obediently sits in the chair next to Kerry's as she works at a zipper.

"What size shoe do you wear?" she asks.

"Ten."

She nods.

"You have the nicest room of all," he says.

"Thanks." Kerry is touched, but also embarrassed by her mother's decorating: paintings on the wall, curtains framing the window, a real rug. No one else's room has a rug, much less fresh flowers.

Johnny fingers the signature scarf tied around the neck of the lamp beside him.

"I like your name scarves."

"It's a souvenir scarf my father sells. It has all the signatures of the presidents on it. Kinda tacky, but tourists love it."

Kerry sits up, unties the scarf and spreads it over his shaky hands.

"Soft," says Johnny.

"Synthetic," she says, finally getting one boot zipped up.

"Every summer, I watched a lady at the fair tell stories from people's handwriting," Johnny says shyly.

"That's interesting," says Kerry, only half listening as she struggles with the other zipper.

"And I've learned on the computer." Johnny continues. "Abe uses only his initial. That means he's modest. The 'A' is linked at the top to the 'Lincoln' and that means he believes in himself."

Kerry has managed to get the second boot zipped and sits up to focus on Johnny. He's rarely spoken in full sentences before now.

"Say more."

Johnny takes a deep breath.

"His writing is stretched up tall, which means honest."

"Honest Abe," says Kerry.

"The letters at the end are squished together, which means he's stubborn to the end." He glances at Kerry, who nods encouragement.

"Do another," she says, bending back down to stuff her pant legs down her boot tops.

"Herbert Hoover has two big 'H's and the other letters are small and hard. He wants to be a big man in control. There's a loose tail on his last 'r' which means he has secrets."

"Didn't he like to dress up in women's lingerie or something?"

A giggle spurts past Johnny's lips and he looks down at his hands.

"I'm not kidding. Hey, do Bush's. The son. There's two Bushes. Here, I'll find it." She takes the scarf and shows him the signature. "Here it is. A big 'G', a runny scribble with a small 'g' looped on the end that connects with a little 'w.' Then a big spineless 'B' followed by a lump and a trailing line. Looks like a whole lot of nothing," she says with a smirk. "What does it mean?"

"Tough in front and weak behind. Big ideas that aren't very good."

"That's too bad if it's true," says Kerry. "Will you do mine?"

"Yes."

She looks around for a pencil and paper but can only find a pen. She ends up writing on the inside flap of the book by her bedside, Jane Austen's *Sense and Sensibility*.

"Here." She hands over the book and Johnny looks at it for a long time. He glances shyly up at her, then back to the book. "Go ahead. I can take it."

"The curls at the ends of your big letters says you like attention." He stops as if for a reaction. She grins and he continues. "The writing lies back, which means you hesitate … to do what you think." She sighs at this and he stops, looking alarmed.

"No. Go on," she urges.

"Yes, okay," Johnny says, speaking faster, "the 'y's have a closed loop on the bottom, which means you keep feelings deep inside. The squeezed up little 'r's mean," he pauses, "… selfish but the vowels are round so that's not selfish, too." He stops, unsure, his wide eyes staring at the open book on his lap.

"You're amazing, Johnny. That was pretty accurate, I'm afraid."

"It's good stuff," he says quickly.

"Thanks. What about yours? Have you analyzed your own signature?"

"I do printing, which doesn't count."

"You can have it if you want."

"What?" Johnny stares at her signature on the book flap.

"The scarf."

"Okay." He closes up the book and puts it back on the table. Then he rubs the scarf's silky material between his thumb and little finger before stuffing it into his pocket.

A GREY SUN hangs over the river and casts soft shadows across the snow. It's windless, as if the cold has shocked the air into stillness. Something by Satie or that melancholic Barber piece, Kerry muses, remembering the game she and Allan used to play. Realizing what she's doing, she abruptly turns her attention to Johnny.

"Your shoes look soaked. Are your feet cold?"

He only shrugs in reply. She smiles at his odd stoicism and he smiles shyly back.

"We should probably head in." They've been out here for twenty-minutes, if not longer.

"I'm okay."

Her own feet are starting to get cold so his must be numb, thinks Kerry.

She suddenly feels guilty, remembering how tired her mother looked when she dropped off the boots, unusually quiet, too. Kerry wondered if her mother wasn't finally getting sick herself, what with taking care of both her and Dad. When Kerry asked how Dad's hip was feeling, her mother seemed confused.

"We're more worried about you, right now," she said, avoiding the question.

Mom should take a vacation, thinks Kerry, and imagines herself and her dad alone together. A warming thought; she's been missing him so much, lately. She could take care of him, which would help keep her mind off herself. She'd asked Dr. Myatt if she could take a day trip to see her dad, but he didn't think it was wise. "Not yet," he said.

Johnny leaves the path to pick up a branch that's fallen from one of the maples, his footprints destroying the snow's smooth uniform height, its illusion of solidity. With the leaves gone, Kerry spots a bird's nest exposed in a high crook of the tree. She wonders if anything's in it — like old bits of shell, a feather. Would the birds that built the nest be returning in the spring? Johnny is tearing off the smaller branches from the large one, dropping them over the snowy ground like scuff marks.

"What are you doing?"

"Making a walking stick."

"Good stick for it. There's cougars where we live and my husband made me one ..." She stops. It's not "we" anymore, she thinks, and Johnny nods in understanding, rips clean another branch.

A flash of purple emerges through the clinic doors. Norma is bustling along the path toward them, wearing a bright purple jogging suit. She's a lesson in contrast against the dove-coloured landscape.

"Kids," she puffs out with a cloud of breath, "it's my job to pass on the news that Dr. Michael is out west for a conference and Monday's session, that's tomorrow, is postponed until Thursday."

"He told us," says Kerry politely.

"Well, I also need to tell you," Norma continues, "the reason we haven't seen our fellow patient, Marcus No-va-kow-ski lately." She emphasizes each syllable, then lowers her voice. "He escaped like a bandit in the night last Wednesday, off to join the circus maybe. Ne'er a farewell. Best of luck is all I can say."

Norma stamps the snow from her whiter-than-snow jogging shoes.

"Course we'll all be kicked out of here before long. Though I heard tell of one of the cooks leaving," Norma chuckles. "So they might never get rid of me."

Without waiting for a reply, Norma briskly rubs her hands together. "Too cold for me, got to get back to my toasty oven." She turns her head to sing over her shoulder: "Don't be late for tea, you two. It's a treat and a half today!" Norma never reveals ahead of time what the afternoon's confection will be.

Kerry watches Norma hustle purposefully back to the entrance, the swish of her nylon pants amplified in the quiet. The sound of a plane landing at Reagan National roars overhead and Kerry's stomach hollows with anxiety. The safe predictability of the clinic is ebbing away from her. She feels like she's being handed the reins to a horse she's not sure she's ready to trust, much less ride. Marcus always initiated things in group. The thought that she'll never lay eyes on him again is disconcerting. And Dr. Myatt — she was hoping to share her recollections of the accident with him. He'd told her to expect repressed memories to return and, now that they have, it feels important to talk about them. Not that she'll be able to do so without bawling like a baby. She tried to arrange a meeting, had tracked him down in the staff room, but he was in the middle of talking to the receptionist, Terese, who gave her such a cold look she didn't want to interrupt. And now he's gone on this trip.

"Where will you go?" Kerry asks Johnny. "After here."

Johnny shrugs, eyeing her carefully. "Where will you?"

She hesitates. "Home here for a while, I guess, stay with my folks. Just until I can think of something ... I loved Vancouver Island but don't know if I could ... go back."

"I just want to be where you are," Johnny says quietly. He reaches for her hand.

She smiles at him, squeezes his hand and brings it to her lips for a kiss. "You've been such a good friend," she says. When she lets his hand drop, it remains suspended in mid-air. He looks stricken. "We'll keep in touch, Johnny," Kerry reassures him, but it doesn't seem to help. She doesn't know what else to say. "Let's go in, okay?"

Near the clinic entrance, Johnny stashes his walking stick behind some tall bushes.

"For later," he says and Kerry nods.

Hootie greets Kerry with a broad grin as she and Johnny stamp their feet on the inside mat.

"Got some colour in your cheeks there, Kerry, darlin'," Hootie says.

Kerry notices Johnny clenching and unclenching his reddened hands. They must be burning cold.

"Come on in and get yourselves warm," urges Hootie. "It's almost tea."

He helps Kerry off with her coat while Johnny hangs back, stuffing his hands into his coat pockets. He looks like a jealous little boy, thinks Kerry. She hopes she hasn't led him to believe their relationship is more than it is.

"Oh, Kerry, darlin', I meant to mention it on your way out. I'm real sorry to read about your Daddy passing on. Such an interesting name he had — Beresford."

Kerry smiles sweetly at Hootie. *What?* She looks to Johnny, who's staring at her wide-eyed.

"Sounded like a good man who did a fine job of his life. Left behind some real gems." He winks both eyes atop a fresh smile and then the intercom buzzes and he steps toward the computer.

"Thank you," Kerry says numbly, her mind struggling to understand. Why didn't she know? Why wasn't she told? When did this happen?

THEY ARE at the bottom of the stairs when Johnny sees his girlfriend's eyes glaze over, the colour drain from her cheeks. Two more steps and Kerry's eyes roll up, up and away. Despite his readiness, Johnny bruises his knees when he catches her, her perfect head only inches from the stone-tiled floor. He, Johnny Bourne, will carry her himself, all the way to Mrs. Carter, the name with the perfect oval shapes and softly slanted letters, the name he trusts. Kerry weighs more than he thought. As he climbs the steps, he feels his arm and back muscles working, imagines them bulking up. He looks down at the woman in his arms, her skin slack in the crescent arcs of her cheeks, her eyes carefully closed. He knows she's not asleep but hibernating, to keep the pain from getting too close, too fast. It's a quiet walk, just the two of them, his breath loud and hollow in the narrow tower of stairs. At each landing, he has to sit and rest, pull her angel heat against his heaving chest. He is relieved that now she won't be going away anytime soon, but afraid that when she wakes she might be angry, might hurt herself. He rocks her ever so gently, strokes her hair, tells her he'll take care of her. When his muscles feel better, he starts again, one step at a time, just the two of them.

When he arrives on the third floor, his hero's muscles are burning. In a voice that won't wake Kerry, he asks the receptionist, Terese, where Mrs. Carter is. Terese takes one look at him and the world erupts with yelling and buzzers, like a game at the amusement park. Big Bryson is rushing toward him, then prying Kerry out of his arms. She wakes with a single piercing scream and Johnny winces, knowing she wasn't ready to wake up. Then Kerry's voice is silent and her body starts screaming.

"Don't hurt her," Johnny wails, watching his angel flail and thrash in Bryson's arms. She is so strong that Bryson grits his teeth.

Mrs. Carter is yelling at Terese to call Dr. Myatt. "And call Mrs. Taylor. Kerry's mother should know what's happening."

His pinky finds its hole and then Mrs. Carter is asking him something, but it's only words and he doesn't hear her.

THE CONFERENCE over, a teacher-training workshop in place for the spring, Michael is in good spirits as he heads to dinner with Isabelle at their childhood home — his mother's house, as he has always thought of it.

He's seen Isabelle only once in the past three years and the ease and familiarity between them takes him by surprise. She seems to have become mellowed by motherhood, and has a more ready humour than he remembers. Tall, blonde and narrow-faced, she looks like a female version of their father. Her husband is also fair, as is their eldest child, Connor. But the younger boy, Galen, has his grandmother's olive tones, her dark-set eyes and hair. The boys call him Uncle Michael and he willingly plays the role, wrestling their small muscles and strong imaginations on the matted floor of the family room, a cheerful addition since Michael's day. There is a kindness residing in these walls, a calm that was non-existent when the house was ruled by his mother. The fireplace blazes with a fire and the former glare of white plaster has been soothed by warm taupes and reds. Arrhythmic jazz on the stereo helps erode his memories of operatic laments, of his mother hushing him as she listened and grew moody. Judging by the disposition of her boys, Isabelle appears to have survived their childhood with her maternal instincts intact.

Michael waits until after dinner when they're alone in the kitchen, him washing, her drying, to ask if she's heard word about their father.

"What father?" Isabelle says dryly.

"True enough."

"Actually, two years ago my lawyer called and told me of an education fund started in my boys' names. Had to be him. Hard to stay mad at him after that. A torn man is how I think of him."

"Torn between?" Michael asks, wondering if Isabelle somehow found out about Eden.

"Between humans and plants," she says, making Michael smirk.

"He did love his work," Michael says. "How old would he be now? Seventy-five?"

"Seventy-eight. He was seven years older than Mother." She looks out the window into the dark. "After she died, I gave up looking for him. I moved on, so to speak. There's only so much energy one can spend on trying to mend the past."

"Hey, that's what I do for a living."

She smiles. "Sorry."

"You and Paul seem to have a solid relationship," he ventures, trying hard not to sound like a psychologist.

"He's straight-ahead," says Isabelle. "And I trust him. That means a lot."

Michael responds with a kiss to her cheek.

"How about you, Michael? Will my boys ever have cousins to boss around?"

Michael pauses. "What makes you think they don't already?"

They laugh together, like old friends.

ISABELLE'S HUG is prolonged when it's time for Michael to leave.

"I wish you weren't living so far away," she says, before letting him go. "It's nice to have some family around. Especially for the boys," she deflects.

Michael agrees, genuinely appreciative of the evening, of the sense of family. As his taxi pulls out of the driveway, he looks back at the house. Tomorrow he'll visit the other house he knew from his youth.

It's early Monday morning when, handing over his room key, he asks the hotel clerk if he has any messages. No news is good news, he figures, trying to suppress the nagging concern he carries for his patients even when he's on the other side of the continent. As if they were children and not adults, he chides himself; half of them are older than he is.

And as if he has any real control over their fates. Despite Frieda's antagonism, Michael is happy knowing she's in charge. He knows she wouldn't hesitate to contact him if anything, however small, came up that he could be blamed for.

On the taxi ride to the rental-car dealership, he checks his cellphone one more time, knowing it won't work where he's going. It's drizzling today, in that non-intrusive yet persistent West Coast way. At the dealership, he chooses a four-wheel drive for the back roads — a white Jeep Cherokee with a superb sound system and, just in case he'll be spending a night or two in the car, seats that fully recline. Only after he hits the highway does he remember that radio reception will be basically nil after the halfway point. Now he can almost hear the crackling hiss from his father's old truck radio when the ride turned bumpy and trees grew so thick and tall they blocked out the light of day.

MICHAEL SPENDS a rainy Monday night in an empty motel — the same one that he and his father used on their trips. The place is virtually unchanged save for a satellite dish squatting in the trees and cable TV in each room. The same Haida paintings, with their confident black curves, hang over the same single beds covered with the same bumpy chenille bedspreads to make those ancient trips seem like yesterday. One of the paintings is of an eagle, one of a hummingbird, and Michael's reminded of a story Eden once told of boastful eagle challenging all the birds to a contest to see who could fly the highest. *The day of the contest, hummingbird hid on eagle's back and when eagle flew as high as he could, far above all the other birds, hummingbird rose up off eagle's back, flying just that much higher and winning the contest.* Michael never knew what to think of her stories, yet somehow they've stuck with him. He makes himself a sandwich from the groceries he thought to buy at the last gas station, then twists the top off a lukewarm beer. After his meal he flops like a kid onto the springy bed, flips through the channels and falls asleep with his clothes still on.

The morning air smells clean from the night's shower, the cold sky loud with the cryptic croaks of ravens hidden in the cedars. A sound, thinks Michael, like the smell of burning meat. Pulling out onto the narrow highway, the sun breaks through the cloud cover and the straight stretch of road, wet from the night's rain, gleams in front of him like long black hair.

After a few hours and a stop for breakfast, Michael reaches the turnoff and the sign of a leaping buck. He remembers this sign. As a kid, he used to expect herds of deer to begin vaulting in front of the truck and was always disappointed. He recalls spying a deer, once or twice, tucked in the woods and staring over but never did he see one leaping, flying like the picture implied. This reminds him of the chicken wire fence Eden built around the summer garden, "the deer fence." It was as tall as his father. When Michael asked her why it was so high, she told him that the deer could clear anything lower. Which means, he thinks, eyeing the woods, they could quite possibly start flying over his Jeep right now.

He turns off onto a pitted dirt road, the four-wheel drive handling the bumps one hundred percent better than his father's old Ford pickup. Michael drives for an hour through a fortress of trees that block out the sun, the radio reception dead and gone. If his memory serves him, he thinks, feeling a child's anticipation, the bottom end of Lake Bernard is around the next bend.

As he rounds the corner, the trees on the right give way and the sun breaks through for a second time that day. The expansiveness of the lake is a relief to the eye and Michael pulls onto the shoulder to get out of the car. The sun skips and darts over the lake's ice-veiled surface. Large spruce trees line the embankment, leaning into the lake like giant divers about to spring. The cold air widens his nostrils and he whistles through the gap in his teeth. His tone is reedy, windy, never the good streamlined sound of his father's that Michael had tried so hard to copy. He surprises himself with an unkempt tune and his body feels lighter, his joints loose. Muscle memory reassociation, he qualifies, then squints across the long mile of water, knowing that the old cabin sits almost directly across from this point. He sees a wavy line of smoke winding out of the trees and his heart beats a little faster. An eagerness, a kind of naive hope, accompanies him as he sits back behind the wheel, and he immediately shuts down.

The thought that his father has possibly been hiding here all these years feels confounding in its obviousness. Maybe his father wanted to be found. Maybe even his mother knew and didn't say anything. It would have been a simple matter of pride in her case. *Why didn't I think to look here?* Michael asks himself. *Why have I kept the obvious at arm's length? Even now. It's taken him — what? — almost three months to decide to finally come here.* He suddenly can't imagine why it's been such a big deal. Two grown men saying hello, how are you, comments on the weather, the hunting season.

Michael parks at the mouth of the road that leads down to the cabin. He wants to, feels the need to, walk the rest of the way through the woods. The smell of dirt, pine sap and chimney smoke peel back the years. The curves of the path are unaltered. The trees are taller, but so is he. Though snows rests in the crooks of branches, the ground is dry, hard with cold; it's the time of year when dirt feels clean. His approach is soft-footed to match the surrounding quiet, his ears instinctively awake to sound. The dipping boughs of evergreen usher him forward like welcoming hands.

Near the end of the path, the firs give way to a grove of aspens and Michael remembers a clearing hidden in the grove that was his childhood retreat, his fort, his submarine, the place he'd go to sort his feelings when they threatened to overwhelm his clarity. He'll visit it later, but first he's anxious to see who's home. An old blue Volvo wagon is parked in front of the dilapidated shed that stores a rusted wheelbarrow, a shovel, rake, hoe, stacks of firewood. An axe is sunk into a stump and he can visualize the arc of his father's arms, the torque in his long back before the sound of the wood breaking open, hitting the ground in two uneven chunks. He climbs the partially rotten steps to the wide veranda, the dry, grey boards creaking under his weight. He loved sitting out on this old porch at night with his father and Eden, watching the bonfire on the ground below, its flames sparking skyward as if this were how stars were made. A neat row of wood is stacked along one wall and at the end there's a large box full of kindling and twigs. Two worn rocking chairs creak in the light wind. He understands, suddenly, that his father is old now.

The screen door shrieks open under his hand and a piece of firewood reshuffles itself. The questioning cry of a raven rings in the trees followed by a sound like dripping water. *The raven is the great imitator and can mimic any sound he likes. To make you think twice and then think again.* Michael raps on the wide boards of the wooden door and a similar knocking echoes in his chest. He gives three more raps, a bit louder this time, before he tries the doorknob. The unlocked door offers no resistance and the cabin's warmth beckons him inside, making him aware of how cold his hands and ears are. There's the smell of something cooking, a soup or stew of some kind.

"Anyone home?" His voice evaporates like steam.

He steps inside the small entryway, where a pair of gumboots and worn slippers line the floor under hooks hung with a yellow slicker and a heavy wool knit sweater he recognizes as his father's old sweater, the one made by local First Nations people. *They leave the lanolin in to repel the rain.* He goes inside to the main room. The same kitchen table, couch, black cookstove and armchair sit on the same faded and scratched floor. There's the door to the bedroom where his father and Eden slept while he slept in here on this couch with the dog named Raven. The door is closed and Michael pictures his father in there, asleep, dead. He crosses the floor but then stops at the sound of his own footsteps. He should wait for Eden, or for whoever made this soup. She'll be back soon enough.

There's a new door off the kitchen through which he sees the corner of a free-standing tub. An addition, he thinks, remembering the rickety outhouse he had to use back when. Late at night, the throw of the oil lamp would make the small enclosure look as if it were swaying and Michael recalls feeling mortified at the thought of it toppling over at a crucial moment and exposing him to Eden, invariably waiting in the dark on the other side. He was always embarrassed, yet grateful that she insisted on accompanying him.

Now, he notices the tongue-and-groove bookshelves. These he doesn't recall. But as he moves closer, he finds the bound books are familiar even before he reads the titles. His father's library of botanical books. He draws a breath. There is a framed photo of a small boy, maybe two years old, sitting on his father's knee. The boy is pointing to whomever is taking the photo, a look on his face as if he wants to be there with the photographer and not with this man with the pipe hanging from one side of his mouth. He recognizes the young man as his father, the boy as himself, the picture obviously taken on the veranda of this cabin. But how? When? His father didn't bring him to Lake Bernard until he was four or five.

Michael turns from the pictures, suddenly uncomfortable at having intruded into someone else's home. His father is no better than a stranger by now. Michael goes back outside, turns up his collar against the cold, listens for a footfall. Maybe the man's not bedridden but out walking. Certainly he's the type to die on his feet, still working. Retracing his steps back down the road to the aspen grove, his old retreat, Michael dodges the whips of branches and makes his way into the small clearing. Enveloped in his old sanctuary, he can feel himself relax. It's darker than he remembers. The aspens have grown and block the light but still the place is more peaceful than gloomy, and the muse of a child's imagination is still present. Michael doesn't recall the large smooth-shouldered rock in the corner; for if it had been there back when, it would have been his throne or desk, a wild boar, a secret door to the underworld. Moving closer, he notices the uneven ground extending out from the boulder's sloped face. Closer still, he sees the thin lettering worked deep into the uncompromising surface. He fingers each ragged letter, letting his hand absorb both the name and its meaning:

ALEXANDER MYATT

1927 – 2002

A shiver of wonder lifts the fine hairs of his neck, then something quieter settles him to his knees. Relief, perhaps, at having his biggest question answered. Disappointment, too, of being let down once again. But this time he's not sure who has let down whom. Michael scratches at his chest, at a disconcerting itch well beneath the skin. He lost his father too long ago to grieve now, he tells himself. Still, he can't help but wonder when it happened. How many weeks, how many days ago?

The dogs come out of nowhere, barking in tandem but staying at a distance. Michael stands to face them. The mongrels are groomed, well cared for and they approach with territorial confidence. He offers his upturned palms and they come forward to sniff his hands, humble their heads for a pat. One of the dogs looks identical to Raven, except that this one's no more than a pup.

"Raven?" Michael says quietly and the black dog's ears prick and his tail wags.

Michael hears the slow deliberate snap of a twig behind him and the dogs leave.

"Her grandson. I've passed on the name," comes a voice that both soothes and unnerves him. Eden. Michael turns around slowly to see the dogs, snouts raised in canine devotion, sitting by their master. A long black braid polished with grey snakes around the shoulder of his father's mistress. The broad face beams a wide smile, and the gap between her two front teeth is far more blinding than the water ringing her eyes.

For a moment he can't move or think. The dog Raven whines into the silence, until finally Eden bows her head and speaks in a small voice.

"Your father passed away ten days ago. Peaceful enough. He would be glad that you have come."

The words sound rehearsed and ring false in the cold air. His eyes fixed on her face, Michael feels his whole body hardening, willing itself to reject whatever comes out of her mouth.

"Why didn't anyone tell me?"

"I wrote you. Didn't you get my —"

"Not about him. About you," he says, nearly sneering.

She drops her eyes, her hand searching out Raven's neck as if for support.

"Your father took you away from my breast when you were just two years old."

Michael turns away, unable to look at her.

"How could I refuse my son the opportunities of the educated? I was young and trusted the wisdom of my lover." Her voice is shaking. "He assured me of your health and happiness. 'He will have a sister to play with,' he told me, 'two mothers to love him.' I did not see you again until you were almost five, when you were suspicious of my eye and my touch."

Michael imagines that her voice is the wind now swaying the tops of the trees and not coming from an actual flesh and blood person. "'It is best that he doesn't remember,' your father told me, 'it'll keep matters simple.'"

The wind has stilled. The trees are a sea of petrified ears.

"I have tried to forgive myself for my cowardice," Eden continues, her voice cracking slightly, "in being unable to claim my own son. You had moved on with your life. It didn't seem fair to you."

Michael glances over to see tears running freely down her face. She makes no attempt to wipe them away. He knows it's his turn to say something, but he can't. Won't. He jerks his head away, surprised by his body's violence. *She has no right*, says the voice in his head. His empty stomach churns with anger.

"I felt I had to wait for you to come to me." She lets her words settle. "It is so good to see you."

By the change in her tone, Michael judges that her little speech is over.

"There is hot food on the stove," she says simply. Out of the corner of his eye he sees her turn and walk away, the dogs following.

Cold enters his bones where his feet contact the ground. Right now, this sensation is the only thing he knows to be real. The renewed rustle of aspens sound like hushed laughter scorning the identity he's worked for years to assemble and make sense of. It lies now on the hard ground, a puzzle that's been kicked apart. He picks up a stick and heaves it to splinter against his father's gravestone.

THAT NIGHT, Michael sleeps in his car. He can't stay but he can't leave, not yet. His dinner is a day-old sandwich and a bag of chips and he listens to some crackling country station on the radio, the only station he could find, until he fears his battery will die.

In the morning, Eden brings him steaming oatmeal, resting it on the hood of the car.

"I would like you to come inside and get warm," she says, making her words loud enough that they can be heard through the closed window and beneath his pretension of sleeping. Then she leaves him alone, still waiting for him to come to her. He is colder than he's ever been but doesn't budge, only turns on the engine to generate some heat. Later that morning, Eden appears again. She tells him she has to take her car into town, and then drives off.

Michael gets out of the Jeep and eats the cold oatmeal still sitting on the hood. He takes a long walk around the lake, then returns to chop firewood and stack it. Anything to keep moving and not think. He finds fishing gear and fishes off a rock through a fissure in the ice, but doesn't bother to bait the hook. He avoids his former sanctuary, now his father's grave. Who's the biggest liar in all this, he wonders. His father? Or which mother? At least one was honestly hateful of his existence.

He returns to the cabin at dinner, hungry enough to eat what Eden offers. They share the kitchen table in silence. The second night, Michael sleeps on the couch despite Eden's insistence that he have the bedroom. She keeps out of his way and the next morning he stays for breakfast. The rest of the morning he chops wood and walks, applying all he knows, all his professional expertise, to sort out his emotions. He tries several times to sit and settle into his body, touch the places that know without knowing, but each time, something in him revolts and he is up and walking with even more urgency.

At lunch, he watches his fists pound on the table like a child having a tantrum. When his soup bowl crashes to the floor, his voice comes out of nowhere. "Spineless, deceptive, self-pitying liar!" Something drops out of his chest and, startled for breath, he bolts from the cabin, down the road to his rented truck. He doesn't care that he's left his coat behind. He just needs to get away from Eden. And his father.

He drives too fast, cursing at potholes and the staring trees. He yells his questions at the sky.

"Was it his money she wanted? How could she hand me over to that bitch of a mother? To someone who could only loathe my existence? Why should I care that I was lied to all my life? That my real mother was some teenager, dumb enough to listen to reason?"

By the time Michael reaches the sign with the leaping buck on it, his anger has played itself out and he's ashamed and embarrassed by how he's acted. He's nearly forty and he acted like a five-year-old. No, he thinks, laying his head against the steering wheel. Like a two-year-old.

∽o∾

ARLENE FINDS it unforgivable, how Kerry found out about her father. Unforgivable. Also unforgivable was that Dr. Myatt was out of town, "on a vacation of sorts and unable to be reached," as the receptionist, Terese, told her. Arlene had had enough of hospitals and clinics by then and was going to take Terese's advice and care for her daughter at home. But when she saw Kerry-Ann all doped up and hanging in her chair, mute as the day she picked up her daughter in Victoria, she'd almost lost it. Almost. She knew she couldn't care for Kerry-Ann by herself. Not yet. She had a husband to bury first.

"I assure you, she's not catatonic," Mrs. Carter told her. "She's just choosing not to communicate for the time being. And we've had to dose her to keep her from harming herself." The nurse seemed terribly apologetic and urged her to reconsider removing Kerry from Rosewood. Still she gave Arlene the names of two local therapists she called "excellent."

Arlene had gone home and called the one person she could think of who might know how to help Kerry get through this. Hugo had cried on the phone, said he'd hop a flight the next day. Told her she sounded far too stoic considering. She appreciated that.

After signing the necessary paperwork, Arlene removed the large objects from Kerry's room — the paintings, curtains, flower arrangements and rug — along with most of the clothes. Then she left her daughter to stay one more night until Hugo's arrival the next day. His flight was to arrive in Baltimore at six in the morning and he was going to rent a car and drive directly to Rosewood. "Don't worry," he told Arlene. "I'll deal with The Girl."

∽o∾

"WHERE'S Big Daddy's Girl?" Kerry hears through the opened door. Something leaps into her peripheral vision, landing on pillow feet. The something — or someone? — has bags hanging off it.

"Ta da!" sings the bag man. His feet are moving toward her chair.

"Hello, Beautiful," he whispers, too close to her ear, and she is lifted forward in her chair and pressed up against him. Why? He sets her back in her chair but his face remains so close that she can smell mint on his breath. Minty bag man. "You know, I remember when you used to be a whole lot easier to lift."

He parades across to the window, his pillow feet hardening, and she hears the blinds clattering open. Light fills the spot on the floor where she stares, bringing out dark red flecks in the grey linoleum. She hadn't noticed them before.

"At least they gave you a room with a view. Loved that film. Now, my doll, let's get down to the ABCs of taking you home."

Kerry can hear the clunky music of things being packed, the chime of hangers.

"Whatever are you doing here in Club Dead? You, the sanest neurotic I know."

She knows this voice, yet doesn't. All the voices she knows have been taken away when she wasn't paying close enough attention.

"No brain, no pain. Always a favourite motto of mine, too."

The minty bag man is kneeling in front of her now.

"Girl, you look like shit, if I do say so. What sort of drugs are you on? I tell you right now, I got better ones."

She feels glasses being put over her eyes and the arms tucked behind her ears. The grey floor is now tinted red. "Here, you need these more than I do. They're all the rage in Frankfurt, and that stare of yours is scaring me, to say the least. Now," a minty hand is lifting her chin, "can that head just straighten up a bit more?"

Keep your head up. Eyes out in front. Too heavy.

"Years of posture training down the pipe. The *peep* as we say *en français.*"

Her chin is pushed up, knocking her teeth together. Chunk. Why does he keep touching her?

"Better close your mouth before you catch flies, dahlink. Oh, what was that teacher's name? The Czech pedophile always after skinny Cindy with the boobs? Karoly something? Well, anyway, the glasses help a lot. Now you just look depressed. Depressed I know. Depressed I can do."

There are crinkling sounds like hard rain. Things going into bags? Or coming out? The red bits in the floor are now black.

"Arlene told me what this hotel is costing you. Could've taken me on a Baltic cruise for that price. If you weren't so fecking stubborn, that is. I'm desperate to see some fjords. Fjords, I love that word. Fjords. It's even refreshing to say."

More hard rain.

"Look what I picked up in the airport for you. A pair of those cigarette pants you like so much, so you can show off your golden arches. And *voilà*, a thigh-length tailored jacket." Something soft slips across her lap. "Feel that, if you dare. Linen and silk. All a nice depressing black, save for the," the spots are suddenly gone from the floor, "ecru camisole. Ooh, you're going to look fine ... from the neck down. Now, let's get you out of that granny gown."

The minty bag man starts to tug at her clothes. She doesn't care enough to resist. She has been dressed and undressed by other hands for months now. He is just more hands.

"You're not helping me," the bag man is singing again. "A little cooperation, pullease."

The glasses are knocked off as soft fabric sweeps over her face. The floor is gone, then back, grey again with dark red flecks. Her skin is cold. Hot, cold, it's all the same.

"I thought Queen Arlene said you'd gained weight. I don't think so. I've gained ten pounds since Germany. They've got pastries to die for called bee stings. Thin layers of pastry, custard and then a thick layer of icing over top trimmed with chocolate. Ooh, I'm going to drool. Then there'll be two of us."

A light clatter to the floor. "Oh shit, my glasses. Cost me eighty euros, those. I know, ridiculous. One could feed a small African nation."

She is being dressed now, the goosebumps on her legs being covered first.

"When you hit puberty, let me be the first to buy you a bra. Jeez, could I have a little help here? It's like dressing an infant," he grunts, pig-like now, and she feels her hand bend precariously in a sleeve. It hurts, but not nearly enough.

The bag man's feet mark a fourth position on the floor.

"There we go. Whoa, fabulous fit. Now if you'd just sit up a little straighter," he says, shoving her shoulder. "And, Girl, we've got to do something about the Barbie look." Her ponytail is tugged up and then dropped.

"I say we chop it off and bleach the hell out of it. Look like the twins we are at heart. We've all outgrown the bun thing. It's allowed now. And unless you learn to speak up between here and the salon, Kerry-Ann Taylor. What's that?" A silver ear blocks her view of the floor. "I can't hear you."

His black boot taps out a rhythm on the floor. "I think I just might have to get you good and mad." His voice deepens to a darker blue. The boot stops. "Always worked for the stage."

The floor is moving away from her now.

"Goddamn it, Kerry." The wheel stops turning. Again there is hard breathing near her face. "Don't do this to yourself. Much less me, who hasn't slept ever since Queen Arlene called forty-eight hours ago. Come on, my friend, the symphony's warm." His voice is urgent, sad music now. Vivaldi's *Winter.* "And when it comes down to it, we're all soloists in this life." His minty head drops into her lap, warm and silver. Shot down, something wets her hand, needs her help. With heroic effort she straightens up to see what sort of animal the neighbour's cat got this time. It's a large animal, a dog, with a silver head, a soft black coat. Cashmere.

"I'm so sorry," the animal moans. "I know what you're going through and I should have come sooner. Shouldn't have listened to that stick doctor of yours." He lifts his head. "Hey," he barks, "you're sitting up straight.

Oh, sweet-faced girl, it's so good to see you. Can you lift those icy-blues and look at me?"

He is squeezing her hands.

"It's okay. You're going to be fine, we're going to be fine."

She can't look at the animal's face but she's happy it's going to be all right, sad that it will heal and leave her. Her eyes feel wet now.

"Tears are good." The dog takes her face between his warm paws, his lips touching against one cheek, then another. His nose too dry. A finger draws on her face. "You got your head on straight, that's a start. I know you're in there somewhere."

She turns her hands palm up on the arms of her chair but his silver head is gone, the floor is moving again.

"Now, my pet, let's pull ourselves together and go face the big bad world. You have to say a proper goodbye to a father who had more grace and style than the late great Nureyev, though probably not quite as nice an ass. 'Course, I never saw your father's ass. Ooh, slap my face." There is the sound of a slap. "In three days is the memorial service and funeral party. I love Arlene for throwing a party at a time like this, so we need to get you back to form."

Barres stream past her ears and there is light up ahead, voices.

"Queen Arlene has asked for my ideas on the buffet menu. It's going to be understated, as is fitting, but still fabulous. No frozen Sara Lee cakes for you, Sweetheart, I'm sorry to say. We could round up a few if you ask real nice like. Then maybe I'll whisk you back to Frankfurt and strap some toe shoes on those feet and get some more mileage out of you. Germans are partial to blondes, as you know, and I promise not to give you any speaking parts."

The friendly dog voice won't stop talking. "Now let's keep the tears and the wine flowing. And, you know, I'm completely serious about the hair." She sees an ear again, trimmed with silver circles. "I can't hear you," he sings.

"You're taking her, then." Another voice. A quick worried one.

"She's mine now. Sorry. But I must say, Fraulein, you have dimples to die for. I can't tell you how much my friend here wanted dimples.

Isn't that right, Kerry, darling? But you should see this girl's arabesque line." A dog whistle rings out around the room. Kerry feels her shoulder being patted. Good dog. "Can't have everything, now can we, Golden Girl?"

"Best of luck to her," says the worried voice.

"She doesn't need luck, she's got me."

THEY GO outside in the cold air, then inside, where there are smells that burn the nose. She is lifted out of her chair and into one with red leather. Brown wood floor drops away on either side, a shelf of brush and combs, a jar of blue liquid.

"We have to cover the mirror," says the familiar voice. "Until the end."

"She asked for this?" a small deep voice, a mole's voice.

"In so many words. May I do the honours?"

There is a tug of her hair, the sound of gnawing and Kerry's head is lighter, a million feather-fine pick-up sticks exploding soundlessly onto the floor beside her.

"There's some weight off those shoulders." A paw squeezes one shoulder. Now her other shoulder.

"And what kind of cut is she after?" The mole sounds alarmed by the dog.

"She wants it just like mine."

A hand mushes her head.

"Cropped close with a just a whiff of bang in the front. But she wants it in gold to offset my silver. Don't you, Kerry," the dog says, two paws now, heavy on each shoulder. "In memory of the Varna ballet competition of whatever year that was. Really, I also should have taken home the gold. I nailed every one of my double tours and ended my à la seconde turns with five pirouettes. Five," he says, in a top dog voice. "A deduction for the run in my tights, if you can believe that. Totally unfair. Now, this girl won the gold but only because she kept batting her ice-blues at one of the judges. Isn't that right, Kerry?"

Her spine knits closer together. The dog is barking too close to her ear.

"Her fouette turns were all herky-jerky, if I recall. But, then I ask you, David, what's fair in this world? Not much."

A light rain sprays her neck and ears. Little tugs and then sissonne, coupé. Pull up and sissonne, coupé. Sissonne, coupé forward and back, coupé, sissonne side and side. Something tickling her face, falling in her eyes, tumbling down her sloped plastic shirt. Sissonne, coupé. After awhile, wet paint slopped on, here, there, over and under. A stinging. More burning smell. And then roaring heat in her ears, the world moving away.

"A little more lift in the front," the dog is saying as he mushes her head some more. "Dazzling colour. Eighteen carat. Wonderful. You are an artist David, truly. Now Miss Kerry-Ann, ready for the unveiling? I don't believe she's ever had short hair," he says. "A Daddy's girl, if you understand my meaning. Gothic section of the orchestra, go. The mirror please, David."

The space in front of Kerry becomes a shade lighter. Fingers, not paws, hold the sides of her head and bend it back. In front of her sits another version of herself, only this one has no hair but yellowy gold feathers stuck to her head like the hairpiece she wore in *Peter and the Wolf*. She danced the Bird and the dog, what's his name now? — danced the Wolf. He, the other face in front of her with the silver head and all the hoops in one ear. Not a dog but a wolf. The wolf. The wolf named Hugo.

"Look, Kerry," says Hugo, his wolf face nestles cheek to cheek with hers. "It's spirited, daring, it's the androg look in all the mags. What do you —" He stops as Kerry straightens her head and looks directly at him.

"Hu … g … go …" The words stutter through her teeth and lips. "You b … bitch."

Hugo leaps around in front of her chair, badly startling the hairdresser, and kisses her full on the mouth.

WHEN KERRY and Hugo arrive at her mother's apartment, Arlene opens the door and does a double take. At first, it looks to Kerry like she's not going to let them in.

"Kerry-Ann?" says her mother, blinking back tears. "You're back. With a haircut," she adds, turning to Hugo.

"Doesn't she look marvellous?" Hugo smiles grandly.

"It's … really bright," says Arlene and Kerry would laugh if she had the energy. "But never mind, you're here, up and talking again." She kisses Kerry's cheek and hugs her. "Hugo, you're a miracle worker." She hugs him, too.

"That makes you Patty Duke," Hugo says to Kerry. He swirls his hand around her head. "With a new do."

"Don't worry, Mom," says Kerry. "I hate my hair, too."

Hugo laughs gaily and Arlene ushers them inside.

"The key is to piss her off," Hugo whispers to Arlene.

"I heard that," says Kerry.

"Nice coat," says Arlene to Hugo. "Is that cashmere?"

AS ARLENE prepares for Beresford's funeral, Kerry is left in Hugo's hands. All Kerry wants to do is sleep and watch mindless TV, take long baths and eat peanut butter. Ignoring her protests, Hugo bundles her up and takes her on outings in his rented Honda Civic. They go on long meandering walks in the National Zoo, Georgetown, Rock Creek Park and along the Potomac. She holds his hand and their conversations wander where they will. To the men they've lost — Allan, Thomas, Kerry's father, Hugo's lover Frederick and every boy they knew at the Academy, except Stephan and the one straight guy, Peter. Hugo talks about Frederick's seeming remission before his death, his "glamorous" funeral and the piece Hugo choreographed and performed for the occasion. Kerry tells him about her time at the clinic, about a boy named Johnny, "simple but deeply understanding, who did handwriting analysis," and about Dr. Myatt, "distant and somehow close at the same time, hot and cold." She doesn't have to explain herself; Hugo has always understood her piecemeal language. "You mean Dr. Stickuparse," Hugo renames him.

The two of them ponder fate and karma, endings and beginnings, and the simple senselessness of life. The next day, Hugo takes Kerry to the Vietnam Memorial, "the crying wall," as he calls it. Kerry doesn't understand why they're here until he places her hand against the cold marble and begins to read out the braille of boys and men, all strangers but strangers with such ordinary, familiar names. And soon she's crying and then he's crying and then tears won't stop. For an hour they lean against the black marble and against each other and weep. They drive home in silence, until Hugo tells her they're going to stop at McDonald's for fries and strawberry milkshakes.

Each day they go to the grocery store because Hugo insists on fresh ingredients for dinner, which he also insists on cooking. Kerry doesn't have the energy to complain and Arlene is relieved to have one less thing to worry about. He makes lamb loin chops, roasted vegetables in a rosemary vinaigrette and couscous with pine nuts. The next night it's poached red snapper, asparagus and scalloped potatoes. He buys Kerry slippers lined with rabbit fur. A stuffed llama. He buys several flavours of Häagen-Dazs ice cream and force-feeds her as they sit side by side, watching the videos he's taken out of the library. They're the old Russian classics — *La Sylphide, Coppelia, Giselle.* She listens to him exclaim over the line of one dancer ("as good as Bujones") and scorn the turns of another ("turned in supporting leg") all the while picking apart the choreography. He makes up what the dancers are whispering to each other.

"The guy in the third row's mine."

"God, your breath reeks."

"I love pudding."

"My hemorrhoids are in remission, Boris."

Kerry can't quite muster a laugh, but she does smile at times. When she needs to talk, Hugo pauses the video and listens.

"I tell myself that I'm nothing special," she says. "That people lose their loved ones every day and not because of a stupid accident either. I mean look how many innocent people died in Vietnam, and on September eleventh, on those planes and in those towers." Kerry nestles deeper into Hugo's shoulder. "And it helps to think of others and not just focus on me and my losses. But still, my body feels like it has these huge holes in it. Like it's missing a lung or a breast and now my father's gone, too … and I just feel so … disjointed."

When she starts to groan, shaking her head and shoulders, he holds her head against his chest.

"Losing people isn't an idea. It's real food and we have to eat it, digest and shit it out. It takes time, though, Girl. Two years, people tell me. In two years, the missing appendages grow back. They're not as strong as the originals, but still they work."

Kerry stops talking and Hugo starts the video again along with his running commentary.

"Time either moves too slow, too fast or disappears altogether," she says and the dancers are again held in freeze-frame. "I prefer when it disappears, since I can't stand to remember the past or think about the future without Thomas, Allan and my father in it."

"A German friend of mine, who's a Buddhist," Hugo tells her, "says that death is only a continuation of our story. That we keep evolving, life-time to lifetime, so that whatever we've learned from dancing around in this body isn't wasted. He calls what continues, 'karmic consciousness.' Fancy words for 'soul' is how I see it. Anyway, I'm voting for reincarnation because then there's still hope that I'll be able to get it right some lifetime down the road. My friend also says that, lifetime after lifetime, we keep reconnecting with the people we love." He brings Kerry's hand to his lips. "I'll be your trained monkey in our next life together."

Her feeble attempt at laughter ends in tears.

At night, Kerry ignores her mother's distraught looks and sleeps with Hugo in the den. With the help of Hugo's little yellow pills, she falls asleep with her ear pressed against his chest, listening to his heart. Da dum. Da dum. Da dum. Da dum. One hard beat followed by one soft. Like a limping walk.

∽o∾

JOHNNY SLIPS into the hall unseen. He's overheard that Kerry Taylor won't be needing a nurse this evening and he is hungry to see her.

Desperate to see her. It's been three whole days of missing her at meals and for afternoon walks, missing her flying legs doing their exercises, her fast card dealing. It's been three whole nights of waiting to hold her soft hand in his and look into the only eyes that really understand.

He cracks Kerry's door an inch and instantly knows she isn't in her bed. He enters and closes the door behind him. The bells around the doorknob are gone. He stands motionless in the darkness, moonlight sifting through the blinds. The silhouette of Kerry's ruffled curtain no longer frames the window and the walls are missing their pretty pictures. The perfect white sound of her presence is gone; the scent of flowers, of her, is replaced by disinfectant. As his eyes adjust, he can see that all surfaces are cleared of her belongings — the crystal vase of fresh-cut flowers, the books, the get-well cards.

His angel has been taken away.

Without any notice. Without planning. Without saying goodbye. Why hadn't Mrs. Carter said anything when she let him play on her computer this afternoon? She would have known about it. Why didn't she tell him?

Johnny doesn't bother to sneak back to his room. No one will notice his walking down the middle of the hall well past curfew. He is now permanently invisible.

The bedside lamp is the only light in his room and it shines down on the orange Frieda left for him three days ago. He couldn't bear to eat it in his worry over Kerry. Its cheery presence taunts him. He imagines a sneer on its tiny orange face. She would have left him sooner or later, even if she had been able to say goodbye. He hears Kerry's voice in his head: *You've been a good friend.*

Johnny takes the orange and rips at the rind with his teeth, spitting ragged strips to the floor. He tears apart the sections, chanting his rhyme and tossing the pieces against the wall.

"She loves me, she loves me not."

He throws each piece with more force than the last and the wall bleeds pale-orange beads. He stops when there are two pieces left.

"She loves me, she loves me ..."

The segments fall to the floor and Johnny's energy leaves his body like air from a balloon, in one great whoosh. He takes the walking stick, the one he had found on their last walk together, out from under his bed. Then he arranges his bed the way he does to look like he's sleeping.

Standing in his bathroom, Johnny faces the mirror. He has wedged the walking stick beneath the lock on the door and against the base of the toilet, good and solid. Now, he feels for the scarf he carries in his pocket, the one he rubs soft against his hand in the day and up against his face when he sucks his finger at night. He feels for her signature in his other pocket, takes the slip of paper out and eats it. He looks in the mirror at his pimpled face and red hair. Then he punches the image above the sink, once, twice, three times, until the image fractures. Shards of mirrored glass fall into the sink and onto the floor. He searches for the sharpest one.

THE ORIGINAL church, next to Kerry's old Catholic school, has been torn down, and the land is now stuffed with pastel-coloured townhouses. The new church, built on the rectory grounds, is a simple rectangular box of ashen-coloured brick. Only a silver cross on its facade distinguishes it from a furniture warehouse. The wan brick continues on the inside, as if there hadn't been enough money in the collection plate for drywall. Gone is the rich dark wood, the carved pillars and rolling archways of the church in which Kerry fidgeted every Sunday of her childhood, fretting over the endless ways to sin. The pale birch altar, plopped on top of grey wall-to-wall carpet, is all straight lines and looks like it came from IKEA. No kneeling rails guard the sacred, no rich brocades drape the boxy chairs and the plastic marbleized baptismal built into the corner reads "JACUZZI" on its side. What beauty remains is reserved for the twenty-foot-high, stained glass mosaics gracing the wall behind the altar, one of Joseph, the other of Mary, and Kerry is grateful for this one sin against pragmatism. A framed picture of her father sits on a low table in front of the altar. It's an old picture, a professional portrait taken when he was maybe fifty, his face in profile, glasses off, a debonair smile on his lips. It's not the face she pictures when she thinks of him, but his eyes are the eyes she remembers, and her heart trips in her chest.

Hugo had helped Arlene brighten up the church with numerous flower arrangements sent by those unable to attend. As he walks Kerry to the pew in the front reserved for family, he snips off a purple bachelor's button and strings it through the lapel of his black jacket.

"I love black and purple together," he whispers.

The Irish brogue and towering authority of Monsignor Quinn from Kerry's youth has been replaced by a fastidious, nasal-toned priest enamoured by the sound of his own voice. It's obvious he didn't know her father. The perfunctory service mirrors the low-budget surroundings and is alleviated only by the heartfelt presence of family and friends and the harmonies of the church choir. Before the sermon begins, Kerry's sister, Patricia, is invited to the podium to do two readings from the Book of Job. One of these was slated for Kerry, but Arlene didn't want to "risk any displays." Hands and voice shaking, Patricia starts reading. Kerry listens closely, trying to glean some meaning or comfort from the archaic talk of alphas and omegas, sin and redemption. Patricia's face mirrors relief when it's over, and she stumbles a little as she steps down from the podium. Next, a family friend tells stories of the "good ole days" and how much they all looked up to Beresford, "who always knew what he wanted and how to go about getting it. His family, though, was always first on his priority list. Never saw a man more proud of his family." Last, and with his father's poise, Richard reads a well-rehearsed but heart-rending eulogy on behalf of the family. This brings most of those gathered to tears and polite nose blowing. The more stalwart, Arlene included, clear their throats.

Kerry, too, sits dry-eyed, observing the tribute to her father as if from a distance. She can't shake the sudden knowledge that she missed the services held for her husband and son last August. There was one in Vancouver, with Allan's family, and one here in Virginia. Arlene had relayed all the details — who had come, the lovely things said — and had showed Kerry the notice she wrote for the paper. Allan's mother sent a long letter describing the sister ceremony, including photos. Kerry has yet to get around to opening the envelope. She's mostly afraid of the pictures, of seeing the coffins, one large, one child-sized. Nothing has come close to solace or closure for her. And now her father is gone, too. These men she loved have been swept from the earth and she can't accept it. If only she could grasp why, the understanding might settle under her feet like an island and perhaps she could stand. Instead she only feels numb and frustrated and alone. So alone.

The sermon, self-consciously savoured by the young priest, wafts past her like a neutral smell. When it's time for Holy Communion, Kerry mechanically follows her mother into the aisle. The wafer on her tongue is as white and bland as the service. The body of Christ should taste like sweat and rusty nails, be tough as gristle, she thinks as she sits back in the pew. A thin pain seems to worm its way through her bones and undecipherable emotion spirits along her muscles like oily balls of mercury. It's suddenly torture to be sitting here, hands folded, doing nothing, pretending that words could possibly address the pain of losing your only child. She needs to move. She pictures women wailing together, pounding their black robes against rocks, furious at this fact of death and beating it down. She needs to move to some edge, touch the wall that separates the dead from the living, tear at it with her teeth and nails.

The organist hits the opening chords of the final hymn. It is her father's favourite, "Amazing Grace." The devotional voices of the choir cause a tiny implosion in Kerry's chest and she closes her eyes. The music moves through her, momentarily easing the struggle and opening small doors that seem to lead to bigger ones, doors that have been held shut for a long time. The concluding notes hover under the vast ceiling before trembling to a close, pinning Kerry precariously to her seat. The mass has ended and the pious priest steps from his ugly throne and proceeds down the centre aisle. The Taylor family falls in behind him and, when Kerry remains seated, Hugo is there, touching her shoulder.

"You coming?"

"I just want to sit here for awhile. You go on." She's breathing hard through her nose.

"You all right, Kerry?" Hugo hesitates, and moves to sit down next to her.

Kerry nods emphatically and pushes his hand from her shoulder.

"I'll come check on you shortly," he says, and kisses the side of her head.

She laces her hands together in prayer, bows her head, listening to the muffled sounds of people leaving. Finally there's silence. She wants to yell into it, call out to that other realm, whatever and wherever it is. She wants so much to feel their presence, hear their singular voices again.

Kerry lurches to her feet. She steps into the aisle, then up to the open space in front of the altar. Letting her eyes close, she hears the choir in her head. She takes her floor-length, pleated skirt in both hands and flares it like a fan, her neck arching back as she lets her breath go. The gold crown of her head swoops down like a body falling from a great height and she pushes over, under and between the music filling her ears. Straining and surrendering, retracting and unfurling, her body burns pathways and tunnels, reaches places where words have no light.

ᥝᥱᦂ

HAVING THANKED people for coming and sent Richard and Patricia on ahead to the reception, Arlene asks Hugo to help her pick out and bring along the nicest floral arrangements from around the altar. As she and Hugo pass through the doors to the church hall, their attention is caught by movement. In front of her father's picture, Kerry is dancing like a wild animal suddenly freed from its cage. Arlene is afraid her daughter's lost her mind once again. The violent fluidity of her long pale arms leaves an afterimage like a hundred strips of trailing silk trying to catch up to two. Her head whips around and around in abandoned pirouettes and her legs, pulled by the sharpened points of her feet, are thrown skyward, circumscribing the air.

Hugo reaches out an arm and gently stops Arlene. She looks around anxiously and sees Mrs. Evans, a church volunteer, hurrying down the hall in their direction, head-bent toward her next duty.

"What she's doing?" says Arlene. "She really shouldn't be —"

"She's saying goodbye," Hugo whispers. "The way she knows how."

A storm suddenly spent, Kerry slowly unfolds until she stands still and upright. She makes no sound as her shoulders begin to convulse and her head lolls back before her knees unhinge her to the floor. Hugo rushes forward, leaving Arlene alone to intercept Mrs. Evans.

"Any programs left in the pew?" comes Mrs. Evan's busy-bee voice.

Arlene's lower lip is vibrating beyond her control and, unable to answer, she turns her face away. Thus far today, Arlene has proudly succeeded at needing only dabs at her perfectly appointed eyes. She held her own watching Patricia's quivering chin behind the podium, gulped handfuls of air during her son's tour de force. Now she pretends to dismiss the grieving contortions of her youngest child. Mrs. Evans moves in with ready-made sympathies and Arlene's eyes prick frantically before something akin to a gasp lurches from her throat. Black tears streak her cheeks as she pushes past Mrs. Evans to stumble down the aisle and collapse alongside her weeping daughter. Hugo's arm encircles her shoulder and she hides her face in his black shirt, careful to avoid his silk tie.

"Crying is so cleansing," Hugo whimpers, then bursts into a wailing so unrestrained it sends Mrs. Evans running from the room.

AFTER THE last guests have left the reception, the Taylor family, plus Hugo, retire with the leftover food and wine to Arlene's apartment. Having already surrendered her dignity at the church, Arlene is into her fourth — or is it fifth? — glass of wine. With her legs tucked beneath her in the large white chair in her living room, she's tired and thoroughly relieved this day is behind her. She sits and listens to her children and their spouses talk about the faces they haven't seen in twenty years, about Richard's eulogy, about the way the priest kept smoothing his hair. Then Patricia tells of the morning Beresford died and how she'd dropped Evan off early to school and rushed over to console Arlene. "But Mom wasn't here, only Richard, because she'd gone to get her hair done!" Everyone laughs until tears jangle in their eyes, even Kerry.

Arlene looks down at her glass. It is suddenly full again, and she realizes that Hugo, sensitive to being the non-family member, has taken on the role of server and bottle washer. Dear Hugo. She can see him through the door of the kitchen, putting plates away. With his proud nose and incisive eyes, his general sleekness, she'd label him a fox, no, he's too tall and more grand ... a wolf.

She sips her wine and watches her granddaughters flit about the dining room, two canaries, in a whisper of make-believe. The two boys, whose animal counterparts elude her, are worn out from the late hour and seek places to lay their heads. Evan finds his mother's lap and Marshall is leaning against his Aunt's chair, staring with primal content while Kerry softly toys with his hair.

Arlene senses Beresford's presence, clear and strong behind her. She reaches her hand to her shoulder and rests it there. A familiar warmth settles over her. Looking around the room, she realizes how her life will continue on in so many faces, in so many stories, and knows that when it's her turn, she'll go without a fuss.

✂◦✂

KERRY EXCUSES herself and steps over Marshall, always her favourite, now asleep at her feet. She searches out Hugo in the kitchen, makes him stop washing glasses and pulls him into the bathroom. She locks the door behind them.

"Miss Kerry," exclaims Hugo, "I was like a proud parent watching you dancing in the church to —"

"Hugo, listen, I have to go back to Metchosin," Kerry says, squeezing his fingers.

"Of course you do, sweetie —"

"No, I mean soon, now, tomorrow. It's time, I have to see that …"

"Now, don't get me worked up again," Hugo says, wincing as he extracts his fingers.

"Hugo, Mom's bound to give me a hard time, but I've got to be there."

He just smiles. "This is the pigheaded girl I know and love."

"Hugo."

"I've got a friend in the airline business."

"You have friends in every business."

"What exactly are you implying, Ms. Taylor? I'm a friendly sort of guy is all," he says in a beguiling tone while slipping an arm around her waist.

Kerry hugs him tightly around the neck, her body sighing in gratitude.

TWO DAYS after the funeral, Kerry leaves for Canada. She promises her mom that she'll call every other day to compare survival notes.

"I have to see that they aren't there," she pleads. "I have to have a ceremony of my own. And I know it has to be there. Don't ask me to explain. You might see me in a week but, right now, I have to go."

Her mother nods. "I've never understood this uncommon child of mine," she says, lovingly brushing the back of her hand along Kerry's cheek. "But I know I don't have to. In fact, I prefer not knowing. To be kept guessing. Life needs its carrots to keep it moving forward."

"Thank you," says Kerry, simply.

Bags packed, Kerry goes into her mother's room to help herself to a sweater for the plane. Opening the drawer, she hits her hand on something hard and she lifts up the top sweater to see a groomed seven-year-old Thomas smiling up at her. She picks up the photo and there beneath is the picture of Allan hugging her from behind. Her mother must have put them away, afraid how she might react but, oh, it's so good to see them. Her husband, her son, whole and perfect and real. She sees from their faces that their lives were decent and good, and the ache in her chest is almost bearable. She replaces them in the drawer and gently pulls a sweater over top.

ON THE DRIVE to the airport, Kerry tells Hugo to remind her to mail the card she wrote to Johnny, explaining her sudden departure. Johnny must feel a little abandoned by her. Hopefully he has some place to go after the clinic. Kerry tells herself that Mrs. Carter will look out for him, make sure he doesn't fall through any cracks. She'd debated whether or not to put her phone number on the card and at the last minute decided not to. Better to stick to writing. She'll track him down next time she's in town, take him to lunch. When they stop for gas, she spots a blue mailbox on the corner and gets out of the car. Before slipping the card though the slot, she kisses it, sending him her angels.

ꜱꜱ

GAZING OUT the plane's window to blue sky above and a sea of clouds below, Michael replays Eden's words in his head. He wonders what sort of time frame he should give his mind to assimilate what his body has understood all along.

As the voice of the pilot announces the time-zone change and imminent arrival at Reagan National, Michael is anxious to get back to his work. Back to his first, overall successful round of patients. Not counting Marcus, that is. He has one more exercise to present, the list of hypothetical questions to help with the transition from the clinic and back into the world. Questions that provide patients with a sense of possibility, of forward vision and daring, now that they have some ground back under their feet. *"If you could choose anywhere in the world to live ... if you could choose any famous historical figure to be ... any profession ..."*

Too bad about Marcus; his answers would have been entertaining. Mostly lies, no doubt. Michael shifts uncomfortably in his seat. He has just realized he still doesn't know his mother's last name.

AS MICHAEL walks up the arrival corridor, he's surprised to see Terese in the crowd up ahead, waving at him. He has no free hand to wave back so he throws her a smile of recognition. She looks almost teary. The last thing he wants right now is a scene. He's hardly deserving of her tears and feels instantly guilty. Her arms are around him before he can even stand his bags upright.

"Oh, it's good to see you," says Terese with a little whine to her voice.

"You, too." Michael hugs her back but doesn't linger.

"I wanted to surprise you, but also wanted to be the first to ..." She takes a sharp intake of air as if holding back emotion. "The first to tell you all that's happened. I didn't want you to hear it from Mrs. Carter or Dr. Scully or anything."

What is she talking about? Someone jostles past. An announcement plays over the loud speaker about a car in a no-parking zone.

"I've got my bags. Tell me in the car?"

A few minutes later, Michael sits in Terese's car in the covered parking lot and she tells him everything.

"I still get all tense remembering that awful nerve-pinching squeal and Mrs. Carter yelling. I've never heard that woman yell like that. The drilling must have lasted for a half hour at least. Apparently he had jammed a stick under the bathroom lock so that Mrs. Carter's key was useless. Made a real mess of himself. Blood everywhere, so I'm told. I can watch it in a movie no problem, but I have no stomach for real blood."

"Is he …?"

"Luckily he didn't seem to know where to cut himself so he was still alive. Passed out from loss of blood but still alive. He's in the hospital now, but Dr. Scully's having him committed."

"Oh, no," groans Michael.

"I think it's because of Dr. Scully seeing Mrs. Carter in such a state. She was really losing it, if you can even imagine it. I know I couldn't. She was talking a mile a minute when Dr. Scully took her upstairs. I heard she's taking time off for once in her life. Bryson says she might take early retirement." Terese's emotionality is unconvincing. "I wanted to give you fair warning that you're expected to report directly to the board to answer to Johnny's attempted suicide and other issues that have been brought to their attention."

"Other issues?" he asks. Not that it matters now, he thinks. His posting is over. Maybe his whole career.

"I accidentally glimpsed a memo from Mrs. Carter to Dr. Scully. Something about her witnessing inappropriate physicality with patients." She looks at him, and Michael sighs and shakes his head. She continues, "Also, a romantic liaison with a staff member. Me, which is none of her damn business. There was mention of our using your office for what she termed 'a licentious rendezvous' whatever that means. How she found out about that I have no idea. She didn't mention the elevator," Terese snickers and Michael resists an urge to hit something.

"There was mention of indecent drawings found in your desk files? I certainly hope they were of me."

Terese playfully slaps his shoulder, and Michael feels himself tensing all the more.

"Her intention was pretty clear and I felt you deserve to know what you're up against. If you need someone to stand up for you, I'm there," Terese blathers on, oblivious to his distress and to what this really means.

"How's Kerry Taylor?" he manages to ask.

"Oh." Terese hesitates. "Well, actually, she's gone home."

"What?" he says with such force that Terese jumps.

"I tried to call you but you'd already left the hotel," she says quickly, guiltily.

And my cellphone? he thinks but doesn't ask.

"Hootie didn't know she hadn't heard the news about her father and gave her his regards. So she had another fit and wasn't responding to anything. Mrs. Taylor thought she'd be better off at home."

"Mrs. Taylor thought that?" he says accusingly.

"Yes," she says. "Don't yell at me, Michael. You came on to Kerry Taylor, didn't you? When she was catatonic."

Michael throws open the door with such force it leaves a dent in the parked car beside it. He rips his bags off the seat, slams the door shut and gives the car a kick. Then another.

"Hey," yells Terese from inside the car.

~o~

AFTER RETRIEVING their bags from the carousel, Kerry and Hugo wait curbside for the bus that will take them to the Seattle ferry terminal. There, they will board the Victoria Clipper that will carry them across the strait to Vancouver Island.

"You live at the end of world," Hugo grumbles. He lists the different modes of transportation they will have taken to get to her house. "Car, plane, bus, boat, taxi ... You doing all right?" He takes her hand.

"I'm all right. A little nervous."

"Which is good. Which is normal. I can't wait to see this little house I've heard so much about."

Kerry smiles weakly and Hugo pulls her into him. A boarding announcement comes over the loud speakers and they pick up their bags and ease into line.

"Never liked boats," says Hugo. "I get bulimic on boats."

"Funny," Kerry says, a smile nudging her lips. "Hugo, I can't begin to tell you," she says suddenly, "how grateful I am —"

"For the haircut?" says Hugo. "You're welcome."

Kerry tousles the glittering shoots of her haircut. "My head is always cold —"

"I know what you look like," Hugo says, taking an appraising step back. "An intellectual dyke."

Kerry smirks. "The antithesis of me."

"Your intellect's as healthy as the next dyke's. You, Girlfriend, have just never been encouraged to use it. And besides, two-thirds of our brain's in our feet. We're dancers."

Kerry looks down at her feet and the line starts moving.

"And as for the dyke bit, ooh, they'd eat you up, with whipped cream on top. And you can bet they know a thing or two between the covers. Don't close off any options."

"But, really, I'm so grateful that you came all this way with me."

"Well, I wouldn't have missed your church routine for all the queers in China," he says as they trundle up the gangplank to the ferry. "Are those whitecaps? In the harbour?"

"You really don't like boats?"

THE SUN'S UP and streaming in the window and Kerry just can't sleep anymore. And she can't just lie here for fear of thinking too much. She looks at Hugo who is passed out on Allan's side of the bed. Even with the Dramamine he bought on the ferry, he was still sick on the boat. It had been dark by the time she and Hugo arrived and Kerry insisted they keep the lights off and go right to bed, knowing that the onslaught of memory would be slightly easier to take in daylight. Hugo, in no shape to argue, had dropped his bags and let her steer him where she would. She doesn't know how many pills he took, but he lay down and hasn't moved since. Now, she kisses the top of his silver head and he rolls over. She gets up, throws on last night's clothes, and walks as quietly as she can to the kitchen. She makes a pot of tea while trying to shield her eyes from the pencil lines on the doorframe marking their respective heights, the date next to each of their initials. Thomas was up to her shoulder ...

She also tries to ignore the swaying branches of the young plum tree out the window, the one she'd planted, with Thomas' help, just last spring. Tea finally made, she grabs her jacket, slips into her boots and hurries outside to stand on the back porch, the porch that Allan had replaced, board by board, and that they had all helped paint. She continues off the porch, across the grass and out to the road in the direction of the shore, hot tea spilling over the sides of her mug.

When they arrived late last night, she'd found the spare key she'd duct taped under the rusted mailbox last winter. She'd been planning to paint the mailbox forest green and then stencil on their last names, "Taylor/ Mason," in a cream colour.

"Ladies first," she'd argued when Allan questioned the order of the names.

She felt bad about the short notice she'd had to give to the tenants who'd been renting the place since August, but they were really nice about it and told her over the phone, they'd already been looking for a place in town. She couldn't tell if this was true or if the woman just felt sorry for her.

The overcast sky has a silvery underbelly that lends a warmth to the bay, Mount Baker a stencil drawing beneath the distant fog. Last night, awake in her bed, she'd listened to the wind bang the loose drainpipe she'd been reminding Allan to fix. This morning is windless and the ocean slaps lazily at the pebbled shoreline.

Kerry's boots sink into the rounded stones, deeper with every step, and her favourite spot draws her into her skin. She'd forgotten how this place grounds her, synchronizes her body and mind and, for a moment, her senses widen out into the view. This place, new to her once, is newer still this morning. She tells herself it's a second start, only this time she's starting alone. She sits down on the beach, eases a niche into the stones and cradles her hot tea against her belly. Prokofiev's *Romeo and Juliet*, "The Ball," she thinks, looking at the sky. Allan would have said Leonard Cohen's "Suzanne." She tries to smile and out of nowhere, a whip of cold wind stings her face. Before she can register her reaction, she's hurled her mug to shatter against the rocks.

"Why?" she screams at the water and sky. "Why, goddamn you, Allan, weren't you paying attention?"

A gull shrieks as if in response and then the world is quiet again. Hot tea has spilled onto her pants and she smacks at the burning sensation spreading over her skin, adding insult to injury.

"Why wasn't I paying attention?" she says in a quieter, harder voice. "If only I hadn't gone for that goddamn cookie. If only I had kept my head up …" She bangs her fists against her thighs. "Why, why, why?"

Kerry buries her face in her hands, her choppy breath loud in her ears. The ocean, refusing to be quiet, to be ignored, relentlessly laps at the shore just beyond her feet. She hears its push and pull, push and pull, and thinks that if she leaves the pieces of her broken cup out here, the sharp edges will eventually be rounded smooth by that sound. She lifts up her head and looks out at the horizon. Tears start falling like easy rain.

MICHAEL LICKS a stamp onto the envelope and looks out his office window at the few deciduous trees. Their leaves are a brilliant newborn green. It's been five months since his dismissal from the prestigious Rosewood Clinic, and his private practice in Port Angeles, Washington, has been slow to establish itself. Port Angeles is a coastal town, blue collar, with a large First Nations population, many of them Salish. His mother's people. His people. It's only a few hours drive to Lake Bernard, but he's not yet made the journey. Eden has written him several times, explaining and even defending the choices she made long ago. Unlike then, she's finally fighting for him. He reaches for Eden's last letter, still open on his desk, to reread the last paragraph:

Your father came to me because I was easy, never asked for much. His wife challenged him more, was probably better for him, but I was grateful because I loved him in place of you. Your father was a good man, but for some reason he was afraid to get his heart dirty. It's a shame to go to your grave without knowing this kind of joy.

Michael has just finished a letter to his mother, his first communication since that day last November. He reads the name on the envelope before tossing the letter in the out-mail tray. Eden Paul. Now he knows where his middle name came from.

The kettle whistles from the kitchen. His secretary, Mrs. Crowden, must be making tea. He's made an office out of the two front rooms of the small house he bought. His practice is partially subsidized by the government because the majority of his clients are unable to pay, and the house arrangement makes living more affordable. Built on a hillside, the house has a view of the ocean. This is the main reason he bought it.

Michael starts doodling on one of the loose papers strewn about his desk. He hasn't dated since coming here, hasn't had the desire to engage women on that level. Today Mrs. Crowden told him she planted her pumpkin patch over the weekend and when the fruit are the size of base-balls, she's going to carve her grandchildren's names in them. "The kids get a kick out of watching their names grow right along with that pump-kin," she told him. "And when Halloween comes, they get to carve a face on the other side."

Her words had taken him back to the Halloween party at Rosewood and as he lifts his pencil from the paper, two round eyes emerge from under his hand. The eyes he met for the first time on that dance floor, eyes that made him question who he was and how he was. Michael opens the bottom drawer of his desk and lifts out Kerry's journal, flips to the page listing her favourites.

Favourite place: Shingle Beach, Metchosin

Michael makes a note to look up Metchosin on a map. Wouldn't be far by boat, he imagines, looking out his window at the hazy land form just visible across the strait. He balls up the paper, shoots it over to the blue plastic recycling box and misses.

∽o∾

ARLENE RUMMAGES in the kitchen drawer for a screwdriver to pry open the sliding glass door in the den. The entire city is on orange alert but she doesn't believe those earnest faces on TV saying a chemical attack may be imminent. She's buying the "may be." She did buy her duct tape, though, along with some extra canned goods that are stacked on the floor of the bathroom closet, the room she's put aside as her "safe room." What she does know, judging from the lineups, is that the hardware stores are doing good business. Which is more than she can say for her scarves.

Dini has called in a panic twice in the last week to see if Arlene is all right and to read off a check-list of "necessary" items with which to stock a safe room. Dini sounded excited by the prospect of being under attack and Arlene had to hold herself back from suggesting she move back and join in the drama.

In all of her fifteen years here in this apartment, the sliding glass door in the den has never been opened. Beresford was too chilled in the cool months and insisted on air conditioning in the heat. They had accessed the balcony from the living room only. Spring has splattered the landscape with green glitter and when she sits down at her drawing table, she wants to be able to smell that colour. It takes twenty minutes of frustrated effort, but she gets it. Sliding open the heavy door, wisps of green air rush around the room, causing the phone bill on the desk to float happily to the floor.

Since Beresford's passing, thoughtful friends have made sure that Arlene's days are full and active. On top of tennis, she lunches daily at the club and has kept up with the latest gallery openings. Recently she's begun a painting course two evenings a week entitled, "The Richness of Watercolour." It's the evenings that she finds the hardest. The hardest and the longest. She spends most weekends at Richard's or Patricia's, though prefers it at Richard's because his house is bigger and Patricia's husband, Bill, likes to sit around in his undershirt and his boy-sized chest under his man-sized head makes her squeamish. Once a week, on Thursday nights, she talks with Kerry in Metchosin.

When Arlene called last night, Kerry-Ann sounded pretty good, definitely less fragile. She's been seeing a female psychologist her doctor recommended and is finding her helpful. "Healing" was the word she used. She was planting her garden and looking forward to trying new things — kholrabi, arugula, kiwi and cantaloupe. Arlene found it hard to believe that kiwi and cantaloupe could be grown anywhere in Canada but Kerry said it wasn't uncommon in B.C. Hugo was coming in August for Kerry's birthday and Kerry thought she might accompany him back to Germany to see the opening of his new ballet, "Phallistic." She is looking into teaching a few classes at the local rec centre come the fall, though she is totally out of shape.

This weekend, Arlene has declined Richard's invitation to stay over, deciding instead to try and shake this idea for a painting from her system. She pours herself a second glass of wine before sitting at her drawing table. Without Beresford here, the sound of the television is replaced by the soft sound of classical music and her untouched hair is rooted in tiny white shoots. She mixes watercolours, practises her strokes and lets her hand wander randomly. At some point, she doesn't know when, her dabbling becomes a beginning.

Hours later, she lifts her head from the canvas, confounded at how seven o'clock is now pushing ten. Climbing off her stool, she stands for a groaning stretch. Draining the last sip from her glass, she regards her painting.

An elongated square of light shines from an unseen source onto a blue surface. Half full with water, a Mason jar straddles the boundary of light while, on the illuminated side, a single rose nods its velvet head over the jar's edge. The red petals arc toward the blue ground, which resembles sky more than anything. The rose looks too fragile to live and one curled red petal, just let go from the stem, is falling into the blue.

"Well, that's depressing," says Arlene. "But it's pretty good, if I do say so myself."

She picks up her empty glass and makes a mental note to look up the deadline for the next senior's show at the Torpedo Factory.

Epilogue

Dear Hugo, thought I'd never again lay eyes on that lovely journal you gave me but guess who showed up on my doorstep the other day? Dr. Stickuparse, as you once called him, my old doctor from back in Alexandria. It was totally bizarre to see him after — what is it? — over two years anyway. I was in the middle of writing a paper for the environmental restoration class I've been taking, when I looked up and saw Dr. Myatt, Michael, at my screen door. It was a weird flashback to see him and I was a little shaken at first, afraid it would bring up old stuff. But he seemed so different, and I didn't go back there.

Apparently Michael was at some conference in Victoria, remembered that I lived in the area and wanted to return my book. It was awkward knowing he'd read my journal. God knows what I said in it. Michael didn't seem to recognize me at first, the hair probably. Short hair's so nothing-easy to care for, I decided against growing it out. Mom says I look like David Bowie and that no man wants to go out with David Bowie. Who cares? I say. Anyway, Michael was as shy as a schoolboy. I think he was actually checking me out as potential "love meat" as you call it. It was all rather uncomfortable. I showed him around — not much to show — made him some tea and, since he'd come all this way, walked him down to the beach. On the way back, we passed Felice, who was driving into town. She stopped, of course, nosy as she is, and had to make sure she knew who the stranger was. She called me later to say she thought he was "seriously hot."

I was surprised hearing that Michael was no longer at Rosewood. For the past year and a half, he's had a private practice in Port Angeles, which is just across the Strait in Washington. Said he worked mostly with local First

Nations people, told me he was half Salish himself. The Salish thing makes perfect sense now that I know. Michael's really interesting looking, with these broad cheekbones and golden skin. His looks are a strange combination of intellectual and rustic, if that makes sense. He's got these warm chestnut-coloured eyes, which I'd never noticed before now. He was way more approachable, more real, than I remembered. Finally got the stick out, I guess. Of course, he was my doctor back then and had an agenda to keep.

In his last letter, Johnny told me that it was Dr. Myatt who got him out of the bin and into the halfway house in Maryland. I give Michael points for that. Johnny's got a job. Did I tell you? It's something to do with making circuit boards. I'm going to visit him when I'm home next month for Arlene's seventieth. Johnny feels like my kid brother by now. I always hated being the baby of the family.

When Michael was leaving, he said he wanted me to know that he had learned a lot from having me as a patient. I didn't pry but I was curious what he meant. Then he asked me if, the next time he was in town, I'd like to go out to lunch or dinner. Yes, Hugo, he was looking for "love meat." I said I wasn't sure, but I'd think about it. I gave him my number, though.

I like the idea of dating a man across the water. That's close enough for the time being. Right now, Hugo, I feel like I'm learning how to be alone for once in my life, even to love myself a little. I'm not such bad company.

I ACKNOWLEDGE the following people who offered their insight and encouragement in the early drafts of this book: Joan MacLeod, Cathy Benfey, Leslie Covington and my writing group, the LFC — Janice McCachen, Carol Matthews, Laurel Bernard, Lucy Bashford, Penny Hocking and Patricia Young — whose collective genius and kindness was and continues to be indispensable. I thank Jan Geddes for her dream about teeth, Sean Virgo for his ribbon tying and my agent, Carolyn Swayze, for liking the book. I especially thank my husband, Bill Gaston, for his overall infectious creativity and, more specifically, for his skillfully offered criticisms; and my editor, Lynn Henry, for being so damn smart and willing to share it.

— Dede

VAL MONTAGUE

DEDE CRANE has been shortlisted for a CBC Literary Award and has had stories published in *Grain*, *Antigonish Review*, *The Fiddlehead*, *Dalhousie Review* and *Room of One's Own*. She is a former professional ballet dancer and choreographer who has studied Buddhist Psychology at Naropa University in Colorado, and Psychokinetics at the Body-Mind Institute in Massachusetts. She lives in Victoria, British Columbia with her husband, Bill Gaston, and their four children. *Sympathy* is her first book.